Jonathan Gash is a doctor specialising in Tropical Medicine. He lectures worldwide on the subject. He developed his love for antiques during his years as a medical student when he supplemented his income by working in the London street markets. He lists his hobbies as antiques and his family.

He is married with three daughters and three grandchildren and lives in Essex.

THE SIN WITHIN
HER SMILE

Jonathan Gash

ARROW

First published in Arrow 1994

1 3 5 7 9 10 8 6 4 2

The right of Jonathan Gash to be identified as the author
of this work has been asserted by him in accordance
with the Copyright, Designs and Patents Act, 1988

First published in the United Kingdom in 1993 by
Century, Random House UK Limited

Arrow Books Limited
Random House UK Ltd, 20 Vauxhall Bridge Road, London SW1V 2SA

Random House Australia (Pty) Limited
20 Alfred Street, Milsons Point, Sydney,
New South Wales 2061, Australia

Random House New Zealand Limited
18 Poland Road, Glenfield
Auckland 10, New Zealand

Random House South Africa (Pty) Limited
PO Box 337, Bergvlei, South Africa

Random House UK Limited Reg. No. 954009

A CIP catalogue record for this book
is available from the British Library

ISBN 0 09 938441 8

Printed and bound in Great Britain by
Cox & Wyman Ltd, Reading, Berkshire

Now, in your land, Gypsies reach you, only
After reaching all lands beside;

Robert Browning
The Flight of the Duchess

If fools never went to market, forgeries
and cracked pots would never sell.

Jean de Malchanceux
(Twelfth Century)

A Story for Roy and Beryl and theirs,
and Matthew, Sarah, Jack, and Charlotte.

To

The Chinese god Hu Ching, patron saint of
jewellers – who gives priceless jewels that
transform ugliness to beauty to those who
humbly dedicate works to him – this work is
humbly dedicated.

Thanks

Susan

1

Women stop you thinking of antiques, forgery, the essentials of life. She proved it, giving me a smiling clout.

'Get to the orgasm, Lovejoy,' she said, breathless.

They nark you as well. 'It's your fault, not mine.'

'Who's the slave here?' she demanded.

She had a point. The slave's always me. I obeyed the selfish cow.

This trouble started with me helping friends, all women. It's how a scruffy penniless antiques dealer gets in such a mess. I would have escaped, only she soared me to ecstasy.

There's nothing to be ashamed of in wanting women and antiques, which is how I landed up being sold in this slave auction.

Shame comes into it. I was scared I'd go cheap and everybody would laugh at how Lovejoy was auctioned off for nowt. In Rome, slaves ascending the auction block must have borrowed a comb, tried to look presentable. Shame is powerful stuff. I'd had my usual bath, done my teeth twice, reamed every pore. I'd put new cardboard in my shoes, and sewn two buttons on my jacket. For me, I was beautiful, but still felt a prat. When they called my name I shuffled forward and stood red-faced to a chorus of jeers. Sweat was neutralizing all my dawn scrubbing. Slaves are ashamed, sure, but they're also angry. Remember that, for this story's sake.

That morning, Jessina Mosston'd caught me in my workshop – a tatty garage in undergrowth. I was faking a Turner painting, *Venice with the Salute*, and swearing at his genius. Life's hell for a forger. The trouble is, you can't tell whether Turner did two, three, or twenty-seven glazes. I was forging Turner's famous secret 'dirty white' sky (Payne's Grey in turpentine with a drop of Venice turpentine oil; don't tell).

Jessina hove in. 'Lovejoy, darling!' I leapt a mile. She stood appraising the painting, head aslant. 'It's like nothing on earth.'

'Ignorant cow.'

She sighed. 'Your charm won't sell you tonight, Lovejoy.'

My brush wavered. Well it might, because Turner would have used his fingers to paint the foreground waterscape. I'd already guessed wrong over rose madder. I was broke, so a trip to London's Tate Gallery to see the original was out.

'Tonight? What's tonight?'

'The charity auction, Lovejoy. You've not forgotten?'

Me and Jessina had made smiles often once. Now, she'd gone up market, worked the yuppie circuits, clubs, leisure centres, all that. Like many rejects, I'm not to remember that she'd actually enjoyed lust in the dust with a nerk like me. Her husband is big medicine in posh motor franchises.

'No, course not,' I countered quickly. 'Only, er, what – '

She smiled sweetly. 'You are Slave For A Day.'

That stumped me. 'Slave?'

'Auction of promises, Lovejoy.' She wore a clipboard and an air of exasperation, the hallmarks of the do-gooder. 'You could have drawn Chauffeur For An Afternoon.'

'You're barmy. My motor doesn't go.'

She laughed with the woman's impassive hilarity. 'An evening babysitting – '

I brightened. 'I'll promise that, love!'

'You already babysit for half the village. It'd upset the mothers' rota. Slave For A Day is ideal.'

I eyed her with distaste. 'What's it mean?'

'Cut the grass, make tea, park the car! Heaven's *sake*!'

'What charity, anyway?' I could discover conscience.

'Haven for the mentally ill.'

Conscience gets a rough time. 'What are *you* promising?' I demanded. These sharks get the awards while others slog our guts out. It's charity's cunning way.

'Timothy's giving a new fitted kitchen.' He's her husband. 'You've so far donated nothing.'

See? Nasty with it. 'I mean you, not your bloke.'

'I'm organizing!' she said, snappish now I'd sussed her. 'It's been weeks of work . . . ' et hypocritical cetera.

'Oh, aye.' Somebody's slave? I'm at everybody's beck and call as it is. 'Swap you jobs?'

'Seven thirty, Lovejoy!' She swished angrily out.

You can't help wondering about women. I watched her lovely shape cross the tangled garden. They're mad at me all the blinking time. There isn't one that can say hello without ballocking me about my life style. Even Michelle the post girl plays hell about women who sometimes stay over.

Turner called. My smile returned. I went to examine his – well, my – use of Naples yellow. It's a kind of law with me, that antiques really bring no problems at all. People are the problem. I make hundreds of these laws up about antiques. I only wish I'd remember some, maybe keep out of trouble.

Blotto, the stout bloke next to me in the village hall, is our village cricket team's useless left-arm bowler. I read his auction list. 'You are Gardening For Three Hours. She's put me down for a whole day!'

Blotto heaved his huge girth round. His mates were in the row behind. 'Lovejoy'll get some biddie wants a rave up, booys.'

They fell about, more merriment at my expense. I glanced round the hall, bored out of my skull. Over a hundred people were in. The lads were making joke bids to our curate, Elton George, who'd drawn the auctioneer's straw. Elton's pace was funereal. A whole hour and so far he'd only done twenty-three. A proper auctioneer would have rattled us back to the boozer like a Gatling.

A scatter of applause greeted A Week's Dog-Walking, to filth the footpaths, five measly quid. Elton was ecstatic.

'Thank you!' he piped. 'Magnificent! Now item twenty-four: Trim Your Hedge.' He blinked his bottled eyes, mirth coming. 'Shears *not* provided! Only the labourer is worthy of his hire!' He snuffled, got a grip as ingrates and sycophants rolled in the aisles at such drollery.

The list was pathetic. Not a single antique. I mean, Deliver A Dawn Breakfast? Wash Your Car? Not one was worth a light. The daftest was Do Your Week's Ironing. Honest to God. Clothes only crumple anyway, so why iron at all? Yet all over the hall people were bidding for an afternoon's typing, a freezer meal for four, a

3

haircut (male) or wash-and-set (female). I could have been down at the White Hart hearing from Tinker if he'd managed to get the badly cleaned antique warming pan I'd sent him after in Beccles. (Tip: when cleaning old copper the traditional way – sea salt wetted with vinegar – don't let it run; the horrible streaks are murder.) I was hoping to snaffle it for a dud IOU.

The hall held unusual affluence. Undistributed wealth is never boring, but I like to see the rich threatened. Posh folk desperate to be seen, councillors with dwindling majorities, politicians wanting tit for tat, golf club hopefuls with desperate wives were all gasping for their pink gins. Is it wealth that makes me feel sardonic? Am I jealous? Mrs Frances Bledsoe was in, I saw with annoyance. And her writer husband, Meredith, who'd inherited half of Suffolk to struggle by on. She avoided my eye, for sexual reasons in her past. And her friend, bonny in a black velvet dress that had cost about my mortgage. She'd glanced at us serfs but looked away when I'd looked. Women are good at that. They are also good at what she did next, saying something quietly to her velvet-hatted pal. Do women ever admit having made illicit love, or not? I don't know, but expect it's the worst.

'And now, Do Your Weekend Shopping! Bids, anyone?' Elton mopped his brow. Even his gavel sounded apologetic.

Chatting absently with Blotto's mate Fez, who works down the harbour, I suddenly came to. Fez had named an unimaginable sum of money, the sort people pay for Canalettos and jumbo jets.

'Eh?' I asked.

Fez grinned. He's like a cartoon mouse, all buck teeth in a chirpy wrinkled visage, wiry as all sea-coasters.

'Straight up, Lovejoy.' He was in to bid for Groom Your Dog If Docile because he has this lame greyhound called Bottlebank that hates him but sires valuable champions. Fez is covered in scars. 'It's moored off the Deben estuary.'

'He paid that for a *boat*?'

'Lovely lines on her, though,' Fez said wistfully, as though morphology justified spending a king's ransom.

Which made me look at the tall elegant gentleman just in. I'd passed him as I'd arrived. He'd been in the gloaming having a smoke, leaning on an opalescent Rolls. A woman in his motor was

4

reading a magazine under soft lighting. I'd wanted her to look up and smile, but they never do what you want.

He didn't look a sailor. Your actual nautical is tanned, hard to rouse on any subject except sea tides and gaff-rigging. This land-lubber was tightly strung. You could almost hear the quivering tension in the man. He wouldn't sit down, though Hepsibah Smith, our gorgeous choir mistress, currently on teas, tried to entice him to a Chorley cake and some Earl Grey. I've wanted her for years.

Some loon bought Prune Your Roses, and then it was my turn.

'Goo it, Lovejoy, booy!' Blotto yelled, leading the catcalls. I went red-faced to be auctioned off.

'Slave For A Day,' Elton squeaked, wondering whether to gavel again, finally thought it too fascist. 'Lovejoy's handiwork is well known . . . ' The double meaning struck him and he coloured. 'And his popularity is, ah, equally, ah, well known.' More stammered doublethink.

How do you face an audience? I stared at the clock over the entrance, but people's amused features kept swimming into view. I swore to get even with Jessina.

'Five pence,' Doc Lancaster called.

Well. Riot city in the old village tonight. Everybody rolled in the aisles. I might have known. Doc Lancaster would make me walk a letter miles away, Mount Bures or somewhere. He makes people take exercise and eat fibre foods, the maniac.

'No bid!' a football club wag called. 'He's shopsoiled!' Pand-emonium. The whole place rocked. I was red with shame.

'Doc'll have you on his owl' rowing machine, Lovejoy!'

'Nurse Prentiss'd have Lovejoy on *her* rowing machine any owl' toime!' from witty Fez. Uproar.

No more bids seemed likely. I gave Elton a curt nod and made to step down. Then it happened.

'Ten pounds,' a woman called. The hullabuloo ceased.

'Twenty,' Frances Bledsoe's black velvet friend said.

'Thirty.' I strained to see, finally saw. The rival woman was the pale blue pastel one I'd seen in the Rolls. Her elegant bloke glared into space.

'A hundred,' after a quick nudge from Frances.

'Two hundred,' from the blue pastel lady.

The hall's silence was chipped into shards by Elton's strangled repetitions. I thought, what the hell is happening? My domestic skill isn't worth a groat. I mouthed the question to Frances herself, but she stared straight through me. The bids climbed.

Five hundred quid came and went. A thousand. Then guineas. I was out of breath. If these birds wanted me to do their gardening, their grass must be like rain forest – unless they wanted me for something else. But I can't do anything else, except babysit.

The bidding ended when Frances's pal, her face white and set, gave in. She maintained her minuscule but fraudulent smile, acknowledging the pastel woman's victory. Elton knocked me down for two thousand guineas, an unbelievable sum.

'Arden,' the lady called, easing our curate's panic.

The hall broke into excited speculation, people standing to see Mrs Arden. The jokes now fell flat. Suddenly there was less humour to go round.

One strange thing happened. Jessina, she of the charitable urge, caught my sleeve. She looked flushed with monetary success, but said a really odd thing: 'I'm sorry, Lovejoy.'

''S awreet, love,' I mumbled, and moved on by. I could have throttled her. I sat, Blotto staring at me.

'What you got that dried flowers ha'n't, Lovejoy?'

Indeed, I wondered, as Elton resuscitated the auction with Mrs Camden's Basket of Assorted Marmalades, indeed, what?

2

The White Hart taproom was seething. Nothing excites like money, does it? Well, nearly nothing. I entered feeling I'd run a marathon.

'Lovejoy. Bless you.' Cyril Darwin's wife, Hilda, isn't a local dealer, but adds to local bafflement. She is starlet pretty without the malice, and every male in East Anglia would give a Rembrandt to land her – antique dealers excepted, of course.

'Eh?' She only speaks when Cyril's given her a message.

'Your gift, Lovejoy! To the mentally ill!' Worse than I'd thought. I got ready to flee from yet more charity. 'So generous, Lovejoy! I've misjudged you!'

'Please.' I basked in her admiration. I don't get much. 'It's nothing,' I added, hoping to God I was right.

'No, Lovejoy. Will you have a drink?' She left her table. My progress towards the bar became untrammelled. 'You must be giving Mrs Arden an absolute monster of a present!' The dealers snickered. I gave them the bent eye past Hilda's glorious shape. 'For her to bid guineas, as auctions used to be!'

'Don't, love.' I went all noble. 'Charity is silent.'

Hilda's eyes filled. '*Beautiful*, Lovejoy! Considering.'

Chris Mannering passed us, slapping my back. 'Put in a word with the Ardens, eh?'

Dog-eared Harry Bateman, following Chris, hoping for crumbs, added congrats. Lily, Harry's wife, signalled to come over but I grinned as if I'd misunderstood. She's crazy for Patrick which is barmy because Patrick only loves Patrick. All have glossy cards claiming they're antiques experts, valuers, accredited, registered, and suchlike. Doldrum Townsend was in, I observed, chatting up Jessina Mosston. He was a parliamentary candidate once, and true to his genes has a penchant for bribery. He's bribed his way into more birds than the parson preached about. His seduction technique is to ask, 'What if I paid for a Mediterranean holiday? Go

7

with who you like . . . ' It's astonishing the success Doldrum gets, and who with. Makes you wonder which of them, Doldrum or the lady, believes they've pulled it off. Both?

My eyes stopped roaming the saloon. These women's hanging remarks worry me sick. 'Considering what?'

'Well, Mrs Arden's reputation.' Hilda spotted Laura Gilleard, a jolly plump girl who'd joined the Antiques Arcade with pretensions of Regency furniture on the strength of knowing a Derby jockey's cousin. I still haven't worked it out. 'Cooee! Laura! Coffee, Jackson's, elevenish . . . Ouch!'

My hand relaxed on her wrist. 'Considering *what*?'

'That hurt, Lovejoy! Mrs Arden's terrible, that's all.' She inspected her arm. 'You gave me a Chinese burn.'

Everybody seemed to know the Ardens but me. This was unlikely and maddening. I'd do Tinker. He's my barker, my warning bell. He was probably kippered in The Ship on East Hill.

'Why?' I waved back to Dolly, just entering. She is bonny, once catwalked for a London fashion house. She loves me, which is a bit galling, but I like her. She's wholesome, sees that you get bran and vitamins, and is given to checking your teeth. It gets on my nerves. The Sunday before, she'd got us both up and nearly to Holy Communion before I woke up enough to ask what the hell she thought she was playing at. She was astonished. It was my patron saint's day. I hadn't known I'd got one. That's all there is to say about Dolly. Oh, she has a marriage somewhere.

A few of the lads were making her blush with lewd comments. She looked gorgeous in her fitted yellow suit. I beckoned her over to save her death from embarrassment.

'Hilda Darwin, Dolly. Dolly, Hilda.'

'How do you do? Good evening, Lovejoy.' Dolly's never out of breath, but looks about to be. 'Tinker bid, but they wouldn't accept your IOU.'

'Bloody nerve.'

'Please don't be upset. The copper pan is in your cottage.'

'They wouldn't . . . yet you got it?'

'Tinker telephoned.' She set her lips in a prim line to show anger. 'I had to speak quite sharply to the manager.'

The dealers were craning to listen and look. Between Dolly and

Hilda, lust was spoilt for choice. Dolly is more voluptuous, pearls dangling from her prominent curves. Hilda is more your elfin winsomeness.

'Well done, Dolly!' I exclaimed. The Dollys of this world always make you talk like Thackeray. 'Would you care for a drink, my dear?' See what I mean? I never call anyone my dear.

'Thank you. Tea, please. Do they have Ceylon Amber?'

Even Hilda stared at that. I pretended to order tea and biscuits to an uncomprehending Eric, our barman, and led the two to near the fireplace. Dolly lives in terror of draughts. I was trying to avoid Tania Pope, an aggressive girl engaged to Big Frank from Suffolk. He's our local English silver dealer and bigamist, on the verge of notching up his tenth – I think – missus. She was livid because I'd declined to be Frank's best man again, again.

'Hilda's telling me about Mrs Arden,' I told Dolly.

'I am fully aware of Mrs Arden's character, Lovejoy,' Dolly said in reproof. 'Reverend Elton informed me.'

'Two thousand guineas.' I was narked she was taking my sale price so coolly. I'd never been worth that. We slaves have our pride.

'I honestly don't know which is preferable, Deirdre Divine or Valerie Arden.'

'Who?' Tania Pope was zooming up, I saw with dismay.

Hilda nodded. 'The other lady, in wrong black velvet.' She digressed at a chance of venom, saying to Dolly, 'The sales at Willie Griffs?'

'No. January's cheap sales at Borrowdale's.'

They settled on a quiet exchange of denigration as Tania surged wrathfully from the throng.

'Lovejoy! You *must* be best man!'

'No, love.' I tried reason. 'I must *not* be.'

'You're spoiling it!' The taproom hushed at her wail.

See what I mean? She's marrying Big Frank, a multiple bigamist, so *I'm* in the wrong? Their minds are definitely odd, no question. 'No, Tania. Big Frank's nine previous wives are the obstacle. And law.'

'You're being unfair, Lovejoy!' et loony cetera.

I was desperate. Dolly and Hilda joined in with amateur sociotherapy, but salvation arrived in the shape of Mr Arden, debonair but harassed.

'Lovejoy? Carl Arden. My wife wants you, immediately.'

Orders, from a stranger, in my own local? 'Say when I've to start, mate. I'll be along. As it is . . .' I indicated my company, secretly working out my fastest exit. 'Tomorrow, nine-ish?'

'Now, Lovejoy. A day is twenty-four hours.' He glanced at a watch that could have bought the parish. 'Start forthwith, or the cheque gets cancelled.'

'Lovejoy,' Dolly and Hilda said in mournful reproach.

'That's me.' I rose amid jeers and hilarity. Once a serf, always. I followed Carl Arden, my hands clasped in jaunty boxer style, but heavy of heart. Jessina smiled wanly. The last thing I saw as the pub door swung to was her pretty mouth giving a silent repetition, *Sorry, Lovejoy*.

His approaching Rolls meant nothing to me, because all motors don't. If it's moving, it's posh and the owner's got gelt. I stood waiting.

'In, Lovejoy.' Valerie clearly had the whip hand.

'Ta.' The warmth was scented with affluence. If slavery included driving this thing at least I'd not catch a chill. My old Ruby's like a wind tunnel.

We moved through East Anglian blackness. I nodded off when we hit the lonely hedgerows near Adamswell. People often come to the valley because it's beautiful, but beauty doesn't count if you're stuck out in the countryside. Fields and forests do nothing for me. Give me a crowded huddle of houses any time.

Probably we made a left turn up through the Pennies. Don't laugh at the name. An ancient queen of ours, dying, once scoured the land for a lovely young lass with brains enough to take her place as bedmate for the King. The only girl woman enough was little Alice Perrers, a humble tile-maker's daughter from Little Penny in 'Silly Suffolk'. The royal lady possessed of such ferocious devotion was our well-loved Queen Philippa, her husband that violent but strangely endearing King Edward III, a mediaeval ball of fire. Young Alice must have been rather special. The King's riotous troubles – Church, Parliament, Rome's Vatican, wars, would-be assassins – were only part of Alice's problems. She also had to mother the King's demonic offspring – John of Gaunt, the Black

Prince, others. No doves among that little lot. Yet Alice of Little Penny village became our adored 'Lady of the Sun'. I'd have given almost anything to –

'Lovejoy. We're here.'

'Thank you.' I woke blearily, only wanting to sleep.

At his order I alighted. He immediately drove off. I waited patiently, but the car's lights dwindled. Silence. My sleepy mind went? Maybe he had to park at a neighbour's? I looked about. I was on the drive of a great house, old-new phoney, trees sparing lawns, a fountain splashing somewhere. Balustraded terrace, leaded windows, plastic olde worlde lanterns, nooky doorways, trellised roses.

'Mrs Arden?' I cleared my throat. Louder. Nobody.

The sough of the night breeze made me shiver. The house was on a rise. A passing motor swished by, pulled by its cones of headlights. A few windows were lit but the curtains were drawn.

See what I mean about countryside? God knows where the nearest tavern was. I couldn't see any crystal cluster of gold lights that gives villages away in this dark land. Arden had told me nothing, the aloof swine.

The front door opened. A woman stood in silhouette. 'Why didn't you knock, Lovejoy?' I'll bet she'd been behind the door tapping her foot with impatience.

'If I had you'd have counted to ten before opening it.'

She laughed at that, really laughed. 'How did you know?'

'Women do. Like they allow phones at least three rings.'

'Come in. What else do women do, Lovejoy?'

'Mind your own business.'

She sighed. 'Yes, you're he, right enough.'

Aye, I'm him, I thought. I'm from the slummy world of split infinitives and no epigrams. We walked along a plush corridor hall into a vast living room. Was this where I was to be enslaved? I stood like a spare tool. She wafted to a monster chaise longue and sank in a flurry of silk. She looked ready for bed, if you believe those fifties glamorous Hollywood spectaculars, like I do. I glanced at the armchairs but didn't sit. Slavery doesn't come alone.

'Light.' A cigarette was between her lips, dangling there in paradise.

'Yes, miss.' Straight out of infant school, I struggled with a gold lighter the size of a domino. She watched me, sighed, took the damned thing and gamely lit her fag.

'That bitch Deirdre's just rung, Lovejoy. Offered me the bid plus, if I'd pass you on to her.'

Was I expected to dance with joy, that my serfdom was now worth even more? And what did Deirdre Divine, whoever she was, also want me for? I was fed up. I was knackered.

'Where are they, missus?'

'Where are what?' She honestly did look blank.

'The antiques. The ones you want me to divvy.' She dragged smoke in, held it, her eyelashes looking twice as long in the pose, exhaled. Breathing does wonders for their shape. I shoved my gaze about the room for safety. Kulaks do not ogle their betters. 'Stands to reason, love. You only bid so I'd divvy your antiques.'

'Is that so?'

'And the profit you'll make will be worth well over two thousand, or you wouldn't have bothered.'

'Can you really do it, Lovejoy?' Her eyes glittered. My heart sank. I knew what was coming.

Her eyes lit from within. I'm not kidding. They truly did take on a luminescence. It's not a trick they can turn on any time, more a sort of luscious understanding of chance favouring them. Infants do it, smiling without a change of expression, showing a burst of love. I've tried doing it in the mirror, and failed. But some shinings are different. Not all are pretty. This radiance was one of the least bonny. I'd seen it before, all too often. It's known as greed. There ought to be a word for a woman's combination of lust, greed, the ecstasy of craving . . . Grust, leed? I shivered.

'This pendant cost a fortune, Lovejoy. Worth it, yes or no?'

'Gunge.' It was an old-looking tumbaga god of pre-Columbian design, on a gold chain. I'll tell you its dark secret in a sec.

Speechless, she tried to unfasten the catch at her nape, angrily gestured me to do it. I walked over and obeyed. She dipped deliberately, making my breathing suddenly engorge at the proffered view. I dropped it beside her and moved away. I was in enough trouble without tumbling into her cleavage. Carl would leap out of the tapestries with the local peelers. 'Fake, dud, sham.'

She finally erupted, 'I have Government assay reports – '

'In triplicate? Cross-checked by Queen Mary College down Mile End Road?' I'd have sneered but don't know how. 'Then you can sell it to some deluded clown.'

She would have risen, had me horsewhipped, but the hour was late and her plans all awry. 'Walk home, Lovejoy.' She stabbed out her cigarette like it was me.

'Can I go?'

That silenced her. She eyed me, gazed at the pendant. It was a genuine pectoral disc, casting back light of that unmilked lustre only true gold shows. A beautiful piece. Her eyes lifted, their gleam different now she believed me.

'Lovejoy. You don't care, do you?'

'For tat, lady? Who does?' I stood my ground, but ached to leave. I'd find a barn to kip until morning, out of this house of bondage. 'Everything's got value – *except money*.'

'So I'm a deluded clown, Lovejoy.' A flat statement.

'Lady, you're worse. You're a pest. You want locking up.'

More quadruple think. Then she smiled, surprising me. It was like watching sunrise. 'Lovejoy, bring a drink, fourth room off the landing.'

'Er, what?' Did she mean for me, or for somebody abed?

With a faint tut of disbelief she wafted from the room without answering. It took me twenty minutes of dithering to work out she might mean white wine, but I couldn't get the bloody bottle open so took her some whisky.

The rest you know.

3

The bedroom could have bought and sold me, which in a way it had. I woke with a mild headache, thinking that women stop you thinking of antiques, forgery, the essentials of life. I remembered her command to ride on to detumescence.

Was I to start work now, seven in the morning, daylight seeping through? Or had I already done half my stint?

She lay humped beside me. I love morning women, all tousled. I love winter women, bundled in thick coats with shell-like faces, or in bed with their hair spreading. A bruise was on her cheek. I went red. It isn't my hallmark, but it hadn't been there last night.

Slavery's funny stuff. Nobody believes it still exists, yet everyone knows it does. Take your great ancient slave revolts, for instance. They didn't *want* to abolish slavery. They were simply takeover bids. Like Vadius Pollion. He was a freed slave who got rich. Did he show compassion for his pals, slaves who hadn't yet made it? Not on your life – he fattened the eels in his eel pools *on live slaves he chucked in to drown and be eaten*! Typical. Even slavery's theorists are phoney. Take Karl Marx. An inveterate snob, he kept his own peasant slavewoman unpaid and penniless, fathered little Henry Frederick on her, then airily pretended the baby was his pal Engel's by-blow. See? People pretend that unpleasant things don't exist, but they do.

Like forgery.

This elegant lady sleeping beside me knew about forgery, like she knew about bossing her peasants, husband Carl included. Not a servant to be seen. But a household this size needed at least five, and she wasn't the kind to rush about basting the carrots before the guests arrived. And Carl the Compliant, humbly zooming off while his missus ravished a serf, must own at least (a) another dwelling, plus (b) a team of abject helots, and (c) bulging moneybags to maintain the whole lunatic charade.

14

Forgery, and the tumbaga pendant. This lovely lady was a crook.

The ancient peoples were more skilled than we credit. Like in jewellery. Tumbaga is an alloy of gold with copper – about four parts to one. The primitive Amerindian folk knew, long before Columbus, how to create beautiful effects in tumbaga. Imagine their delight. They dig up a mess of lode, crudely smelt it, and it looks like utter crud. Then they shape it to, say, a disc five inches across, like Mrs Arden's 'pectoral' (think of a decorative breast jewel in miniature). It still looks like disappointing dross even if it is flecked with gold. So the ancient goldsmith does a brilliant piece of craftsmanship. He does depletion gilding.

Say it like that, it sounds as if he covers the top layer to hide the patchy grot, right? Wrong. He collects some plant juices that contain oxalic acid. (We forgers nowadays use strawberries or rhubarb.) He steeps the pectoral in the liquid. The thing begins to look worse, covered with filthy dark scales. But this ancient gold worker doesn't despair, knowing it is merely the surface copper changing. He heats the jewel, and hammers it gently. He does it again and again. And something truly wondrous happens. The gold is left there *alone* on the surface, gleaming and pure!

It's not like electroplating, where you *add* a gold layer. It's not like gold plating, where you *cover* a rubbishy object with slim gold sheet. No, depletion gilding rids your masterpiece of the undesired muck – in this case, copper. It leaves pure gold.

The importance of this to the forger? Nothing new is added! So any tests you do on a piece of jewellery will prove it to be *as ancient as the original alloy*. Get it? However sophisticated your tests are, down to millionths, your fake will be proved genuine. That's why this ancient technique is coming into its own again. I've shown three amateur goldsmiths how to do it. Five years ago, nobody was interested.

If you don't trust your own depletion gilding, you can use Mother Nature, a well-known crook. Make your piece of jewellery from some tumbaga, then simply bury it. The soil will corrode out the alloying metal from the superficial layer, letting you dig it up later and polish it to show only the pure surface gold. And all as genuine as the original metal in the alloy – *and as ancient*! Better still, the 'sinker', as we call this technique, alters modern solder. The soldering is displaced by your gold, so no amount of eagle-eyed 'expert' examination will reveal your con trick.

Isn't art wonderful? The answer's yes – if you pay a hundred quid, say, for a small rough chunk of Columbian alloyed ore dug up last Tuesday and sell it this week as an ancient gold pectoral for ninety thousand. It's not quite so wonderful if you're the buyer, because you've paid a fortune for a laugh. The trouble is that posh books have a way of giving these processes grand names: 'surface enrichment' and, inevitably, Frenchify it to *mise en couleur*.

Her hand slid onto me, taking my breath and sanity away at a stroke, so to speak. I looked. She'd been watching me all this time. Women are sly.

'I never saw a man's brain work before, Lovejoy. It explains . . . your passion.'

'I can't afford it.'

'A slave doesn't pay, Lovejoy. Seeing you thinking is like watching fireworks. I ought to make you remember your . . . position here.' She smiled, raised the bedclothes to inspect her handiwork. 'Duty calls.'

Another of my laws is that a woman never pays up front. It's why they carry purses, so they can prolong the delicious agony, the wrenching act of forking out for something they have decided to grab. I should have remembered that law, too, but didn't until death came as a reminder.

An hour later I'd had a bath, dressed, and discovered two other benefits of slavery. The first was a bountiful breakfast, served by Evans, a pleasant lass who'd have been gorgeous if she'd had a diet of her own grub instead of serving it to passing strangers. Too slim by a mile, but able to swish among the porcelain without catastrophe. I liked her. The mistress of the house dazzled in cream print, everything matching, her composed features brilliantly smooth. Nothing fake about the diamond hair slide or the immense Singhalese ruby ring.

The second was Mrs Arden's next command. She observed me noshing the meal, chin on her linked fingers. She made no attempt to disguise her languid air of the woman roused from bedded love.

No messages from Carl, late of this address. She just watched, occasionally beckoned peasants to replenish my plate, more toast, mushrooms, be sharp about it. Odd, but women like evidence of a man's appetite – make that plural, appetites. I can't understand why, but it's a global truth, like leaves being green. A woman in our village, Connie, who I babysit for, used to strive might and main to switch the light on when we made smiles just to search my face, exclaiming with relish and clasping me afterwards as if I'd given her a year's holiday. See? You'd think they'd have something better to do. It's no good asking. I asked Connie about it once. She just called me stupid. Where was I? Mrs Arden's imperial imperatives.

'Ta, love.' I leant back, declined another fry-up.

'Lovejoy? What do you like doing best? Not that,' she put in quickly, 'a set task, work. Until evening.'

'Well, run errands, sit for babbies. I'm good at them.' I glanced about. The spotless breakfast room was the size of a hangar. I said lamely, 'Sweep up.'

'Antiques?' she suggested.

I brightened. 'Antiques aren't a job, missus.'

'What are they?' It was sheer curiosity.

'Life, love.'

'Both? Or did you mean love in the vocative case?'

God Almighty, declension country at breakfast? 'Both.' I really didn't know. Still don't.

'Then you can check Carl's collection.' She saw my face light up. 'It's no good, Lovejoy. There are sophisticated alarms.'

That narked me. I honestly hadn't thought of stealing a single antique. I said, 'Antiques are robberies that everybody swore could never happen.'

She stayed snooty. 'Evans will show you to the library. Lunch at one precisely, tea at four. My husband requires details of your mortgage debts before dinner, seven thirty.' She rose with that smooth motion women do. I got up, all clumsy angles trying to be suave.

'Er, debts?'

'Yes.' She hesitated as if about to say more, but moved to the French windows. Evans leapt forward with a lace shawl.

'Er.' I knocked over a chair. 'What debts? I've got none.'

'That you owe on your cottage, whereby you defraud building

17

societies in Ipswich, St Edmundsbury, Lavenham. And all your fake IOUs.'

'Missus?' I called, not knowing how much I was supposed to reveal in front of the serfs. 'I didn't think I was going to get . . . '

'Paid, Lovejoy?' Mrs Arden turned, lovely against the cold morning sunlight streaming from the garden. 'Consider it an advance.'

I wallowed, helpless. I wish women would explain things. 'Advance on what?'

'Services to be rendered. Show Lovejoy the collection.'

'Yes, ma'am.' Evans actually bobbed a curtsey as her boss swept past. Luscious legs, I noticed. In the press of bedroom events I'd not had time to get really going at my own pace and direction. Maybe her lady's hunger was sexual repletion from the rude and licentious plebian masses? It happens. I mean, look nearer home. In our village, at Elaine, Margaret, Josie, Betty the teacher, Connie, others. Why, only last week Olivia, our curate's wife, invited – 'This way, Lovejoy.'

I followed. She'd got good legs, too, but I'd gone off her. Never called me sir. I felt peeved. I suppose one villein can always spot another. Still, by the end of the long corridor I was trying to chat her up and got cold-shouldered. Women should be more trusting, but they aren't.

By nine that night I was in the Antiques Arcade just before closing time, having earned my freedom by enduring painfully polite meals, including a moribund nosh with Carl making county-set dullisms at a repro mahogany table as long as my garden. I'd given him a list of all my debts. He'd pocketed it without a glance. His antiques were porcelain duds and fakes, the product of greed gone wrong. I was blunt.

As the hire car dropped me off by the war memorial, I was worried sick, and desperate to find Imogen, the one person who might know what was going on.

4

The place was deserted but for Loafer. Even so, the very air of the dingy Antiques Arcade was like wine to me. It's nothing more than a corridor under a glass canopied roof. The lighting's quite wrong, fluorescent strips that go flickery at the wrong time. The dealers have partitioned nooks. The poshest belongs to Loafer Pod, a wino with no means of support except Verola whose work station (*sic*) is a yard near the Welcome Sailor, a tavern at East Gates where merry lads go to enjoy her, er, companionship.

'Wotch, Loafer.'

'How do, Lovejoy?' He wasn't surprised. Winos aren't, by anything. He was trying to sweep up. His area's the size of a confessional without the holiness.

Loafer Pod would be a friend if he wasn't a dealer. Women say he was handsome, past tense. Starts out impeccably dressed every morning, looks like nothing on earth by the time the pubs open, and is a shattered relic by late evening, as now. I took the brush from his shaking hands. 'Nobody about, Loafie?'

'Verola's at employment.' He says it like she's at a vicarage party. 'The rest are gone an hour.' He made a pretence of searching for a glass. I shook my head, and he guzzled a bottle with relief. 'Heard about your auction. What was she like, your white slaver?' He belched while still swilling. I watched the bubble of eructation ascend into the liquid. If I tried that I'd choke. 'She's a right cow, she.'

'Oh, she was okayish.' I observed his imbibing skill with admiration. He hadn't stopped swallowing while speaking. Was it a trick? Ventriloquists do it all the time. Or maybe they . . . Hang on, my mind demanded sternly. How come Loafer Pod, kept by the nocturnal doings of his Verola, knew my erstwhile opulent boss? 'How come you know her, Loafie?'

'Come in here last week, she. Tried it on over a piece of porcelain. I'd done a scoop, ground out the maker's mark and enamelled in a new one. Should I have used gold, Lovejoy?' He didn't wait for an answer. I knew the plate, a Spode copy he'd tried for weeks to sell as genuine Josiah Spode of 1814. They say it's still in genuine production, so watch out. (To scoop: to grind out the modern mark, then draw the false mark on; the giveaway is the little roughened hollow instead of a glaze-smooth surface. *Never* buy without running your finger pulp over the mark.) 'She had some expert trolling along. Writer for a drossy glossy. Went through the Arcade like senna pods.' He shook his head in sorrow. 'Know what, Lovejoy? Antiques'll get a bad name. Look at the finds lately.'

There had been a recent spate – not too strong a word – of finds of Roman weaponry and Early Christian silvers locally. We usually get dribs and drabs hereabouts, being Rome's first colony in Britain. But the shoal of finds had brought every moonspender in the country bleeping our fields with their electronic wizardry. Naturally, there'd been trouble. Two knifings had made the local bobbies paranoid. They always blame drugs to newsmen, but know it was antiques all right. They'd busted into six dealers in town, plus others in the villages. I said, 'The shivers were the Brighton circus, Loafie. It wasn't us.'

He spat expertly into the flagged floor. A shiver is one who uses a shiv, a stabbing knife, to further private arguments. 'Try telling the peelers that,' he said with feeling. 'They caused this mess.'

I suppose I ought to explain about the Arcade. There's maybe a score or more dealers. Some have a curtained plank and a chair, no more, while others, like Loafer Pod, have a glassed bay off the main thoroughfare. Verola has an arrangement with the owner. At the time of going to press the owner is Woody, a caff proprietor bent on corrupting East Anglia's nutrition with fry-ups of solid saturates thinly disguised as food. He makes a killing, Tinker jokes of Woody's nosh. The Arcade has no locks that any decent burglar'd notice. The last out's supposed to key up, to stop couples fornicating in the Arcade after the town's lone cinema closes. The council's Watch Committee, morality-riddled vigilantes who thwart reproduction among all known life forms except bloodstock horses and gun dogs, pays a hireling to check the dud Yale hourly through the night vigil.

Happily, he's bribable. Verola knows to what degree, 'tis said.

Some dealers default on payment of Woody's extortionate rent as a protest against his policy of dereliction maintenance. I'm one, if not two. I use Margaret Dainty – lame, pleasant, a husband vaguely somewhere, respectable – and Loafer Pod, to 'hodge', as the trade says. To hodge is to give one's antiques to another dealer who simply keeps them to pad out his own inferior stock. Should your hodged stuff sell, why, he'll honestly give you a pre-agreed cut, usually half to two-thirds (we don't go in per cents, tradition being more trustworthy than anything decimal). I provide occasional services, about which more anon. The Arcade works pretty well, though it's a dead-and-alive hole. You wouldn't go there hoping for your genuine astonishing find of a John Constable, but you might chance a buy for an antiques-loving uncle. My point is, I know everything there about the local antiques scene. My barker, Tinker Dill, antiques snooper in tramp's clothing, sees to that. Except suddenly now I didn't.

'She's into gold, Lovejoy. Silver at a pinch.'

'She? That woman peeler?' East Anglia had suffered a series of five police promotions in a twelvemonth. One was a career lady called Melanie Laud, of impossibly high police rank. Inevitably she'd been dubbed Maudie Laud. She came with the 'mother' – slang, meaning the warning word – of having pulled some major antiques bust in the Midlands. Local lads blamed her for absent friends.

'Maudie? Not her. I mean the cow who hired you. Gold mad, she. Her tame expert put her to rights.'

'Was he any good?'

'Not bad. Mrs Dainty said he wasn't just a woman.'

A 'woman' is any prospective buyer, not a dealer or collector. Odd for Loafer to talk up a bird like Mrs Arden. I'd known him years, and he's a dour 'caller', as we say of a dealer who denigrates everybody.

How come I knew nothing of this? 'She come in often, then?'

'She was everywhere this past fortnight. Homed in on gold, then left no matter what colour the rest of us fetched.' Colour is a load of showy antiques to catch a potential purchaser's eye.

Curiouser and very narking. I put his brush away after sweeping the gunge into the corridor with a flourish. It's difficult to judge tidiness. I mean, Dolly keeps tidying my cottage up. She's always hard at it. Tidiness to me is like weather, there somewhere but not worth mentioning. I looked about.

Yes, somebody seemed to have gone through Loafer's stall. And they'd done damage. They'd smashed a small Lowestoft jug, now worth less in smithereens. Loafer had the bits on a piece of brown paper. Some travelling 'antiques fayre' might give him a couple of quid if he stuck it together. He'd be better off having it enlarged, by forming a fake of it on the outside, to contain the damaged pieced-together jug. A clever forger would leave a small area showing, to entice the unwary.

'What'll I do with that, Lovejoy?' Loafer asked. He uncorked another bottle of wine somehow with his teeth. I really envy people like Loafer. He fell, still drinking.

'Tell you in the morning, Loafie.' I helped him up. 'Christ, pal,' I said, gasping. 'How far you got to go?'

'To the Welcome Sailor. Verola'll be finished soon.'

'I'll get you there.' I didn't want to promise, but was trapped.

We locked up. I posted him into the Welcome Sailor ten minutes later. Another odd thing, though. As we blundered past the Priory ruins Loafer said something else about Mrs Arden. I'd mentioned her country estate near Lamarsh.

'Her didn't always live there, booy,' he said. He still carried his bottle. 'Lived Upchurch way. I met her first husband in the dox shop.'

Dox shop, the detoxification centre for hardened drinkers. 'He still about?'

He spat across the road into a shop doorway. I'd have applauded if I hadn't been holding him upright. 'No. Passed on. Some sort of chemist.'

And that was that. I caught the last bus to my village, made it home by half eleven. All the way I was thinking, *I didn't know.* Where was Tinker, the idle old nerk?

She was waiting for me.

My cottage stands on our village's outer edge. The narrow lane descends to a little vale – copse, a stream, some fields – and a farm valley of obnoxious rurality. I plodded up my path and was fumbling with the Suffolk latch when I paused. I thought for a second I'd heard Tinker cough. It's a salvo, roaring up from his diaphragm into the universe to silence life forms for three leagues around. I stood on tiptoe to see the roof lights of the Queen's Head but they were out. Tinker doesn't hang around shut pubs. The racket must have been some badger or hedgehog. I shrugged and went in, lit the lantern with a match. My electricity was cut off, the electricity company mad about some bill, the selfish swine.

I stirred the ashes in the grate. Hopeless. The fire was out. I went to the workshop for my primus paraffin gadget (I use it for annealing silver alloys when forgeries or repairs to antiques are needed). Ten minutes, and I had a pan of boiling water. I'd no milk, because the milkman had caught the Scrooge complex. I shook a piece of cheese in hot water, getting a milky fluid in the lantern glim. I used that. Two tea bags left, a lump of sugar miraculously surviving on the bluetits' string in the porch, and I was in paradise. Tea, at home. The place isn't much. One main room, a curtained alcove of a kitchen, a small bathroom and loo, a thatched roof. It looks abandoned from the road, not altogether a disadvantage.

'Lovejoy?'

The shock made me drop my hot mug. I leapt a mile. 'You silly bitch!' I stormed to where she stood in the doorway, but two constables shone torches in my eyes. I faltered. 'You made me spill my tea!'

'Wait,' she told the darkness over her shoulder.

Maudie Laud was in plain clothes. About thirty-middle, brownish hair, plaid suit a little long, earrings, really lifelike.

'I under arrest?' I didn't trust her. She knew it.

'No, Lovejoy. A couple of questions.'

'Me first. Got any milk or sugar?'

'These shivers. Two dealers were knifed over some ancient finds from nearby fields. A small chalice, late Romano-Celtic. A gold torc, pre-Roman British tribal.'

'I don't help people who spill my last hot drink. Dawns take time coming.'

'They were the cause of the fights. You divvied the finds?'

'Yes, constable.' She didn't rise to the insult. 'In The Ship, East Hill. For three quid and a meal. The fights started after I left.'

'So I believe.' She came and sat gingerly on the divan. 'You haven't made your bed, Lovejoy.'

See? Another ten minutes she'd be washing the curtains, and I'd not find a thing for weeks. 'I've just got up,' I said, nasty. 'I'm usually in bed by ten.'

'How was Mrs Arden?' Her smile was all Sweet Ida.

'Your lads carry a tea flask?' I asked, buying time. This was getting scary. I mean, everybody was in on some game they thought I was playing too but wasn't.

'She is reputedly Dynamite Lil in bed.'

'Now, Sergeant, I never betray a lady's confidence.'

She eyed me. 'So I hear. But I don't believe anything I hear.'

'Nor me.' I scuffed about for more hot water. I could maybe rescue a tea bag from the bin. What did they use in wartime, burnt acorns? Plenty of oaks about, but exactly when did acorns grow? Just my luck for it to be the wrong time of year . . . She'd said something almost practically nearly vital. 'Eh?'

'I said what's this about a holiday trek?'

'You've got the wrong bloke, love.'

'The surgery has you listed. Sunday.'

What now? Charity was proving a right pest. 'I'll kill Doc Lancaster.'

'The good doctor says medicine holds out no hope for you.'

When doctors turn comics it's the end. 'Ask your grassers, love.'

'I told Doctor Lancaster I couldn't quite see you in a caravan.'

'Eh? Oh.' That was different. I could tolerate a ride in a motorized caravan, a picnic on the lawn then home.

She tapped her handbag. 'You didn't sign up with Mrs Divine?'

Gone midnight, me knackered, and they come at you with this dross. Is it any wonder you get narked? 'Tell you what, love. Set one of your Plods on watch at the gate. Let me kip, okay?'

She thought a moment, smiled, and made for the door. 'Very well. Lovejoy, why are you so poor, you having the magic touch for antiques and all?'

'Kind ladies help me back to poverty.'

Her smile faded. 'Some games are not for innocents, Lovejoy.'

She tells *me* that? They left, no silent snooper left to lurk at my non-gate gate. Was she bluffing?

I surveyed my cottage's interior. No grub, except a mouldy piece of pie under an inverted saucer. No tea, sugar, milk. No acorns. I lodged a chair at the door, dowsed the candle, undressed and went to bed. Caravan trek? She was a frigging nutter.

5

Jacko's coal lorry wasn't functioning next morning, so I started the forlorn trudge to town. Jaunty pensioners waved at me from the buses wafting past. It was what folk call a 'nice' day, as if there's any other sort – they mean sun, warm, blue sky – and for once I was glad. My usual bum-balls-armpits scour was cold as hell. I'd drunk some warm water, using my pan-on-lantern technique, but water for breakfast doesn't go far. I walked round to the old church in case Tinker had dossed in its ancient vestry, but no. (You break in, incidentally, by a weighted string, several turns round a piece of wire.)

The phone box at Braiswick was unvandalized, by some oversight, and I got through to Dolly. She took twenty long minutes to come. She can't concentrate. Only last week she'd forgotten to lend me the train fare to Norwich and I'd had to hitch a lift on the trunk road. I got in, told her about the police visit.

'They asked me about Mrs Arden. I don't know why.'

'Have I to find out anything, darling?'

Not bad. I looked at Dolly's morning prettiness. She moved in different circles, maybe even in Mrs Arden's. I needed somebody there. 'Yes, please. The meadow, love.'

Before I go on, I've nothing against wealth as long as nobody suffers and the rich don't get uppity. Divisions are really great. They create business, trade, collecting fever, and, truth to tell, antiques. It's just that folk can get carried away. They really can. When they get so toxic that they burn homes and ride about in funny white sheets and knife rival football supporters, all that carnage stuff that begins in exclusivities of colleges and councils, then it's time to call a halt. Even patient blokes like me get narked.

'Which meadow?' She tutted in annoyance. A queue of cars had formed behind us at the station roundabout, all expressing impatience. 'Can't they wait a single *minute*?'

'Sty's yard, love. A meadow's a place where antiques are auctioned, impromptu. Not buttercups and daisies.'

'Is Sty's that incense place under the viaduct? I hate it.'

See? Already hating a place before she knew we were going there? 'That's it, love.'

She glanced at me. 'Hand off my knee, please. I'm driving.'

'It was accidental!' I said, indignant. 'Look, if this is too much bother, give a friend a lift . . .'

We bickered all the way through the villages to Sty's gungy temple. Today's meadow. If Tinker wasn't there I'd throttle him.

We halted outside the Temple of Relevant Harmony. Its resemblance to a junk yard – bashed cars, chunks off excavators, in a muddy tangle beneath a viaduct – is made authentic by signs announcing discounts for cash. Sty always has a couple or three amateur engineers hunting for special bits. They sometimes actually buy rusting axles, old batteries. I know one who's building a replica of Campbell's *Bluebird* motorboat, and he lives in a third-floor flat near Edmundsbury. It's in his living room. Like I say, amateurs are strictly crazy paving. Always interesting, but off the wall.

The Temple was an adjoining shack, as weird as it sounds.

'Want to come in, love?' I didn't mean it.

'No, Lovejoy.' She recognized the gift in the offer and smiled. 'Did you miss me?'

'Eh? No. Mrs Arden made me stay the night. She kept me busy.' I bussed her but she drew away.

'Busy, Lovejoy?'

It's stupid trying to kiss a bird when she's withdrawn to glare, and you advancing with your lips stuck out. Bussing's not complicated, put your lips together and suck, for Christ's sake. 'See you, love.'

'Lovejoy?' She was mad for some reason.

Big Frank's old Rover was here, and Liz Sandwell's motor. I was in for a lift to town. 'I'll make my own way, love.'

'What went on, Lovejoy?' Anger makes women speak metronomically. 'I want an answer this instant!'

A familiar cough gravelled into the world. Tinker's corrugated roar dopplered over the country, quelling the by-road's traffic sounds. I waited as it finally sank to chugs and whines. It ends with a rasping inhalation, Nature pivots back, and the universe is safe. There he stood.

'Thought you'd vanished for good, Lovejoy. Morning, missus.' He shuffled across, a relic in a stained old army greatcoat. His trousers were frayed, his wizened old visage a crinkled walnut, teeth like a blackened graveyard amid stubble. The glories of old repasts stained his mittens, chin, garments. He stank of beer. No Beau Brummel, but the best barker in the business.

'Wotch, Tinker. I've a bone.'

'Aye?' he said, as near to a snarl as he could manage on a blood alcohol just breaking its dawn low. 'I've one with you an' all, Lovejoy. What you mean shacking up with that posh bird as bought you? I had word about the Ipswich gab?'

He meant the pan. A gab's an auction. 'Dolly told me.'

'Something's going on, Lovejoy, and we're out of it.'

Dolly called in her nuclear-critical voice. It doesn't half penetrate.

'Don't I just know it, Tinker,' I said bitterly as we walked into the Temple of Relevant Harmony. Its incense stank to high heaven. Indeed, I hoped it did just that. 'I cursed you, leaving me in the dark.'

'Me?' He was outraged, fumbled a tin of beer from his overcoat's poacher's pouches. He flicked its hooped seal and swilled, his chicken-neck Adam's apple yo-yoing. 'I've been chasing you like a blue-arsed fly – '

'Morning.' Sty came to welcome us. 'The lady with you?'

Dolly was steaming with fury in our wake. I closed the door on her. 'Just somebody asking the way.'

Sty is spherical, which is saying something for the ultimate health freak. His health's different from Doc Lancaster's in that Sty advises no exercise, constant gorging, unbridled sexual licence, and the stimulation of illegal enterprises. He weighs twenty-six stone – 364 pounds if you're transatlantic; God only knows what if you're a kilogrammer – and looks every ounce. He wears enormous caftans woven by acolytes, of which he and his Temple have an abundance. He always surprises. This time, he was bald as a bladder of lard. He has quadruple chins. One ear lobe dangled under the weight of platinum links, which ended by being sewn (as in stitched) into his shoulder. He looks a right daffodil, but you daren't say.

'Wotch, Sty. Glad you're over the anorexia.'

He raised a hand like a second feature Navaho and intoned a babble of nonsense, eyes screwed into his rolls of fat. His upper arms flabbed obscenely.

'You may now enter.' A furious knocking sounded on the door. 'You sure that lady's not with you?'

'Positive. How many, Sty?'

'Seven. One stranger, vouched for.'

Tinker grimaced at me. Hard to spot, are Tinker's grimaces, his face being what it is, but I signalled for silence. I don't like strangers at meadow auctions either. The trouble is, these days money talks loud. Two of Sty's Temple Vestals sauntered pneumatically by. I've known Sty some time, and still haven't seen a single one tender any sacred flames. They always carry a Staff of Relevant Life – I won't say what it's shaped like, if that's all right. I lust after one called Momenta, but she stares through me. They live in small caravans and trailers dotted round the field. Sty flits from one to the next, as a bee pollinates wayside blooms. Tinker says it's easy to guess which one he's kipping in; it's the one that rocks all night.

Sty had the usual meadow arrangement, the antiques laid out on trestles, where applicable. The two pieces of furniture rested on plastic sheets.

'It's in the cloister,' Sty explained, meaning a few upright poles with polythene overhead. Otherwise it was open to the elements. A nubile Temple Vestal stood by in white raiment – a sheet with gold crosses adorning the hems – with one breast exposed. Sty smiled at my interest. 'You still admire Momenta? Greek ideals, Lovejoy. So many Earth rituals predate Hebrews, Persia, Christians.'

'Hello, Lovejoy.' Liz Sandwell is from Dragonsdale, a bonny lass unfortunately matched with a rugby giant. We'd made smiles when he was playing away. 'I see you like Sty's . . . decor.'

'I was only saying hello,' I said, narked. 'It's polite.'

Liz propelled me away from Momenta. 'You've heard of the expert Simon Doussy? He's here!' Such breathy excitement is usually reserved for royalty, sex or wealth.

The man was talking with Big Frank from Suffolk, about being best man, I shouldn't wonder. He was smooth, tie just so, the sort you see in departmental stores as floor walkers, hired for their wavy hair. Florence Hughes was there, all sequins and black lace to prove that she would never grow old (a word forbidden within gunshot, for she was still being twenty-nine). Dunno what women have against age. Older women are preferable, all things being equal – and are usually preferable even if all things aren't, if you follow.

'Is there any Georgian in, Liz?' Florence was a clue.

Liz smiled sweetly. 'Perhaps La Hughes can recognize some early Regency piece from her childhood!'

'Here, Lovejoy,' Tinker growled. 'Them girls have nothing on. They'll catch their deaths of cold.'

'Leave off, Tinker.' Kim Doyle and her live-in deficit, Tolly, no surname, were in. Rumour said that they were unsourced, meaning having unidentified backers. I left Liz and crossed to Kim and Tolly. 'Wotch, pals.'

Kim was all dimples, very fetching. She dresses like a cowgirl, fringed leather and buckskin leggings. Some days she seems all bottom, other days it's bosom and legs. Today she wore a kidskin cloak with a Celtic clasp. She looked good enough to eat. 'Lovejoy! You made it past Momenta!'

'Got a drink, Lovejoy?' Tolly said without much hope.

'No, Tolly. Tinker hasn't, either,' I added quickly, for Tolly is your actual New Age forager. He's on the dole, cadges off buskers. Those I don't mind. But I can't forgive a dud thief. He once stole his own lawyer's briefcase at court. He also stole some oxyacetylene equipment to do Dorrard's Bank in the High Street – and was really narked when the peelers found him next morning, still trying. He'd stolen welding equipment instead. Yet he lands a glamorous bird like Kim Doyle. She concentrates on silver, porcelain, some paintings. Odd that Sty'd invited them. Had they friends here I didn't know about?

'Lend us a note, Lovejoy?' Tolly asked, his one greeting. He dresses like a marauding Brigantean, rough leather tied with thongs, silvery studs. I couldn't help wondering about his festering teeth and Kim's succulent lips. Aren't folk odd?

'Time, worshippers!' Sty called. He has a falsetto voice, but is no eunuch. 'Deals on the nail!'

Which was an insult. The one good thing about antique dealers is, they honour their bargains or die. 'On the nail' means to pay ready gelt, from the Bristol Exchange's four ancient pillars, The Nails, whereon you plonked your money. Liverpool Exchange had a copper plate, The Nail. Limerick Exchange had a giant three-foot-diameter copper plate known as The Nail. There's nowt new. I drifted, to soak up the antiques.

Meadow? Maybe because it's like a temporary fair in a real meadow. The important point about a meadow is that you can't be sure the stuff's not nicked. Which means that you have to assume it's *all* stolen. So, buy in a meadow, then sell fast. After that, you're in the clear. That's why antiques are beautiful. This potpourri was a spread of about thirty antiques, lookalikes, fakes, distresseds and relics, plus . . .

Florence said, 'It's a load of tat, Lovejoy, isn't it?'

But an antique had spoken, as clearly as if it had sung out. It was a silver bowl, but not simply that. I wiped the silly grin off my face and tried to look bored though my soul chimed like a berserk campanile. I could hardly look at the superb silver. No lion mask, no ring handles, certainly not massive – only weighed about thirty ounces. But it was worth Sty, his entire Temple of Whatnot, his Vestals – even Momenta – put together.

Tinker was complaining to Sty, 'Them girls should get dressed. This weather goes to your chest . . .' Florence was asking me about some fake George II kneehole desk: 'Are those handles right, Lovejoy . . . ?' And Big Frank was coming over to look at the silver bowl. It was among cutlery, a chamber candlestick – that's a squat upright candlestick in a small flat pan, all silver.

'Genuine, Lovejoy?' You've to crane up to talk to Big Frank. He's silver mad, wouldn't cross the road for a Sheraton. Despite his obsession, he knows less about silver than he does about women, marrying as he does with cavalier disregard. 'Shouldn't it have a cross on the stick?'

'Sometimes. That'd be late Restoration, if genuine.'

He nodded, not downhearted. He'd make it genuine 1680 in a trice. He is the illegal owner of many ancient silversmiths' dies, wherewith to hallmark any fake crap. He makes three thousand per cent profit. 'Somebody's gone over the top with the punchbowl, eh?'

'Mmmmh.' I mentally apologized to the beautiful antique monteith. 'The base was original, but just look at the top.'

'Usual balls-up, some nerk putting too many makers' marks on,'

Big Frank grumbled. Fakers always have more trouble getting marks off than putting new ones on. Removing a mark can take three weeks of solid fettling. 'See the marks on the rim and base are different? Idiots.'

'Mmmmh,' I said, looking bored. 'Not much here, is there?'

'No. Disappointing. You met Mr Doussy, the Impressionist collector?'

Now, this was from our silver expert, a man who's made it his life study. Yet he strolls away from the one piece of silver that could buy the neighbourhood. Which proves that your average antique dealer's knowledge lies south of the comic strip. For the monteith is rare, rare.

They say the name comes from an eccentric Scotsman whose cloak was deeply notched. The monteith has nothing to do with him, being simply a silver bowl whose notched rim allows you to hang drinking glasses *inside* the water-filled bowl. It's a simple glass cooler, nothing more. But they are unbelievably rare. The whereabouts of most are recorded. The commonest mistake is to sell them as punchbowls. If you see one, sell your granny and go for it. They emerged about the 1680s. Some – I've never seen one – have a detachable rim like a collar. The Victorians tended to fix the collars permanently to the base, a friendly silversmith naturally imposing his own marks. Antique dealers like Big Frank naturally assume that some cunning faker's enthusiasm ran away with him. My hopes rose. Florence was looking in a mirror on an Edwardian washstand, junk (the washstand, not Flo).

'Like your frock, love.' When fawning, praise their looks.

'Lovejoy! You noticed it's an original!' She gushed perfumed delight. I strained for air. Nothing stays ungushed around Florence. But older women have an inner wisdom, however barmy, that younger birds don't even begin to understand. And they bring a little mercy, the essence of the successful woman. Where was I? The monteith.

'Look, love,' I said, making sure we were remote from the rest. 'That punch bowl. I *think* ... ' I dwelt on the word ' ... it's a friend's.'

'Rotten luck.' She tutted sympathy. 'Trying to buy it back?'

I did my forlorn look. 'Big Frank's in. My friend'd pay good money for it.' I filled up at the thought of my mythical old mate. 'He's in a nursing home. His family aren't good. His son's a swine . . . ' I choked back a sob, believing my own tale.

'Poor man! He'll *need* his little treasures, in a home!'

'I knew you'd understand.' I smiled with utmost sincerity.

'Oh, I *do*, Lovejoy! It was the same with my Great Aunt Faith! My cousin Jane was *so cruel* – '

The Florences of this world rabbit on. You have to be firm. 'Would you bid, love?' I told her an amount that widened her eyes. Suspicion glimmed within. 'It's my one chance, love,' I wheedled.

'Why don't you ask Liz Sandwell?' she demanded quietly. 'You're always around that bitch.'

'Florence.' I went all frosty. 'Don't speak of ladies like that. If you won't help an old gentleman – '

'I'm sorry, Lovejoy. You've got the cash, though?'

Lancashire Law, they say in the north; no stake, no draw. The consequences of default can, I assure you, be dire. I was frightened, bidding on a meadow without the money.

'Certainly,' I lied, throat dry. 'I won't forget it.'

'You won't forget it because you and I will have supper tonight.' She waited for my synapses to clang.

'Love, my pleasure,' I said, pure honesty shining from my eyes. She let me go. Tinker shuffled over. 'Tell Dolly to wait. Matter of life or death, keep her here.'

'Stop sniffing around posh bints, Lovejoy,' he said, censorious. 'It'll end in tears.'

'Get gone.' I went towards Big Frank and the suave gent. 'This is your friend, Frank? Lovejoy. How do?'

We made polite mutters. Simon Doussy sussed me. I didn't need to suss him. He could only be the 'expert' who'd lately accompanied Mrs Arden. He looked cool, in place.

'Pleased to meet you, Lovejoy. I've heard a lot about you.'

So why I haven't heard a thing about you? my mind went, but I grinned and nodded, the country oaf. I could see he was disappointed. 'All bad I hope?' The goon's response.

'Seen anything you like, Lovejoy?' Mr Urbanity.

'I like everything. You?'

'A bit here and there.' The sparring done, he swooped. 'You're the divvy. For what?'

33

'My divvying comes and goes,' I said, woebegone. 'Wish it worked all the blinking time.'

He didn't believe a word. I could tell. He asked my opinion about an Argand oil wall-lamp, double chimney and a cunning central oil reservoir. They were a major advance before gas lighting. The valuable ones have Wedgwood jasperware mounts, Matthew Boulton doing the originals for the Swiss inventor. I said it might be original, and deliberately got the date wrong. I said it was before Aimé Argand's patent got revoked in 1780. I should have said 1784.

He didn't correct me, didn't even inhale as if about to, but he knew, he knew. I went to stand with Liz. Sty started the auction with an incantation while we stood like lemons in various attitudes of school-prayer reverence. Then Sty called out, 'This thing?' while a Vestal indicated the antique, and we were off.

There were few competitive bids. Liz Sandwell got a tin tobacco jar with a domed lid, quite good. Kim bought the furniture, mostly dross. Florence competed without real hope. The prices were reasonable, as always at a meadow auction. There's no sense messing about with low bids. It's a selected audience, so the starter bids are very near the eventual knock-down price. Everybody just puts on a quizzical expression as if to say, That it, then? and somebody nods and it's on to the next.

Big Frank got the silver chamber candlestick for not quite a song. Simon Doussy got a teapot made without a lid all in one. He'd hardly glanced at it, a sharp-eyes. Liz had recognized it as a Cadogan teapot, called after the Honourable Mistress Cadogan, who sent an Indian greenware piece for Thomas Bingley at Swinton to copy. Nobody took much notice of these funny teapots until the Prince Regent was tickled pink when, out visiting, somebody served him a rum toddy from one. (You fill them upside down through a hole underneath, set them upright. The tea can't run out even though the hole's left open. A tube is wound round inside, allowing the tea out of the spout when you pour.) It wasn't daft, for the tea stays hot longer. Try one. Collectors go for those decorated in relief with peach flowers, fruit and foliage. Lately the prices of Cadogans in pearl with a green ground have gone ape. I don't understand demand. It is hell trying to outguess public whim. I like things to stay constant without sudden crazes. Like sex.

The monteith came up. I could hardly breathe. Big Frank bid a token fortune, Florence chipped in with my maximum amount – me with my heart pounding – then just before consensus the swine Doussy gave a casual, 'Oh, I think maybe a hundred higher, what say . . . ?'

Florence darted a glance at me, a clear giveaway, the stupid cow. The auction went on, me staring dully, my disappointment so profound I was almost suicidal.

We all drifted, chatting or pretending to. Florence said to meet her at the war memorial about sevenish.

She whispered, 'I'm looking forward to our evening, Lovejoy. I simply *love* a good meal.' She lives on double meanings. I responded with a merry jest.

Dolly had gone, a stroke of luck. It would have been a stroke of bad, had Florence got the monteith, for I'd have been lynched on the spot. See what I mean about women being thoughtless? They ought to get organized instead of flying off the handle for nothing. I spent a few seconds talking to Momenta until other Vestals prised me loose.

Big Frank gave me a lift. Tinker went with Kim and Tolly. All the way to town Big Frank complained because I wouldn't be best man. He made me feel a right worm, so I agreed. I extracted a promise, though.

'I want to see your divorce papers *before* church, Frank. None of that it's-in-my-other-jacket like last time.'

'Right, Lovejoy. I promise.'

'And if there's more than eight sets of relatives and three objections when the priest asks about impediments, I'm out of it.'

'Right, Lovejoy.'

One thing, I thought bitterly. I can still bargain.

6

Getting downhearted isn't fair. Oh, I'm not one of these folk who's forever depressed at the economy, youth's mad values, oil slicks. I'm as concerned as anyone about the razor-billed guillemot or whatever, sure. But I don't wake screaming because Peking has a traffic problem. I'm a soul of bright outlook. Women help. Antiques help. That's only another way of saying that life helps.

So why my dispirit? I trudged into Woody's caff to take stock. Something was rotten.

'Here's Lovejoy, booys!' Harry Bateman called, joyful to be handing it out for once instead of catching it from his wife, Lily, mistress of Patrick the Strange. He started up on an imaginary trumpet, '*Pa-paaaa, papapa-paaa-papapa* . . .' to wholesale laughter. The place rocked in its welter of fag smoke and fumes of saturated fat. It did little to lift me as I asked the waitress, all six feet of her, for a pile of toast.

'You've the money, Lovejoy?' Lisa adopted that provocative pose, one foot advanced, hip out of line. I swear she only does it to get me going.

'Course!' One thing I didn't need today was another failure before breakfast. 'Look, Lisa, just because you archeologists can't get to the treasures first . . .' She's a digger, always despoiling the graves of our ancient ancestors. It's known as vandalism, if you're not posh. If you go tribe-handed and have a letterhead in Albertus Bold, you're immune. I asked, quiet, 'What're they singing?'

She coloured. ' "The Slave Chorus", from *Aïda*.'

'Ta, love.' Opera'd be nice, if it wasn't for those burdensome chunks between songs. No wonder I felt soulsore, off course on my own pond. I was now scared worse.

The place suddenly fell quiet. Denny was in, offering bargains. 'Deals on wheels!' he kept calling. His expertise is rumoured to be transport – trains, bikes, motors, scooters. His wife left him last August, to bring him to his senses, but he was thrilled and stuffed her space with yet more tat on spokes. She lives now with a fertile boatman in Rowhedge.

'Morning, Lovejoy.' Doc Lancaster slid in opposite. My low spirits nose-dived.

He's not actually a bad sort, more misguided. He's one of those tallish, cool Englishmen you see in the tropics, never fazed by aboriginal dialects, droughts, or the tumbu fly. Dry of wit, his main flaw is that he's hooked on health. Like I say, mania comes in many a guise. No wonder the caff went quiet. I saw two dealers surreptiously extinguish their cigarettes. Joe Chance, a wandering dealer who lived on the knock (suddenly appearing at your door with money 'for any old thing you'd like to sell, lady . . . ') even covered his meal, a mishmash of eggs, grease-riddled bacon and charred sausages in a sea of congealing lard. It looked delicious. Nessie Packard, a recklessly obese treen dealer, gave Doc a smug greeting over her pious slice of wheat toast. He returned a smiley nod. He's up to everybody's game, knows full well she moves on to gins and massive chocolate creams for elevenses.

'Morning, Doc. No, sorry.' I said it all in one from habit.

'Sunday's trip, Lovejoy. Biggest contributor goes.'

'Oh, aye.' I eyed him. 'Won't take long, will it?'

'Shouldn't. Wales isn't far, cross-country.'

That made me gag. 'Me? *Wales*?'

'You'll love it. An air-conditioned charabanc.'

'It's two hundred miles, for God's – '

'It's four hours, Lovejoy. Sleep in luxury, then home. It's not the North Pole. You can't let the charity down now.' He saw my plate come, the tea, Lisa stand waiting, felt the terrible pause. 'Don't you have an unhealthy intake about now, Lovejoy?'

'Yes, well.' I felt my face redden. 'I've taken your advice, Doc. Eating, er, polystyrenes. I'll go jogging if my leg mends . . .'

He sighed, nodded to Lisa. I whaled into the grub, offering him half a slice in token politeness. He refused it, thank God. I was starving. 'One other thing, Lovejoy.'

That froze me. Offhand remarks spell doom, from gentlemen concerned with the Common Good.

'What?' I felt shaky. Usually I'm only like this after heavy-duty wassailing. Maybe Sty's had unsettled me, because a charabanc jaunt was no threat. You get these feelings. It was probably hunger.

'Will you phone in, say how it goes, Lovejoy?' I realized with astonishment that he was embarrassed. I'd never seen a mortified doctor before and must have gaped. 'No reason, just that I like to take an interest.'

Should I take pecuniary advantage of a doctor suddenly discountenanced? Conscience dealt with, I summoned Lisa and told her double eggs, bacon, fried bread, eight more slices of toast. 'Proper butter, Woody,' I called. 'Your waitress shorts me with maggy ann.' He made a rude gesture, coughing flakes of cheroot into congealing beans. 'Well,' I told Doc, 'Woody keeps proper butter for the Plod, only gives us margarine. It's not . . . ' I brightened. A word came to my rescue, '*democratic*. You want me to phone, right?'

'If it's not too much trouble.'

'Okay, then.' I honestly couldn't see what the fuss was about. Then my mind went, Aha! Sly old Doc had a bet on! Doc Davis in Dedham was his rival. They went to international matches at Twickenham, bet on all that rah-rah stuff. If Doc Lancaster got the bent word from me *before even the trip had finished* . . . ! The cunning swine. He soared in my estimation. Maybe medical schools did teach something useful after all.

'You'll find the team pretty friendly, Lovejoy.' Doc rose, leaving some notes floating on the table's spillages. I snaffled them, a frog with a fly.

'You coming too, then?' I gave back, narked. Charities charge everybody else for their own piety.

'Don't be silly. I've the practice. Hope your leg mends.' He smiled at my blank expression. 'To go jogging like you said.'

'Oh, ta.' I grimaced at an imaginary twinge. Trust him to pick me up on a casual remark, malevolent sod.

He left with a wave at Lisa, who looked after him through the window. I could tell she'd like to make smiles there. Strange, but you don't usually think of birds having carnal lusts the same as us, do you? She plonked the vast Woody's special down and stood waiting. Blithely I pulled out the notes and with a flourish peeled . . . No I didn't. I slo-o-o-owly removed one and handed it to her, gaping as

38

it left my hand. It was of a denomination I didn't normally see. Now, whatever inflation's done, you can get all Woody's culinary efforts on one plate for less than a fiver, easy, repeats thrown in. So why did the notes Doc Lancaster had dropped on me each outweigh that? For a *breakfast*? Even I couldn't nosh my way thorugh a fraction of this gelt. I thought, came to no conclusion except that I was unhappy.

Like I said, time to find Imogen. She's a dancer, and as unemployed as dancers always seem to be. First, I'd find out about Wales, where certain people wanted me to go. The library called.

Our local library's the pits, so I got a lift to Ipswich. I asked for Wales, including language.

'Welsh under *Foreign*,' the assistant said airily. I knew I was in for a high old time.

'Welsh is the only language that *isn't* foreign, love,' I told her, but she was too learned to suffer learning.

There seemed to be two distinct kinds of books. One claimed that Wales did everything in all history – America's Declaration of Independence, explored the planet, Thomas Jefferson was Welsh, so was Montezuma, King Arthur, his Round Table, everybody else that mattered. The other kind claimed that Wales actually *didn't* do everything but *would* have – but for bad luck/oppression/paganism/ Methodists/poor weather, etc. In five minutes I was fed up. I persevered.

And learnt that the Welsh are great genealogists, their families extending to the ninth degree of kindred. I come from close Lancashire folk, but even we only reach the fourth. And the Welsh claim descent from every king you ever heard of, Welsh or not. If he wasn't Welsh, well, he probably was anyhow. All Welsh are descended from princes, Egyptians, God-knows-who. But no popes. Wales was founded by the Trojans fleeing from Troy (yes, that one), ancient Phoenicians, et aristocratic cetera.

Wales's 8,000 square miles, I read, inspired the world's greatest musicians. Wales has a trillion breathtaking world records. Prince Madoc of Wales discovered America in AD 1170, and the Daughters of the America Revolution have erected a plaque to tell his arrival in Mobile Bay, Alabama. The Mandan Indians spoke Welsh to prove it, but are now extinct. Dylan Thomas wrote sourly of the Land of My Fathers, 'My fathers can bloody well keep it!' Yet it was in Wales that the first steam train, Trevithick's, rumbled out of Merthyr at a giddy five miles an hour or so in 1804. Sickeningly, a Welsh squire holds the record for shooting 'sporting' animals – over 5,100 'rabbits, etc.' in a 'standard' seven-hour shoot. God knows what he did on a 'good' day.

They truly did colonize. They failed in Brazil, but pulled it off in Patagonia. There, their Welsh-speaking colony in 1865 gave women the vote. They lost a gunfight with Butch Cassidy and the Sundance Kid, who quarrelsomely arrived for reasons best not gone into. The purplish dragon of Rome's banners is really the red dragon of Wales. Endemic slavery hung about longer than anywhere else. Wells are not holy in Wales, whereas elsewhere they are dressed in flowers on May Sunday – you hang a thread or pluck of wool on the nearby alders, for the luck. Wales actually has cursing wells. God, I thought, reading on in alarm, I've to watch my step.

Differences were everywhere. Poetry's inflexible mediaeval Rules of Twenty-Four Metres has decided if poems are any good. And Good Queen Bess, the Virgin Queen, was delivered of a healthy babe near Llangollen, a terrible secret. Less secret is that Queen Elizabeth the Second is actually one of the Gorsedd of Bards of the Isle of Britain, robes and all.

Merlin the Magician is Welsh. As are all known religions. I flicked the pages faster, because Welsh religions are unknowable. I mean, Baptists, Methodists of (reputedly) a good dozen stripes, chapels of over forty persuasions, Welsh Anglicans, Reform sects, Nonconformists doing battle with Unitarians. My head spun. And they all persecuted the poor old Quakers. I gave up, like I'd already done with Welsh politics. I honestly did try to plough through the records of a Swansea by-election, but every bloke seemed to have his own party.

The language, though, underpins our own. English dissected reveals tons of Welsh, even though it was bad-mouthed as the Victorians rushed to anglicize it. It happened to all lingos and dialects, home and overseas, suppressing mostly by derision and school punishments. I remember getting thumped myself for talking dialect, what I'd thought was English, my first day at school. School is there to clout you, in Wales as elsewhere.

Tiring, I concluded that Welsh traditional law, of the ancient Prince Hywel Dda, was beyond comprehension. I also learnt that the flamboyant Prime Minister Lloyd George was actually a sly old coot who sold knighthoods (£10,000) and peerages (£100,000) on a sliding scale, and got stocks and shares by means not yet fully understood. His (beloved) English mistress and (maltreated) Welsh wife had a lot to put up with. An old manuscript told me that if you could build a house in twenty-four hours on common land, the plot became yours forever, free.

That was it. Ancient Celtic folklore was founded on fairy tales, fantasy for storytellers. The Romans obliterated it in Anglesey. Harmless enough when a Victorian lady invented a 'traditional' fancy costume. I find it rather pretty, and no reason to march on Rome, if you follow. There are some really curious facts, though. How come that the dark-haired Welsh called the blond Vikings *Y Cenhedloedd Duon*. The Black Nations?

The library assistant shook me awake. I blundered out, knowing enough about Wales – so I thought. They seemed a rum lot, but who isn't? Wales seemed bland enough. Four Sunday hours on a charabanc, then home by evensong, same day if I wanted. Easy. Uneasy.

7

Having no motor's inconvenient even with Dolly's mobility. I phoned her at the voluntary library, arranged to meet her twoish. I found Tinker forlorn outside the Woodman and said I had to go to Imogen's. He was censorious, hating postponing the next tavern.

'We've to earn some credit at Postern's. Viewing's today?'

'Word's got about, Lovejoy, about them IOUs.'

'Here.' I pulled out Doc Lancaster's bounty and gave him three. 'Don't forget to eat.' How he survives on only beer beats me. Logically he should be dead. He gaped. 'Lovejoy. What you done? Maudie Laud's – '

'It's safe coinery, Tinker. Doc Lancaster paid me in advance, wants the nod on this Sunday.'

Tinker cackled so much he set himself coughing, hawked up phlegm, spat between two prams. It hit a dog between its ears. It snarled, mystified, went on its way in a state of mistrust. He blotted his rheumy old eyes on his sleeve. 'Doc got a bet on, eh?'

'Meet at the Three Cups. We'll show folk we've got gelt.'

'That Imogen should cover up. She's not decent.'

'I'll tell her,' I promised. I never do. She'd think I was off my head. I conducted him into the Trinity Walk alleyway, and climbed the Dance Academy's grotty staircase. I could hear clapping, Imogen's exhortations, tinny piano music, and feel the quivering boards. Gingerly I knocked.

A glass partition separates the office – a chair, desk, battered cabinet, phone – from the exercise floor. It's the entire Academy, apart from a corridor with old metal lockers and loos. No showers, no baths. It's pretty spartan. A score or so women in leotards – Tinker's state of undress – were leaping and clapping to Imogen's calls while a diminutive lady with a bun and a lace blouse played on the old upright. I'd got Im the piano cheap.

A bonny red-haired girl was on the phone in a temper. 'I'll call you back,' she was saying. She saw me. 'They've arrived at last. Where is it?' She looked beyond me.

'There's only me. How long'll Imogen be?' She observed me with a knowing sneer, as if she'd expected her dance teacher to be mixing with lowlifes.

We waited in silence. I watched the dancers. They were naff. Some were old, others smart and crisp of movement. Imogen was as slender as ever, cheering them on. I suppose every dance teacher has to pretend that terrible heartiness. I hummed the melody, wondering why the angry lass looked familiar. I'm dynamite with faces.

The music laboured to an end, the dancers making it within a couple of bars. Im came in.

'Lovejoy! How very nice to see you!'

'Wotch, Im. Only called on the off chance.'

'Look,' Miss Charm snapped, rising. 'I can't hang about – '

'Meg, please,' Imogen begged. I felt awkward and dithered. 'Just think – '

'I've already thought.' The girl swung out.

Im rushed, calling downstairs, 'You'll phone, promise?'

'I might!' and she was gone. I looked askance at Im as she returned to dry her nape, head sideways on like they do.

'Sorry about that, Lovejoy.'

'It's okay, Im.' Meg the Morose was probably some friend's daughter passing through. None of my business, but curiosity drives you mad. 'Love, will you be free any time? I've something on my mind.'

'I heard, Lovejoy.' She was faintly amused, but I could see that Meg's stormy exit had depressed her. She was normally a lot bouncier. 'Your slavery. I don't trust Mrs Arden.'

'It was grim,' I said nobly. 'I was the last to hear.'

'Don't sulk, Lovejoy.' The first of the women came out of the changing corridor, flinging on coats, dropping handbags and bits of gear. 'Here's impossible. Where?'

'The Three Cups.'

'See you there. Give me a few minutes.'

'Right. Ta, Im.' I left among the departing women. They asked if I was joining the class. I said maybe, soon as my leg mended. I limped to show a football injury. They sympathized, said dancing was great. I ducked away from these lunatics into Lord Benton's Walk.

Which was how I came to spy on Meg, who was speaking angrily to Simon Doussy. They were in a small alcove in the wall of old St Nicholas's church. It's still used by snoggers of an evening. I've used it myself, when the bird was worried about being seen. I halted, stared unconvincingly into a florist's window, watching their reflection.

The odd thing was, I knew her from somewhere. And she'd expected me to come with someone, which was really odd. Somebody else, bringing 'it'? She'd looked behind me, so the package was precious, because only then do delivery people go in pairs. The second oddity was that her manner had definitely changed when she'd heard my name.

Doussy persuaded her to get into a car at the corner of Wyre Street. I was by then eeling through the alleyway towards the Three Cups. I'd wondered if Meg was one of Sty's Vestals. I'd ask Imogen.

Tinker was in the Three Cups when I arrived. Unfortunately, so was somebody else.

The Three Cups is the place I told you about, plumb in the town centre. I like it. There's an old Saxon church opposite – successfully vandalized by our council into a folksy museum with Tudor-type music plinking and goonish wax models that schoolchildren sketch in 'real living history' class. We're progressive, acres of car parks replacing superb ancient architecture to prove it. The tavern's old as our hills – older in fact, because we had a recent earthquake, 'recent' being the 1880s. Tinker likes the Three Cups because it's got beer.

But some folk are much less admirable. One of them's Gee Omen, diamond merchant extraordinaire to his glitzy friends, pillock to those like me who hate him.

Two years ago, he gave me a lift home from Corby where I'd advised some women wanting to sell pottery for an old people's home. They'd got hold of nine Bellarmines. I said I'd help. Daft me. Bellarmines are nicknamed 'greybeards'. They're ugly stoneware, crude salt-glazed things you wouldn't shake a stick at. Except they're highly sought by collectors. Bellarmine was a dour cardinal well hated in good Queen Bess's time. People imagined his gruesome phizog in the moulded face mask. They're only bottles, hold from a pint to a gallon. These Northants ladies had the rare 'pottle' bottle – half-gallon – so made a killing when I'd divvied them as genuine.

I'd been waiting at the bus stop when Gee Omen stopped his vast silvery motor. Accepting lifts is a kindness that I rarely bestow. I hardly knew the bloke, just seen him around at exhibitions of Victorian jewellery. I find you have to pay a fare. During the journey to East Anglia he wore me down asking about Continental ferries, truckers on the A12 trunk road, the night shifters who'll deliver antiques illegally anywhere, all that. I finally started to close up. The sod chucked me out for not being more forthcoming. That, I didn't mind. But something happened that put me off Gee Omen for life.

We were at this roundabout on the Cambridge outskirts, Gee narked at my reticence. I could tell he was in a temper. In the darkness a hedgehog slowly started across the road, rocking to and fro. Gee drove straight over it, even as I said, 'Mind that . . . !' And the bugger laughed, 'Three points!' smacking the wheel in self-congratulation. I didn't speak another word, merely said my thanks. I watched his motor go, and knew hatred.

Seeing him chatting, buying friends with drinks from his manyfold wad, my heart remembered the stone in its centre. I didn't smile. He greeted me like a long-lost brother. I just signalled Mary the barmaid for a drink in the taproom.

'Mary, darlin'!' Omen called. 'Lovejoy's swill's on me!'

I gave Mary the bent eye, Just you dare. She quickly pushed the glass into the taproom. Tinker followed me shamefacedly.

'What's good old Gee on about, then?'

'Ferreting, Lovejoy.' Tinker coughed up a great gob of phlegm and dribbled it into an empty glass. Everybody went queasy. I wanted to apologize but, cowardly, didn't say a thing. 'On about some tom.' Tom is jewellery.

'He'll have a hard time. Mrs Arden's blotted it up.'

'He's milking the museums.'

During the past decade, museums and galleries had suffered from

Government cutbacks. They began to sell 'excess items'. Sensible folk like me created uproar, to no avail. They went on selling. And they did it stupidly. Like, if they had three Roman bronzes from Camulodunum – Rome's first-ever colony in Albion, the Isle of Britain – they'd flog off two, to anyone sweet of tongue. Such persuaders were mostly Gee Omen. He gave the trustees a written promise to sell them back to the museums on demand. Then he lit out for the Continent with the country's heirlooms. This deception the trade calls 'swearing'.

'As usual. They got anything left?'

'He's sworn a few pieces out from Suffolk.'

Europe's common market's really great. Its creation absolved governments of troublesome responsibilities, like protecting cultural heritage. Don't misunderstand me. I'm against nationalisms. I am, however, for a little fairness. I detected Tinker's reticence and shelled out for three pints and four pasties. He'd eat, with ale to irrigate solid calories.

Gee Omen's not his real name. I'd sussed it out as 'nemo' yonks before – no-one in Latin.

'Eh?' I asked Tinker between coughs and spits.

'That tart as bought you, Lovejoy.' He cackled, opening his mouth to reveal a cavern churning pieces of meat, potato, immersed in a slop of ale. I looked away, nick of time. 'She's his pal.' He plucked my sleeve, came closer for a secret confidence. In a voice like a factory hooter he whispered to East Anglia, 'She's hump-and-dump, Lovejoy.' And in case the coast had missed the point, he explained, 'Fucks, then fucks orff, understand?'

'Aye, Tinker,' I sighed. I'm burdened by friends.

'Screws,' this paragon of eloquence emphasized, 'then blues.'

'The Postern auction, Tinker,' I said, to shut him up, though he'd actually given me an important warning. 'What's in?'

'Nothing, Lovejoy, except a bloody glass thing. From the vicarage, Mersea Island. Never seed such. Like a huge chess piece, letter in the middle, ends sticking out – '

He stopped because I'd grabbed his windpipe. 'Tinker,' I told him quietly, 'just nod or shake your head, okay?' I slowly relaxed my grip and let his colour back. He wheezed, came to with a thunderous cough, spat across the taproom into the fireplace. 'Glass crown on top?' He nodded, swigged a pint in one go. 'Goblet at the top, glass lettering in the middle like Cs and Vs, their feet projecting?' His nod raised my hopes even higher. Excitement took hold.

Formerly East Anglia's trade – like that of Yorkshire and Leith – was muchly with the Baltics. Look at Culross, in Fife. Once a great walled burgh, palace and all, rich on salt and coal, then virtually a ghost town, it is now a respectable village. Like East Anglia, it has mirrored the Baltic trade. On the whole, Scandanavian glass was pretty mundane, except for Sweden, which filched Italians for Stockholm. It was the gifted Scapitta who got things moving about 1676 in Kungsholm. He chucked it up after a couple of years, but left a factory that flourished until Waterloo. Now, his ornate goblets sometimes emerge from attics hereabouts, a countryside memory.

'Who was there, Tinker?'

'Postern's? Florence, Liz Sandwell, that poof singer from Eltenham and his butler, ought not to be allowed, Big Frank's Tania, that forger with three wives. And a couple of barkers, stewed,' he added with prim disapproval, 'on flash.'

Flash being home-distilled liquor, I could imagine. But Tinker's news was interesting. A definite Scapitta piece is priceless. If it was a Kungsholm piece *after* Scapitta scarpered, it was still worth a fortune. And it takes a really skilled glassworker to make a replica . . .

'Tinker. I'll go to Postern's. If Imogen comes, tell – '

'No need, Lovejoy.' He quaffed my unfinished drink. 'She's just arrived, talking to Gee. He stays in her house near the Priory.'

I glared. 'You stupid old sod. Why didn't you say?'

'You never asked.' I ordered him another three pints. He could drink a brewery dry. 'Know what I think, Lovejoy?'

'No?' I bent close, uneasy, for ghastly new revelations.

'It's not decent,' he megaphoned. 'Unmarried woman, taking a man in. It's a carry-on – Lovejoy?'

But I was gone, signalling apologies to Imogen who looked up smiling. She was with Gee Omen.

You can always tell when a woman sits by a man what they are to each other. At least, sometimes always. Imogen and Omen were sharing more than cornflakes. I wanted Imogen's gossip, but not at such cost. I rushed into the shopping precinct, but was waylaid by the singer from Eltenham, and his butler.

8

There are friends, and friends you steer clear of. Sometimes I find myself nipping from alcove to gateway, nook to cranny, desperate to avoid this last category. Het up, I became careless.

'Coo-ee! Lovejoy!' a voice trilled.

I continued on, looking at shops and smiling at prams.

'Chuckie! Fetch Lovejoy!'

Grainers Walk, an alleyway leading to the market, could swallow, but too late. A hand clasped my shoulder.

'Lovejoy.' A bass voice vibrated the cobblestones. 'Come along, like a good gentleman.'

'Chuck,' I pleaded skywards where Chuck's face hovered. 'I'm pushed. And my leg – '

'Raddie is waiting, Lovejoy.'

'I'm coming!' I swear blokes his size don't think the same as us. He can't understand that we are at risk in a pub brawl. He's serene. Mayhem never touches him. Nor, I might add, does it touch Raddie.

The crowd parted as I was hauled along the pavement. Raddie was arranging himself in the lights of Sommon's jeweller's. The lights are those focused things that make the gems glitter. And no gem more glittery than Raddie. Raddie for radiant, he says.

He purred. 'Ever seen me so glamorous, Lovejoy?'

'Er, aye, Raddie,' I said. 'Great.'

'That all?' He rotated, admiring himself. Chuck stood.

'It's the most superb . . . ' Christ, was the word ensemble, that women use? '. . . ensemble, Raddie.'

I had to go canny because I killed his cousin once. You don't re-open old wounds. If admiration was called for, admiration I'd give till the cows came home. The pedestrians passed by. Local yokels smile with a strange fond knowingness, spotting Raddie. I'm always pleasantly surprised: women think him a mischievous child playing naughty dressing-up tricks (no pun intended). Chuck stands checking attitudes.

'You really think so, Lovejoy?' Raddie murmured, dragging the corners of his mouth down. 'I've gone *maddissimo*, haven't I, Chuckie?' He darted me a malicious glance and tittered. 'Dress is beyond *scruffs*. But we butterflies have to, well, *fly*.'

He looked a right nerk. Mascara'd eyes, false eyelashes, I suppose a wig (his hair hadn't been long or magenta), an orange cloak in sequins, thigh boots like a pantomime principal boy's, he'd have been laughable but for Chuck. Raddie's diminutive, Chuck's enormous, bull-necked, head shaved to a polish. He's your impeccable London butler in tails, black tie, patent leather shoes. Chuck drives Raddie in a Rolls big as Guildhall. Raddie deals in Roman to Early English jewellery. He appeared about twelve months ago from the Continent. They live near the lighthouse, in a converted Martello tower.

'Who did your colours?' I smarmed, not wanting talk to turn towards missing relatives. 'Magnificent!'

He fluttered his eyelashes, swirling the air. He pointed irascibly at some innocent shopper who Chuck removed by simply lifting the astonished bloke out on to the pavement, leaving Raddie all the mirrors. 'I had a *wretched* time with some mauve seersucker.'

'Er, anything you want, Raddie?' I was impatient. A fortune waited at Postern's.

'Yes, dear heart!' He dragged his loving gaze from his reflection. 'Sunday. Caravans, the raggle-taggle gypsies O.'

I laughed, but my mirth dwindled. This was now weird, when somebody as unlikely as Raddie beamed in.

Raddie batted me playfully with his luminous fan. 'You *are* going, Lovejoy?'

Best to be honest. I shrugged. 'I'd like to oblige, but – '

'Chuckie, dear.' Raddie returned to his reflection. 'Advise.'

Chuck placed a hand on my head, a sort of advisory hand, if you follow. 'Lovejoy?' His bass voice woke the pigeons up in Holy Trinity's squat Saxon tower. I felt narked. Those feathered sods could go wherever they wanted without bonecrushers like Chuck coming the heavy. It's not fair.

I grinned affably. 'I'm going for sure. I meant I wasn't sure of the starting time – '

'You know,' Chuck boomed. 'The Moot Hall.'

Raddie smiled in a way I didn't like. Clearing my throat for air, I gently withdrew my head and backed away. 'Right, then, Raddie. Hope it goes well, eh?' I hesitated while Raddie twirled, eyeing his cloak's hem.

'Bye-hee, Lovejoy.' He minced off towards the fountain, Chuck behind. I watched with great wariness until they were out of sight, then tiredly made my way to Postern's corruption-riddled auction rooms that smelled of stale sweat and woodworm. I reached it like a drowning sailor reaches land, in sore need of normality. For normality read antiques.

Raddie's a singer at the Marquis of Granby. No mention of relatives, thank God, whether alive or the other thing.

Postern's changes hands every Budget Day. Threadneedle Street investors, sloshed in wine cellars, decide to launch out on the stormy seas of antiques. They arrive mesmerized, craving the giddy gelt made from the world's mania for antiques. Every newspaper, pension fund, union savings company, resounds with tales of megamillions made from a threepenny splash. Like that Florida geezer who laid out two hundred quid for Giorgione's *The Three Ages of Man*, then coolly snaffled Leonardo Da Vinci's *Christ Amongst the Elders* for one and a half grand. It happens to everybody else, never me. The old placies, though, stay the same, musty, dusty, and crusty.

Postern is of the waistcoat-and-chain brigade, moustache, lazaroidal, scrawny faces, pinstripes. I think they buy blokes like Postern from a defunct batch made in 1911 and found in a cellar.

His thin-lipped smile died. 'Lovejoy. Wait.'

'Eh?' I'd not had this before. 'For what, Pozzy?'

'There are gentlemen in.' His smirk mingled admiration with fealty.

'My money's as good as theirs.'

'They pay, Lovejoy. You default.'

Silent, I stalked off – then nipped past the ironmonger's into the auction house yard. The whiffler – an eminently bribable shifter of assorted antiques employed by the auctioneers – was having a smoke, heels on a fake Sheraton pouch table.

'Wotch, Bert. Why's the place barred?'

Whifflers come in two sizes, the rotund corpulence and the funereal cachectic. Bert's the latter, chain-smokes – he's caused two fires – and picks losers at York Races.

'Posh dough. The Continong, Lovejoy. Not the likes of you.'

'Who are they?'

He eyed me with sour hope. I put on a show of shrugging off the whole thing. His hope of bribery died.

'Brussels. Pals of the guv'nor's friend Doussy.'

Were they indeed? 'We locals are Pozzy's stock in trade, Bert.'

'He let in Flo Hughes.' He sniggered at my angry frown.

'Bloody birds. It's always me out in the rain.'

He relented. I was postponing his destitution at the bookie's. 'Slide in, Lovejoy. Don't say I let you.'

'Ta, Bert. I owe you.' I eeled into the office, shushing Maureen, a middle-aged cynic I've wanted for years. She rolled her eyes, ignored me. She's always busy, proof there are female workaholics.

The auction rooms (why plural when they're one big space?) were filled with junk in varying states of disrepair. Immediately I saw two favourites of mine that kept recurring. I faked them two years back. One's an ancient rocking chair in red and white hickory. This is American wood, genus *Carya*. I'm told it's a pretty tree. Its wood is elastic, lovely to turn on a lathe or for doing bent work. (I don't mean illegal, I mean physically curving.) But, excited at getting hold of some seasoned *Carya*, I'd also made a mediaeval half-tester, that is, a wooden bed canopy. At the time I didn't realize the wood was hickory, so quick as a flash I aged it and sold it on. Every dealer in the Eastern Hundreds has had it at some time or another. Sooner or later they erupt at mediaeval furniture made of pre-Columbus wood, and round and round the poor things go.

Two men strolled among the crud. They wore overcoats with furred collars, homburgs. I'd seen one before, ordering a shipping container load from Long Melford.

Florence Hughes was looking at a pelerine in Ayrshire whitework – think muslin with varied needlepoint infilling and pretty designs. Scotch work, William IV to mid-Victorian days. I'm always narked at how cheap these worked pointy capes and children's bonnets sell. Some day, antique collectors'll see sense. I sssss'd quietly at Flo, who came across with the vigour of the fraudulent. I drew her behind a dud mid-Edwardian wardrobe.

'You're early, Lovejoy,' she said approvingly.

'Eh?' Then I remembered I'd promised her. 'Oh, just making sure . . . Look, love. Them blokes.'

'Mr Twentyman and his diamond merchant friend?'

'Er, aye, him.' Twentyman, London rep for the auction house near Hanover Square. I recognized him now. One of Lloyd's of London's 12,630 'Names' – insurance moneyers – who had lately gone on to the breadline or ducked out. Gone are the good old days when Lloyd's Names cabled to the San Francisco earthquake claimants in 1906 'Pay our policyholders in full.' But, *diamond*? 'Suss them for me?'

'You'll be on time, Lovejoy?'

Women never trust me. It's a flaw in their characters. 'Don't you trust me?'

'As far as I could lob you, Lovejoy.' She pulled my cheeks and plonked her moist mouth on me.

'Gerroff, silly cow.' I yanked myself clear.

'They've horrible taste, Lovejoy,' she said, checking with the woman's slick everywhere glances. 'They picked up a horrible glass goblet. Postern let them wrap it. Twentyman said to the foreigner, "Mustn't forget what we came for!" They had a laugh.'

'Postern saw them lift it?' I could hardly believe this, but Florence wouldn't lie.

'Great ugly glass thing. Useless in a normal household. He put it in their motor.'

Which explained why Postern was stationed by the door. To keep an eye on a valuable piece of antique Swedish glassware. For an auctioneer to fiddle so, this is very, very naughty.

Slipping out, I strolled by the picture-framer's on Peter Street, then up past Postern's windows. He was still there. I gurned at him. But I really wanted to feel emanations from the big Bentley parked illegally on the slope. I almost staggered under the impact of the unseen radiance beaming from the motor. I don't know how, but I got myself past. I was getting hungry. Dolly might want to get me something to eat. I had some money, but food is a woman's job. They do little enough as it is.

9

Antiques is packed with mysteries. Some are ancient. Like, why is the Bayeux Tapestry called that? It's an embroidery, not a tapestry. And was made in Kent, England, not Bayeux. Other mysteries are secret and recent. Like, why *did* the Prince of Wales and Mrs Simpson (yes, her) in their secret tryst in Hungary, in 1935, secretly telephone an antique dealer, Mr Pick, late at night from their secret room in Budapest's Hotel Donapalota? My own problem was all these once-rich entrepreneurs. Stupidly I went to find Brad at the boat race.

The town is set on a hill. Below flows a river. It winds a bit, floods now and then, has ducks and anglers, is mindbendingly dull. Constable painted it. Other than that, forget it. Not one antique shop on its bonny banks.

Brad is a boat-and-ocean man. That means barmy. Talk about gaff-rigged sloops and he's your man. He has a serious workshop. Buys jeweller's powders, corundum and such, polishes precious stones, works a lapidary's rotary polisher. We'd never had an epidemic of gemmologists in the Eastern Hundreds before. It niggled. So, find Brad, ask a couple of questions, and I'd know where I was. I could get on with my grot-riddled life of penury.

When I arrived, the children's boating-pond had been closed for the river races. These are crippling non-jollities to me. People's daftness only needs some excuse to spread like the plague. Across the meadow marquees had been erected. Ice-creamios, roll-a-pennies, stoves selling mushy black peas, fortune-tellers, balloon vendors, the whole shoddy mess of folk pretending they're having a great time. It beats me.

'Quid, Lovejoy.' The burly man on the gate stopped me.

'I'm only going into the park, Ratbag.'

'Entrance fee.' Ratbag because he shoots the rats along the river-banks with an airgun. He hates them, does it to preserve something or other, dunno what. 'For charity.'

See? Charity makes everybody else holy and you Scrooge. 'What charity?' I hung on in case it was the cats' home.

'Mental Health Unit.' He stood, ticket poised.

'The Royal Charter says the meadow's free,' I grumbled, paying up. 'The bloody war was fought over it.' Hereabouts 'the war' means King Charles I's Great Civil War.

Ratbag told me Brad was down at the river. I moved, mystified, among the children, morris dancers, white-hatted bowlers, the throngs milling about the flower show and home-made cake stalls. A riot. Had they no homes to go to?

Somebody grabbed my arm. 'The male swan's creating hell! It's swiped Old Jarge into the wet.'

'Not me, mate,' I told him, cheering up. 'I'm the lead boatman.' Nobody deserved a ducking more than Old Jarge. He's not the rural rustic he sounds. He's the town council's organizer.

'Sorry.' He vanished, still calling for help.

Five boats were already in. Victorians had dammed the river with a weir, to form a pool. No barges use it now. Once, it was where the Roman barges discharged their cargoes from Gaul. So far has our civilization advanced that it is now used solely for these boat races. Four furlongs upstream, to a ruined mill. The winners do it a second time, the losers being freed to drink themselves gormless in the beer tent. So the day goes riotously on, until in a grand final – by then everybody's sloshed senseless – one boat splashes home. It gets a song sung to it and floral tributes. I saw Brad's team among the willows. Old Jarge was wiping himself free of mud, surrounded by a twitter of benevolent ladies. A huge cob glided balefully in midstream, eyeing all with hatred.

'Jarge,' I called blithely, 'your megaphone get wet?'

He ignored me. I cheered up. A good omen. I declined home-made treacle toffee from some uniformed little girls, paid them a quid not to sell me the damned stuff. God, it looked evil.

'Hello, Lovejoy. You entering?' Brad's nautical blokes were all slogging away. I've yet to understand what they actually do. I think it's all sham.

'No, Brad. Hurt my arm . . . ' I always scupper his invitations.

He was waxing his boat's bum. 'Heard about your slavery. Grim work, was it?'

'Okay.' My grouse cut him short. I was sick of jokes at my expense. 'Anybody after tom lately, Brad?'

He stopped what he was doing and eyed me curiously. 'Real tom? No, except the buyers.'

This was the difficult part. 'Buyers in, then?'

'Collared the garnet-and-gold unearthed at Burstall. Not much of a piece, but rare.'

This late Romano-Celtic or Anglo-Saxon had been found by a moonspender – an illicit treasure searcher on Suffolk's bounteous pastures. I was narked it hadn't shown up at Sty's auction, especially after the hassle at The Ship pub on East Hill.

'I heard it was well-nigh ruined in the dig.'

Brad grinned. 'You should have asked them about it. They're staying at Mrs Arden's.' His mate Colley laughed.

'Ta, Brad.' I started to stroll away, a model of disinterest. 'Just curious.' I paused, narked, to get my own back. 'Oh, good luck with the race. If you're short of that white beeswax, let me know.'

And meandered on my merry way. I heard Old Jarge demand, 'Wax? Competitors waxing their boats *will be disqualified*!'

'Lovejoy!' Imogen linked my arm. 'Come to my dancers.'

'Just on my way,' I lied easily. 'Superb event, eh?'

'I'm coming to see you off on Sunday. Those lovely horses!'

'Eh?' I gaped, asked what she was on about as we traversed a series of guy ropes between tented stalls.

'The trip, Lovejoy.' She pursed her mouth in what I can only call an aggravating manner. 'I only wish I was coming.'

'What about Gee Omen?' I wasn't narked, but she was bonny.

We'd stopped for some reason. 'Gee? He's just gone into partnership. Him and his sightholding.'

'Well, a bloke and his work,' I said lamely, and put my mouth on hers. Gee Omen was a sightholder? We were mostly silent, until I broke away gasping. She glanced about, breathing stealthily, a woman planning infidelity.

'Not here, Lovejoy. I'll be finished here sixish.'

'What about Gee?' I could have throttled her, but needed to know.

'He's meeting his partner Simon Doussy. He'll be late.' She sprang away with that furtive falsity women employ when nearly discovered, and said brightly, 'No, Lovejoy! I simply don't have time! Perhaps later . . .'

And we emerged, talking casually as if we hadn't agreed on mutual ravishment. Folk are cunning. I'm thankful I'm not like that.

There were three nick-nack stalls – Margaret Dainty, Liz Sandwell, and a fragile little lady with a piece of porcelain on her stall. I found myself gaping at it, shuddering from its vibes.

Some of the most lovely porcelain jugs ever made came from the Midlands, Pinxton, near Chesterfield. Valuable, atrociously rare in pristine state, they still turn up. Luckily the press of folk was so great that Margaret and Liz didn't see me buy the luscious thing. It had that magic oil-on-water sheen that's a very strong hint. The painted flowers screamed of William Billingsley. I was shaking, but didn't know if it was because of what Imogen had told me or the little jug. Liz called after me asking what I'd bought. I smiled disarmingly, and escaped to see Brad's boat get disqualified for waxing. I got an ice-cream.

Sightholder. She'd said her bloke was a sightholder. Now, a sightholder spells diamonds.

Speaking of diamonds – who isn't? – they're no longer a girl's best friend. Everyone's saying it. Diamonds are *not* forever. Because there's a glut, a mighty one that won't go away. The world's awash with diamonds, and looks likely to stay so. Once, diamonds were paradise. Possession meant bliss, affluence, and the bitter admiration of your rivals. Stick a diamond on a lady's finger, she swelled with pride. The more dazzle, the greener her jealous friends. But in the early 1990s diamonds sickeningly proved you can't trust anything. Or, indeed, everything, 'everything' being the combined greed of the world's greatest superpowers, plus the world's most formidable cartel, plus politics. For nations everywhere shored up the world's diamond markets. The price was kept up there in the stratosphere. You'd think nothing could unglue such a financial empire, right? No, wrong. Crooks did it. And include politicians, governments, plus even me. Oh, and thee.

Remember those diamonds-forever halcyon days before August 1992?

Any tome on gems will give you the 'facts', those well-worn myths we all learnt and, in a sordid way, loved. The diamond facts: native carbon; found mostly as isolated cubic crystals; the only mineral with a Mohs scale of ten, maximum hardness. India supplied the Ancient World, then Portuguese Brazil three centuries ago. Then South Africa, Zaire, Angola, the Soviet Union, Botswana. Tanzania came up on the rails, China's Hunan Province, Australia, with South America doing its stuff.

Okay so geographical far. But diamond prospectors have hidden worries. Diamonds must be wrenched from the earth and polished. Not easy, because diamond mining was only economic if the diamonds were one in twenty million. (Get it? You dig, smash, wash, and search twenty tons of solid rock to find one-thirtieth of an ounce of gemstone.)

Except it's not even that easy. For first you have to know where. Then you have to recognize the stuff. History's littered with stories of prospectors who dug in the wrong places, or made 'miracle finds' of Scotch mist. And diamonds don't come all sparkly like in *Snow White and the Seven Dwarfs*. They come up looking like the twenty tons you've shovelled aside. Worse still, your diamonds might only be industrial-quality gems, worth practically nil. Of course, you might be lucky, like little Erasmus Jacobs who started South Africa's diamond rush by finding his 21.7 carat glittering diamond, and set the Victorian world agog. But might be only means might not be.

Nowadays, diamond investors are likely to be unlucky.

For the Soviet Union fragged. Governments shredded. Politics back in the 1990s changed from wholesale to piecemeal. Human greed, fuelled by hope's sad longing, altered for ever the stolid, solid world of diamonds where money and beauty reigned supreme. Like balloons do, it went pop. And it was the garimpeiros did the popping. The great De Beers people sweated in the ultimate nightmare, as diamond merchants blamed recessions, retailers blamed governments. But the garimpeiros – the universal word for treasure rustlers, wealth-crazed wildcat prospectors – screamed delight. They literally undermined the globe's diamond cartels in the biggest diamond bonanza the world has seen. De Beers *borrowed*. Even the plain words make me wince. It's like saying God's got lost. Don't misunderstand: diamonds aren't a huge industry – only one diamond miner to every thirty gold miners, after all. But the money is beyond belief.

Once, diamonds were simple: countries digging them up cut a deal with the secretive CSO – Central Selling Organization, London, the virtual handmaiden of De Beers, nooked away in London's unprepossessing Charterhouse Street. Botswana, for instance, simply sells the lot to the cartel. This controlled the flow of the precious diamonds that everybody wants. So the price stayed high, and every country mining them made a fortune. Bliss for the international cartel, bliss for the countries owning the diamond fields, right? Yes, way back then. But in Angola the garimpeiros suddenly realized they were not being policed much any more. Towns mushroomed as a thousand gun-toting prospectors a day trudged in across porous borders to Luanda Norte, and the Wild West was reborn.

It was odd of God to lend a hand. But He did. Just when the diamond world really began to panic, the Almighty, always a joker, sent the worst droughts of recorded time – and the diamonds suddenly became fifty times easier to spot in that old alluvial gravelly soil! Illicit diamond mining became a digging delirium, a tunnelling turmoil. And the CSO – four-fifths of all traceable carats subject to their stern rules, remember – spent hundreds of millions buying up the flood of new extraneously mined diamonds. (Incidentally, holiday in Belgium, to see the diamond rush's European terminus.)

Then, when diamond merchants were mopping their foreheads in relief, thinking it all over, the Soviet Union did its stuff. The old USSR used to play along, fourth in the world's diamond-producer league. Okay, the KGB nicked some superb gems, and good old decent Switzerland smarmed its bank-vaulted way into the KGB crooks' hearts by storing the smuggled stones, but basically it was stable: Yakutia – you've to call it Sakha Autonomous Republic now – in Siberia mined virtually 100 per cent of that nation's diamonds, and trickled them out at the correct rate. Happy bankers flourished everywhere. Very important, really, because whereas Angola grubs up something over a million carats a year Russia does ten times as much.

The rest of the diamond story you know: how USSR's élite but unpaid regiments joined the unemployed; how their special forces, including the famed *Spatsnaz*, disbanded into lone mercenaries scrapping in the Balkans or new republics. And how secret crimes were committed – like the mysterious death of Mr Nikolai Urkin, boss of Russia's most efficient diamond mines, who fell so very 'accidentally' from his high window into the dark Moscow street that nobody knows about, that didn't get properly investigated or explained ... See what I mean? You can think about diamonds in general and it's like a merry game. But dwell on one particular aspect, it's death and corruption. It'd worry me, if it wasn't normal.

All money's relative, isn't it? The USA thinks nothing of blueing twenty-three million dollars on one toilet for an astronaut, and a cool two hundred thousand dollars on a toothbrush holder (the toothbrush is extra). And what do I get for being sold for a day? But, to be a sightholder is an Oscar plus a peerage plus a fortune plus film starlets plus everything. The ultimate, in diamonds, so to speak. It all hinges on how diamonds are actually sold. I mean, even if your land yields glittering diamonds every square yard, you just can't dig them up and sell them, no. You take them to London. Specifically, to the CSO. And not everyone can walk in and simply buy. You have to be a sightholder. *And there's only about a hundred and fifty in the entire world.*

It's been written about everywhere, so I won't go on. Glossy magazines, thrillers, films, all harp on the great secret vaults in Charterhouse Street, and the selling 'sights' they hold.

Basically it's simple. If you're a sightholder, you get invited to come to view the new release of diamonds. But then the simplicity ends, for you don't just pop along when you're ready, go two floors up in De Beers, and pick what you want. You have a front man, a London diamond broker, whose job it is to tell them what sorts of diamonds you're hungry for. Then, you know what? On the appointed day, you turn up with your broker, all eager – and get handed a tiny package. Because they're all heart, you're actually allowed to open it and look. Inside, is a selection of uncut diamonds.

Now comes the crunch. You've got to buy the lot. Or not. At the price they say. No debate, no haggles, no let's-talk-prices. You humbly pay up, and depart rejoicing (or, possibly, seething). If you think the stones aren't good enough, you can walk out. But then what? Where's your business? What do you tell customers who want a diamond necklace? *And what if the CSO cross you off their list?* So you pay up. You've seen those small cardboad boxes that babies' bootees come in? That's how your diamonds are packaged. No plush velvets, no gold-edged leather cases. Cardboard. The box, the trade jokes, is free.

That's all there is to it. Umpteen thousand millions of us on Planet Earth, a hundred and fifty sightholders who are allowed in, and five diamond brokers to do the brokerage. Okay, there's a synchronized mini-sight in Kimberley, and one other in Lucerne, but you get the idea. A handful of people control diamonds. And you and me're on the outside looking in.

And Imogen's lover was a sightholder?

It's not blasphemous to grumble about God's quirky humour. But sometimes the Great Architect really does make you gasp. His great bounty gives control of all diamonds to one massive Corporation in the hands of, unbelievably, one family, the Oppenheimers. To prevent another writ, I must record that they're nice blokes, charitable to a fault. They give stable employment to a good twenty thousand and more. But *all* legit diamond marketing in the lap of *one* clone? Like I say, God's merriment is weird. And it gets quirkier. Guess what else they own? The answer is a rare yellow precious metal; you dig it out of the ground. Good old God gave them gold as well. Some quirk.

10

An antique dealer's life is rough, if you're any good. If you're a sessile trundler who whimpers on, then you're wasting everybody's time. I decided to stir things up.

So I went to watch Liffy nick a posh motor car, and saw Florence. My heart warmed. She was dithering in front of Raddie's new window. You can spot a woman eager to buy a mile off. She becomes a huntress. Get between a dragon and its aim, and you're for it.

Liffy's nothing to do with Dublin's river. It's short for lifter. He can lift – i.e., nick – anything. Five years ago he lifted a house. Honest – lock, stock and doorways. Took him two days. By the time the parish realized, it was gone. He got arrested, but the Plod's only interested in breaking and entering. Liffy stayed baby-faced, all what-me-sergeant? They let him go. He said he'd tipped the house in a landfill, which was a fib. I sold it for him to a parson creating an Elizabethan village, and parsons don't pay honest gelt. What with forking out for Liffy's dismantlers, the lorries, Sordid Bell, our bent lawyer, the money evaporated.

He's a loner. I saw his hallmarks by St Peter's church. Liffy's cousin's lad Dashboard was tying his shoelace by the traffic lights. The traffic wardens aren't about on fair days. Liffy's own wheels, a motorbike with a sidecar, was the giveaway. I crossed to Florence, to enjoy the fun.

'Lovejoy!' She only gave me a tithe of attention. Her eyes were on Raddie's display. Mine were on Liffy's reflection. He doesn't look about, just strolls by. He opens the cars with a coathanger. The car alarms he strangles first squawk. Dashboard tied his shoelace for the dozenth time, shaking his head. A car droned off towards the Castle. Hardly anybody about, the world gone to be counted. 'That white hand and shell's lovely, Lovejoy. How much duck?'

Duck is discount. 'Oh, say a quarter.' She grimaced. I got the point. Raddie charges women more. 'I could send Tinker in for you.'

'Would you, Lovejoy?' She batted her eyelashes, wafting gales of perfume. I reeled but manfully stuck it. 'Is it naughty?' Naughty means a fake.

'It's bonny,' I said grudgingly, then listened to my chest. One day, I suppose doctors will investigate us divvies. I stood near to the window, held my breath. A definite chime, like Sunday bells across the estuary. 'It's sound, Florence.'

Her face shone. I feel guilty at naked hunger. Why did she need money so desperately? Her husband had gone off with some younger tart, which shows how barmy blokes are. It's no good telling women that youth isn't everything. They think they know better.

'English?' Florence was saying. I smiled, because Dashboard straightened up. They were going for a Rover. I called across the roadway.

'Liffy. That Bentley, okay?' I grinned feebly at Florence and explained, 'Just a joke, love.'

He shrugged, which motor was all the same to him. His skills know no bounds. He nodded, whisked inside the silver Bentley with hardly a hitch-step, and fired its engine. Dashboard – small, but a clever twenty-eight year old – trotted over, slid inside and drove it sedately away. Liffy casually walked to his motorbike, and drove towards the Castle. There would be a small scene at the gate. Ratbag'd call the Plod. Who would witness Liffy on his motorbike. And somewhere tonight I'd have the opportunity of examining the diamond people's motor at leisure.

'Lovejoy?'

'I'm looking, love,' I said, narked.

Her piece was a woman's hand, cupping a shell and resting the dorsum on a second, inverted, shell. Lovely white biscuit porcelain, they were mostly made from slip, which is creamy clayey stuff, really fine ceramics. They say the Yanks copied English methods in the 1840s. They did it superbly. I loved it.

'See Tinker, Florence. Tell him I said get it for you.'

She filled. 'You're kind, never mind what they say.'

'Then you'll sell me your collection, love?'

Her face fell a mile. 'I wish I could, Lovejoy. I need the money for something really big. Gwyn took the collection.'

Gwyn, her no-hope husband, failure at any cost. I was broken-hearted. I'd lusted after her collection of William Howson Taylor ware, from Birmingham Tile and Pottery Works of 1898 on. It sounds derisory saying that Taylor simply made pottery buttons, tiles, jugs. But he was mesmerized by the immortal John Ruskin, and suddenly shazammed into the greatest studio potter of his day. At his renamed Ruskin Pottery he slogged, no holidays for the best part of forty years. He invented processes and glazes – *and kept them secret*. Refused fortunes, and went silent to his grave. You'll never see a simpler vase than a Taylor. All sorts, dappled or lined glazes, lovely colours, each valuable item costs a mint. Okay, so people scorn 'art nouveau'. Let them. I was almost in tears. Why couldn't Florence simply put up with a lifetime of sordid sorrow, keep her dud hubby and her collection? It wasn't too much to ask, for Christ's sake. Women have no sense of priorities.

'Lovejoy. You shouldn't have made Liffy play that joke on Imogen's feller. His friends were so nice when I asked – '

'You *asked*?' I almost screeched it.

'Yes!' she said brightly, silly cow. 'You told me to find out. They were happy to explain. They'd come for early jewellery, silverware, gems. They saw the glass piece and bought that instead.'

She was concerned, but only because she thought I'd got a headache. Do you believe women? Having ruined everything, she trotted blithely off to find Tinker. I turned, and bumped into Nurse Siu Lin. She's at Doc Lancaster's, shapely, distrusts the ground I walk on.

'If you need medical help,' I said, 'you've had it.'

She is all teeth and dimples when she smiles. She walks with speed, every stroll a twenty-kilometre Olympic. 'Thought you'd be in training for Sunday, Lovejoy.'

In spite of myself I found I walked along, trying to keep abreast. 'Look, love, what *is* this Sunday thing?'

She stopped. A police motor slowed, accelerated on past. Maudie Laud glanced at Nurse Lin, not at me. Everything was odd lately, so what's in a glance?

'You really don't know, Lovejoy' she marvelled. She's from Hong Kong, so I've a soft spot for her, even if she does help Doc Lancaster to make us all dead of health.

'What actually happens?' Simon Doussy and his posh mates were now talking angrily with a police constable. Maudie Laud was reversing, ten-point turn to reach the scene of Liffy's crime. Nurse Lin eyed me.

'It's very therapeutic, Lovejoy. It's encounter-with-therapy motivational adventurism . . .' I heard, in all her crap methodology, some ominous nouns: 'fortnight', 'report', 'psychosomatic'. She was describing an extraterrestrial escapade, which is just not me.

'Look, love,' I said. 'Nobody's sadder than me, but I can't go. I'm not ducking out. It's my bedridden Uncle Erasmus. I've promised to go and see to him. Tell Doc I'd go like a shot – '

Dolly's motor drew up. 'You *can't*, Lovejoy,' Nurse Lin was wailing as I climbed in. You have to adopt the foetal position to get into Dolly's car and crouch like a neonate. 'The horses are ready! The patients – '

'My apologies, love,' I said, signalling to Dolly. She managed three gear changes a yard, but definitely forward. 'Maybe next time,' I bawled. I would have bussed Dolly for her superb rescue, but could only move a hand.

Dolly said primly, 'I'm driving! And never in public.'

'Sorry, love. Accidental.'

'Your hand is never accidental,' Dolly said sternly. I could have eaten her. 'My husband is home, Lovejoy. What are we going to do?'

One thing I hate is this plural women use. Possessions: they talk singular, I, me, all that. Problems: they switch to the plural, what're *we* going to do.

'Drop me at the Post Office, love.' I did a quick think. 'I'll send a telegram. My pal'll know how to handle George.'

'Frederick,' Dolly said, the pest. 'My husband's Frederick. It's time it was out in the open, Lovejoy,' she said soulfully.

'Yes, dworlink,' I said, with sincerity. But what the hell had I got to do with her husband, for heaven's sake? I think women are getting even less organized than they used to be.

Maudie Laud had me pulled in as we reached the village. For once I was glad to see the peelers, and bade a fond so long to an outraged Dolly. The police car drove me to safety.

11

These cops. The Plod motor streaked into town wahwahing.

'How many pedestrians d'you lot kill a day?' I asked.

The assistant uniformed idler leant and thumped me in the face. My head spun. All I could see were swirling dots. 'That's enough from you, prat.' The motor rounded a bus. Oncoming traffic screeched.

'In the county, I mean.'

They're so undermanned that they have only one idler per car. His job is to watch the driver drive, and knuck citizens. This yob brought blood to my lip. I hoped it was prominent.

'Stop, Mac,' he said. 'The embankment. I'll do this fucker.'

'Seriously.' I tried to sound like those TV newsreaders that can't read the idiot boards. 'What've you got against people?'

He unclipped his seat belt to clobber me. I bobbed as best I could, but keeping my seat belt legally fastened.

'Cross,' the driver remonstrated, offhand, 'we're in town.'

'The bastard.' Constable Cross caught me two good ones.

Pedestrians were looking into the motor now, at a traffic light. I made a great show of mopping the blood from my face. I wound the window down, said to a kindly old dear, 'Love, can you call a policeman? These kidnappers – '

The car took off, G force pressing me against the upholstery. By now my nosebleed covered much of it. I'd spread it about. Cross was examining his hands. My cheekbones had cruelly grazed the skin.

We pulled into the cop shop yard by the roundabout. There's a ruined Roman temple standing proud of a green tummock next to the cop shop. Satan always gets the best tunes.

Slyly I didn't undo my seat belt, and stayed somnolent when Cross snapped, 'Out.' Mac was more alert, almost looking awake. I closed my eyes. I'd streaked my hair with nose blood.

'Oooogh.' Not my best groan, but convincing. Few pass by because there's only the Salvation Army and the tax gatherers. Still, any witness wouldn't come amiss.

Cross leant in to yank me out but the seat belt held. Cursing, he reached across in a stink of sweaty anger. I did my groan.

'Crossie,' the driver said, 'watch it.'

Eyes closed, I released the press clip as Cross gave a super tug. We catapulted out like corks from a bottle, me sprawling. I was really proud. A messy but superb performance.

'For Christ's sake, Crossie,' the driver said.

Feet clomped close, with voices. I did my groan. The two Plods babbled explanations in which truth didn't quite make it. I was lifted. I collapsed in a heap. All fell silent. Then Maudie's voice said, laconic, 'Get him inside. You two, inside.'

'It was like this, ma'am –' Cross began, lies to the fore.

'Noitwasnotlikethis,' Maudie said, one word. 'Clean him up. Doctor on call. And you – disciplinary charges forthwith.'

'Yes, ma'am,' some nerk intoned. 'Written reports, booys.'

For a bird with a soft delivery, she made her voice prophesy untold harm. My blood, what bit I had left, ran cold. She departed. Nice legs, for the Old Bill. I allowed myself to be carried, making sure my head did a lot of lolling.

The process took a full hour, time I could have used. I wondered if I might get paid for my suffering. Money is dear bought – it costs more than I can afford. And law delays justice until the suffering have suffered to extinction. The police surgeon was noncommittal and brusque. I was offered tea by an apprehensive policewoman. Maudie came in – I was on a wooden bench – and sat opposite. I was astonished she wasn't covered in silver braid.

'Lovejoy. You're useless, fake-wise. Everything the hard way.'

What can you say to crud? 'Listen, missus. If I wanted to make money from fakery I'd nick Leamington Spa railway station's wooden benches from their waiting rooms. Twelve. Convert them into three sixteenth-century court cupboards, that goons call buffet cupboards.' I smiled with delight at the thought. 'Nick their two tables as well, I'd knock you up two brace of joiner armchairs, Great Civil War period.'

'Stop it, Lovejoy.' She was the most assured bird I'd ever met. 'I am going to put a few questions. Be precise.'

'Eleven,' I said, through swollen lips. 'Tell Cross.'

'Eleven what?' She glanced at the tape recorder. The charade includes taped interviews, the time-place-date-observer bit jokingly specified in the Police and Criminal Evidence Act.

'People killed by police motors. Cross was having a laugh.'

'The events will emerge in the inquiry.' She was laconic. I wondered if they all went to acting school for promotion. 'What is the relationship between you and Mrs Arden?'

'You know, Corporal. She helped a charity, and bid for me.'

She didn't know whether to believe me. Now, this was new. She'd believed me not long since. 'And Carl's lady friend?'

What *was* this? Good old Carl had seemed ballbroken, reduced to ferrying scruffs for his missus. Could such a serf secretly be pleasuring a bonny lass? These things happen, I've heard.

'Look, love. The county set's not my scene.'

She eyed me, her gaze latching on blood in my hair. I'd deliberately not washed up there to keep the sympathy vote. 'Very well.' The Plod have two different minds rattling around their capacious noddles. One mind's humdrum, how-much-is-petrol mundanity. The other mind hates trust, wants to hit everyone with savage abandon.

'Eh?' I gasped in disbelief at what she'd said. 'Sorry, Constable. Didn't hear you. Your lads beat me deaf – '

'You heard, Lovejoy. What is the specific gravity of gold?'

'Gold?' I said stupidly, wonderment cubed.

'As compared to diamonds. Confine your reply to fact.'

Lost, I hurt my face with a frown that made me yelp. 'Gold?' I made cautious inquiry. Cunning to the last. 'You mean as compared to diamonds?'

She said nothing. See what I mean about peelers? She could easily have offered a helpful comment, It's like this, Lovejoy . . . to oil things. She sat still as a stoat.

Gold? Diamonds? The gold mention was to put me off, right? Stray brain cells grappled to synapse ideas but failed.

'Diamond's density is 3.52. Gold's miles off, 19.3, give or take a yard.' She stayed mute. I waxed on, gathering steam. 'As different as can be. Odd, really. Diamond's so hard the miners used to try smashing crystals with a sledgehammer, thinking if it withstood the blow it was true diamond. Except,' I said with genuine sorrow, 'they didn't understand crystal cleavage. Gold has no real cleavage. It's softer, 2.5 to 3.0 on the old Mohs scale. That doesn't mean,' I explained, watching her face for clues, 'it's a quarter as hard as diamond, which scores 10.0. It depends how you test it. Ordinary talc scores one, gypsum two, then soft old calcite three. Gold's a mite softer than calcite, okay? On the Knoop scratch scale, though, diamond's *thirty times harder than gold*. See?'

Silence. What the hell did she want? Investments?

'Diamond doesn't stretch,' I resumed. 'But gold's so ductile that a single grain – 5,760 grains to a pound weight – can be drawn into wire five hundred feet long!' She didn't applaud, to my annoyance. 'Gold leaf is quarter of a millionth of an inch thick! You have to polish diamond, takes an age . . . ' My saga went lame. 'Gold loves being twisted. That's why torcs – gold collars for ancient British kings – are twisted more than other metals could stand. Drop gold into a stream, bury it for three thousand years, up it comes bright as a button!'

Watch it, Lovejoy! my adrenals shrieked, spurting adrenaline in a gusher. Treasure hunters wouldn't thank me for blabbing of the pre-Roman torcs. She spoke.

'Could an ancient gold torc be excavated, then made into ancient jewellery, chalices, cups?'

'Yes,' adding the swift disclaimer, 'I bet.'

'And for it to be done so carefully that even the very best scientific investigators could not prove it modern?'

'Yes. Only supposing, mind,' I added.

'Just as I, too, am only supposing that you might know these things, Lovejoy.' I didn't like that. 'Diamonds . . . ?'

'You can't age diamonds, love. You can only age their setting, the jewellery of which they form a part.' I brightened. 'But you can fake a diamond. That help? Some new simulants are great. The older ones are easily detected. Give themselves away by refracting double when you look through, as if you're squinting.'

'Can you age gold?'

I was becoming interested. 'You can add trace elements, of the sort that contaminate gold from the ancient world.' I caught myself. 'Don't you have tame scientists? The ones,' I added nastily, 'in your secret laboratories near Chislehurst?'

A glimmer of amusement showed. 'Thank you, Lovejoy. Now, why is there so much charity work on my manor?'

A knock sounded. The policewoman came, whispered. Maudie's lips thinned, a promising sign.

'He will be out directly,' she said in fury. 'Lawyers, Lovejoy?'

Lawyers? I have no lawyers. I have tax gatherers, homicidal constables, creditors, women badgering me to get married . . . Dolly! Dolly had lawyers, dentists, accountants. She kept lists of them in a red notebook, blue for engagements.

'Thank you, Bombardier.' I made my way to the door. She made no demur, just accompanied me to the corridor. From there I saw Dolly clutching her handbag, pretty as a picture, between two besuited gents in postures of disapproval. I asked shakily, 'Is it safe, Sergeant? They won't beat me again . . .'

Dolly leapt forward with a cry and extricated me. I tottered out to her motor while the lawyers chanted their rituals and fluttered papers.

'Darling!' Dolly said, torn between fire-bombing the police and caring for me. 'The Chief Constable will hear about this!'

With a groan, I told her to phone the Home Secretary. It was a joke, but Dolly told me she already had. We drove sedately out. I told her to take the hospital route.

'Love,' I said. 'Who is Mr Arden's lady?'

There was ample time on the two-mile journey. Dolly's driving has a comatose air all its own. At an empty crossroad she stares forty times in each direction in case of lurking motors, then putters forward in first gear – by which time, of course, a column of demented motorists is trailing behind, coronary arteries clanging.

'Knee, Lovejoy,' Dolly said sternly. 'I'm beginning to think you're not quite as injured as you appear,' she said, pretty mouth set in rebuke. Lips are odd. Some women thin their lips and it's a threat. Others do the same and only look delectable and make you think lustful thoughts. 'I said *knee*, Lovejoy.'

'Sorry, sorry. I overbalanced. Carl Arden?'

'Mrs Deirdre Divine is disgracing herself. It's a public scandal, and her husband hardly cold in his grave. I blame the wife,' she threw in with crazy logic.

Of course, I thought. Women always blame the bird. Logic is for losing track of. 'Poor thing,' I said, to keep her going. She inched up, a heady ten mph.

'Mrs Arden was irresponsible when her first husband started to drink. Didn't stand by him a single minute!'

'God rest him,' I said piously, wanting more.

'*Such* a clever man – a scientist, metal chemistry, I think. Did wonderful work, despite his weakness.'

Dolly has only three grades of calamity. The 'weakness' is due to one's own intransigence: Raddie's sexual proclivity is an example, drunkenness and the Methodist persuasion others. More severe is the 'disappointment', which covers harlotry to financial fraud. Dolly's sternest condemnation: to 'misbehave', encompassing murder, high treason, and failing to feed your garden bluetits by eight thirty. I like Dolly, and not just because she'd just sprung me from Castle Otranto. She meant a wino, confirming Loafer's account. And a metal chemist, maybe gold?

'Poor man,' I murmured.

To the traffic's joy, she parked and rummaged for tissues. 'You're so sweet, Lovejoy. So badly hurt, and you still show sympathy!'

Put that way, I was so touched I almost welled up myself from finer feelings. She sniffed herself dry.

'Now, Lovejoy, let us get on.' She pulled out with cool disregard of other vehicles. 'Why the hospital road?' She smiled demurely. 'Because there's a layby there? Lovejoy, you are incorrigible!'

'You guessed!' I lied with a shrug. 'We haven't had a good – '

'Lovejoy!' she said, scandalized. 'Language!'

'Sorry.' The two blokes who'd been knifed were likely to be still in hosptial. I tried to think of a way of postponing snogging with Dolly until we reached the cottage. Something pleasantly innocent would occur to me, with luck.

12

The hospital's gone ineffably modern, so patients can catch legionnaire's disease free of charge. They spent so much money installing air conditioners that they haven't the money to take them down now they've proved lethal.

'Look, Dolly.' The hospital car park only has room for two prams and a three-wheeler. 'I wanted somewhere to talk.' Women think speech is an infallible index of feelings, whereas I don't trust words.

'I understand, dear,' she said mistily.

The Bentley would be across the Channel by nightfall, so I had to get a move on. But this hospital visit was important. 'Look, dwoorlink . . .'

'Yes, Lovejoy?'

'You know how I feel, Dolly. Always have, ever since we met in the vestry.' She is our church treasurer. 'It's just that . . .' I gave a really genuine passion-riven hesitation. 'Well, your husband.'

She sighed at my inner beauty. 'You're a lovely man, d'you know that?' Well, yes, but I needed to get inside the surgical wards. 'So compassionate!' I hastily looked compassionate. 'But if we're to make a life together – '

'I'm so glad you said that, Dolly.' I looked so glad, because the town bus entered the hospital drive. We were blocking it.

Annoyed, she started the engine. 'I'll park on the road.'

'Love,' I smiled brightly, 'there's a canteen. You park, I'll be waiting. This is too important to interrupt.'

I shot out as her motor kangarooed off, and went in.

'I'm from Doctor Lancaster,' I told the receptionist. 'Message for those two blokes brought in after the stabbing.'

'Access denied,' she said in that monotone jack-a'-backs use on underlings. 'Ward Three is under police guard.' She was used to subservience. But I had the habit of a lifetime. I grovelled, really thrilled at such an august personage.

'Thank you, Mrs Prescott,' I said. 'I'll tell the police surgeon no.'

She had to come running. I almost made the door. 'A message from the police surgeon?'

'Shhh,' I said quietly, trying to sound Special Branch. 'Don't send word. I know the way.' That shut her up.

Among limping orthopaedic patients and trolleys bearing the moribund I reached a quiet backwater where a policeman stood lusting at passing nurses. I waited with the hospital visitor's inscrutable patience – hands folded, leaning on a wall. Within ten minutes he deserted his post and headed off. A pause, then I sauntered into Ward Three. No nurses, except for one scribbling at a desk. One door gave passing rogues a clue: 'POLICE NO ADMITTANCE'.

The door had a porthole glass. Inside, I drew the curtain across it, hoping the vigilant constable wasn't. One bed, the occupant dozing. He didn't look ill.

'Wakie wakie, Des,' I said quietly.

He zoomed awake with horrified eyes. 'Wha . . . ?' He looked for his police protection, then quietened as I shook my head. I was pleased there were no bleeps and dripping tubes. Hospitals make me shudder. 'Who're you?'

'Stay cool.' I was disappointed. Other people say these Americanisms, they sound really good. When I say them I sound pathetic. I saw contempt rise in his eyes. He had me sussed. I drew up a chair and sat. If the peeler bothered to return, he'd see me sitting, posing no threat, though that wouldn't stop him from battering me senseless in the pursuit of his calling. 'We want the word, that's all. Blow by blow.' I leant forward. 'Your version. Not . . . ' I nodded at the vacated bed.

Understanding crept in. You don't need to make blokes leap to conclusions. Half a chance, they leap with abandon. Look at Dolly.

'What's Sass been saying?'

I put on a show of innocence. 'What do they tell me?' I did my lean again with a wintry smile. 'Just imagine I'm . . . Fraud Squad.'

He smiled at that, raised himself with a wince that I felt. 'Sass wus on time. We did the wheels okay, sussed the pub just right.' I looked at the floor, nodding. It was all a bit Fagin-in-the-loft, but the nerk kept going. 'The dollybird fingered the bloke. We starts the scrap all right. It'd have gone brill, but for this poofter who starts screaming.'

'You sure she fingered the right bloke?'

'Leave orff,' he said with weary scorn. 'I bin doing rumblows 'fore you wus outer yor egg, son.'

A rumblow is a fight that isn't a fight, to provide distraction. But why exactly? All I know was, some Brummy blokes started a scrap about some finds from Suffolk.

'Nothing else?' I did my over-the-shoulder glance.

'Look. Sass chats the bint up. She says the one they call Wolfie got the Stonehenge. We do the deal. He makes to scarper. Sass sez not on your life. This Wolfie geezer does his nut, this poofter starts screaming. Some gorilla moves on us. Sass pulls his shiv. The rest is in the papers.' He sounded bitter. 'Tell Si we did it to the letter, okay?'

Stonehenge is ancient treasure. 'The right bird, though?'

'Tits, red hair, miserable cow that Meg. Tarts oughter be in school.'

'True,' I said, rising. 'I never came, right?' Too much. I'd done too much. Actors say: Enough is too much; wanting more is just enough.

Suspicion clouded his eyes. 'What's the name?' he asked.

'That's mine,' I said, trying for Maudie Laud's laconic manner and missing by a street. I reached the door. 'I'll tell Si it sounds to me you did right.'

He glared, not knowing if I was from his boss. Si, Simon?

Feeling I was catching up at last, I stayed and played with the children scattered on white ward linoleum. I played them bowls, but the little sods beat me hands down. I complained to the nurses that they cheated, but they only laughed. The infants laughed. Kiddies and birds take no notice. But it's not fair to cheat. I never do, except when it's vital. I'd have won ten-seven but for a little swine called Jerry.

'Get on with you,' the sister scolded when I grumbled.

'My wood was in!' I groused. 'You'd have to be blind – '

'Jerry nearly is,' she said, like she'd told me he was tall for his age. 'He's good, isn't he?'

I swallowed, said I had to go. I told the children so long. They shouted to come back and they'd play me bowls again. I left feeling utterly down. Some days it's always big snakes, little ladders. Or even no ladders at all.

Meg is Imogen's pal. Now, Im is Gee Omen's lady. And Si, Simon, is Gee's partner. He hired the two Brummies, Des and Sass, to go to The Ship and buy the precious pre-Roman finds illicitly excavated by the night hunters. Mistakenly – Meg's mistake – they'd approached Wolfie who, of course, is the only undercover bobby our town's got. He's so undercover, in fact, that he's practically famous. No wonder he'd started swinging when this Sass bloke pulled out his sly knife to enforce a deal. And no wonder Raddie started screaming. Which had made Chuck put the miscreants severely into hospital. Okay, except for one thing.

Where did all this treasure-buying money come from? And why Simon? Or was it his own gelt, or his pal Gee's, diamond sightholder? Was it to corner the market? But who in his right mind went chasing diamonds when the international market had fallen like a, well, stone?

And I'd seen Meg before somewhere.

When I got outside I didn't see Dolly. Mind you, you'd miss that tiny car of hers if it was parked near a brick. Gone home in a temper? I sighed, caught the bus.

'Liffy!' I spread my arms wide, as if he was a narked cow.

The window slid down. 'You rotten sod, Lovejoy.' He's got one of these nose-picker's faces.

I was a picture of innocence, there between the lane's hedgerows. 'I got pulled in by Maudie. Sorry. Anyway, didn't I put you on to the Bentley? It's worth a mint. Get it over the Channel, lad. Blondes, beds and bullion.'

'Nearly got me done, Lovejoy.'

'Listen, Liffy.' I got heated. Why do people never trust me? 'I was in Dolly's motor, right? But I act as decoy, let them take me in, knowing you were waiting here. They do me over, but do I complain? I've still blood on me.' I yelled, working up. 'I get myself done over rotten – '

'Okay, Lovejoy. I owe you. Sorry, mate. And ta.'

That cooled me, but only a little. I saw my cottage door ajar, and guessed Tinker had been. Me, the iceman. 'You left this Bentley in my undergrowth, right? Then they'd blame me if they called, right?'

'Don't go on, Lovejoy.'

'That's two you owe me. Any antiques in it?'

'Nothing, Lovejoy. It's clean as a frog's arse.' Grumbling, he disembarked. I undid the boot, the bonnet, searched the glove compartments, the wine cooler, radio, doors.

'I did the door panels, Lovejoy.' He shrugged at my quizzical look. 'Foreigners and drugs, what not, you know?'

'No tom? No documents, Liff?'

'These.' He pulled out some travel documents, a Hook of Holland ferry pass, a small notebook, insurance, tat. I handed it back, disappointed, but kept the notebook to shufti.

'Liffy. Were you at the ceilidh in The Ship?'

'The Brummies as got knifed?' He grinned at the thought, an undercover peeler scrapping out of a crime. 'Yeah. Saw Wolfie fight for his honour. A laugh. He'd have got knifed like a colander but he hacked Raddie's legs. Then Chuck, and the sky fell in.'

A laugh indeed. 'Any witnesses?'

He fell about. 'We all had our eyes shut.'

'See you, then, Liff. And ta.'

'Pleasure, Lovejoy.' He grinned at me from the opulent interior. 'Here. Your plump little tart. I wouldn't mind having a chew, when you've done.'

East Anglia's never short of Beau Brummels. 'Cheers, Liffy.'

'Cheers, Lovejoy.'

The great saloon car drifted away looking like a church in search of a parking space. I sighed. I sometimes really wish there was such a thing as an antique motor car. They'd be beautiful, if they weren't modern crapology. 'I'll keep you in mind, Liffy,' I said, like some sad epitaph, and went in to wait for news from Tinker. He should have bought the Parian ware from Raddie for Florence by now.

Inside, I read Untracht on jewellery until the day closed and I had to hunt for candles. Long after dark I remembered I'd been going to see Imogen. And Florence. But I was worrying about Liffy. I kept seeing his face grinning cherubically, saying his Cheers Lovejoy and driving off.

Had I done wrong?

Dolly came, bringing seven pasties and a primus stove with tea, milk, sugar, bread and butter, which staved off one hunger at least until nightfall and time for her to satisfy a second hunger. She checks the windows for an hour before she rapes me, in case nonexistent hordes not stalking the lanes stop to look. She wedges chairs at the door, for the same non-reason. I don't mind. It's what they do. But didn't my urging Liffy to nick the silver Bentley put him terribly at risk?

Odd, that a woman's best gift is sometimes oblivion. That night, it didn't come.

13

It was early. I woke to a patter of rain. Still dark, the room cold. Dolly was sleeping with the woman's intensity, a serious job to be done.

Hands inside for warmth, I stared unseeing at the ceiling. Why do we? We might as well keep them closed. I couldn't get Liffy out of my mind.

It was time I saw Mrs Arden. I wasn't sure why, because I'd finished with her. Yet she seemed the prime mover. There were other mysteries. I mean, what did elusive Deirdre Divine have to do with anything? And Mrs Frances Bledsoe'd pointed her rich lady friend at me then cleared off, no longer associating with riffraff like Lovejoy.

Not only that, the Swedish glass piece with its priceless air had vanished from the silver Bentley. So where was it? Nobody would leave a thing like that in a parked car. Yet they had.

Dolly sighed, turned over. I dragged the blankets back. That Sunday jaunt seemed to be growing in size, time, variety. Horses had been mentioned. Any horse was bad news. 'Caravan' means camels, a mobile home, or a gypsy's painted dawdler that poets write sonnets about. I was definitely no gypsy type, campfires and roasted hedgehogs, squirrels for pudding and nettle soup.

No, thank you. I'd reluctantly agreed to go, thinking it a kind of posh ramble in a charabanc, a pint at a tavern before the evening snog. But a fortnight? Not only that, but Nurse Lin had hinted that I was somehow responsible, kulak to gauleiter at one bound.

And my lustful dream of a trip with some elegant ladies had vanished. Now I'd be lumbered with nutters, loonies from the booby hatch. Doc Lancaster had given me funds, very kind of him, seeing he desperately wanted me to go while he did sod all.

That word echoed in my cavernous skull. Hang on, I thought with sudden interest. Doc Lancaster *desperately* . . . Mrs Arden *desperately* wanted me to go, didn't she? Imogen wanted me to go. And Raddie. And Nurse Siu Lin, but she was crackers about Doc Lancaster so she would. And Dolly, also desperately, because it would be sweet and other Dolly-type words that were her irrefutable logic.

All that desperation. Why did the world want *me* off with the crazies? It didn't make sense. The other worrying point was that Maudie Laud with her Keystone Kops was gnawing the same bone. And wherever I went Simon Doussy seemed to be already there, smiling, nodding. And Gee Omen. Odder, these big buyers had all suffered lately: Gee in diamonds; Twentyman in Lloyds' insurance tumbles; Simon Doussy – didn't Big Frank say he collected Impressionists? If so, Doussy had lost fortunes skating on that thin ice.

Then this rumblow, at The Ship inn. The Old Bill's undercover man Wolfie brawls with crooks, yet I get questioned. And all about some ancient golds dug up hereabouts that I hadn't yet seen. And Meg, Imogen's friend, chats up the ubiquitous Simon Doussy, and happens to point out to the Brummy knifers the wrong bloke. So who was the right bloke?

Suddenly it's like I'm watching a kabuki play blindfold with commentary in lost Tasmanian. I gazed in the pitch to where Dolly slept beside me. She of the upright, uptight morals always helped. Being entirely woman, her help was peculiarly hit or miss. Her reasoning was a strange mutant all her own, but she was all for me. Hers was the weird type of help that people give children, like those Thermogene pads slapped on your little chest to itch you to distraction, or those lunatic ointments that ran down to sting your eyes. My Gran used to say, Lord, spare me my helpers. I know how she felt.

Right. Reason assuaged by having realized it was all beyond me, I cast my leg over Dolly – lucky they have a waist, just right – and slept the sleep of the just.

Then Dolly woke me with some terrible news. It was Sunday.

She wouldn't drive me to Mrs Bledsoe's. I honestly don't know what gets into Dolly sometimes, because Mrs Bledsoe belongs to the same clubs, societies.

'Bloody great.' I was bitter. Dolly dumped me in town. 'It's a matter of life and death.'

She gave me her glare, which is truly horrendous, a frown and a tut together. 'Please do *not* give my regards to Mrs Bledsoe.' She gunned her engine, preparing to drive our town traffic mental.

I gasped in outrage. 'Dolly! You're so, well, *blunt!*'

She said defiantly, 'Mrs Bledsoe harbours . . . *feelings* for you.'

Reeling at such frankness I said, 'Dolly, I'm shocked – '

'Please excuse me, and be at the start by two.'

Off her motor crept, causing vehicular consternation for miles. Well, he travels fastest who travels alone. I'd no intention of being anywhere near the start. I wasn't going.

Tinker was sloshed half out of his mind at the Welcome Sailor. He grabbed my arm, ordered three pints on me, and drew me furtively down the taproom bar.

'Lovejoy, for Gawd's sake! What you been up to?'

'Nothing,' I said in a panic, quickly reviewing my blameless life. 'The Old Bill hauled me in, but – '

'Women,' he proclaimed in his foghorn whisper. 'They're gunning for you. Oughter be in church, the lot.'

'Amen.' I agreed. 'Any idea what for?'

'Jessina Mosston, snooty bitch. Florence; she come earliest. That lass who's always no frock on.' He meant Imogen. 'And her red-headed girl, Meg. Dunno what you done, Lovejoy, but I'd steer clear of her for a coupla year.'

'That's enough to be going on with.' I paid for the beer.

'And that Mrs Arden and her blokes – '

'Blokes?' Plurals are the pits. 'Who? Carl, big posh motor?'

'No. That Doussy wally, Gee Omen, a foreigner doing his nut.' A wally is a dealer. 'Mrs Arden called at your cottage.'

Escaped by a whisker. 'Those Suffolk gold finds. The police –'

'And that Mrs Divine.' Tinker cackled. 'And her pal, posh bint you used to shag rotten.' At my affronted stare he fell about, rheumy eyes streaming. 'With the huge bristols. You used to be knackered all bleeding day.'

'Tinker,' I interrupted, broken, 'shut your gums. Did you get that Parian ware for Florence?'

His face became prim as a Victorian granddad's. 'From that poofter? Aye. Oughter be locked away. With his gorilla.'

Homo sapiens shares 98 per cent of genes with other primates. But this only makes you wonder who's the ape.

'Raddie knocked it down to a quarter 'cos you'd sent me.' I was astonished. The trade discount's 20 per cent. 'It was a lady's mitt holding a shell.'

Raddie, desperate to please me? Desperation was still about. 'Who entered the glass piece at Postern's?'

'Dunno, Lovejoy.' His expression cleared. 'I seed Mrs Arden's husband with it yesterday after the Castle fair.'

That shut me up. He hawked and spat phlegm into the tavern fire, almost putting it out with a prolonged hiss. I smiled apology at two ladies trying to chat by the warmth.

This news gave me urgent visits to make, now I had some priority. First, ask Jessina Mosston, who'd thought up the Auction of Promises. Then Deirdre Divine, Carl Arden's side piece. Then maybe Valerie Arden. It was too risky to confront Simon Doussy. I didn't trust him from afar. Closer could be worse.

'Here, Lovejoy,' Tinker said as I rose to go, leaving money to ensure his survival. 'Hear about Liffy?'

That froze me in mid-exit. 'Liffy?' I said stupidly.

'Got topped, son. Dropped orff.'

'Liffy? Not . . . *Liffy*?'

Tinker searched my face. 'We friends of his, Lovejoy?'

My chest had become a glacier. 'Sort of.'

He groaned. 'Oh Christ. We gotter do summink?'

'Not yet, Tinker.' I swallowed, tried to anyway. 'How?'

'Stopped in a layby. He took fire siphoning petrol. Fag ash dropped in, burned him and his old Morris.'

'A Morris motor?' Liffy doesn't smoke. 'God rest him.'

'Amen.' Tinker piously bowed his head, then yelled at the barmaid, 'Miss! Get off your fat arse.'

The air on East Hill inhaled better, but only until the recollection of Liffy's so long, 'Cheers, Lovejoy', came to mind. Then it was hard to breathe. Liffy never had an old Morris. He only pinched classy cars. I walked up the slope and caught a taxi from outside Mark's to the home of Mrs Bledsoe, she of the remarkable figure attested by Tinker. I saw Tania beckon frantically from the museum steps. She even ran after the taxi, but I've been chased by faster birds and still got away on crutches.

The news sickened me. I didn't know if I'd done it by neglect, murder by omission. But Liffy was gone. Where was Dashboard? Why hadn't Liffy been puttering safely home on his motorbike?

Mrs Bledsoe wasn't in. A serf spurned me at the front door, which I'm used to, but they also refused to take a message. I got the taxi driver to phone for Mrs Deirdre Divine's number. His call-car service found out her address, Artillery Street by the Falcon Arms.

14

The area is down the Hythe, the town's docks. Nothing like Liverpool, just a muddy estuary by flat sea marshes with samphire whiskering the sea lands. Birds hang about there, gaped at by twitchers through complicated lenses, and cold onshore winds set the tethered boats clinking like tinkers' barrows. On the water you meet small two-thousand-ton ships from the Continent. The drab warehouses, on their last legs, line the harbourside road that heads for town with relief. It's there that New Town begins – 'new' because it flourished after Queen Boadicea burnt the joint after a disagreement with Caesar. It became newer still when Cromwell spotted that the town guessed wrong in the Great Civil War. Terraced houses cover the area, two parishes only. They're unpretentious, back gardens but nothing much in front, cobbled streets, small chapels, cramped pubs.

This didn't quite match my image of Deirdre Divine. She'd looked glam the day I got sold, a Knightsbridge model taunting the lower classes. And a friend of the carnal but aloof Mrs Frances Bledsoe *couldn't* be a lady of modest means. I asked the taxi driver if he'd got the right place, with its slate roofs and chintzy curtains.

'Cold feet?' he snickered. 'I know every yard here, booy.'

He dropped me in troublesome drizzle. You can't just hang about in terraced streets. In villages you can stroll, admire flowers or the ancient church. I entered the Falcon Arms, got a drink. I put my edginess down to Liffy's passing. Or maybe the charity that wanted to send me off with cartloads of nutters.

The taproom was quiet. Two old blokes played shove-ha'penny, another worried himself sick trying to get double twenty. The publican honed glasses, strolled his sentry behind mahogany.

'These houses all look the same.' I told it like a defeat.

He chuckled, nice old chap with a football medal on his watch chain. 'Messenger, are you?'

'Aye. Sunday, too. Wrong address, twice.'

His head tilt made the offer. 'In this street?'

'Mrs D. Divine, elderly lady – '

'Not much,' he said, the admirer's admission of envy. 'Give me her any time. House on the alleyway to the old foundry.'

'Fall for my charm, eh?' I swigged my drink.

That gave him a laugh. 'Landgrabbers afore you, booy!'

'Just my luck. Ta.' I strolled out. The rain was in earnest. I hate getting my head wet, so hitched my jacket up. A motor swept past with that susurrus posh cars make.

At La Divine's number I knocked. No porch, no shelter. I must have looked a state when she opened. Her smile died instantly.

'Yes?' Her peremptory manner proved she'd been expecting somebody else. Or somebody who'd just left and forgotten something?

'Er, I came to ask about the auction.'

'The auction? You want Jessina Mosston. She organizes those.'

'I wondered . . . ' I had to stop. An inner bonging made me.

'Are you ill? What's the matter?'

Not exactly overwhelming compassion, merely a don't-be-ill-on-my-doorstep dismissiveness. She was delectable, a plain cotton skirt and twin set. I thought of the antique she had in there – the door lets straight into the front room. I took a flier. I gave a rueful grin, like she'd seen through me. 'I just came to see the glass piece, the Kungsholm.' Well, something was beaming seductively in there. 'An offer . . .'

She said, 'It was lent solely to help the charity.'

'Wait a sec, missus,' I said, but to the oak door.

She knew me. I caught a bus from St Leonard's old church, thinking of the big motor that had left Mrs Divine's as I'd shown up. I wish I knew more about cars. Was it Carl Arden's? What colour had it been, blue? I sat on the bus, thinking. Minimal evidence, sure, but the publican said some landgrabber had already got there. Carl Arden was a property speculator. And real estate lately was a world of sandshiftery.

When I alighted, a plain-clothes Yorkshire bloke called Corran with a brewer's goitre made me sit in his car.

'Look at these, Lovejoy.' He showed me photographs.

'What for?' I didn't look at the big glossies.

'So's I can go off duty.' He told the driver to drive anywhere in town. Very few people were about the Sunday pavements. We pulled in by the bicycle shop. Its window held a huge black quint. 'My great-granddad used to ride one,' Corran said reminiscently. 'Sixty mile an hour they reached on the old Doncaster track.'

A quint's a five-seater cycle. Two wheels, five sets of pedals, no brakes on an untouched version. Seven-man monsters, too, raced spectacular races at the turn of the century.

'Then you shouldn't have mucked the road laws about, Corran. That horrible thing's got handbrakes, lights, a dynamo.' I hate depredation. 'It didn't have, once. Law is the new vandalism.'

'Barmy bugger, Lovejoy.' He wheezed, lit a fag and coughed to test the flavour. 'Clock Liffy's picture, then you can go.'

Liffy's name pulled my eyes down. The charred thing was like a corroded statue in glistening mud. A boxer's stance. I shoved them away. They fell.

'See his motor, Lovejoy?' He was putting the horrible photographs away when he flashed one right in front of my face. I couldn't avoid seeing the old Morris. Its burnt skeleton clung to morphology. 'A feller dead of burns assumes the stance of a pugilist.' He wheezed a chuckle. 'Quote from forensics.'

'Can I go?' My police sentence.

'Liffy wouldn't be seen dead with less than a Humber Supersnipe.' He gave a belly laugh. The car shuddered. 'Hey, get it? Wouldn't be seen dead?'

I got out, or tried to. He clamped a hand on me. 'Lovejoy. Maudie asks what you think happened, that's all.'

'Antiques are my game, Corran, not killing folk.'

'Forgot how peaceful you are. Killing people's for others, reet?'

'Yes.' I made the pavement with relief.

'Mind you, Lovejoy,' the sod called after me, winding his window down to spread the good news down the High Street. 'You killed Raddie's cousin. Nobody else.'

Swearing in blind hate, I retched, managed to pull myself together pretending to inspect a secondhand tools shop window. I felt clammy. I marched off against the wet wind. Dolly was there when I reached the Arcade. I practically fell into her motor's fuggy interior, and sat with eyes closed trying not to see Liffy's blackened figure, crisped beside the motor he would never have stolen in a month of Sundays.

There's no such thing as an accident. You can't escape blame, because there's no such thing as an excuse. These days we evade the consequences of our actions. We're all correct all the time. I don't know anybody who isn't. So how come the world's in a shambles?

'Dear?' Dolly said, placing her hand on mine. From Dolly, that was an emotional striptease. I think she'd heard about Liffy. 'Have you had anything to eat?'

'No.'

'Then I shall see you are properly fed. I've forgiven you.'

'Ta, love.' I'd forgotten why I needed forgiveness.

She took us to the George carvery, then back to the cottage. If I'd been up to my usual level of scatterbrained vigilance, I'd have spotted the prelude to betrayal, but I wasn't so I didn't.

After we dressed, my compassionate loving helper sacrificed me to the worst of all possible worlds. There's an old English proverb: you can't turn bees, women, or swine. It means that they do exactly what they want, and the rest of us just go along.

15

'It's a surprise, Lovejoy,' Dolly said, smiling.

'I don't like surprises.'

'You'll love this one. You see.'

She drove her tiny car with concentration, looking hard at the gear stick deciding whether to change. I remained coiled like a dead spring, hoping for somebody with a tin opener.

Dolly has a sense of impending doom because she's no longer eighteen. You know what I think about older women – the best tunes are played on old violins. Not that younger ones are undesirable. But the one doesn't displace the other, which is where women of Dolly's vintage go wrong. In sum: women are never past it. But try telling them that, they think you're having them on.

Dozing set me dreaming. She'd woken me too quickly after love. A woman wants to leap piping into the world alive. They don't understand that a man's different. It's like – well, you know the word as well as me. If we're allowed to wrestle with spectres a few moments, then we emerge remembering only the happy love. But if the bird insists on rousing her bloke without more ado, to prattle and have a laugh, then she gets the sailor's elbow, the nudge-splash verdict, bewildered and wondering why. Older women learn.

The word's death. It's close to the soul. Made me think of Raddie's cousin.

It started with a Pembroke table.

A small breakfast table, called after 'the lady who first gave orders for one', Sheraton said. But it was probably Henry Herbert, the ninth Earl of Pembroke, who pegged out in 1751, who originated the design. This inventive 'architect earl' was noted for his elegant taste. Small, with two flaps, it has a couple of small drawers.

It is the most faked piece of furniture on earth, has been for two centuries. I've done several.

There are a couple of tricks about Pembroke tables that will explain my innocence. Solid mahogany Pembrooks – it's variously spelt – are valuable, yes, but those with serpentine (think wavy) edges to the little flaps are much more so. The second thing is that, when the good Earl did his design and his lady ordered the prototype, the American 'lyre' Pembrokes style took London by storm. Cut to Charleston, where American makers started making them as fast as they could go. And some of them were curiously distinctive. Look underneath, the two supports were lyre shaped. This spin-off was a riot. Everybody loved them.

They still do.

Example: you buy a plain genuine Pembroke table, Sheraton's own work. Solid mahogany, but no lyre supports. Plain non-wavy edges to the flaps. But you can't help thinking how *more* valuable your Pembroke would be *if it had serpentine edges and lyre supports*.

So you alter it. Now, this is easy. If it had inlaid surfaces, complex veneers, or if it was elegantly crossbanded, then you'd be barmy to attempt it. You'd be ruining a perfect genuine antique. But, a plain one? To some crooks, with minds like gaping pockets, a plain Pembroke is an invitation to plug in the electric bandsaw.

What follows is murder. The legs are replaced by lyre supports. The table's straight flaps are waved. Often the work is so crude it defies belief. The genuine antique is butchered.

Which is where I come in. I'd been asked by a dealer called Jerningham to commit this felony on a plain Pembroke. He did this sort of thing – bought genuine old pole firescreens, made them into pairs of small circular tables. He bought old hourglasses, aged the wood, used some recycled old window glass. You get old glass by paying nerks to shatter the casements of Georgian mansion houses. The Old Bill thinks it's an attempted burglary, and are relieved nothing is stolen – except they're too idle to check the glass shards.

Well, Jernie had this Pembroke. He wanted the lyres, the serpentine edges. I refused, with abuse. He had a shed out Peldon way as a cran for illicit secret storage.

Now, the one thing that puts customers off is fire. I mean, who likes a dealer whose premises keeps metamorphosing to ash? I checked out Jernie's cran. It was empty except for some old school desks he was trying to convert to davenports. I decided to put him out of business, and serve him right.

There's a pal I had then, a peterman – fire raiser, with explosive skills. I asked him for a small explosion with a delayed fuse. I wanted time enough to alibi my way to some tavern. On last Saint Lucy grey -- 'longest night, shortest day' – I broke into Jernie's shed and placed the gadget in one of the desks. No antiques about. Jernie was in the Midlands. Off I eeled to the White Hart, hugging myself with delight. I'd put paid to Jernie's at a single blow.

But Raddie's cousin was a thief. Cro-Cro, he was called. I didn't know that he had earmarked Jernie's shed for burglary – not realizing that Jernie had taken the Pembroke north. As I was in the tavern building, an alibi Sherlock Holmes couldn't have cracked, Cro-Cro, a simple bloke who'd never had a job in his life, was that very moment stealthily entering the shed, slickly removing the desks . . . And was being blown to blazes by the fire bomb that exploded when he was halfway to his motor.

There's no such thing as excuses. Have I said that before?

All good intentions achieve their opposite. Jernie was in the clear, but warned off. He's now a famed dealer in the Midlands. Raddie hasn't said a word about it to this very day. The police have. And the lads hereabouts talk of it still.

Tinker's never said a word. I was questioned, as the Plod always do. My pal the peterman was posted abroad the day after, lost his life in some foreign country where wars were starving the populace wholesale. The Plod was Corran. He brings it up when he wants to be nasty. He blames me, on no evidence. It was shelved. But everybody knows.

It happened last Christmastide, feels a thousand years ago.

Dolly shook me. I tried to fling my leg over her, but was bound fast. I struggled, bathed in sweat.

'Darling!' She cradled my face. 'It's all right.'

Daylight. The interior of Dolly's walnut-sized car. Outside, people in drizzle, Doc Lancaster, Town Hall steps. For a second I tried to discipline my pounding heart. Dolly mopped my brow, now the silly cow'd made me think it was the apocalypse.

'I'll be fine. Give me a minute.'

'Maybe we should have rested after . . .' Her colour heightened. 'I do hope I didn't hurry . . .' Syntax was a problem. She'd just ravished me to a grease spot, and propriety had to be served at all costs. 'What I mean is,' she reconstructed, 'perhaps I should obtain a tray of tea.'

'Dolly,' I said wearily, 'you haven't sold me off?'

'No, Lovejoy!' she said brightly. 'You're leaving with Lancaster's mental patients!'

'You mean yes, Dolly,' I translated harshly. 'Why?'

'Because it's what you really want to do, Lovejoy,' she said, eyes misting up. 'In your *heart* you *want* to *help* these people. I'm so proud.' Et holy cetera.

Friends always know that my aim is to serve their ambitions.

My head was splitting. 'Why the hell don't you do it?'

'Now, Lovejoy,' she purred, her lovely face smiling, 'you'll enjoy every single minute!'

Smiling people were knocking on the car door, all ready to explain how much I would enjoy this crappy jaunt while they did sod all, in my very best interests, of course. I got out.

Dolly came along. 'Can I stay and see you off, dear?'

'Please do, love.' The quicker the better. What I saw waiting made me swear a secret vow. First bend in the road, I'd be off through the hedgerows like a hare, alone, and safe from my helpers.

Doc Lancaster stood there like a spare tool, definitely edgy. Nurse Siu Lin stood with them, combative in stance, smile a foot wide. The parish mayor – warped shrewdness supervising dereliction – stood there in the chain of office he'd invented. He's a portly, balding bloke with a laboured grin who stores influence like a dromedary does fat. Fawners stood about wanting things to go wrong to prove they, not lovable Chairman Gordon, should be running things. A cluster of folk huddled in doorways as the rain began. The playground of the world.

Merry Mayor Gordon advanced, grasped my hand, and spun me as the camera flashed and clicked. 'Good luck!' He leapt into a vast saloon and was driven off at speed. Indecision thickened our moribund Sunday joviality. Now he'd gone, hate became less clear cut. We looked about.

Faces gazed down from a charabanc. The loonies?

'Name age sex domicile occupation?' the photographer's girl asked. Her clothes were tatty. Flashbulb Fred was clicking away.

'You look knackered, love,' I said. 'Nip home for a kip.'

'Do you hope this trip will raise social awareness . . . ?'

I walked past to Doc Lancaster. 'Hello, Doc. Look. I'm not seriously going through with this, am I?'

'We certainly are, Lovejoy!' Nurse Lin replied, switching to plurals for obligation. 'We have a responsibility to the patients. You agreed.' She added, 'All is prepared!'

No help anywhere. I followed her on board.

'This is Humphrey.' Nurse Lin indicated a mid-thirties bloke. I eyed him, prepared to flee. Tidy, casually dressed, hat, thinnish stubble. He stood looking through me. 'Humphrey, this is Lovejoy. Say hello.'

'Hello.' An educated monotone.

'This is Rita. Say hello, Rita. She's the life and soul of the party, aren't you, Rita?'

'Hello, Rita,' I said in dull reflex, then caught myself. About twenty, slim, in a print schoolgirl frock. Her mouth was a gargoyle's under greenish makeup. False eyelashes, rouge wronged her skin. An infant's first go at cosmetics. I'm not good at telling wigs, but her fair lopsided pile gave grounds for suspicion.

'Hello.' She smiled wonkily from scatty makeup. Nurse Lin grasped me firmly. Nurses grab like a derrick.

She propelled me down the coach aisle. 'Phillida. And Arthur!'

A bespectacled lass sat nursing a baby. Its look asked, You in on this lunacy? I gave it a nod, one prisoner to another.

'How d'you do, Lovejoy?' Phillida gave me a normal smile. My spirits rose. The infant gazed in derision. I was hurt, because I'm pretty good with infants. They know I'm a pushover.

'Hello, Phillida. You coming too?' I tried bravely.

'Yes. Quite an adventure for Arthur!' The babe ignored her, bored out of its little skull. Its belly dwindled musically a full octave. Clearly I was in the presence of a master. 'Sorry,' Phillida said with a mother's apologetic look. 'He's windy.'

'It's okay. I'm a village baby-sitter.' I backed to avoid Arthur's niff. He really did pong.

'Mr Lloyd,' Nurse Lin said. An old bloke, bank-clerkish in attire, didn't respond. Nor did an elderly lady shaking and dozing, 'Old Sarah,' I was told. She looked like a duchess. 'Senile, I'm afraid. And our hypomanic, Corinda.'

'Hello, Lovejoy!' Corinda was laughing, clapping, tapping to a radio. She looked from a music hall, spangles, low-cut blouse. Nurse Lin gave me a warning glance.

'This is Boris. He's shy.' A young man sat at the back, face in a book, thick bottle specs. He didn't look. Well, I didn't want to meet Boris either.

Some seemed not all that barmy. Nurse Lin made me shake hands with a slow country bloke. Heavy boots, corduroys, bowler, inverted pipe smoking, Thinnish overcoat far too long, muffler round his throat. I smiled. 'Lovejoy.'

He gave the curtest nod. 'Luke. I'm in charge.' That was that. A true countryman. I crossed him off my potential list of oddities. I went out for the big farewell.

'Dear?' Dolly stood primly there, handbag in both hands. 'How very proud I am! Such a noble cause.'

'Now, Dolly.' She dabbed her eyes. 'It's my duty to help the less fortunate.' I was almost in tears myself.

'I know, dear.' She braved herself. 'Promise, Lovejoy.' She took in the distance between us and rain-soaked humanity. It was safe. She whispered, 'Darling.'

'Not here, Dolly.' I can't resist becoming primmer.

She nodded, collected herself. 'Quite right, Lovejoy. Behaviour. Telephone, and I shall bring you home. Take care. Mr Luke seems most capable. And control your temper. Your bag I've packed for you, with ... ' she blushed '. . . clean underpants and socks. Six pairs. Plasters for cuts, toilet rolls in the flap pocket.'

A great Rolls cruised up. Mrs Arden alighted, advanced like a queen donating her presence. Carl carried an umbrella over her. Nobody applauded, but we came close.

'Lovejoy! Ready to leave, I see!'

Our grovelling welcomed her gushing condescension. 'Thank you for your support, Mrs Arden,' Doc said.

'My pleasure to help, Doctor! The great quest! Isn't it exciting? In fact,' she added, her eyes giving mine a swift flick, 'I might pay a brief visit myself! Renewing the experience!'

My throat, dry from anger, now dried from the oldest craving of all. I saw Carl stiffen. They have a million sayings for a woman scorned, but none about blokes. Carl the cuckold, hated me, even with Deirdre as compensation.

A morose photographer spoke. 'I want a shot.' Rain dripped off his beard.

His girl spoke from behind her specs. 'We want a shot.'

Even the loonies – sorry, passengers – might be better company than this lot. I sighed, made to buss Dolly a so long but she leapt away at my frank display of lust.

Luke was driving. I went inside with my case. I wasn't going to be around long enough to take this departure seriously. The photographer's camera flashed. Drenched spectators waved. We drove off, to Wales. I settled back. I'd hop off this rotten bus in ten minutes, and it could go where the hell it wanted, without me.

16

In the excitement of the warm bus I nodded off. I remember us swinging along the A604, and hearing little Arthur yelling, causing Corinda to screech like a, well, maniac. Sorry. Old Mr Lloyd was static, staring. The old duchess was dozing. Boris was furtive.

The bus stopped. I awoke. Blearily I looked out at a country bus stop. Suffolk still. I recognized the Boar's Head at Vallancey. Luke shut the engine off, got down to talk and sign a district nurse's clipboard. A gentleman dressed like a verger boarded with prayer book raised aloft. He paused and burst into 'All the Way My Saviour Leads Me'. Then somebody else. Meg the red-headed harridan who hated me and whose boyfriend, Simon, burnt Liffy to death because he'd nicked a motor.

She flounced grumpily into a seat. Was she our guiding spirit? Lovejoy the Ingrate, I went to sit beside her.

'Lovely Wales,' I sighed like I loved the thought.

She eyed me, saw I was sincere, and nearly smiled. It would have been her first. 'You feel the fondness?'

'Oh, aye.' My eyes filled. 'That longing.'

'*Hiraeth*,' she put in mistily. She shone. 'Longing.'

'That's it,' I said, thrilled I'd penetrated her antagonism. I knew the word from the song. 'Heer-aye. I've longed for valuable striped Welsh ware for years.'

'Antiques?' She rounded on me so savagely I almost fell off. 'You barbarian! I'm talking of the Principality's soul!' She lapsed into Welsh, cursing.

When I'd settled down – her still muttering – I wondered what I'd done wrong. Look at the opportunity of picking up some Welsh antiques. It was logical, for heaven's sake.

'Listen, love.' I chose my words. 'Think of a caveman. He found he could shape clay into a cup, that it got hard when baked. Then he learned that a glaze made it watertight!' I honestly couldn't see why she sat glowering. 'He'd invented technology! Then he tried slipware, using clays that burnt to a white-grey colour for decoration on the russet pot.' I tried, but it was uphill work. 'About the Civil War time, they used powdered lead glazes. Maybe from the old Roman silver mines in Wales, eh?' She suddenly turned and stared right into me. 'Think yellowish, think striped, and you can buy your own caravan!'

'Lovejoy,' she said, voice tight.

'No, love,' I said magnanimously. 'No need to apologize. We'll maybe find one together. Think! Welsh ware looks so amateurish, you can pick it up in junk shops. A single plate worth a car!'

'Lovejoy,' she said. 'If you loot the Principality, I'll see you gaoled. Understand?'

Her eyes were live coals. I swallowed. 'Yes,' I said meekly. Except I didn't. I'd been tactfully praising her country folk, for God's sake. Some people never recognize tact. I left her.

For a second I sat, then slithered down. I was by the emergency door, side rear. I'd already swivelled the handle experimentally. Now I swung it, fell out, as the bus started. I managed to close it, stepped behind the bus shelter and listened in rapture as the charabanc left. Its noise receded. I was a dozen miles from home. I'd walk. I gave them a minute, then stepped lively. Free!

There was a small country garage about a mile from the Boar's Head. I might be able to phone, rustle up a lift.

Walking in the countryside is rubbish. I strongly advise against it. You put one foot in front of the other, then do the other leg. Slowly, the scenery changes. East Anglia has no pavements except in towns. Motors squeal to a stop, the driver staring in fury. Horseback riders – Jesus, there are shoals – trot over you, the nags too stupid to watch their feet. You're forever leaping into the bloody hedges (thorny hawthorn, thorny dog rose, et thorny cetera).

But to escape Meg's merry band it would be worth it. I was tempted to rest at a bridge over a brook, but decided no. Best to pike on.

It's hereabouts that you get the treasure hunters. Find a patch of ground. Buy an archeological map. Get a pal with a metal detector, and you're off. Make sure you've got a quick getaway. The farmers hereabouts hate poachers. The law hates night marauders. And the constabulary, being failed criminals, hate everybody. The trouble is our crazy eleventh-century Treasure Trove law. The coroner's jury must decide if the original old Romano-British owner, way back then, *lost* the treasure or *hid* it. Ever heard anything so loony? Like wondering why your ancestors in AD 200 don't write any more.

I've been done myself under the Theft Act, for walking on somebody's farmland with a metal detector in the candle hours. 'Equipped to steal', the law decides. I ducked into the hedge while an enraged motorist fumed past. Excavating treasure goes in spurts. Like the Hoxne Treasure, a sensational Suffolk hoard. It's superb, numbering thousands of separate items, coins, necklaces, cutlery, bracelets. Naturally, everybody reads of this wonder, and starts digging that very morning. Metal detector sales boom.

It's down to money. I don't understand the stuff, not really. But if you crave it, why not sell pop stars' sweat? They say it's fifteen pounds a bottle; the fashion started in the USA. Sales are soaring. Or sell forgeries, or fakes on commission. It's often done, and you're in the clear. Money mesmerizes. Folk don't merely want to sell granny's old mangle (value equal to a second-hand car). They want an Old Master painting, the *châteaux*, casino, and girls that go with it. It's greed.

Which raises the question of why so many folk seemed desperate to keep me on this deranged scheme, wandering the leafy lanes with idiots. It was odd. It was a syndicate. The Ardens, Simon Doussy, his diamond sightholder Gee Omen, Raddie, Jessina Mosston. Doc Lancaster, too? But why me? Why Wales?

The garage hove into view. I plodded up, spoke to the girl. She was reading a glossy, chewing gum, listening to a deafening trannie. Irate at being interrupted, her only transport was an old motorbike. I said excellent; perhaps one that actually went . . . ? She said she'd phone a friend. I waited outside. The countryside, I assure you, didn't change. Thirty minutes later a great vehicle glided on to the forecourt like a stately galleon. A swish lady spoke.

'Now don't be stoopid, Lovejoy,' she said. 'Mrs Farahar.' I looked accusingly at the garage girl. 'Her people work on my husband's land. Get in.'

'Does this constitute an offer?' Luke must have a car phone.

She smiled. 'Yes!'

Which took me aback so much I got in. It was like being inside St Paul's, but plush. We were moving. 'Colonel Farahar is inspecting another farm we've just bought.'

'Quite a spread, then?'

'Some acres.' She wore that TV smile American women always wear. There was a big Land Rover following us.

'Who's your mate?' I asked. 'Bodyguard?'

'We've had a few incidents lately. Childish pranks, not serious.'

'Mmmmh,' I said. 'That's countryside. Danger everywhere.'

'I expect you to be on our side, Lovejoy. My husband demands loyal service. Understand?'

'Listen, lady. I've toted a gillion loonies for a thousand miles – '

'Fourteen miles, Lovejoy, from your cottage.'

'That where we're going?' I asked hopefully.

'No. We will visit my home. Your presence on the trip is essential.'

'Will I learn why?'

She considered that, brilliantly smart in a leaf-green suit. Her knees were edible. I had to stare away. Temptation's always too much. Guilt's easier. She said at last, 'Yes. But not yet.'

Notice anything about wealth? It gives a holy feeling in the abstract. But think of the people wealth owns, suddenly you're on lunar landscape. Money creates that mysticism when seeing the huge Pearl River or Derwentwater – you're witnessing the transcendental. You're emotionally lost. That's why people who win unbelievable lotteries or the football pools go mental. They're bewildered. I knew this woman, a pleasant lady, lived next to my Auntie Agnes, and she won the pools. Over half a million pounds. Happiness? Hardly. I was in my auntie's kitchen (she stored a forged Russell Flint painting I'd just finished) when the newly rich lady came steaming in. 'Why didn't you say hello, Agnes? You walked on by!' And my auntie said sorrowfully, 'Sorry, love. I didn't want to seem *after your money.*'

See? Money causes problems. The lady went to Spain, spent like a drunken sailor, was flat broke in a twelvemonth, her phalanx of new laughing lovers leaving her stranded. It's the natural history of flood money.

So we ordinary people invent a kind of hate for the rich. And why? Because we sense something deep down about real wealth. *We couldn't cope.* The point of all this is, we kulaks worship *abstract* wealth, and hate people with *real* money. Can I prove it? Instantly. You get on a train. On the seat are two magazines. One concerns the problems besetting the Exchequer, charts of fiscal policies. The other shows a superb girl dripping with precious gems and carries the headline RICH GIRL IN MONEY BLITZ AS HURRICANE RIPS HOTEL. Which do you pick up? You *ought* to choose the former. But you don't. Nobody does. You want to read how the spoiled bitch got her comeuppance. See? Worship and spite.

There's a survey in Paris, on the very, very rich. It covers fewer than a thousand European homes, to see how they live, what they buy.

'Missus,' I said as the motor swanned up to the grandest mansion house I'd ever seen, 'do you make a clean sweep of hotel rooms for shampoos, bath salts? The super-rich do.' The Paris survey.

'One doesn't use hotels, Lovejoy.' A serf opened her door. 'One has one's own town houses.'

Silly me. The helot looked narked. I'd opened my door unaided.

The house was majestic, a true Queen Anne manor that hadn't been mucked about. It felt friendly, regal. Lawns that writers call sweeping, drives curving between fountains. A lake glinted, an ornate summerhouse, a red brick wall with espalier shrubs. Fields showed a farm with a curl of smoke. Monarchs of all they surveyed, these Farahars. It always irks me that mansions get their blossoms earlier, as if God's keeping in with the moneyed class. A heraldic shield bragged over the main door. A heraldic flag flapped disdainfully from a mast. Rich rich.

The rich rich ignore fur coats and sports cars, I remembered. And it's not enough to be blue of blood to be topsters. The Farahars might have scooped the pool, decided to repossess the old mansion. Such things do happen. Wasn't the once American President George Bush supposed to've hailed from Messing, way back when?

Mrs Farahar preceded me. I followed, a lapdog. The place was sumptuous. Something covered with a beige cloth was on the coffee table. I staggerd as its unseen radiance beat into me.

'Wotcher, Raddie.'

He didn't rise, simply drooped his wrist. 'Lovejoy. Consorting with riffraff, Vana dear?' He wore a turban, bright silver lamé, with an ostrich plume dyed emerald green. He wore a nose ring, the emerald glittering. His suit was a match for Vana Farahar's, rusty pink and blue stripes, cossack pantaloons and Turkish slippers of yellow fur. He looked a prat.

The covered piece lay there.

'That will do, Raddie. Behave!' But she said it friskily, loving his reprimand. 'Lovejoy's come to be persuaded.'

'Can I see it, please? I don't often get to see something genuine and original.'

She was taken aback. 'That fast?' she said, marvelling.

The beige was easily lifted. A piece of silver, flat, the corner only of an original tray, properly called a lanx. It looked oddly similar to the famous one excavated in the 1720s in Risley Park in Derbyshire. There were pagan scenes, beasts, a rider on some animal. I held it by the cloth. On the reverse was EXUPER. EPISC. The fragment ended in a rip. 'Spade through it?' I asked. There'd been a Bishop Expurius who'd owned such lanxes, in the pagan fourth century when Christianity was just coming. I had to blot my eyes for sudden wetness. I'd never seen anything so lovely.

Vana Farahar was staring. 'My God,' she said.

'Where's Chuck, Raddie?' I asked.

'I'm cross with Chuck. He brought the wrong liqueur. I've sentenced him to three songs outside.' Raddie makes Chuck sing melodies as punishment. I can't understand their relationship.

'Do sit down, Lovejoy.' Mrs Farahar had that lovely contoured grace women have. It tore me to give the lanx up. A manservant came for orders. I said orange juice, please. Raddie giggled, tsssstssss, into vodka. 'That piece?' She pointed to a fragment alone on a plant stand. I went to look.

The silver carving was superbly aged. I lost interest. 'Gunge, lady.'

'Coffee, Wilson.' Vana Farahar swept her hair back. It's a lovely gesture, always fascinates me. Even twenty-month girls can do it. I gape to see a woman taking her hat off. 'It's high time you were less of a problem, Lovejoy.'

'Me?' I was honestly startled. 'Others cause problems.'

Raddie did his tsss-tssss.

'You promised to join the trip. You escaped. That's trouble.'

I rose, enraged. 'Listen to me, you posh bitch.' I was yelling. 'Frigging charity games belong to you and your playmates.' I grabbed the phoney silver lanx, shook it in her face. 'And you have the gall to think I'll be mesmerized and I'll do as you say? Honest to God.' I flung it across the room.

'Oooh, *reeee-yull*!' Raddie squeaked, applauding.

'Miraculous,' Mrs Farahar breathed. 'He really *does*.'

Raddie sipped his vodka. 'I told you, Vana, silly cow. He's a divvy. They're basically weird.'

Which from him . . . 'Look, missus.' I was weary. 'I want out. Force me back to that mental zoo, I'll skip.'

'He really did it!' she was still saying. 'Not even to *look*.'

'Where'd you get the original Romano-Celtic lanx?' I asked. 'Some market overt?' She looked blank. 'Any old street market is a market overt – meaning you can't get arrested for buying something stolen there. Scotland's different. So is – '

'Wales.' A military man strode in. Stout, fiftyish, decisive, laundered. Colonal Farahar? He took a frosted glass from a manservant. 'A market overt is any street gathering of vendors. Buy something in good faith, you're in the legal clear.'

He sat, eyed Raddie with loathing, me with distrust.

'The City of London's a market overt each weekday,' I added. 'Buy a stolen Old Master, you're safe. They can't ask for it back.'

'Is that right, honey?' Mrs Farahar said. I looked, wondered why she hated him.

Colonel Farahar saw my glance, recognized it for what it was. 'Boot sales, Lovejoy?' It was a prompt.

'Boot sales aren't market overts. Nor garage sales for charity.' I added that last bit just so he'd know. 'I was just leaving, Colonel. Hope your scheme goes okay.'

I was out when Raddie spoke. 'You can have the lanx, Lovejoy. Though why *you* deserve a priceless slice of Romano-Celtic history, I can't imagine!'

My feet wouldn't move. To my horror they turned me round. I almost exploded at their treachery. Just when my mind gets its priorities straight, something betrays me. But my willpower was still under control. I opened my mouth to say go to hell.

'Have what?' I heard me say. I thought, that's not right.

'True, Lovejoy. We've got all three fragments, better than the Derbyshire find. It's yours, if you'll go.'

Slowly I drew a breath. Mrs Farahar had risen, as if to pour coffee, and moved behind her husband and Raddie. She looked at me above their heads, and slo-o-o-owly cupped a breast in her palm, laid her fingers on her mouth, and silently blew. She poured, strolled gracefully back. Women think they can have everything they want. My mind sneered at her crude attempt to bribe me, with my will of steel.

'It's a deal,' I croaked.

Farahar gave a curt nod. 'Right, Lovejoy. You can have the silver thing.' He smiled.

'Deal!' I said, to my fury. Everbody except me was smiling.

Syndicates puzzle me. Whether for diamonds, silver, dollar bonds, or an antique dealers' auction ring, a syndicate is simply a way of ganging up on the rest of us. Greed always ends in betrayal, being uncontrollable. Think of it. You simply *can't* call a mob of malicious murderous hoods a syndicate, and expect it to be a collective St Cuthbert. Here were Gee Omen with his Continental diamond connection, Simon Doussy, lovely Valerie Arden, Colonel and Vana Farahar, Raddie, Sty too, for all I knew, plus lesser mortals, all in on something highly illegal. Why didn't they go for some legit antiques? Anybody can drop a line to the Vatican Commission for Cultural Heritage, spiritual overseer of 97,200 churches (chuck in Sicily, that's one every two and a quarter square miles) and legitimately buy the 10,130 of them up for sale. Okay, so you promise to use the holy basilicas, chapels, shrines, for 'culture' (the Vatican's word, not mine). But sold churches change overnight into gyms, pop discos, boutiques. *And their antiques vanish*. My law is that syndicates start with sin. Don't ever forget.

17

Farahar, in uniform with five bands of ribbons, drove me.

He stopped by a flat expanse of nothing. In the distance, a few buildings. We were at some sort of perimeter, wire mesh between us and the boring terrain beyond. East Anglia is flat as a model's bodice. Somebody had concreted the whole pancake.

'Five minutes,' he said.

He talked about his origins. Arkansas, but 'Welsh way back. Grandparents emigrated, hard grafters, Lovejoy.' He almost dashed away a manly tear.

We got out of the car and strolled beside the fence. It was a mile high, electrified. Then I saw a falconer, and knew. Military air force bases hire falconers to keep away birds, which have an unpatriotic habit of getting sucked into aircraft engines and bringing them to a bad end.

'That why you got yourself posted here?'

'Sure is.' His eyes were glowing. I thought, hello, here we go. Crusaders are ten a penny, all harping on conquering something somehow. 'I'm back at my roots.'

If you say so, I thought. I only bothered to listen in hope of learning how to reach the delectable Vana.

'I promised my old folks to one day repossess the land of my fathers. They were driven out by persecution.'

'Great!' I said heartily. 'Well, Colonel, I'll be off.'

He ignored that. 'My expertise is geologics. I've solved the world's greatest mystery.'

Oh aye, I thought. Which? The Holy Grail, Stonehenge? I was so excited I yawned.

'Where,' said this goon, 'did Stonehenge come from?'

Everybody knows. 'It's a mystery.' I was innocent as a lamb.

'Lovejoy,' he said portentously, '*I've found out.*'

'Good heavens!' I'd nearly nodded off.

He was gratified. 'They came from South Wales!'

'No!' God give me strength. Master of the bleedin' obvious.

'It's true! The standing stones are of a particular composition. Stonehenge has thirty-four so-called *foreign* stones. Of them, twenty-nine are dolerite, that people call bluestones. The other four are rhyolite boulders, with one sandstone. The significance?'

'What, Colonel?'

'Dolerite exists in Devon, Cornwall, North Wales, too. But the Stonehenge stones are conclusive. They're from the Preseli ridge, South Wales!'

'That's stupendous!' I cried. You have to humour nutters, when they're paying you a priceless Romano-Celtic silver, plus Vana. He'd obviously read H. H. Thomas's monograph.

'I knew you'd be astonished, Lovejoy.' He went grim. There was a shrill whine, and three jet planes streaked across the grey skies. Thunder rolled up their wakes, thumping my eardrums until I felt like screaming. The bloody old fool was looking up in rapture. Another wave of American war planes shrieked overhead, battering us.

Quiet returned. He was transported. 'Wasn't that the most beautiful sight in the goddamned world? War on the wing!' He hummed a tune. My hearing crept warily back into my head. '*They* gave me the clue to Stonehenge, Lovejoy!'

'They? The planes?'

'Sure did. Contour analytics. There are two peaks in the Preseli range of South Wales, ten miles inland from Fishguard. Foel Drygarn and Foel Feddau. Between them stands Carnmenyn, a hill with a group of cairns. That's where they came from, Lovejoy.'

'But the effort, early man cutting those monoliths – '

'They had to, Lovejoy.' He'd stopped now, oblivious. 'Primitive man stood watching on Drygarn Fawr. All around him was winter, ice, snow. No food, only the cold. The sun had gone. Then, suddenly, the sun would rise at last – a direction of 110 degrees – behind Darren! Winter had ended!' There were tears in his eyes. I felt ashamed. Barmy or not, he believed. 'Spring arose, summer! Life returned to the earth!'

'Then?'

'Then, Lovejoy, one evening, those ancient watchers would climb the same mountain. The sun died behind Freni Fawr's grim mass. And their souls chilled, for winter had come, to grip the world in ice. Midsummer solstice too, sun rising behind Corngefallt, would be a morning of huge significance.'

'Colonel,' I prompted. 'It seems to me – '

'No, Lovejoy. It cannot *seem*, not nowadays. We are protected from starvation. We *know* the sun will rise. We have the technology. Ancient Man hadn't. He just prayed that tomorrow the sun *would* return, and not plunge the earth in midwinter forever.'

'Stonehenge?'

'Was a calendar, Lovejoy. It was built with stones, from the most magic part of the world known to Ancient Man. The place where the mountains were a kind of solar calendar.'

'They shifted them?' His was one theory. Others said the ice shoved them to Salisbury. Pick any idea from a million.

'The stones came from Wales, the place of magic. My homeland.' He sniffed, overcome. I yawned, also overcome.

'Great,' I said in. 'You've cracked it. Write to the Royal Geographical Society.'

'No.' He started us towards the motor. 'Do you know, in a research report on UK's tourist attractions – amenities, info, presentation – guess which came *last*?'

Go on, I thought. 'Go on,' I said. 'Not . . . ?'

'Stonehenge! The greatest source of clues to the dawn of *Homo sapiens* – scorned by its custodians!' He set his face grimly. 'I see you're a man of sentiment, Lovejoy,' he told me, which I already knew. 'I must do more than write a report. I must do something.'

'What exactly?' I couldn't see what he was driving at.

'It requires money, Lovejoy. But it is already begun.'

'Well, er, good luck.' Flint-eyed sex-charged Vana was married to this visionary?

'I won't need it, Lovejoy.' He swung in, fired the engine. 'All I need is for you to obey orders. Then all else follows.'

In a war picture, I'd have snapped, 'Roger!' As it was, I didn't say a word. He drove me about ten miles, where Luke's charabanc waited on a village green. I said ta, climbed aboard. Luke gave me a don't-abscond-again look. Meg started a passionate lecture on responsibility. I was asleep in seconds.

18

The coach stopped. Phillida dropped little Arthur on me. I blinked awake. They'd all disembarked. We were near a rugby ground. A rim of tall greyish hills, few trees. God, countryside.

A greyish horse cropped the grass, between the shafts of a gypsy caravan. Not original, a repro made by Dealing in Manchester. It looked tough. I wanted evidence that the bloody thing would crumple within a furlong. Worse, another caravan stood beyond it, a black horse noshing. Colourful, acrylic paint for God's sake. And two more beyond.

Luke and Meg were looking at a map. I got out to negotiate deliverance, carrying Arthur.

One caravan was predominantly blue. One had a pinkish front. Green, yellow. Blokes in blue, birds in the pink? Well, the quicker we departed the sooner –

'. . . Lovejoy will drive last. I'll head group conferences, as psychiatric nurse.'

'You're off your frigging head, Meg,' I said, then went red. I'd best watch how I phrased things. Barmy, loony, dimwit, idiocy, cretinoidal, the normal vocabulary of the know-all, must be shelved among these, er, folk. 'Me? Drive a horse?'

'It simply follows the others.' Meg was exasperated.

'Good.' Which meant I could scarper and the psychiatric nurse carry the can.

I went and kicked the caravan wheels. Luke turned aside with a chin-jerk of exasperation.

'Get aboard, Lovejoy,' he said. 'Me first, blue caravan, Humphrey and Boris. It's where you'll sleep. Then yellow with Mr Lloyd, driven by Ifor.' He indicated Preacher. 'Meg's green, with the old lady. Last, Lovejoy's pink-top with Rita, Phillida and the babe.' I drew breath but the swine got there first. 'Rita knows horses.'

'Luke,' I said, really depressed. 'There must be some way – '

'Say goodbye to the lady, Lovejoy, and we'll get started.'

Beside our charabanc stood a Rolls, Valerie Arden smiling beside it. I went to her. No driver. She was stunning.

'Just came to say a fond farewell, Lovejoy.'

Why more women don't wear amber I can't say. Expense? It is definitely out of fashion, which proves fashion's ignorance. Her colours don't sound right – a fitted wash-grey suit, tight high neck, skirt – with deep-red burnite amber necklace, matching brooch and rings. Glorious. My mouth watered. I'd never seen so much burnite. It is rare, hard red amber exported from Burma. She even wore a comb of it, and a bossed catch on her grey sealskin clutch bag. Its hardness is only 3.0, but when you're carving (use stainless steel) it generates so much electricity that your forearms go into spasm. I once went to Doc Lancaster thinking I'd got polio. He chucked me out, laughing, callous sod.

'*Pinites succinifer* amber,' I said. 'Will you marry me?'

She laughed. 'We *shall* get together. You met *dear* Vana and Franklin?'

'Aye. If I stay with this mob, I get an antique.'

'Don't call Vana that,' she said sweetly. 'You *will* be rewarded. I promise.' She had her hand on my arm, quickly bussed my face. 'I'll be at the rehabilitation unit in Mynydd Mal.' She drove off.

First time I heard that name. I wasn't to forget it.

The horses were gigantic things. Pulse, Ash, Cotton, and Barley, stupid names. I sat wobbling nervously on the caravan's seat. I could hear Rita and Phillida chatting inside, Arthur wisely talking to himself. I took the reins, pushed the brake like Luke did.

He flipped the reins once. I saw Preacher flick his, praying away, then Meg. Timidly, I flapped mine. My horse started with a jerk, following the green-topped caravan docilely enough. It felt odd, rolling slowly along with iron tyres making a racket beneath. We trundled out on to the roadway.

For those not in the know, a horse can be very hypnotic. They seem just mobile scenery, trotting past your garden. You call out, 'Afternoon, love,' to the pretty rider, and keep out of the beast's way. You might give it an apple. Finito.

But driving – if that's the word – a horse is mesmerizing. It's also silly. You hold these leather strips. The horse's ears occasionally flick forward. Its head goes up and down. The hooves are another gripping diversion, going clop-de-clop-clop-de-clop. Its bum moves. Its tail swishes, but for no reason. And that, said Alice, is that.

Worse, after a century of this tedium, I glanced back – *and we'd only gone four hundred yards!* I could still see the tall rugby posts. I groaned in agony. We clopped another couple of years, travelled twenty feet. Dolly'd never catch up.

'You all right, Lovejoy?' Meg called back sternly.

'Yes, Meg.' I thought of Doussy's notebook that Liffy'd given me, and took it out.

Going plod-plod after a while becomes fascinating. I found myself trying to remember that rhyme, all the months of the year, one word each. Snowy was January. Then Blowy? I vaguely recalled April as Showery, May being Flowery. And the old poet had written them in threes, season by season. My cousin Glenice used it as a skip chant when she was five. 'Hoppy, Croppy . . .'

'Lovejoy?' Luke was shaking me. 'You dropped off, booy. Take care.'

My caravan had skewed across the road, the horse was chewing a hedge. 'Sorry. Didn't notice.'

He waved a couple of cars past. 'You dropped this notebook.'

'Ta.' We hoofed off, me determined to stay awake. I knocked on the door behind me.

'Didn't want to wake Arthur, Phillida,' I said. 'A word?'

'Yes!' She knelt. The drifting scenery showed only fields and whatnot, and the road ahead. 'Arthur's flat out.'

I drew her beside me and closed the door. She relished the view. 'Love, where're you from?'

'Oh, we've all only just met, Lovejoy. Isn't it exciting?'

'Delirious. You're not from one . . . clinic?' I hesitated, what with the stigma of mental illness.

'No.' She wasn't embarrassed. 'My doctor said this was a splendid chance. I'm just nervous, Lovejoy.'

We talked of infants. I made her laugh with tales of my baby-sitting. But after a mile or so I had to say it. 'How long you been a fork-lifter, Phillida?'

'A what?' She looked at me all smiley.

'Fork-lifter.' I pointed two fingers downwards as if into a pocket. 'Subtle-monger. Big dipper. Howffer. Pickpocket. Knitter. Knitman.' Knitter, for knit one, purl one, drop one.

She laughed. 'Oh, you mean this? I *found* it.'

'Ta.' I took the notebook back, put it into my pocket the side she was sitting. It's safer. Your pocket furthest away from the dipper's the one to watch. She was dynamite. I'd employ her any day of the week. She was also a regular, good explanations if rumbled.

She said, untroubled, 'This trip's just what Arthur needs! Fresh air, new people. He's taking interest. Creatures in the fields, countryside, people, birds!'

'Aye,' I said. 'One long whirl. Do you know the others?'

'Only Rita. The thin man was in our psychotherapy.'

Words like that chill my spine. I wanted her to say they were safe, wouldn't go ape with a hatchet.

'Boris has problems, though. He's on tablets.'

God Almighty. I eyed the caravans in front, wondering if the loon – sorry, bloke – was peering through some pinhole planning a chain-saw massacre. I prayed he'd keep taking the tablets. But what's a nutter's promise worth?

'And . . . ?' I tilted my head back at the door.

'Rita? She's asleep.' Phillida was cheery. I liked her, at least one normal in the pack. 'There's nothing *wrong* with us, Lovejoy. Rita's just sad.'

Sad I could cope with. Phillida was easy, Humphrey no bother, and Luke was sane with his country lore. I wanted a mobile phone.

One odd thing. When flicking through the notebook, an address had caught my eye. I recognized the name, Polkahorn, of that Polkahorn rugby ground. It was the first address. I thumbed, found the last. Mynydd Mal. Valerie Arden had said Min-nith. There was an address in Polkahorn, Tippett Antiques, and the word *church*.

Desultory chat for a quarter of a mile's numbing trundle, and Arthur erupted with a scream of fury. Phillida went in. I wondered how we cooked. Was it all kitted out, stoves and things? We'd streaked past a tavern. I was getting famished. Was there some way of contacting Luke? Short of dropping off and walking to him, no.

The book had one name that stood alone. Dolaucothy. I tried saying it softly to myself. Odd name. Welsh? It wasn't local. Or were the other addresses antique dealers on route?

What had Meg said, when rowing with Imogen at the dance school? Something about Imogen not wanting Meg to go. I couldn't remember. My Gran's trick was to try not to remember – aha!

'Flowy!' I exclaimed, delighted. 'Snowy, *Flowy*, Blowy! Then it's Showery, Flowery.' Five out of twelve wasn't bad.

Gripped by the excitement, the horse broke wind with a growling noise that even little Arthur would have admired.

Horses, being horses, want a quiet life. Give them a tailboard to follow, they plod on for ever. I jumped down and walked alongside. The nag didn't mind. I climbed up. It didn't mind. I sang, whistled, and got back clip-clop. I told it various things. I shouted abuse. I told it to stop, hurry up, slow down, gallop. The dumb beast plodded on, our wheels grinding beneath. We were now passing various cottages, Polkahorn outskirts.

And in a window stood two brass candlesticks. A woman was looking out. I leapt, ran to tell Luke my horse was limping. All waggons stopped.

'Limping? Near or off? Hind or fore?' He came to see the animal, bent and picked up a hoof.

'I'll get it some water,' I offered helpfully, hurried to the cottage door. It opened, a pleasant housewife with what my old Gran would call Celtic colouring – raven-black hair, azure eyes. I told her our horse needed a drink. She let me enter.

'Heavens!' I said. 'Those candlesticks! My granny's!'

'Are they indeed!' She brought a pail, smiling.

Try to choose between a woman and antiques. I mean, a woman has a sin within her smile. But so do antiques. Find one, you've found sin. The trouble is I go red easily.

'Well, no,' I lied, starting to stammer. 'I saw your face. I told the boss the horse was lame so I could meet you. He's an antique dealer, see.'

Her smile was quieter, lazier. 'Take the pail.'

'Oh, aye.' I found Luke checking the horse's feet. I offered the pail to the nag. It showed no interest.

'Lovejoy. We've gone one mile. This rate, we'll be six months on a fortnight's journey.'

'Don't get narked.' Honestly, show compassion to dumb animals and what do you get? 'Only trying to help.' Boris was staring down. I grimaced, seized the pail.

She waited indoors. 'Fine, is it?' The candlesticks were on the table, a commemorative mug between.

Now, some antique brass isn't. Because it's latten. Ancient brass candlesticks are the most missed bargains in the kingdom. To know why, think of the metal.

A couple of years before the 1588 Spanish Armada, household brass hit Merrie England. Read the wills of that period. They make a sharp distinction, between brass and latten. For that first brass century until about 1690, the metal was simply copper alloyed with calamine. The founders of the time moaned and groaned. It was hell to work. They hated it. Make some, if you don't believe me. It's a pig. Tough, friable, with a surface pitted like a coke clinker. Now, latten is merely the word for ingots, solid chunks of this rotten old-alloy brass that were hand beaten into sheets. Brass founders sold these sheets for making candlesticks, bed-warming pans, horse brasses.

Now, calamine brass, though naff, is highly prized these days. And the lady's candlesticks were ugly, deeply pitted, of sickly colour, with hardly a gleam. To the people of Good Queen Bess's time, pretty awful, but all they could afford. To me, unutterably gorgeous. I glanced at the caravans through the window. Luke was already striding to his driving seat. Boris was looking out.

Which made me force my gaze past the delectable woman/candlesticks, to the mug. There's a boom in gloom. The mug commemorated a split in a royal marriage. Some collectors actually go for misery. Never mind joy. They lust for a bust showing tragedy and pay through the nose for cups of woe. This one was virtually brand new. It wasn't Boris's face. So why did I think of him?

'Love.' I took the lady's hand. 'I'm Lovejoy. Can I see you? I'll come back this way.' Luke called impatiently.

'When?' She glanced about. 'It's a bit difficult, see.'

I whispered, 'I've got it! Put these candlesticks out of sight, and the mug, right? Tell your, er, bloke you've sold them. I'll bring the money. Maybe we can . . .'

Luke himself came thumping on the door five minuts later. I fore-stalled him, rushing out and leaping on my perch. 'Sorry, Luke. I, er, spilled the water and had to . . .'

He gave me a dour glance, mistrustful swine. I waved to the lovely Bronwen until the cottages were out of sight. My spirits rose. Maybe this wouldn't be wasted time after all. I'd get the latten sticks for a song. The nauseating mug I'd tolerate, then sell it to some misery for a fortune.

We rolled into Polkahorn proper about twenty to five, just in time to get me arrested. Heaven teaching me not to enjoy myself so much.

19

A few little Polkahorn lads tried swinging on our caravan tails. Luke went berserk. I only grinned. I'd done it often on coal waggons and brewers' drays when a kiddie. The nag didn't mind.

We didn't arrive like Western heroes riding into Tombstone. A few folk were around. One or two muttered about gypsies. The traffic was scarce Sunday stuff. We stopped on a patch of green grass. A bobby hove up and said we'd to move on. Luke clicked his horse up, and started off. I hauled on the reins, narked. My horse looked over its shoulder, narked. It knew only to follow the dead lantern up ahead.

'Move on.' The peeler judged me balefully. I judged him.

'Tell me why.'

He strolled ponderously. 'Because Polkahorn doesn't want your sort. Beyond the signpost by dusk, or else.'

'Lovejoy.' Luke paused a hundred yards off.

'I want a pee,' I told the peeler. 'And to do some shopping.'

'On your own head.' He strolled away, grinning at the lads. A dozen or so. 'Don't rough him up too much,' he said. They grinned, clustered closer. My heart sank, recognizing vigilante righteousness. I jumped down.

'Anybody get me a newt?' I asked quietly.

They looked blank. 'Newt?' one said.

'Some dead-nettle? A plant called valerian? Passiflora?'

With the theatrical gestures of a bomb-thrower, I beckoned them closer. Furtive glances, licking lips, I could have been a politician. 'There's somebody hereabouts called Tippett, right?'

They looked at each other. Their average age was about fourteen, same as their IQ, but bruisers.

'And a bone of an ox,' I put in for good measure.

'Tippett? Yes.' They shuffled as one made the admission.

'Antique dealer, he means, Jem,' a little one said.

'Shhhh!' I was Guy Fawkes on the way to the Gunpowder Plot. 'Mustn't say.' I grinned, clandestine. 'There's a couple of quid in it. Bring them before dusk.'

Jem was reckoning profit, the way born leaders will. 'Tippett's an incomer, done nothing for Polkahorn.'

Not local, this Tippett. I could see Polkahorn's mighty police force staring. 'I'll leave your bobby be, for the whilst,' I said, giving absolution. 'But he'd better not push it.'

They dispersed, most going with Jem. Valerian is a plant used as a tranquillizer. Passiflora I'd heard of vaguely in the same connection. Dead-nettle just sounded superstitious. I hoped Polkahorn's newts were fleet of foot. The ox bone I could throw away once we'd moved on from this dump.

The little town was what's called picturesque. A river, bridge, riverside black-and-white beamed houses, 'Tudor' in style. A couple of pubs, a motor or two parked near the church. Luke was gazing at me, at the bobby, the town. I waved him on to the greensward.

'Lovejoy?' Phillida emerged. 'I need a few things for Arthur. Have we time?'

The shop was only over the road. 'Sure. We camp here. I've to go to church.'

Arthur eyed the world balefully with an infant's implaccable dislike. Luke came up.

'Luke. I'd get the waggons. I'm to evensong.'

'What about the copper?'

'Forget the Old Bill. Tell him it's all arranged. The women are going shopping.' I drew him to one side. 'Listen. Where do we normally, er . . . ? I mean, a caravan's cramped, isn't it?'

'We carry portable loos, no baths. Use the public ones.'

'Right.' The Duke of Wellington always said to pass water at every opportunity, and he was a stickler for form. I mean, he sent Lord Hill to rebuke Colonel Tynling of the Guards at Bayonne in 1813: 'Lord Wellington does not approve of the use of *umbrellas* during the enemy's firing . . .' So be elegant, but not namby-pamby. Dozy East Anglia locks its public loos at dusk, so you've to constipate until 9 a.m. 'Tell the peeler to leave those loos open.'

The church was grand, thirteenth century, flint-and-mortar, the flints napped vertical to face the weather. Odd, they stay shiny, century after century.

'Church, Lovejoy?' Luke said. 'You a churchgoer?'

That made me almost pause, because he knew nothing else about me either. 'Be about an hour, if the sermon's short.'

The church had superb beams, a lovely wooden reredos, and a forged ciborium. It was Holy Communion that evening, so Luke *et al* could add ten minutes. There was a meagre congregation.

One woman caught my eye, though. Thirtyish, costly with that primness fashionable women manage without a struggle. She came in with Reverend Will the fat parson, probably his wife. She looked about a third his size, which made me wonder how they achieved the perfect friendship. The rest of us hoi-polloi numbered some twenty or less. Good organist but a rotten organ, modern repro, positive-pressure manual. They'd be ten a penny if they didn't cost a fortune.

In church, my attention wanders. When a lady's handbag emits a constant chime, if there is such a thing, I can't for the life of me concentrate on higher matters. Antiques became everything. By the sermon, I was almost deranged. I'd have killed for her handbag. It was modern, more straps than an Arab satchel.

The ciborium, when we few tiptoed to the altar rails, was a poor fake. Not even silver. Somebody had made it of silvered copper. These fraudulent days, you can get polish that will impart a real genuine coating of silver over practically any metal object you polish. Be careful of the edges and recesses if you want to swap your auntie's best silverware secretly, because they're a horrible give-away. Practically every church in the country nowadays is selling its plate off for hard gelt, and substituting it with base metal lookalikes. Some parsons do it honestly. Others keep it secret, ho-ho.

But there are secrets and secrets. I mean, who is the Kingdom's fastest solver of jigsaw puzzles, at the time of going to press? None other than Her Brit. Maj. Elizabeth Two, that's who. Naturally, we're not allowed to know this secret because the time trials were very secret secrets. Another secret is that her dresses' hems are weighted with lead in case a breeze gets cheeky. Other secrets are wide open, like church silver.

It's not anybody's fault. Silver itself is to blame.

Back in July 1992, London's bullion dealers awoke into a really happy day. They were asked to sell silver. Thrilled, they set about this merry task. It had languished a bit lately. Today would be money for jam, because silver is sold in a face-to-face one-to-one secrecy. Nobody else there. A simple handshake, and a million ounces of silver zooms. And nobody else knows. Secrecy rules. (Actually, New York is the exception. There, the traders share a sort of bullring, complete with showy TV screens.)

Suddenly, that terrible morning, dealers realized they'd been had. Nothing illegal, but every secret deal was duplicated throughout the world. And it wasn't a few ounces here, a few there. It was stupendous, over six hundred tonnes.

The silver price tumbled. It tumbled again. Further. Kept going. Suddenly, the plug fell out. Back in the happy old soaring days of the Bunker Hunts, silver was over thirty-five dollars a troy ounce, touched a dizzy fifty-two dollars. It had declined since, but now it really did plummet, touching three dollars ninety. Worse, the Yemenis went home. They are – were! – traditional silver buyers, for that hard-working lot love the stuff. Banks unglued. People who a few days before had been melting their Georgian silver into bullion were now badly frightened. They tried to sell at giveaway prices, and were left begging friends to help. I don't understand the international bullion markets. Who does? But a blob of metal worth a fortune one day and peanuts the next? Who wants it?

The heady days of 1979 are long gone. Now, silver is almost too dangerous to handle. Except, of course, for the rare ancient silver relics dug up from East Anglia or East Europe. Where was I? In church.

Because I couldn't not, I found myself kneeling close behind the pretty bird. Her handbag beamed spirituality. I could hardly stand for the last hymn. I have to follow the words in the Ancient and Modern, and bawled Bunyan's *To Be A Pilgrim* with enthusiasm. The service done, I hung back. The lovely lass paused decoratively, spoke to the parson, who was giving us smiling farewells.

As she made off I emerged into the dark. Well, it had been worth a go. I crossed to the caravans, light now coming from their windows. The Plod was still glaring. I often wonder if they're taught glaring in police schools, like thumping. Luke was on the grass. The horses were untethered, whatever's the word, noshing in nosebags.

'Doesn't the straw get up their nostrils?'

'No. Enjoy the service?' He was at one with the night, the goon.

'You don't enjoy services. You just go. Rotten sermon, pinched from Cranmer.' We were a few feet away from the caravans. 'Luke. Life with the raggle-taggle gypsies, Oh isn't for me.' It came on to rain. I stood under a tree. There was a pond nearby. 'What do they drink?' You can't help thinking what a rotten life it must be.

'Clean water from the churchyard tap. In,' he added in the awkward pause that ensued at this news, 'a bucket.'

'I'm famished. Is there a caff? Polkahorn's a dump.'

'Those lads left you these. I paid them three quid. What you want a newt, a bone, and some plants for, Lovejoy?'

'To stop the sods heaving us into the pond, like the bobby encouraged them to. Superstition works sometimes.'

He chuckled. 'I was all ready for a scrap. Your sudden holiness was to prove you weren't some cranky wizard? I like it, booy.'

Waiting, I listened to his chuckle. It was very practised. That 'booy' wasn't quite right. And he'd been very, very cool for a bloke about to take on a dozen country lads. They'd have marmalized me. 'These all nutters, Luke?' I was suddenly fed up. I should be home, working out Mrs Arden and Liffy's death and the supposed gold finds and that Doussy. I had a headache. 'What I mean is, what's this *for*?'

He shrugged. 'A charity scheme. I'm hired, Lovejoy.'

'Volunteer, me,' I said. 'I'll go to the loo.'

'Toilet paper under my driving seat, any amount.' He sounded proud. Things fell into place.

'What were you in for?' I asked, chancing my arm. 'Prison.' I felt sorry at his silence. 'Just a guess. People on remand squirrel away shampoos, soap, loo rolls. They're not allowed to buy them when convicted.' He said nothing. 'Are you?'

He shrugged, moved quickly on without umbrage. I admired his cool. I had a pro on my hands. 'I'm just careful. We'll eat in an hour, Lovejoy.' He didn't smile. 'I'm cook. Be on time.'

'Promise.'

Tippett's shop looked drab, forlorn. Its one exterior light hadn't been cleaned since the last plague of moths. I knocked. A belligerent tipsy bloke let me in.

The dingy antiques place had nothing to commend it. I must have been down, feeling bad about Luke, I suppose. I viewed the interior. 'Tippett? Show it me. If we do a deal, fine. If not, fine.'

'Lovejoy?' a voice said. She was as gorgeous as when I was behind her in church trying to raise my thoughts above my umbilicus.

'Aye, lady.' I watched Tippett dither. Maybe the parson's lady was one more member of the unending Arden syndicate? He looked shopsoiled. Failure always embarrasses me. I know it so well.

'Lights,' she said. She stepped to a small table – late Victorian, ruined because its top was replaced by a modern wardrobe's joined sides – and took a tissue-wrapped object from her handbag. I reeled, kept erect from politeness, reached a cane-bottomed chair in the nick of time.

'Please look, Lovejoy.'

Tippett came to stand beside me, bemused. A true antique dealer. It was a small porcelain figure of a lady in bed, with a clownish bloke grovelling at her feet. About 1820, our Coalport imitated Meissen – but Coalport's figures were softpaste, not like Meissen's hardpaste originals. Beware – it's one of those odd examples where the fake is rarer and costlier than the genuine antique original. I relaxed, loving it.

'I buy it?' I asked her.

'Possibly,' she said, so smoothly I knew that she was a regular. She was a real 'zuzzer', one who slyly steals antiques for silent sale to passing dealers. She must have nicked the church's ciborium, heaven knows what else.

'Watch out.' Tippett suddenly pushed to the door, and opened on the knock. 'Constable! Can I help you?'

'I want Lovejoy, Tippo,' the Plod said heavily.

Just when things were looking up. 'Me? What have I done?'

'Your woman's been arrested. Shoplifting. Come along.'

The lady was relieved but puzzled. I told her softly, 'Mrs Will. I'll be back and buy. Okay?'

She nodded, and let me get taken to the station.

20

Phillida's face showed streaks from a waterfall of tears. Arthur carolled, unmoved by the tragedy. The cop shop wasn't up to much – threadbare carpet, worn chairs. Maybe Polkahorn's yobbos and maidens were law-abiding?

'What gets me, George,' I told the peeler, 'is that single bulb. Standard issue, are they?'

'Statement, you bastard,' said this charmer. I went to greet Phillida – where was Luke? She thrust Arthur into my arms. He felt like a tank trap, all girders and wooden beams. He also bubbled and sloshed. Suspicion hit me: only part of Arthur was Arthur. He sang, belched, dribbled, warbled. He niffed.

'It's ridiculous, Lovejoy.' She resumed weeping. 'I accidentally gathered some *buttons*! Adjusting Arthur. He likes being carried a certain way. They arrested me! Can you believe it?'

Well, yes. Babes are on hire by the hour. The age of theft is upon us. Prams, infants, and sympathy, they're the best to shoplift in Marks or Woolworth's. From what I'd glimpsed of Polkahorn's shops, each was family run, no shoplifter's paradise. On the desk lay thirteen plastic strips of buttons, six in each.

She must have seen my face. I shrugged, adjusting Arthur so his legs could piston elsewhere than my groin, and looked down at the sudden clattering. A screwdriver. Four boxes of condoms. Three bottles of shampoo, colours various. A child's penny whistle, B flat. Toffees, a box of handkerchiefs, a dinosaur game, a manicure set, an egg timer, alarm clock, two fountain pens. I sighed, gave her Arthur.

'That is proof of shoplifting,' the Plod intoned.

'Phillida,' I said, 'frisk Arthur. Give it back.'

'Good heavens, Lovejoy!' Phillida laughed breathlessly. 'You don't think for one minute that I – '

'They yours, love?' I asked a determined aproned matron. She glared at me with eyes bottled in wire-framed specs. Glaring seemed Polkahorn's thing. 'This lady is from a mental institution. We're going to rehabilitation.'

'Mental?' the lady asked, suddenly scared.

Phillida laughed with incredulity. 'Heavens, what a *fuss*! It's all so easily *explained* – '

I said to the police, 'Look. No magistrate'll sentence a young mother with mental . . .' You can fill in the rest. I waxed sad, lyrical. I invented case histories. I told how some shop had started criminal proceedings and been firebombed, petrol through the letterbox . . . We left twenty minutes later. I was furious with Luke.

It is on record that Christie's 'Special Clients' section features an exquisite bird on the desk who, as auction day approaches, dons ever-lower necklines and ever-shorter miniskirts. It's also a matter of record that the best predictors of Hong Kong's stock market are the *feng shui* mystic diviners. They use sticks, sand trays, birds in cages. Not a computer in sight, yet they out-perform all known stock exchange analysts. In other words, life is a series of illusions. To prove it: which bank, established 1692, recently employed an exorcist to rid its London offices of ghosts? Answer: the Queen's bank, Coutts, that's which. Therefore nothing is quite what it seems. I went for Luke because he was phoney.

'Why the hell didn't you tell me about Phillida?' I'd dragged him from the caravan – first time I'd seen inside. 'How many more surprises?' I bawled like a stranded seal.

'Keep calm, Lovejoy.' He was untroubled, just stood there. 'It's all the same if you're going to push off.'

'It bloody well is!' I paced like a wrestler about to go for it. 'I'm bloody sick of you and your loonies!'

'Then go, Lovejoy.' He didn't even shrug. Now, very few blokes behave like this. I stifled my anger, glanced inside the caravan.

Humphrey, tall and languid, was reading a book by a dim electric light. Beyond him, Boris sat tapping his knees with his hands, over and over, staring.

'Will you let me?' I asked. 'Or will I be brought back?'

'That's for your absence to decide.'

See what I mean, appearances? Luke, garbed like a yokel, talked like some maverick politico. I knew instantly that if I took a swing at him he'd flip me casually into the village pond. I finally managed a nod.

'Where do we sleep?' It was too late to go anyway.

'Bunks. We're not too crowded.'

'And grub? I'm famished.' Now he really did shrug. I supposed they'd eaten while I'd been at Tippett's antique shop. There was a pub still open thank God. Phillida was already in her caravan, probably pilfering Rita's things. I headed disgustedly for the Rose and Crown, Polkahorn, and slipped round past it in the dark.

Tippett's antique shop was shuttered. A red box on the wall signalled electronic alarms. It would be phoney. No antique dealer wants electricians knowing his layout in detail.

There's always a cran – nooky lodgement for leaving antiques after hours. I found it round the back. A light was on at the second floor. There was a vague sky glim from the riverside lights. I shifted my head, side-side and back, for night vision, and saw the slit in Tippett's wall. Antique dealers would wrap up small handies – antiques dinky enough for your pocket – and post them through the slit. So Tippett must have a cran with larger entry.

Cursing Dolly for not arming me with flashlights, I stumbled about the yard. Tippett's cran turned out to be a wash house now converted into Fort William. I listened inside my chest for a chime but felt nothing. No antiques in store today, then. Rule One is that a home cran is always linked with the dealer's house. It was locked but the back door astonishingly wasn't.

This meant visitors. There's nobody more paranoid than an antique dealer. I slipped in, listened.

Hardly anything, just a murmur. Stairs are a nuisance, but I had to go up.

An aroma caught my nose, made me smile. Somebody was being naughty, using phenolformaldehyde. It's a common trick: paintings in oils take up to thirty long years to solidify. Add phenolformaldehyde, they harden a year *every single day*! But the pungency is a giveaway for a couple of weeks. So Tippett was a forger, hey?

The stairs didn't creak by some miracle. The door was shut. It was odd to hear Meg's angry voice. Eavesdropping's horrid, but I defy anybody not to do it. Test it. Next time you're on a train, take out some photographs and see what happens. *Every*body cranes to see, ticket inspectors, nuns in the next seat, the world starts rubbernecking. They'll do anything to glimpse your damned pictures. Pass a couple snogging in some alleyway, your head swivels like a turret gun, right?

'I can't stand the cow, Dad.' Meg was blazing.

'Don't say that, love.' Tippett sounded cowed. A man trying to argue with his daughter. 'She's been good.'

'My mother's a bitch! I wouldn't have anything to do with the rotten mare if it wasn't for you. That's why I agreed to Florence coming in. If it wasn't for Simon I – '

'Listen, Meg.' Real anguish. 'There's still time. I'll buy you a holiday. You could be in Toronto, your Uncle Jack's, when the balloon goes up.'

'And let that sow queen it?' She said something Welsh and vicious.

'Please, Meg. Imogen gets carried away – '

'Carried away?' Meg slammed something down. 'She's shagging Omen. And sniffs around Simon like she's on heat!'

Well, I left then, too scared to stay. Florence? Meek old Florence Hughes was a tea-lady, a part-timer in antiques for pin money. What did she have to offer a scam this big? And Imogen Meg's mother, Tippett her father? Gulp. I'd once come between a mother and daughter, and believe me shellfire's kinder. It had been a nightmare of evasion, seduction, lies, a losing battle with the daughter bent on raping me at all costs. I still drive round Norwich, never through, in case.

The caravans were somnolent. The horses were standing nearby, a blanket thing over each. I glanced at the church. An alabaster knight, feet crossed to show he'd made the Holy Land, lay near the lady chapel. But I was too tired, and anyhow the thought of stealing some of the precious stone honestly never crossed my mind.

'Isn't it time you went to bed?' I asked the nags. They didn't even look my way. I had a pee near the tree, and climbed the caravan steps. A torch light was on. One bunk lay empty. I stripped.

The bunk was hard and inhospitable. A huge motor started very quietly as I dowsed the glim. I never notice vehicles much, but vaguely remembered a few cars parked by the riverside. Possibly courting couples, commercial travellers saving hotel expenses? I gave up, turned on to my side, wishing I had Dolly, or Elaine, Jessina or Tania, Cerise, Betty or even Janie –

'Night, Lovejoy,' Luke's voice said from opposite.

The sod had waited awake for me to return. I was narked. Maybe you're vigilant, pal, I thought, but you just wait.

That night I slept funny. I usually drop into sleep like a penny off the edge, but this time I kept dreaming. Have you ever dreamt in two sections, like watching two films, knowing that you were only dreaming so it was all right? Like that.

Slipping in and out of one dream then the other, I slumbered fitfully. One dream had really happened a year since.

There was this crowd. I was waiting to cross to the Antiques Arcade, Woody's caff, somewhere. A monstrous press of people, flags, buskers, town councillors trying to look honest, the whole she-bang, bunting across Head Street, a band. Somebody was coming to town. Now, there's real royalty and lookalikes. I mean, there's a bonny Queen Maggie – of Redonda, a miniscule guano-covered blob named by Columbus. She runs a furniture shop in Bolton, Lancs., bless her. Fine, okay, don't knock it. On the other hand, there's Royalty, cap R.

She came in a great entourage, was welcomed at the town hall by robed grovellers. Young, gracious, right royal, the crowd exclaiming. I eeled through. Something primitive stirs at the sight of royalty. It's as if Her Highness was somehow family. Maybe that's what royalty is, mutual ownership? Families, my old Gran used to say, you can't choose. Choose politicians any day of the week, and ditch them quick as wink if you've a mind.

Looking bonny, she answered the mayor and his minions. That's the trouble nowadays, politicians behave like royalty, and royalty tries to look like politicians. All around me, people were talking – isn't she nice, never mind That Scandal, how many years between her and her brother the Prince, isn't she like her uncle. Suddenly the photographers thrust. I was sent flying, into one of the royal's groupies. This aide was a slight tough chap, smart suit. It was he who hauled me upright.

'Watch out,' he said, smiling. 'You'll get arrested.'

'Sorry, sir.' I went red. Her Highness looked round.

'No harm done,' he said. 'Don't blame the photographers.'

That was it. My dozy mind played the dream over and over. It wasn't much of a cliffhanger. Anyway, dreams are stupid. The only thing was the face of the aide who raised me from the red carpet. It was Boris.

Smiling, hauling me upright, joking, dusting me down, following HRH in. Over and over, between snippets from the second dream, the aide-de-camp Boris.

My other picture, as I sweated and turned, concerned Humphrey. His face was pictured sideways on under some headline. I couldn't read the terrible words. He was shamed, though people were pleased with him. How could this be? He was trying to avoid being photographed, tortured, while people applauded.

The image was grainy, like some old daguerreotype. A newspaper picture? Except I don't read the papers, like I no longer read *Toytown*. Recently? Aye, recently, my dozing mind answered. Then Humphrey's tormented countenance would metamorphose into Boris's smiling face as I sprawled for the hundredth time under the royal feet . . .

Demented, I wrestled the night into my first dawn on the hoof.

21

There's something about waking early in a camp. Even in a tiny market town. A horse-drawn cart had crossed the bridge about four o'clock. I lay awake thinking. The others were snoring – not Luke; he'd be like Hereward the Wake, kipping one eye open in case the Normans came clanking up. Boris snored, Humphrey seemed to sleep sad. No noise from the other caravans. Little Arthur was waiting to blow, like Krakatoa.

Thinking of women, the lanx was the ultimate lure. It's impossible to convey the exhilaration. Think of it. Centuries pass, then hey presto! There was the Derbyshire find nearly three hundred years ago, true. And since the fifties there'd been others. But a lanx isn't just a tray, any more than a woman is just a woman. This one had shown visible clues – mixed pagan deities frolicking among early Christian emblems and saints. Which saints? Which emblems, and why? Further, whose inscriptions? Such scraps are the keys of history, of nations. As I say, like women. The lusts for antiques and women are one and the same. Remember that. Where I was born, they still come to blows over Mary Tudor.

A car droned through. Somebody trudged along the river footpath, hawked up, spat into the water. I sneered. Not a patch on Tinker. His coughs would awaken the dead in Polkahorn's churchyard. His phlegm would have blocked the weir.

You've only to see something so glorious as a priceless – well, two-million-quid – silver artwork, and your mind demands, hang on, just a sec, what the hell? I'd heard of a monstrance being dug up last year – the huge display piece for the Host, in radiant gold. Then somebody'd told me about a patten, a small gold winged tray communicants put under their chin. Then Tinker heard of a lavabo bowl . . . But here comes the first concrete evidence, a fragment held by the perfumed, compelling Mrs Farahar. Was she all posh-frock-and-no-knickers, as old ladies scathingly call a sham, or was she real?

Then, land?

There are mysteries in land. I believe a country imposes its stamp on its folk. It's spooky. Go to Glastonbury, and your soul's forever looking over its shoulder wondering. Stonehenge brings an odd peace. A hyperactive city bloke I know goes to Stonehenge at holidays, just stands there for four days, rain, snow, hail or blow, says it's rest. See what I mean?

There's a place called Flag Fen in Cambridgeshire. Go there, you come away mystified, like when you've made love for the very first time. You wonder what life's all about. You stand looking at the low wet ground in that mist. How come the Ancient People built huts, huts by the score on a vast wooden three-acre platform, in the middle of a huge marsh? The effort was prodigious, driving enormous oaken posts into the mud, then weaving spillikins between. The bafflement doesn't end there. The Old Folk then lobbed all their precious possessions into the waters. It was no whim. They kept it up for 1,200 years, age after age. Sacred brooches, priceless (to them) millstones were smashed and splashed over. Dogs were sacrificed and plop went Fido – *always on the seaward side*! Gold rings, bangles, jewels, carvings, the lot. To the Ancients, the stuff was literally priceless. Why did they *do* it? To propitiate the water gods 'because the Ice Age' melted and the North Sea rose about 1300 BC and scared them? Dunno. But it's scary. Sacred to them means sacred to us. It's no good rabbiting on. See, and feel, for yourself.

Sometimes, there's too much, like in Japan. That kingdom has 700,000 ancient ruins. The going rate of excavation runs at 8,170 a year. You'd think that'd be enough, right? Not so. Kyushu's supposed to be where Japan started, so diggers there were overcome when they discovered an ancient burial jar, over three feet tall. Celebration time, fame for the archeologists, cameras, the lot . . . Then they excavated another! Jubilation! Then another. Then a hundred more. Then two thousand. Agony tinged ecstasy. One huge burial urn over twenty centuries old delights Curator Elsie, who's responsible for storing it in the Saga prefecture there. But two thousand? What can Elsie do when yet another daily truckload deposits fifty more on her museum's doorstep? Answer: break up restored burial jars into pieces again, for space.

It gets worse. What if you discover the one true ancient Yamatai kingdom? Superb, right? But not if you want to build a new industrial enclave on that very spot. Then you're into the endless battle of jobs versus culture and backwards reels the cortex. One lobby screams, 'Think of the national heritage!' Opponents yell back, 'You want us to live in a frigging museum?' It comes down to grave robbers versus international financiers. And, what about us, who just love seeing, touching, these wondrous sacred items? The answer's a crude noise, a raspberry. That's why I hate curators, archeologists, and self-seeking city councils. It's not just Japan. Egypt's in a worse mess. Go inside our own Victoria and Albert. Owners of antiques are excused Government death duties – if they hand their treasures over to the taxman. You can inspect the records of tons of such 'gifts'. You can even see them – *still unwrapped*. Some system, eh? Sorry to go on. It's the old problem of sham, writ large, writ sly.

A huge motor whispered close, stopped. No door slammed. I stayed where I was, staring at the caravan ceiling. Pretence is the perennial problem. See a lovely bird, you're captivated. Nothing you can do except hope she'll make smiles with you. You receive her magnificent gift of love, but the question remains, who is she really? That's why older women are best. They know who they are. There was once a great place built in 806 AD, in Italy. Chapel of San Vincenzo, the largest church on earth, supposedly ordered by Charlemagne. A chapel is holy, pious, place of prayer, okay? But this place was occupied by 1,000 monks, plus their servants, in terrific splendour. See? Pretence. Think pretence through, there's no such thing as motive.

Murder protects a pretence. It feeds it, enables it to survive. Otherwise the mask would fall, revealing . . . what?

Sighing, I rose silently, decided to see what Mrs Farahar wanted. It was a mistake, I knew. Women give you paradise, but some still leave you worse off. I don't understand why it seems logical to court them, but off I went. Like I say, it's not easy being a pushover.

Out on the wet grass, I saw the huge Bentley in the faint dawn. I walked across, disappointed to see there was somebody with the superb Vana. Her husband was smoking an enormous cigar at this hour.

Once, experimenters put several families into primitive surroundings. Dank fields, children and all. If they wanted a house, they had to make it. For food, they had a handful of barley. Couple of flint axes, some old leather to start off, and that was it. To live like the Ancient People. They stuck it for a *whole year*! Wet, shivering cold, hungry as hell, they rubbed fire, learnt flint-napping, caught beasts, cooked nuts and roots, grubbed in undergrowth. Know what they longed for? Not a lovely warm bath, not TV, radio, Saturday markets. Know what it was?

Wellingtons. Those boots that collect half the footpath when you're out for a stroll. Wellies. See how fragile civilization is? The Age of the Caveman's nearer than we think. It's a wellington boot away.

'Hoppy, Croppy!' I got. The engine hummed gently.

'What's that?' Farahar barked, cigar on the wobble.

'I'm remembering a rhyme. It's stuck in a groove.'

'Want to talk, Lovejoy?' It's my least favourite phrase. Every soap contains the phrase: *We've got to talk*, as if you need a UN conference.

'Which? Fair and foolish, little and loud?' Vana suggested.

That had me thinking. 'Long and lazy, black and proud?'

'Excellent!' She was really pleased, 'The last two!'

'There's more,' I said, leaning down at the window. 'Women's colours and shapes in eight pairs. My cousins skipped to them. Poems are easy, like "The Twelve Months", one word each. You can just look those up.'

'Why don't you, instead of going round and round?'

'That's cheating,' I said sternly. 'Like, there's three colours you can't rhyme. I *think* they're orange, purple, and maybe silver.'

Farahar gave a bellow. 'What in hell's this gibberish! Lovejoy, ETA at Sunderhill, evening.'

'Sunderhill.' I didn't know that, so how come he did?

'Encamped, 18:00. Victuals, toilet, night roll, 20:00 hours. I expect – '

'None of your Yankee crap, mate.' I was fed up. Everybody knew everything but me. 'And don't give me any of this Yanks-invented-baseball either. It's in Jane's *Northanger Abbey*, begun in 1798.'

'No English literature on the moon, soldier.'

That shut me up. Mrs Farahar smiled, enjoying keeping score. Women are always counting. They live by it. 'Until later, Lovejoy.'

The Bentley whispered away like an airship feeling land. I returned, stood watching the river. The Bentley would have been Liffy's sort. No old Morris Oxfords.

'Know what?' I told the nags. 'I get you lot mixed up.'

'Ash is the chestnut,' Luke said. 'Pulse is taller, blotchy. Cotton is small. Barley's black and proud.'

'Don't they get tired standing up?'

'It's how they sleep.' He was amused. Already I'd been amused at twice, and the dawn not here yet.

'What do they have for breakfast? Same old oats?'

'Mmmmh. Humphrey's getting ours. Eggs, bacon, fried bread, cereals and skimmed milk.'

When I turned, I had to really look to see him. It was as if the bloke was camouflaged.

'Boris?' I asked. I felt miserable. 'He up yet?'

Luke hesitated. 'Boris takes his time,' he said. 'You're in charge of Arthur. Phillida must report to the police.' We walked slowly to the waggons.

'Sunderhill, I'm told by passing strangers. That right?'

'Correct,' Luke said. 'A good road, put a good hoof under us.'

'Is there really a final destination?'

He smiled. 'Bound to be, Lovejoy. Bound to be.'

Once on the road, I decided to get on the right side of Meg. I thought it would be easy. I talked a reluctant Humphrey into driving Pulse.

We passed a roadside touristy place. A lady was wearing traditional Welsh costume, tall black stove-pipe hat, apron, wide skirt. She was selling teas and cakes, and those Welsh carved love spoons. I jumped down.

'I'm gasping,' I told the lady. 'Like your frock.'

'Ta, *bach*.' She was laughing. 'I thought you were more travellers. We've had nothing but.'

'That so?' I would have chatted on but Meg was impatient. I was narked. The stall lady was bonny and knew how to smile.

We plodded past, me waving from beside Meg and calling to have the kettle on next time. She laughed. 'Get on with you!'

'Lovely to see Welsh costume, eh?' Instantly into my ingratiation mode. 'Have you ever worn it?'

'Yes.' Clip-clop, clip-clop.

We were entering mountainous terrain. 'That a standing stone?'

'Indeed.' A great stone projected from a steep fellside. 'The eisteddfod. They commemorate it with a stone.'

'Good old Iolo,' I said, working hard to get my badges back. 'He must have been a marvellous chap.'

'Iolo Morgannwg,' Meg said reverently. 'To speak with him the oldest language of all Europe! It's not like *Yr Iaith Fain*, the "thin tongue" that is English, that steals any word it chooses. We can read the Welsh of the Middle Ages like today's. Who can read Chaucer without a dictionary?'

'True!' I grovelled. I had to take the reins and pull a bit. 'Iolo the genius, eh?'

'I'm surprised you know about him, Lovejoy.'

'Me? Oh, Wales has always interested me, love.' Even if lies come cheap you shouldn't waste them. I tried to remember the gunge from the library. 'Stonemason, wasn't he, from Glamorgan?'

'Yes.' She listened, smiling. It was a pleasant smile, with that hint of sin within. 'Wasn't he wonderful? Triumph of resolve over persecution!'

'Indeed, love.' I grinned. 'What a lad! Always stoned on laudanum opium!' I laughed, shaking my head. 'The biggest hypochondriac ever. Is it true that Dr Johnson gave him the cold shoulder in that London bookshop? Rotten journalist, though.'

'Lovejoy,' Meg said.

Struggling, I was eager to impress her still more. 'Daft old coot! I love a faker. All those old manuscripts Iolo forged. When he invented the Gorsedd stones and bards, he just used green and white ribbons tied round your arm.' I fell about. 'But he was bright. Never went to school, lucky bloke. Yet he invented the whole fraudulent ritual from a standing start in 1819! His Ma taught him English and Latin.'

'*That will do!*'

'No, love. Hang on.' I could tell she was choking with laughter. I concentrated, guiding Ash. 'Ned – his proper name was Edward Williams; he hated it – drank thirty-six cups of tea a day! Fantastic! I wonder if they gave him tincture of opium in Cardiff gaol? Good flautist, though, they say. Hey, Ash!' The nag pricked up his ears. 'Iolo would have walked! He wouldn't ride, from respect for his fellow creatures. Nice chap, eh?'

'*Lovejoy!*'

'Had a share in a trading ship out of Bristol,' I coursed on. 'So what if he was a crackpot? He liked being a grocer and a librarian mostly.'

She fell on me, clawing and scratching, howling hatred. I flung the reins and leapt off. Luke hauled to a stop and came running back. Boris's head poked out while I backed, trying to escape this flailing harridan. Luke and Humphrey hauled her off eventually. Boris calmed the horses. Preacher started up, 'A few more marchings weary . . .' Corinda jumped out applauding. Rita tried to shush us, but Meg was still frothing at the mouth ten minutes later.

We resumed the journey. I was left to drive the pink caravan, by popular request. Little Arthur got the casting vote by proving that he could scream twice as well as Meg. I was mystified. I mean, I'd given her a true summary of druidical culture and Iolo its inventor. I'd thought she was lapping it up. Can you credit it? Try to please some women with tact, and that's what you get.

22

Whatever they say, driving a horse and cart's not hard. You hold the reins for the sake of appearances. Beats me why they have driving championships.

A few village children chucked at us, making my horse, Pulse, shy. I shouted that I'd kill the next little bugger who chucked anything. Except I thought better of it. Some youths in one village threatened to burn us out. I was puzzled. We'd done nowt.

'We don't want you travvies here,' one bawled.

'We're not,' I shouted back. 'We're a mental unit.'

They roared at that. Not pleasant good-heavens-just-listen merriment, but the howling kind you hear from crowds. A local peeler cycled up, and pedalled slowly alongside until we cleared the village. First time I've been glad to see the Plod.

About an hour after, we were overtaken by a crumbling pantechnicon. It could hardly make the one-in-fifty gradient. Its engine sounded like my old Ruby in a headwind, pistons wheezing, bald tyres whimpering. A couple of goats peered blandly from the tailboard. The great thing managed to groan ahead, tail lights dangling. It was struggling to be an antique, but would never make it. A parrot swung in its cage. The pong of charred cooking and chattering racket was left on the country air. Two women waved. A grinning bloke glittering with alchemic silver and black jewellery on leather made some sign.

Now *there's* travvies, I thought, grinning and waving.

Travellers of the New Age, travvies, are almost a new phenomenon. Except they're not. Our old kingdom has always had gypsies. Caravan folk – tinkers, variously Romanies, gyppos, diddicoys, pikers – became partly sedentary over time. Winter, they stay in some housing estate. But come spring, they take to the road, do odd jobs, forage.

Except the New Age dawned, about 1970. Everybody took sides, and the battle was on.

The village inhabitant's view is: instead of a few caravan folk who want to sharpen your kitchen knives, some five hundred people invade in a column of decrepit vehicles. Dogs, cats, maybe a herd or two. They smoke exotic drugs, leave rubbish and stinking night soil. They're parasites, bleed social security money dry. They block drains, ruin Nature's ecosystem, pollute streams. Their vehicles would be confiscated by the police if driven by law-abiding residents, but they drive anything they like. They have Mohican haircuts, and leave villages covered in debris, dung, shit and corruption, broken windows. Then they move to the next village, and do the same thing.

That's the staid inhabitant's opinion, unanimous, *nem. con.*

The travvies' own view is different: what's wrong with freedom, they demand. We have our own chickens, moving where God directs. And everybody gets engine trouble, right? And loyal subjects are entitled to welfare, right? Okay, they concede, so there's 24,000 of us roaming the roads. So what? Mother Nature provides the trees, so why not cut a few down for firewood? The Public Order Act of 1986 is therefore unjust, and brutally oppressive on a peaceful community. And why must everybody live in a semi-detached house with a mortgage, just to please politicians?

Those are the argument's two poles. Me, I'm in-between. The 'decent upstanding taxpayer' resident barks, 'It's not about freedom, it's about filth!' and talks of marauding spongers who spread disease, drugs, and destruction. The travvies saying that they have a right to live as they please. They reply, 'Castlemorton wasn't our fault . . .'

Which is the core of the argument.

It happened in Wiltshire. Come summer, travvies gather at off-the-cuff festivals, the renowned, feared 'fezzies'. The police blocked off some roads in Avon. The roadies teemed over the hill – into Castlemorton. Now Castlemorton, if you've never been there, is a quiet postcardy place. Good history, nice people, bonny site – until battalion after regiment after columns of vehicles and 20,000 travvies wedged into the town centre. Anybody wanting quotes for their news service got them free. 'Like the Goths and Vandals . . .' etc., headed the list. 'Lawless depravity' came next, then 'The Government/police/army/council, etc., ought to X or Y or Z . . .' where those letters meant any sort of punishment you wanted to inflict. This, note, in peaceful old Albion.

Reconciling liberty and obligation is hard. For me, it isn't so much the travvies or their lingering traces of flower power. It's the phoney element. I was telling Phillida, who came to sit by me.

'The Old Bill – police – say that the ravers actually aren't travellers at all. Just middle-class druggies on Ecstasy. They hold deafening rave parties days on end. Then they go home. They even have private newspapers.'

'Don't the local authorities make them turn their transistors down?' asked this lovely innocent with spirit.

'Mmmh,' I mused. As bad as Dolly. 'I hadn't thought of that.' I expect the one police constable, gazing bewildered at the mobile nation-tribe hadn't thought of it either.

Phillida added, 'Incidentally. Does Boris's face seem familiar?'

'Dunno,' I said casually. 'He's from your, er, unit.'

She thought. 'No. Actually, I think Humphrey's face is familiar, too.'

'Mmmh?' I said. 'Dunno.' The moral was to stop thinking.

Phillida was pleasant. I let her drive a bit while I held Arthur. We sang, but the weather turned cold and she took him inside. We came to a row of country cottages, so I called out to Luke. We paused, and I knocked to ask for some milk. Three doors, before one opened.

An elderly lady sold me a pint of sterilized. I got invited in for a cup of tea. I could sense Luke fuming with impatience, but you have to be friendly. I sat and talked about old times. I heard that a family four doors down had some silhouettes on their mantelpiece.

'Little cutouts?' I exclaimed. 'My Gran did those!'

'On dark red,' she said. My heart leapt. 'One is lemon coloured. But very old. They're dated, Emlyn was telling me.'

Giddy with desire, I knew the date would be between Victoria and George III. Coloured backgrounds are rare, though silhouettes are common. They've got to be, because silhouettes were made by travelling artists right up to modern times. Every country market had its own silhouette cutter. Look for coloured (not white) backgrounds, silhouettes on glass, signed/dated works, different tones –

133

hair and clothes in colour, or done on ivory. My favourites are Sarah Harrington's. She was a travelling silhouette cutter who carried a portable cutting machine (half-a-crown a likeness, and cheap at the price). I took the neighbour's name, said I'd be coming back this way. I'd pay plenty.

Luke was impatient when I returned. I got told off, not to leave the caravan on any pretext whatsoever. I smarted under the criticism, waved to the old dear. I was narked. What's wrong with trying to help people? I'd paid her an interesting visit, and brought little Arthur some milk. I'd been superb value. It only goes to show that people don't appreciate helpful folk like me.

When we stopped at noon, I went to an inn and used their phone. I couldn't get Tinker but got Dolly third try. She was breathless, thrilled. After reassuring her that my socks were aired, that the caravan central heating/air conditioning were superb, I got down to it.

'Love,' I said, 'I had to hear you. Any message?'

'Shhh!' She was at the hospice library. 'Yes. Mr Dill. May I read from notes?' She sounded standing at a lectern. 'Mr Corran questioned one Dashboard about one Liffy. Did you get that?' I said yes. She conversed briefly with somebody about a book. 'Are you still there, Lovejoy? Some collectors from Hawksley called twice about a frog's teddy bear . . .' Her voice went doubtful. Paper crinkled. 'I didn't have my spectacles. I couldn't possibly accept *his* note, so unutterably *grimy* – '

'Dolly, love. The rest?'

She read painstakingly, 'Sty's meadow vanished – can that be right? And no news of a glass pot. Finally, your Flint painting of bints washing is a problem. Does it make sense?'

'Dolly,' I said, 'I love you. I'll ring again.'

The weather improving, we all took the air. Nosh was soup and sandwiches. The sleepy old lady I called Duchess, the only person I've ever seen who looked like one. Old Mr Floyd, his fingers pill-rolling and shaky, was listening to Preacher's noon hymn 'Follow On!' and mouthing along, '*Down in the valley with my Saviour I would go . . .*' Corinda was dancing a voluptuous tambourine flamenco while a distrait Meg tried to make her keep her blouse on.

Boris was in hiding, Humphrey in huge sunglasses. Rita looked fed up. I sighed. Normally I'm used to a better class of riot. I fed Arthur, and thought.

Russell Flint was hated by art critics for 'sugary' paintings. The trouble is, the public love them. Unscrupulous forgers, who know that this genius mostly used five hues on 300-pound-weight paper, can make a fortune. Art critics everywhere praise him now he's dead. The 'glass pot' presumably meant Simon Doussy's Swedish glass. Useful, knowing it had vanished. Sty gone?

The teddy bear collectors. This mob of obsessionals had lately been tormented by rumour. Nowadays, when a single old teddy can command the price of a house, it's not surprising that the most famous teddy bear of them all is priceless. It's the one from the *Titanic*. This tiny little scrawny toy is every antique dealer's dream. It's known as the Gatti Bear, from its owner Luigi Gatti. He was caterer in the *Titanic*'s First Class à la carte. His little lad Vittorio gave him the teddy. You can hold the tiny thing in one hand. It's a Gebruder Bing toy, German. It survived the icy waters of the Atlantic, was returned to the bereaved Gattis in London, and miraculously survived a direct hit in the Blitz. It's in Ribchester Museum of Childhood.

A year ago, a desperate yokel claimed he'd nicked the Gatti Bear, and would sell it in the White Hart. Well, it was like a football crowd. I couldn't get near the place for arctophiles, teddy bear collectors. Merrythought's of Shropshire make replicas. Every so often the rumour of the real Gatti Bear's theft circulates. Quite false. For me, I can't stand the merchant freighter *Californian* steaming blithely on even though Captain Lord's crew, rotten sods, actually saw the *Titanic*'s distress flares from only twenty miles off as the poor folk sank beneath the cold waters.

'Eh?'

Phillida had interrupted. She was smiling. 'I said it's an interesting story, Lovejoy. I think *you* spread that rumour about the valuable teddy bear.'

The next few minutes were spent in establishing my honesty, and are therefore superfluous.

23

Two hours after what should have been teatime, we stopped in pouring rain. I was hungry as hell. Little Arthur was asleep with Phillida, the lucky little sod. Meg was furious, Rita weepy, Humphrey depressed, Boris invisible, Mr Lloyd staring, up-and-down Corinda was somnolent in profound gloom, the Duchess wet through, and everybody too miserable to care. The horses looked bedraggled. Preacher was silent.

We were in a farmyard plagued by cats. I went to give the Duchess a toffee I'd nicked from Phillida's theft bag. The Duchess was sitting on the caravan floor when I knocked. Corinda was sitting on a bunk looking at the rain.

'Wotcher, love,' I told Corinda. I'd never seen her fully dressed before. 'Toffee, Duchess?'

A puddle of fluid trickled from the Duchess. I sighed, called for Meg. She came with ill grace. I did the lifting, she the changing. When the old lady was dry I took the soiled clothes and put them in an earthenware pot I found in the farmyard, filled it with rain water. I borrowed some washing powder and hot water from the farmer's wife, a pleasant, dark-haired bird. She said I could hang the Duchess's clothes up in the barn. It was hanging the sodden clothes up that I felt odd, and came upon a shallow bowl underneath an enormous plant pot. I pulled it out.

The Duchess was alone when I went back. Luke and Meg were preparing grub. I could smell it, unappetizing.

'Dry in a trice, Duchess, all right?' She made no response. I think they listen. It's not their fault they can't show willing. 'Into the changeable weather, eh? My old Gran used to say, With the help of the Almighty and a few policemen!' I laughed. She said nothing. I leant closer. 'Duchess. We've made a find.'

From where I was sitting, under the eaves, I could see Meg take some stuff into the farmhouse. Luke was in the blue caravan. I saw Boris talking animatedly as they got the paraffin stove going. I thought of him in Royal Navy uniform.

'We're a rum lot, eh, Duchess?' I bit a piece of toffee off and fed it to her. She sucked. 'Duchess?' I lowered my voice. 'We've found a Nantgarw! Don't tell, okay? This is between you, me, and baby Arthur. Split three ways.' No answer. 'Nantgarw porcelain's superb. But,' I added hastily, 'don't take sides. If Billingsley *did* nick the Swansea pottery's methods, it's their business, not ours.'

Arthur bellowed his imperious bellow. I told the Duchess back in a sec, and raced across. I made Arthur's naff milk feed up, and raced us to the Duchess, breathless. 'Here, love. Feed him while I plot.'

The old lady didn't move, so I positioned her hands. Arthur's little belly parped a monotone. I got the teat into his mouth. He gave a grunt of relish. The Duchess actually altered her position, looked.

'The plan, troops,' I said. 'In the barn, a porcelain's being used as a plant-pot holder. Swansea porcelain *never* shows crazing, that fine cracking.' I scanned the area for spies. 'Know what pigskin's like? Exactly like that bowl! Very, very rare! Confirm it by holding it up to the light, okay? If it's a hazy yellow translucency, we're in. I feel it's a genuine antique. I'll ask the farmer's wife can I use the old barn crock for Arthur's pudding. She'll agree. We'll buy our own mental hospital!'

Arthur belched. I burped him by shouldering, then gave him back to the Duchess. She resumed feeding him. I was thrilled. 'Babes are the best for old folk,' I said. 'We let you crones get away with being lazy, see? Now, a song!'

In the deepening daylight I sang 'My drink is water bright, from the crystal stream'. Arthur finished his bottle. I propped him up on the Duchess. We belted through the chorus, Arthur warbling milkily. I actually caught the old girl looking *at* and not through.

'Now, lady and gentleman,' I announced, 'we sing the old temperance hymn "A Song for Water Bright". One-two-three-four.' We thundered it out.

'Lovejoy!' Luke, in the doorway like an avenging gunman.

'We're singing,' I said airily. 'Any requests?'

He left, shaking his head. Arthur needed changing. I did the deed as we blessed the world with 'The Lips That Touch Liquor Shall Never Touch Mine'. Phillida came for Arthur at supper time. I winked at Duchess and went to wheedle the old pot. The lass was carolling away in her kitchen.

'Was it you singing?' she asked. 'I've not heard them old Sacred Songs and Solos for many a year!'

'Oh.' I went bashful. 'We sang them at home.'

'Do you know "The Ship of Temperance", *bach*? It's lovely.'

I cut her trill short. 'Sorry, love. Can I borrow a couple of old pots from your barn? For the nappies and all.'

'Indeed to goodness!' she cried. 'Take them and good riddance! My Bryn's forever going to clear them out, but does he?'

She beamed, then chilled my heart with her next words. 'You might be lucky, too!' she said. 'One of the girls has just been. Found an old bowl in the barn. Tells me it's valuable! When my Bryn comes back, I'll make him have it valued.'

'Marvellous!' I said. Good old earwigging Meg. 'Your husband away? Actually, I'm a registered valuer for, er, Sotheby's.'

She laughed. 'Get away with you!' I left via the barn, but it now felt empty. The Nantgarw porcelain piece had gone, Meg really protecting her heritage.

After a grim meal – a coarse soup, potatoes, greens, soggy fish fingers – I went to the farmhouse. Temperance singing works up a terrible thirst. The farmer's wife welcomed me, and let me see the bowl. It was a delight. I told her the story of the South Wales potteries. She gave me some heady home brew, plus a couple of meals. I discovered that I liked Wales. I only realized it that night.

Next morning the drizzle was worse. The horses were fresh, having had shelter in a real stable. A couple of farm lads who hove in at cockshout gave them some proper nosh. I was whistling as we got going. The farmer's wife waved me off.

'Bye, Pattie,' I called. 'See you on the way back.'

'Bye, love,' she called. 'Do, if you've a mind.'

Meg finally broke at mid-morning. 'Lovejoy!' Her hissing voice. 'Did you sleep in that farmhouse?'

'Me?' I was indignant. 'What on earth makes you . . . ?'

Pulse nodded on. She had to stride alongside. 'I didn't hear you leave, that's what!'

'Look, Meg. These endless accusations.' I sighed a sincere sigh. 'Just dole out your pills and leave me be. Okay?'

'Did you wheedle the Nantgarw off her, Lovejoy?'

'Meg,' I said, broken, 'I've never betrayed a lady's confidence. As for that porcelain, think the worst.'

'I'm warning you, Lovejoy,' Was all she could manage before Luke called her back to her caravan. Preacher was in the lead today, giving us 'Sweet By-and-By'. I joined in, thinking happily of the Nantgarw piece I'd slipped under little Arthur's wicker cot. I sang really brilliantly, but Phillida ballocked me for making too much noise. Trying to be cheerful's a mistake in some company.

That morning, three old buses filled with travellers overtook us. I'd counted sixteen so far, all heading in the same direction. Were things looking up?

24

A tranquil caravan holiday in pretty countryside is a waste. I'll keep to the vital bits.

Noon nosh was a complicated shambles. See a gypsy camp, it's a sea of tranquillity. A little kiddie running about, a dog rooting, a woman putting a pot on, the bloke whittling. Generally dozy. An hour later, it's the same. Sessility, the mundane. Us? We were like a Dickens slum, and barmy.

We'd stopped at a tranquil hamlet. Its main feature was an old gallows, to cheer us up. I looked at us thinking, God.

For a start there was Boris. Fit as a flea, hiding from the world, arranging things – bits of paper he kept refolding. Like, he'd touch the window, every inch, dot, dot. Then he'd lift his heels in a rhythmic beat until I found myself doing the bloody thing myself. He didn't speak.

Humphrey of the hangdog smile sat mournfully watching the bacon and eggs fry. He'd got it going on some ramshackle gas stove. Thoughts of explosions alerted my mind. Humphrey spoke. 'Bread fried or toasted?' He made grub sound like the *De Profundis*, but I almost wrung his hand at such civilized words.

'Both, please. We enough to go round?'

Luke gave me a look. 'Humphrey is head cook and bottle washer today, Lovejoy. You tomorrow. Hello, ladies.' Rita entered. I gaped, then composed my features. Phillida came trotting up and shoved Arthur at me. I turned him the right way up. He glared at me, winded. I almost apologized before I caught myself. Why is everything my frigging fault? He blew a gale of flatus in reprimand, grunting satisfaction.

'Have one on me,' I said.

That set him rolling in the aisles until he choked, which earned me universal blame. His chin was soaking wet. I'm convinced that doctors haven't got their priorities right. Why don't they find out why cherubs' grot spreads so? I'd only just got Arthur and already we were soaked from his dribble.

The caravan's interior was magic. It expanded. Bunks folded, benches appeared. Hammocks stowed, tables sprouted. A sink, I swear, emerged from a small side table. We even had ornaments, little brass vases, one with some small blue flowers. But the showiest item was Rita.

She was garish. Now, I like makeup. Women never use enough, dunno why. They don't understand, they can never put enough on. If one ounce equals beauty, then twelve ounces equals twelve times more, right? But women are very sparing. This noon halt, Rita had plastered her emerald green eyeshadow on. Rouge on white on moisturiser covered her cheeks. Her eyelashes raked the air. Her lipstick made huge crescentic scarlet rims. She could hardly raise her cup for the false mandarin fingernails that projected. They sparkled gold and silver spangles. You needed eyeshades just to pass the sauce.

'Do you like my new skin toner?' she asked brightly.

'Terrific,' I said approvingly. 'Glad some women know how to use cosmetics.'

'I *never* use too much, Lovejoy!' Phillida said frostily.

Much you know, then, I said to myself. Arthur was crooning, kicking me in the groin. His drenching grot had the disturbing knack of flowing up against gravity so I got soaked whichever way up I held him. I fed him my fried bread until Humphrey roused to rebuke me. 'No, Lovejoy. Arthur has his own food.'

Phillida was mixing some gruesome powder. It stank. Arthur eyeballed it with loathing. 'He loves this.'

The meal wasn't bad, but I sensed we were all tired, or wary, or doubting the whole enterprise. After nosh I changed Arthur's nappy, washed his bum.

'He's like an eel,' Phillida said, watching me. She had a bag of gear, including cream and talc. I carried Arthur to her caravan.

'He's not. An eel wraps itself round your arm.'

'You're good, Lovejoy.' She was working things out, arms folded.

'He's good with me,' I corrected, wrapping the nappy's sticky end round tight. I buttoned his grow-bag about him. I don't reckon they're well designed, cause gangrene quick as look.

'We link with the reporter soon, Lovejoy. We'll be famous. A daily special. A spectacle!' She sounded thrilled, silly cow. 'I'm really looking forward to meeting them.' Photographs? No wonder we'd all been on edge.

Luke was harnessing the horses. For so few straps, it seemed a complicated business. Antique horse harness has recently had quite a vogue, but our nags' gear was a disappointment.

'Their harness is too new for you, Lovejoy,' Luke said. He was getting on my nerves.

'It never crossed my mind!' I gave back indignantly.

'Like at the stocks, the gallows on the green?'

'Look,' I told the evil-minded burke, 'can't I take a look without you jumping to conclusions?' I didn't realize he'd seen me looking.

The stocks were modern. They'd probably moved the originals into their town museum to stop tourists from locking themselves in. The gallows felt original. I shivered. Odd that the guillotine in contrast was regarded as totally humane. Everybody has such opinions on capital punishment. I've heard pub rows where opponents, telling how Sanson's assistant guillotiner in 1795, eager to show the severed head of a victim in France, tumbled and was himself ironically killed by the fall. I've even heard Scotch folk go proudly on about how the Scottish Maiden, a seventeenth-century precursor, was so much more efficient. Dr Guillotine's name only got stuck to it because he made a speech in France about how *kind* it was. Some collectors are desperate for 'grimmies', and offer fortunes for anything connected with horror. I've been asked outright to nick the Scottish Maiden from Edinburgh Castle. Like I say, nowt as queer as folk.

'You all right, Lovejoy?'

'Aye.' I was narked. I didn't need solicitude from the likes of Luke. 'Allergic to horses, that's all.'

He was a dab hand, backing the nags into the shafts and stringing them in. We were on the road in an hour. I kept a weather eye out for Mrs Arden or Vana Farahar. Did women always return to the scenes of their seductions? I wanted Dolly's pleasant, worried face. I wondered who would come, friend or foe. I wanted a phone box. I wanted out.

With faith in my plodding nag's ability to follow the caravan in front, I let go of the reins and jumped down. I walked along, looking up at Luke, said after a bit, 'I'm not really into all this.' I indicated the countryside. 'It's a frigging desert. Not a house for miles.'

'Two farms, two hay carts, six labourers,' he corrected. He hadn't needed to look, just knew by osmosis. I wished he'd smoke or swear or something. Humphrey dropped down beside me and jogged off ahead, wearing a tracksuit.

'I mean, why can't we just go there by train?'

'That wouldn't be news. Or calming.'

'Can I make a phone call?' There was a public telephone ahead by the side of the road. A car overtook, the man leaning out of the window to shout anger at hobos.

'Why not, Lovejoy? Tether Ash to my caravan first.'

Delighted, I ran on, got through to the White Hart and left a message for Tinker, telling him to find Dolly and get her to Sunderhill. I rang Doc Lancaster, but he was out. I told Nurse Siu Lin to tell him I was looking after his loonies and sick of it. She said good. Useless.

25

'. . . off this green,' the tweedy bloke was shouting.

People always set me wondering. Some can shout without raising their voice. Hardly a decibel, and they're foghorns. Makes you wonder how some whisper to a bird along the pillow. Beds like a parade ground.

'We're doing no harm,' Luke was saying as I walked up. Our caravans stood in a crescentic laager on a greensward. Sunderhill was a rich village one street long. A nearby clubhouse boasted with a massive green sign. Six shops, one tavern, and chintzy, chintzy cheeriness. Luke clearly saw it as Rorke's Drift, waiting for the impi to attack.

'Keep moving.' A policeman strolled up. 'No disturbances.'

Corinda emerged in a voluptuous nightdress, and paraded enticingly. Meg rushed about on the spot, if you can. 'These patients are socially disadvantaged individuals oppressed by condemnatory counter-evaluative community imbalances . . .' I think I'm making it up, but am not sure. Maybe she meant what Luke said.

'Listen to me!' the bristly bloke bellowed. 'I'm Major Destry, club secretary. I will not have idiots on my territory! Do you understand?'

'We're doing no harm, sir.' Luke, patient.

'That's enough!' the peeler decided. 'Clear off. You've got five minutes to up sticks.'

'Lovejoy!' Meg tore about flourishing limbs like a windmill. 'Lovejoy! This is an oppressionistically motivated subjugation of . . .' et sociological cetera. She was an urban brawl. I appeared to listen.

'Lovejoy?' Destry howled. 'You the leader? I categorically demand that you remove this outrageous – '

'Very well, sir,' I said, my voice subservient.

'What, what?' he barked. He shot a look at the constable.

Meg went primaeval. 'Lovejoy! That is condonation-wise anti-communal . . . ' I took her fury. Luke looked quizzical. The Plod looked glad, Destry inflated.

'Five minutes!' he thundered. 'See them off, Linzell!'

'Right, Major!' the bobby said. He looked apologetic as authority receded. 'You heard the man.'

Meg was in tears. 'Why is community disapproval . . . ?'

'Meg,' I said evenly, 'shut your frigging mouth.' She gaped. 'Constable, I'll handle things.'

'Right.' He left, righteous swagger in his saunter.

'Luke,' I said, 'brew up, eh? And see if anybody's got some grub. I've not had a mouthful for three days. I'll not last.'

Meg was drawing breath for wordage. I ignored her, went to watch little Arthur. As peaceful a domestic scene as you could wish for. Meg pulled me round, screaming abuse.

'That was the most despicable submission to self-serving commandatorialistic dictatorialism I have ever . . . !' She slapped my face. I caught Arthur's eye. He was sucking on his bottle thinking, Oh well.

'Not in front of the children.' I drew her round the other side of the caravan. A car hummed past, faces regarding the colourful gypsy encampment. I waited until it had gone. I stalled her with a forehander that made her head spin. I spoke quietly.

'Listen, Meg. This shambles is the last thing on earth I want to be with. You're the least pleasant bird. I dislike you, this trip, and your lunatics. Understand?'

She gazed at me. I had her coat gripped about her throat.

'You're useless, Meg. Your mind's full of claptrap. You're also why we're pushed from pillar to post, treated like dirt.' I shook her. Her eyes rolled wildly. I could see she was thinking, this isn't happening, not to me with my sociology. 'Now, Meg. I am willing to stay. But you must make an effort on these poor bastards' behalf. Which means occasionally thinking.'

Not a peep. I let her go. 'Give us a shout when tea's up, love.' I followed the major into the club grounds.

It's an interesting fact that we're all convinced by preconceptions. Often it's not our fault, but sometimes it is. Like, Henry VIII gets a rotten press. I can't honestly see why. His love letters are beautiful. All right, so his passion got deflected, but that's passion's fault, not his. He did wonders for government. He had 381 musical instruments – *and could play them all*. But mention him, you get sly grins as if at a lewd joke. So we assume that church people are holy, bankers friendly, politicians truthful, nobles noble, that professors actually do profess. It's all codswallop. Everything's fraud. I'm as bad, except when I'm pushed, like now.

The sports club had a large car park. I walked the entire spread, line after line. Satisfied, I went through. Several tennis courts, all on the go in that most boring of all games. White flannels, bonny skirts. The clubhouse people were taking drinks on a terrace of manky modern furniture. Golfers were at the second most boring game. I watched, mystified. Major Destry was hectoring some seated club members already into their third cocktail. There was much laughter. He saw me, swelled a few cubic feet, and marched across.

'I thought I told you – '

'How many, Major?' Group activities always mystify me. Team spirit has a lot to answer for.

'Members?' He hesitated, trapped by administration. 'Four-nine-two, waiting list one-sixty.' Pomp refuelled, he resumed command. 'Lovejoy, I want your mad gypsies out!'

I smiled with diffidence. 'Might I ask a question, sir?'

'Very well!' I reeled from the decibels. Members smiled; a scruff getting his deserts.

'Have you any more?' He frowned. 'Antiques, Major.'

'What are you talking about?'

My furtive stoop wasn't good. 'Silver, trophies, that painting.'

A steely glint showed in his eye. 'Into the committee rooms.'

I followed him up steps and along a corridor lined by display cases filled with trophies, golfing memorabilia. I wanted to examine a couple, but he kept firing ominous looks my way.

'Wait here. I'll be back.' He shoved me into a room.

'Very well, sir.' He'd gone to phone the police. Idly I roamed the room. A set of old golf clubs was in a glass case by the window. You could see waiters to-ing and fro-ing, ladies reclining, gentlemen chatting. Such quaffing and regaling made me realize I was faint with hunger.

Major Destry reappeared. 'Lovejoy!' he exclaimed, as if startled to discover me exactly where he'd left me. 'A friend's coming shortly. Don't mind waiting, I suppose?' Clearly, he'd phoned the Plod, exactly as I'd planned.

'No, fine. Chance of a sandwich, sir?'

'Certainly!' He belled, ordered cheese and pickle. 'Ah, come far, old chap?' Clearly a master of deception. 'Good, good!' We sat like bookends. I found myself nodding as if to the weightiest of utterances.

Silence. The sandwiches came, but they weren't much use. The bread was gossamer, the cheese so freed of sinful fat that it was non-cheese, which for cheese is a handicap.

Destry's eyebrows raised. 'You're hungry, what?'

'Aye.' I repeated this, hoping, but he didn't send for more.

We waited, each in our own rehearsal. He was planning to denounce me to the local Special Branch as a scoundrel wanting to thieve all his club's antiques. I would retort that we loyal subjects wanted to rest our weary bones, and that I would tell the newspapers how nasty this posh club had been. It might swing it. A tall sporty gentleman came into the room, carefully closed the door. I watched his arrival with alarm. I was about to start bleating that my remarks about nicking their antiques were only a joke, when something stayed my tongue.

'This he, Pinkie?' Not him, like any normal person would have said. Now, grammarians are unknown among peelers. Hope flickered.

Destry rose. My spirits rose quicker. I know doubt when I see it. The O.B. never, never ever, experience doubt. And they never allow it in others. I enjoyed the silence. Silence is like time, different in patches. It's really quite interesting stuff. If only scientists wouldn't insist that time is a constant, and silence a homogeneous absolute, they'd get somewhere, but they do so they don't, if you follow.

'Yes, Winston. I've told the staff we're in session.'

The Winston man smiled. 'Shrewd, Pinkie.' He stood over me. Lank hair, smart Lovatt jacket that cost as much as the green fees, cuffs shot to show diamond links. 'Name?'

'Lovejoy.' A crook's veneer fades in the presence of other crooks. My spirits were now flying.

'What do you mean by coming here a week early?' He was erect with disapproval. 'System, man. Chain of command.'

'I know, but – '

'Furthermore, Lovejoy, *we provide*. And expect monies as arranged.' He glanced at his pal. 'No deviation. The, ah, goods are due to you in ten days, not before.'

'Fine,' I concurred. 'Go ahead. Don't mind me.'

'Then why are you here?' Winston became exasperated. 'If you want the antiques early, we can't agree.'

'No.' I'd blundered into some scam. This pair didn't look as though they could run a booze-up in a brewery. Mind you, I've yet to see a clubhouse committee that's straight. They're as bent as churches nowadays. Look at Mrs Will.

They endured a pause. 'If a new percentage is earmarked, we want to know what extra we'll get.'

'Look,' I said. 'About these antiques – '

'No, old chap,' Pinkie Destry cut in. He'd become overheatead. '*You* look. Over the past seven months we've provided forty antiques. Those from members we've handled for a decent commission. Those from the club we've substituted with your fakes.'

'You were paid, don't forget,' I interrupted, narked.

'I know.' Destry raised a hand to shut me up. 'But *we* took the risks.'

Bloody cheek of the man. I was about to respond when suddenly I got a grip. I wasn't in their scam at all. But you can understand my annoyance. Amateur crooks want jam on it. *And* they want approval for bating their club's store of antiques. I sadly relinquished my thespian role.

'I don't take any.' The moment had come.

Destry would have bellowed in anger, but Winston was quicker. 'Wait. Lovejoy, why are you here?'

'With the bedlamites. We want to park on the green. I came to threaten a public row, that's all.'

Winston's anger reached white heat. Destry recoiled.

'I was not aware . . .' he stammered, faded. I was shaking my head.

'Sorry, Pinkie. I told you up front. You fell for it.'

Winston straddled a chair and leant his chin on the back to inspect me. We all used the silence for harsh but profitable thoughts.

'Then who else are you?' he said at last, with quick wit.

'Antique dealer, conned in as a publicity gimmick.'

'A gimmick, Lovejoy?' He snapped his fingers. 'Antique dealer? I've seen it, the local rag. A mental unit at Mynydd Mal?'

'That's it.' He didn't say any more. Destry was itching to prattle more inanities. 'How much're you getting?'

'Twenty per cent.' I almost fell out of my armchair.

'Then you're too thick to bother with.' I didn't move.

'True, Lovejoy.'

'Look, Winston. Antique dealers won't give you 'flu for less than 33 per cent. And if it's your antique – okay,' I butted in on myself hastily, 'okay, I know they're not yours *technically*. But you must demand two thirds of 90 per cent of the face value less a tenth, right?'

They looked blank. Pinkie hopped from foot to foot. Winston's mind whirred. 'No,' the latter said finally. 'Tell us.'

'First,' I said sadly, 'a reckoning. You will soon be found out. Somebody honest will phone Scotland Yard's Art and Antiques Squad. Or the Theft Preventative Council Art Register in Yorkshire. Or the Thames Valley Police, one of the nine Plods with an Art and Antiques Theft Squad. You'll leave in handcuffs. You let me walk down your corridor.'

'So?' Destry looked blank.

'God give me strength.' Some criminals should never turn to crime. Honesty's easier. 'Where your fake vases are. And faked old feather golf balls. And your forged painting of the Royal and Ancient final. And your dud silver fruit bowl.'

Winston's lips thinned in a smile that would have been menacing under different circumstances. 'Good guesses, Lovejoy.' We all didn't want to speak. He said eventually, 'I had a friend. Army days, compulsory sport. He played golf.' I knew what was coming, but listened along so Pinkie could catch up. 'He was the unluckiest golfer I knew. Even when the ball was teetering he missed the damned putt. Unbelievable. Yet his approach shots, driving, all masterly. Finally we dropped him, he lost us so many championships. A jinx.' He'd caught the understanding in my eyes. 'Know why?'

'He hated golf?'

'Spot on, Lovejoy. Weird, o' course. Absconded with the commandant's wife, scandal hushed up.'

'Heavens,' I said. He sounded pretty normal to me.

'Divvy!' he exclaimed. 'That's the word for you chaps. In a trance, you can tell what's fake?'

'Spot on.' Their dated slang was contagious. 'Correction: only works for the genuine. Fakes are your business.'

'Price, Lovejoy?' I liked him, a born leader. 'Remember we've taken risks, and been disappointed in the revenue.'

Crooks always moan they never get a fair deal. 'The caravans stay. We get free meals, baths, lounges.'

Destry turned puce. Winston nodded. 'You leave when?'

'Ten o'clock. With,' I added, 'a token of regard. That Page's clock.' Neither spoke. 'It's about four feet tall – '

They seemed relieved. 'It doesn't go,' Winston admitted.

'It won't without water. It's a clepsydra, 1900.'

'Is it valuable?' they asked, had the grace to redden.

'Not much.' I stood. 'I'll also save your bacon. Get rid of that wax model.'

'That statuette? It was our founder, 1890. We daren't.'

'It's cheapo paraffin wax. Your original was worth a mint. Whoever talked you out of it did well – for himself, not for you. He will have sold your S. Percy wax wall plaque for a new car. Famous Regency wax modeller, old Percy. Did major historical figures. Whoever donated it to your club as your founder was fibbing. Georgian apparel, not Victorian. Didn't you notice?'

'Will it give us away, Lovejoy?'

'Sooner or later even Wales must have a few hot days. Cheap paraffin wax melts. Old Percy's figures never do.' They went quiet, Destry in panic, Winston fuming. 'Your antique dealer was naughty. He bought your precious Regency wax model and gave you a penny-plain copy. The faker's Rule One: fake dear, never cheap. He diddled you.'

'Did he now,' Winston said in cold anger. I was suddenly glad I didn't play golf, that 'good walk wasted'. I'd hate to play against him in case I won. 'What can we do?'

'Hire a classy faker to do one in laburnum heartwood, coated with proper wax. For God's sake use old paints.'

'Anything else?' I know a mad bloke when I see one.

'I'll call after this jaunt. Maybe you need me.'

They walked with me to the door. The Winston bloke halted. 'Sir Winston Delapole, Lovejoy, club president. Your name and address?'

'Lovejoy is both, Sir Winston. And don't worry about getting nicked – only one crime in twenty ever gets a conviction. Ta.'

'You are very welcome,' he said courteously. I walked out and across to the caravans. Funny thing, though. I could have sworn I saw Doc Lancaster driving off.

Luke, on his waggon steps, held an enamel mug. 'Tea's up, Lovejoy.'

'Ta, mate.' I went and sat, took it. Meg stormed up.

'Lovejoy,' she said. I knew she'd been practising syllables. 'I shall have you placed under arrest the instant we reach the next village, in thirty minutes precisely.'

'Right, Meg,' I said, 'But we're staying.'

'Staying?' She jigged in distress, an administrator with a defective in-tray. 'But the authorities distinctly – '

'They've changed.' I turned to Luke. 'We can all use the club-house until ten tomorrow morning. Evening meal's in the restaurant, seven thirty.'

Meg erupted. 'Lovejoy! To spend our finances is utterly – '

'It's free, Luke.' I ignored her. There's only a limited number of eruptions you can take in a day. 'Tell them not to break anything,' I told him as he jumped down. 'Oh, except a small plaque in the vesti-bule wall alcove.'

That surprised even Luke but he only nodded, then went on. Meg started speaking again about then, so I went to play with Arthur.

26

That last evening of sanity was pleasant. Meg's behaviour really did set me wondering who was barmy. When I did try being kind and public spirited our doomed relationship went downhill even faster.

It happened after supper – prawns in a tin chalice, incomprehensible pie in inflatable pastry so you never had anything to chew, vegetables, a pudding that went nowhere. I collared a couple of extra meals, but felt really aggrieved. You shouldn't have to forage just because you're hungry. They got the message. The boss waitress started slowing. 'It's marvellous to see somebody eat,' she told her underling. If I was running that place I'd serve proper helpings instead of minuscules that you can't give a decent gnaw. Where was I? Sex, and helping people.

'Meg,' I said, seeing her counting her charges back in the gloaming. 'There's a couple, erm . . .' Shrill cries of carnal activity rent the night air. A couple of club members were at the windows staring. Nobody was doing anything about it.

She rounded on me. 'Lovejoy, it's time you deleted your subjectionistical attidunisings from your reactionary mind-set – '

'Great, sure, fine . . .' I melted. I'm lost. She didn't know who was bonking and honking. What if it was one of our – I mean *her* – loony ladies getting ravished against her will? But she knew best. Common courtesy called for somebody to cross the grass, like I was doing, to check.

It was Rita, trying to fight off some rapacious goon the size of a tram. He had her pinned down. I could just see her face. His hand was clamped over her mouth. He was oblivious. She was struggling. Her knickers were about her knees, her clothes torn. I could just see where to hit by the clubhouse lights. I moved carefully so I didn't clobber Rita.

The cobble I'd picked up smashed the swine's head.

152

Astonishingly he kept moving, reflex, I suppose. I whopped his head again, cursing as my finger got nipped. He went limp, his pale bum showing. I kicked him off.

'It's Lovejoy. You okay?' Then I noticed her head was bald. There was a thing like a drowned cat on the grass.

She was weeping, struggling into some sort of order. I yanked her up, swearing at my finger, got her wig. The hair felt strange, synthetically alive. I almost yelped. Caravans lights were starting to glow. A few people were wandering, talking. Meg was tallying away. Administrators make me puke.

'Bloody cobbles,' I grumbled to Rita. 'My finger doesn't half hurt. Can't see a bloody thing. Countryside's the pits. No lights, know what I mean?'

She was weeping. I heard her moving about.

'That sod should've needed only one swipe,' I grumbled. 'Know what a waiter said? Called us freeloaders. Best publicity that club's ever had.'

The clodhopper was heavy. I dragged him as far as the roadside. As he was still out cold, I kicked his side in. (You use your heel to punt, not your toe, on ribs; a Liverpudlian taught me that.) I'd had so much dinner I was breathless.

'Ready, Lovejoy,' her voice said. Her wig was on, mercifully.

'Come on.' I reached out. She found my hand. 'Watch my finger, love. People who grumble get my goat. That waiter! *We* put bread into *their* mouths, yet the swine criticize us. Can you credit it?'

'Lovejoy,' Rita said, stumbling. That's the trouble with rural things. Take your actual grass, for instance. You'd think it would get a grip, and grow level, but no. 'When I was sixteen, my hair – '

'Eh? Oh, aye. Hair's a pest. I can never keep a comb. The most prized possession of the old bishop-saints in the early church was their comb. The exact significance . . .'

We entered the camp. Meg marched on us. 'Lovejoy! I demand an explanation!' She glared at Rita's dishevelled condition. I tried to show her my finger.

'Got a plaster, love? This nail hurts.'

She uttered a crude expletive. I gave up, said goodnight and sat on the caravan's steps. It was about ten thirty. I heard Humphrey and Boris moving about. The night settled. Cars started up in the clubhouse grounds.

Some motor's brakes dragged tyres to a slither. I heard voices, conversation, I half listened. I was sure it had been Doc Lancaster, taking off. No Mrs Arden, no slinky Deirdre Divine, no Mrs Farahar. My finger hurt. Where I grew up, we had decent rectangular man-made bricks to hurl, and man-cut Derbyshire slate you could skim at each other. These God-made cobbles were useless. No wonder decent folk got their fingers hurt. God's record on justice is the pits.

The caravans were silent now, glims dowsed. I heard somebody mutter a goodnight. The wood creaked, somebody flopped into a bunk. I couldn't help thinking of Liffy. Sorrow's no good. Jessina Mosston's husband sold posh motors. Somebody public-spirited drove the yobbo away, presumably to hospital.

Bedtime. I went in. Boris was snoring, Humphrey almost, Luke silent. If he wasn't an ally, he'd give me the creeps.

'Night, Luke,' I said, slumping into my bunk. 'If you weren't an ally, you'd give me the creeps.'

He almost snuffled a laugh. Or not. I fell asleep instantly. My last peaceful day.

Before anybody was up, I entered the sports ground, found a couple jogging round the track. Waitresses were laying tables, a groundsman gloomily seeing how to doctor the greens before the inter-club match. I dropped a stone into the ornamental pond, startling a couple of huge fish.

'Carp, Lovejoy,' Luke said behind me. 'Morning.'

'Morning.' The blighter was everywhere. 'Bad sleeper?'

'Average.' He stepped on to the flagstone and peered to see the bottom. 'Herons'd clear these fish in one night.'

'Really?' I was offhand.

'They won't like the blood, Lovejoy.' I looked. Their black backs were hard to spot. 'On the stone you dropped in.'

'Blood?' You have to cling to innocence, or you're sunk.

'You searched for the stone. It had blood on.'

Did the sod have night vision too? 'Look out,' I said. 'Your friends are up.'

Preacher was addressing the horses today, a change from distant hills. He was dressed as a parson. Corinda emerged naked, made for

154

a patch of gorse. Meg came flying after her with a blanket. Little Arthur squawked with imperial anger, deprived.

'Did your persuasion extend to breakfast too, Lovejoy?' Luke asked. He was merely curious. If I said no, he'd feed everybody without rancour. If I said yes, the same.

'No.' I watched him, curious. And he did just nod. 'I meant yes,' I said. He looked a moment, said fine. You can always tell an expert. You may find their presence disturbing, but you've got to hand it to them. 'Off at ten. Want to stay longer?'

'Ten's okay.' He gauged me. 'You're some wheedler, Lovejoy.' I got the feeling he'd shot blokes for less.

'The nags, Luke. They properly fed?'

'Yes. You feed a horse two hours before shutting in.' He sighed when I didn't follow. 'Shutting in's getting them into the shafts, Lovejoy.'

'All right,' I said, aggrieved. 'Keep . . . calm.' I'd almost said keep your hair on. I went in for breakfast.

The notice board had a stern notice to all members. I'd never seen so many initials, degrees, titles, in my life. One of my party had stolen a valuable plaque from a wall alcove during supper the previous evening. The secretary demanded its return forthwith. Good old Phillida. I went to complain. There was only cold toast, thin as rice paper. What good's that?

'Here he is!' The head waitress emerged, laughing.

'I've waited hours,' I grumbled. 'Breakfast's at seven.'

'Five to, Lovejoy.' Her mates peered out to share the hilarity. 'Tea and toast?'

See how women nark you? I'd been trying to put her in her place. 'I came to ask if there's a nosh bar anywhere near.'

She exclaimed in Welsh, and retired. I could hear them screaming with laughter, some bloke joining in as they finally stirred their stumps.

The waitresses waved us off. I think they'd been pleased to see so many weirdos all in one go. I wouldn't have minded staying longer. I fancied the laughing waitress. But Luke had his schedule, and we rolled out as the clubhouse clock struck ten. No sign of Sir Winston Delapole or Destry.

We followed the road, which led down to a watersplash then up along a bare hillside. The country was starting to look strange. It unnerved me a bit. You could see for miles when finally we clopped to the crest. Lean over, look back at Sunderhill, you'd hardly notice that there was a village there at all. It worried me. Civilization is rarer the further you go from houses. And antiques dwindle to zero.

Trees seemed fewer. Rivers increased, but had shrunk to steep swift streams. The roads became careless, as though they'd forgotten the route. They made inexplicable detours round fields for no reason. We travelled miles for yards. But I liked the air, and the nags' patience.

The clubhouse had given us jugs of coffee. We issued it up and down the line. The few cars that passed us were interested now. A couple of folk put heads out to enquire who we were. It was pleasant, really, but no way to live.

A maniac arrived at twenty past one.

We were having our nosh. Corinda, our naked lady, joined us dancing some finger-snapping antic, which set the Duchess keening. Meg got them settled and eating the sandwiches the laughing waitress had supplied. Preacher ate a formidable quantity of grub, then delivered a sermon on the mount. Humphrey didn't show, Boris took his grub and stood with the horses, who'd been 'shut out' as we caballeros say. Meg harangued Rita, pointedly sat between me and Phillida.

The maniac came in an electric-red saloon with whitewall tyres and more lights than Christmas, parping his melodic horn. He stood tall, wide of grin, teeth looking row on row, blond of hair. He greeted us with political bonhomie, slapping shoulders.

'Welcome to Wales!' he cried, pumping hands, waving to me though I was within reach. 'Welcome! Calvin Jones says it from the heart and the *Brynvach Register and Chronicle*!' He gave a great laugh, more shrill than I expected. He looked a born athlete, with the sincerity of a newscaster.

Luke said hello. Meg seemed relieved. There was some talking. I didn't listen. Rita was trying to brew tea on the paraffin stove. I saw Humphrey duck inside. Boris had vanished. I was holding Arthur,

'All of you in one line! Photo opportunity for the *Register*!' Jones shouted.

'I'll try!' Meg flew about, knocking on caravan doors. Preacher didn't stop preaching. The naked lady wanted to strip, but Meg stopped her. 'Not now, Corinda!'

'How many of you are there? Calvin Jones strolled the camp, a warrior inspecting his band. He stopped by me. 'The baby crazy as well?' His laugh was terrific. He glanced round, encouraging us all to laugh at such wit. I don't often dislike a bloke on sight, but knew this was for life.

'He,' I said.

'What's he say?' he demanded of Meg. She smiled along, an ally at last. 'Hee-hee-hee!' Another winner. Meg simpered. Was she buttering the goon up for maximum publicity? She was losing friends by influencing people. 'Right! Atten-n-n-*shun*!' He beckoned to his car, and out cringed a girl with a mass of cameras, batteries, tripods, enough for a satellite. My heart sank. He'd brought a smudger along.

'Where, exactly?' Meg was thrilled, pulling us about.

'Does Tee-Hee understand anything?' Calvin Jones pointed to me. 'Olwen. Get that one with the brat across the paraffin campfire. Okay?'

Olwen came at a run, hurriedly turning lenses the way they do. She crouched, arranged the mugs, teapot, would have arranged me and Arthur. I warned her with a raised finger. She coloured slightly.

'I'm sorry,' she said. 'Is this all right?'

I shook my head, but she just looked desolate then photographed me in any case, twisting the lens, peering. Not even an antique, I thought disgustedly. I shielded Arthur. I wasn't having him made a fool of.

'Make Tee-Hee smile,' Calvin bawled. 'No sour shit!'

'Yes, Calvin!' Olwen clicked, a fifth, sixth.

'Lovejoy.' Meg said. 'Calvin wants a *cheerful* picture.'

'Lovejoy!' Calvin Jones really did fall about, slapping his knee and pointing. 'Feature, Olwen! Keep him a miserable bastard. Get the brat. Then stand him up.' He clapped his hands. 'Chop chop!'

Olwen scurried, Meg scurried, the world scurried about the golden wonderlad. He laughed at his own wit.

Meg tried to extract Humphrey, but he'd gone. Boris had vanished. I thought, Boris isn't so dumb. I caught Arthur's laconic gaze fixed on me. His eyes said, Now, Lovejoy, he's done nothing, so don't get mad. Which goes to show that infants aren't dumb either. I allowed myself to be hauled with the rest. Phillida reached for Arthur but he squealed with rage. I kept him. We formed a dismal line against the backdrop of the dark hills. Olwen flashed. Preacher kept on about the Lord's smitingness.

'Hey, Olwen! Get that one dancing!' Corinda was spinning, beginning to strip. Meg dithered, torn between dashing to protect Corinda's modesty and wanting to please Calvin Jones. 'Let her strip, Meg.'

I whispered to Phillida. She looked at me. 'Really, Lovejoy?'

'Please, Phillida,' I said dolefully. 'I've no skill.'

The reporter shouted, 'I want her starkers! Any of them eat things like grass or manure? Olwen, one along the line.'

He talked into his machine. Something caught his eye, and he strode grinning to Luke's waggon. He leapt the steps. 'Hey, Meg! There's one in here! Get him out. I want the lot!' He sprang down. Luke stepped forward quickly. I saw Luke relax when it was Humphrey, not Boris. Luke hadn't seen Boris slip away. But I had, and knew where to look, at Boris near the boulder by the scree. Clever Boris wore a taupe bomber jacket.

Meg brought Humphrey. He stood dispiritedly, head down.

'Right! Only the loonies this time.'

Luke stepped away, and Meg. Luke signalled, but I stayed in the line-up. The reporter shouted, 'Caption it: *Them one side. Us the other!*' More merriment. Meg seemed strained. Luke's gaze on the hillsides, quartering then sectioning the terrain in a mute traverse. Gunners do that, methodical, never forgetting where their eyes touched. He hadn't worried about Humphrey, only Boris.

'That one. Make him look up!'

'Yes, Calvin!' Olwen made Humphrey look into the camera.

'Wait!' Calvin strode over, peered, glanced at Meg. 'Hey, Meg! Can this one answer real?'

'Yes.'

'Is he that doctor? I recognize him.' Calvin grinned, delighted. 'Olwen! We've found a zinger! He's that doctor who went crazy,

158

beat two patients up, man and wife! Get his face, then the rest gathered round him, okay? I'll get a Sunday supplement! The glossies!' He would have capered, but was too graceful. His handsome features chiselled a splendid smile.

The rest of the visit was unremarkable. Calvin Jones did his stuff. Olwen the smudger photographed her mate seated with and without us. He wanted to hold Arthur ('Me showing the kid stinks, okay?') but I wouldn't let go and he gave up. He prattled into his gadget while Olwen packed. He said so long to Meg. I went to Olwen as they got into their car.

'Excuse me,' I said, standing there like a lemon with Arthur. 'Can you take my picture with little Dwight? And his mother.' I dragged Phillida.

Calvin Jones thought. 'Might be useful,' he decided. 'Kid among the loonies.' He inspected a colossal wristwatch. 'Nope. Time. Stand clear.'

I ripped up a bit of grass and stuffed it into my mouth. Calvin braked. 'Hey, Olwen. Get it! Chop chop!'

In a flurry, Olwen took me against the car with an instant camera, Calvin grinning from his driver's window, me with a mouthful of grass, Arthur looking at me because he knew, Luke full of misgivings because he didn't.

They embarked. I went to thank Olwen, opened her door, made a speech of gratitude. Phillida helped Olwen get her things straight on the back seat.

We watched them go. I took Arthur in because it was blowing colder. In her caravan I waited. Phillida followed, beaming with repletion. She unbundled two cameras, a camcorder, seven reels of film, a handbag, and a belly purse that shops call bum bags for money.

'Marvellous!' I said. She went shy.

'Thanks for your help, Lovejoy,' she said. 'We could make a team.' I swear it was sexual excitement. Her skin looked like English peach.

She handed me the camera Olwen had used, hell of a size. I marvelled at how she'd nicked it. But kleptomaniacs are blessed with a skill we do not have. I extracted all the tapes, films, and swapped them for Arthur.

'Would you change him, please, Lovejoy?' she asked.

'Sure, love.' I got his nappy bag and wipes. 'Er, could I have my notebook back again? And my money, please?' She'd moved in a telltale way, something over one arm, a giveaway.

'You must have dropped them, Lovejoy!' She returned them. I noticed on the bunk shelf a plastic medicine bottle with Doc Lancaster's name on it. I don't know if it was Phillida's kleptomania, but I felt decidedly odd. Maybe it was the new worries I'd acquired. I said so long to Arthur and left for safer territory. As I went to watch Luke shut in the horses, I noticed a wooden case slung under my waggon. Very neat. I smiled, pleased that Major Destry had been so quiet about handing over the Page's water clock.

We moved on after the horses had rested. Boris reappeared and followed. I was last, Pulse hauling. Boris walked about two furlongs behind us all the way. We camped about six o'clock.

Which brought me to the ancient Chinese tea ceremony.

27

We drew up in Luke's laager style and were settled by seven, half a mile from a tavern, the Tudor Arms, by a steep hillside, small freshets rushing to a burn, an old bridge crossing the confluence. Sheep hung about. A collie dog stopped, looked, came waggily to join us. It didn't bark, tongue dangling. Luke tried to shoo it away and failed.

'You from the Tudor Arms?' I asked it.

It woofed, settled down, belly in the road. Corinda emerged unclothed. Meg did her blanket dash. Drizzle began. The lead caravan disgorged Preacher, who went determinedly towards the pub. Duchess began beating her head with a fist. Luke tethered the nags, started fetching water in pails.

'Lovejoy?' Luke paused. He had a bag of brushes. The damned nags already shone. 'That pub any use?'

'We've insufficient resources!' Meg shouted. She seemed to hold the purse strings. 'The charity's not for freeloaders!'

'Right!' I called affably. 'Come on, Tudor.' I followed Preacher. Boris slipped into his caravan. I wondered about Boris, but then my mind had done a bunk days back.

The tavern was smoky, eight people in. The Welsh silenced. Preacher had vanished. I asked for a glass, two pasties.

'No pasties, love.' The lass weighed me up.

'Right.' I could see pasties behind her. 'Sandwiches, then, please. Flour cakes, Cheshire cheese.'

'Sorry.' She was as calm as a lake. 'None of them either.'

'Then just a pint, please.'

'No dogs, love.' She had lovely colouring. I could have eaten her.

'It isn't mine, see. Just followed.'

'Came in with you.' She was so sure. 'Landlord's rules.'

'Oh, right.' I paused, not moving. 'Incidentally, miss, did an old bloke come in a moment ago?' There was a small teapot in a glass case on the wall, with a blunderbuss, a curious combination, and a small brass plaque.

'Yes, love.' She leaned forward, deliberately provoking. 'Old frock coat, prayer book? I sent him packing.'

Somebody spoke in Welsh. Chuckles rippled. Somebody capped it softer. Everybody laughed.

'And the old lady with him?'

'He come alone.' I waited. 'Alone, wasn't it, Ieuan?'

If I knew nowt else I knew country superstition. 'He believes he walks with a lady. Long dress, poke bonnet, black shawl. Calls her Rebecca.' Smiling, I shook my head inviting dissent. She'd stepped back a pace.

'No. Definitely alone. Nobody with him, was there, boys?'

'I think he came from the ruined cottage on the fell.'

The barmaid became frankly agitated. 'There is no ruined cottage.'

'Sorry. My mistake. Thought I saw a stone slate-roofed place. Even smelled odd smoke.' I turned and saw the cased blunderbuss and teapot. 'You got the flintlock back, then. The old man'll be pleased. Tudor?'

'Odd, *bach*?' a man asked. He wore a suit, smoked a pipe.

'Well, a peat fire.' I was offhand, going anyway. 'Still, nowt as queer as folk, eh? Night.'

'Wait, *bach*.' The barmaid's words halted me. She must have had some signal. 'Here it is! Two pasties, wasn't it?'

'Ta, love.' I opened the door on the wet. 'But I couldn't give my friends offence.' Friends I made plural.

Falling over Tudor, I trotted after Preacher. He was marching up the road, talking to the air, Bunyan's *Pilgrim's Progress*, I think. I walked with him, nodding sagely. At camp, Luke quizzed me with a frown.

'Well, you lose some, Luke.' I shrugged.

'Don't worry, Lovejoy. I'm boiling stream water.'

As it happened there was no need. The Tudor Arms sent sandwiches, cheeses, a ham, an urn of tea, milk, a dozen eggs, butter, nine loaves. No fishes.

Luke looked at me when the two lads from the Tudor Arms had gone. I didn't return his glance.

162

'Selfish sods,' I grumbled, as he got to work on the grub. 'Not a single pudding. It's not a lot to ask, for God's sake.'

It was nearing midnight when I walked down to the Tudor Arms. The bloody dog was under my feet. Twice I went headlong, so finally I grabbed it – no collar, just when you need one to threaten – and hissed, 'Tudor. One more word out of you, I'll do you, hear?'

It followed chirpily, looking up, tongue lolling.

People were saying goodnights, '*Nos da! Nos da!*', with wise cracks. A motor started, turned down the road. I knocked.

The quiet besuited man came to the door, stood. I was under the porch light. He peered up the road.

'Evening,' he said. Some bird called behind him from behind the bar curtain. He reassured in Welsh.

I said, smiling, 'Just me, saying thanks.'

'You are welcome.' The silence hung about a bit. He ahemed. 'I didn't want you to get the wrong impression, see.'

My smile lessened. 'I began to wonder, Ianto.' His name was above the door, licensed to sell wines and spirits. 'I could joke that I've come for my gun, for the gates.'

'The gates?' he said thickly.

'Indeed.' I quoted from Preacher's bible that I'd consulted, 'Verse sixty, chapter twenty-four ... "Let thy seed possess the gates ..."'

He completed the quotation in Welsh. I smiled, entered on his bidding. 'Come, then. Sit you. Will you have one?' He sounded apologetic. Tudor sat at my feet.

He poured some brew. It almost lifted me off. 'I apologize. Your health, *iechyd da.*'

'*Iechyd da!*' He started off in Welsh. I flagged him down.

'I apologize for pretending. I've come to repay.'

'Apologize? Repay?'

'Rebecca, the cottage ruins, the smoke. All made up.'

'I guessed as much.' He was unfazed, poured more of the deep plum-coloured brew. I guessed sloe gin. Last winter had been a blackthorn winter. 'No harm. Taught us our manners.' He was calm and no mistake. 'You know history?'

'I'm Lancashire,' I admitted. 'It was us throned Welsh Henry.'

He laughed. 'Let's say you made a contribution, *bach*.' We meant Henry VII. 'The Rebecca rioters are still famous here, how they dressed in women's clothes and burned the tollgates.'

We talked over a few points of history about the uprisings, Ben Ludd, the Scotch Cattle.

But I had to get to antiques. 'Your blunderbuss, Ianto.'

'Ah, many's the offer I've had! Why, a Llandeilo dealer offered a hundred pounds! I'm tempted, I can tell you!'

Christ. I nearly fainted. 'Glad your willpower was up to it, Ianto. The gun's worth much more. But nothing like the teapot.'

'Teapot?' He actually got up and switched on lights to gape. 'I've nearly thrown it away a time or two.'

'Don't, Ianto.' I beckoned him to the chair by the fire, and started to earn our keep.

Making tea is easy. You wet dried shreds of tea leaf, and that's it. The most popular drink in the world. Simple, refreshing. Of course, marketing people make rules, *Wait exactly seven minutes*. Much they know.

Go back a bit, and suddenly it's not simple. How come that the ancient peoples of Asia, the Americas, Africa all developed their own indigenous teas? Today we all follow China's Ming Dynasty method. You steep tea leaves in hot water, decant and swig. The good old Ming more or less invented our present teapots, lids, handles, spouts. There's nobody more crazed than a teapot collector. Before you start deriding these obsessed folk, please remember money. And human skill.

Because, just as among painters there's Turner and Rembrandt, and just as among furniture makers there's Sheraton, Hepplewhite, Chippendale, so to teapot collectors there's a Rolls-Royce of teapots. For the Yixing – as it's now written, instead of Chinese ideograms – county of Jiangsi Province produced dazzling works of genius. Antique dealers call them 'Jisha' pots.

They differ. Greenish, reddish, blackish, purplish, with painted or cut decorations, they have a sort of sandy look – hence that 'ish' on the colours. They usually carry a potter's mark, and are astonishingly small. And there once lived the greatest teapot maker of all time. His name Sha Dabin, a name to be burned in the memory. He lived in the late sixteenth, early seventeenth century, the Wanli period. A tribulation to underlings. Rumours still persist: elegant, something of a dandy, austere, made few friends, the lone genius. Boss.

In case Ianto thought I was getting carried away, I told him how it's done. You first go to Huanglongshan, in China, for the necessary red, yellow, or purple clays.

You leave your hotel, and dig down 330 feet for the rock-hard clay. You cut and haul chunks of it. You stack it in blocks, to be weathered for a year. At time of monsoons, floods, you dash out and protect it.

After a year, you slice wedges off the main weathered mass, and grind it to powder. Mix it with water. You compress it small into bars. These, you guard with your life until the powder solidifies. It feels plasticky. It's well over a year since you started, but you don't care. You want that priceless teapot. You squeeze out every molecule of air.

You shape your pot. You can't do it with computered precision tools, only the traditional wood, the clay exact, accurate as a laser.

Then you can laugh, if you're not too knackered, because you've got your original teapot, like the immortal Sha Dabin did it.

'There were others who followed the master,' I told Ianto. 'Chen Mingyuan's trick was to imitate bronze. You can't believe the little spouted thing isn't metal.'

'A teapot?' He still hadn't got it. 'How can you tell?'

'Good lad.' I liked his instinct. 'You can tell by spectrographic analysis, chemical fractionations for trace elements, everything from electron spin resistances to aesthetic judgement.'

He looked from the case to me. 'And you?'

After a pause I said, 'I'm a good guesser, Ianto.'

He thought. The tavern fire had died. Tudor was snoring. Ianto cleared his throat. 'Are you wrong sometimes?'

'Words in songs, aye. The smiles of women every time.'

'Antiques?'

'Look,' I said, rising, toeing Tudor awake. He came, wagging, shaking his coat. Why do they do that? 'I just came to say thanks, no hard feelings, eh?'

'No indeed,' he said. 'As we've drunk, have you a name?'

'Lovejoy. I'm accompanying a crowd of . . . convalescents.'

He nodded. 'I heard. Mynydd Mal? I hope the bother near Sunderhill wasn't too much for the sick ones?'

'No ta. Folk were kind. One thing. Tudor. Whose is he?' I didn't want to get done for nicking a wolfhound.

He looked at the creature. 'It lived in a cottage beyond the hill that accidentally burnt down. He lives wild. Until now. Good guess about his name, Tudor. Made quite an impression.' He smiled. I'd thought it was my superstitious junk that had prompted his generosity, when it was a stray cur's name. 'You've won a dog.'

'Just my luck.' I knew these 'accidental' fires started in holiday homes, to deter profiteers.

'Lovejoy?' He opened the door. 'That teapot you haven't looked at. How much would it go for?'

I got him off the hook. 'At the right auction, with its provenance, in the original untouched case, a historical relic, oh, about worth your pub, Ianto. Good night, *nos da*.'

'*Nos da*, Lovejoy. And thank you.'

'I've done nowt. Tudor.'

With the Tudor Arms helping, we made a reasonable start next day, meaning the grub was hot and plentiful, though it rained like I'd never seen it. Our departure was bedraggled. Ianto stood in his porch with a couple of women to wave as we passed. I drove last. I called out, 'Hey, Ianto! Wales holds the kingdom's rainfall record, nigh three inches in thirty minutes! But why *all* the bloody time?'

He laughed. 'No criticism from you thieving English, Lovejoy!'

'Which from a Welshman,' I cracked back.

He fell about, shouting abuse in Welsh. I heard a man's laugh from the caravan ahead. Boris? Luke?

We rolled out of the valley and clip-clopped slowly up the hillside, avoiding the village ahead by a detour. I saw Boris slip over a dry-stone wall and start along on shanks's pony.

That set me wondering, as little Arthur crooned inside my waggon, about the people on this journey. Humphrey was a doctor who'd beaten a patient up? Then Boris, vaguely familiar from my dream, skulking along like a ghost dogging our wheeltracks. Preacher, already into his second sermon, drove the second caravan. Mr Lloyd was talking to himself, or not. I'd helped the tight-lipped Meg to wash him.

Rita was garish today in a frothy print, the tablecloth sort, with Phillida and Arthur, in my caravan. Corinda had been caught in a strip ballet, and now slept. Meg had dosed her. Duchess today was trembling. I'd borrowed Arthur and played his finger game to make him laugh. She'd calmed a bit.

It got me thinking. We weren't the menagerie people seemed to think. I felt guilty. I'd called them, I mean us, a cavalcade of dingbats. I'd cursed them as loonies, nutters, insane. I'd done nothing except grumble.

Then yesterday Olwen and the odious Golden Boy, reporter to the world, had treated us like a zoo. It was new. Oh, the Old Bill calls me a thief, forger. And I keep getting arrested for fraud, and sometimes there are killings and I sometimes get unfairly blamed, but this was the first time I'd ever been regarded as mental. It was uncomfortable.

Listening to Calvin Jones, I'd felt anger. Calvin Jones made rage feel really pleasant. That worried me more. It's when trouble starts.

I'd no mac, so was gratified when Phillida brought me out a thick waterproof and a floppy sou'wester. They had some stranger's name inside, but so? We plodded on.

The weather worsened, the rain torrential and the roads awash. We pulled in after two hours at a disused solitary chapel to shelter in its lee. The horses had been patient, just trudging and pulling. The windows were broken, the roof toothy where slates had slid away. Squalls obliterated the view, though I could tell we were on a scrubbily wooded hill with the ground falling steeply in undergrowth.

Luke came in a yellow oilskin. 'We'll camp, Lovejoy.'

He went to talk to the others. I went to the chapel doors. The front was impossibly barred. The side door was easier, an old padlock you open with a hook. I went in, crunching glass underfoot, calling 'Hello, any-none!' which mumpers and baggies say protects against the laws of trespass. There was a fireplace.

'Hey, Luke!' I showed him the piles of rotting wood.

'I don't think we can burn those pews, Lovejoy.' He saw I was tapping the pulpit, the lectern.

'No,' I said, most sincerely. 'Only the wood that's rotten, eliminate woodworm and fungi. We'll be *protecting* the place.'

'You sound like a manual.' He went to bring the others in. I continued tapping the pews, the wall panels, scanning the roof truss, the pelmets. I'd not done a fake seventeenth-century court cupboard since the chapel furniture had run out. But with this amount of solid heartwood, matured over 150 years, I might even try a couple of long press or parlour cupboards. Or I'd settle for a selection of tables, including a table dormant. Of course, there's wood and wood. Two mere splinters sold for 18,300 dollars last year. What I call the 'Grail Factor' had upped the auction – the Vatican authenticated them as slivers of the True Cross. And a secret Swiss collector (it was Edward Mannheimer) collared at Christie's a wooden mechanical calculator, same month, for a cool 7.7 million pounds. The tills overtaking holiness. Luke re-entered. I stopped thinking sin.

The others entered, silently looking around at the chapel. I said sternly, 'Listen everybody. This place is holy. We mustn't scratch, mark, or deface the furnishings. The Almighty doesn't want his stuff mauled, okay?'

My voice echoed slightly. I caught Luke's sardonic gaze. Why is there no trust? Preacher shot into the pulpit and began a quick sermon. Corinda entered at a drenched tango. Luke and I started the fire, got the paraffin stove. I thought longingly of the priceless Chinese teapot, and wondered guiltily if Phillida was any good at nicking wall-mounted cases. She went on a tour of inspection. I hoped everything was screwed down.

'Just how good's your mum?' I whispered to Arthur.

He eyed me with a gummy grin, dribbling spit. I knew what he was thinking, mistrustful little sod. During his wash he peed a little spout on to my chest. I should have stayed in the storm. It would have been drier.

We stayed there longer. Corinda did a dance, a lot of whistling through her fingers and shrieking. Meg tried to stop her, glared at me when I clapped. Mr Lloyd sat and was fed. Duchess managed a mug of hot tea. Preacher thundered denunciations, pausing to drink.

Luke showed me his map, traced the way we had come. Mynydd-Mal was in a brownish region, contours closer, habitations far apart. Meg joined us, sulky.

'You know where we go once we're there?' I asked.

'Yes,' Meg snapped. 'And while we're speaking, don't think I've forgotten my threat.'

Luke started to say something but I interrupted. 'We ought to rearrange the caravans,' I said. 'Luke first, me last. It's barmy – sorry, unwise – having Preacher in the lead.'

'If you're insinuating, Lovejoy,' Meg flared, 'I'm a trained horse-women for psychiatric institutes.'

'Mmmh, mmmh,' I kept saying, but she wouldn't let up.

As she was still rabbiting, I wandered the chapel. No stained glass in these spartan chapels. A plaque commemorated the 'passing to America to found the Kingdom of Wales' four names, the 1870s. Four intact windows, leaded. Several other plaques, roll calls.

The far window looked over the valley. The map had showed a stream and a waterfall. I peered out. I saw somebody move among the undergrowth. Boris? Likely to get sodden in the teeming downpour. I looked round. Boris was giving Mr Lloyd bread dipped in soup.

That left Humphrey. Walking in the storm down a steep hillside? I moved. Meg angrily called, 'Lovejoy. I want matters settled – '

Round the side of the chapel I trotted. No path. Vegetation hugged the slope. Rivulets skipped like running mice. There was a tarn below, I knew.

'Humphrey?' I called. No answer. I hurried to where I thought I'd seen him. 'Doc?' Then I shut up. He was incognito.

There was a shiny line near a bramble. Somebody had slithered. I pushed down. I'd come out with no oilskin and sou'wester like a fool. I went on, saw somebody, and began to jump. It's the safest way to go down a wet fellside, like you're actually frolicking. You go in fits and starts, never at a speed you can't control but still going headlong. Bushes whipped me. I held my arms in front of my face against the blackberry and whinny gorse.

'Humphrey! It's Lovejoy!' I saw the greyish frothy gleam of water below. I rushed on. 'I'm warning you,' I bawled. 'I can't swim, you bastard.' Falling now, tumbling over and struggling to my feet to charge on down.

He was standing there, the frigging loon, on a crag projecting over the tarn. A waterfall rushed beside him. He had one foot in the runnel, one on the stone outcrop.

'I'll come in after you, Doc!' I yelled. 'And I can't frigging swim, you swine!'

I rushed him, caught him round the middle and we both went tumbling. He had to lodge his foot against the rockface to stop us. We scrabbled to the solid stone, me covered in mud and scratches, him serene.

'Christ.' I was panting. He was calm. 'I thought I was going. Ta, Humph. I'd have gone in if it wasn't for you.'

He looked over. The tarn was about thirty feet below, but fangs of rock stuck out. He'd have been done for.

'I was just looking at the path,' I said. 'Missed my footing. Did you hear me shout?' I got my breath. 'Yelling anything that came into my head. Lucky you were there.'

'It's coming down in sheets,' he observed.

'So it is.' I snapped my fingers, remembering. 'Oh, Humph. Do you know anything about babies, Arthur's size? Only, the way he's breathing. I've tried talking to Phillida, but I can't get through. Meg's too mad to listen. Would you mind giving him a shufti?'

'Not at all.' He started up the hillside. At the finish he had to haul me. I felt a right duckegg.

He went into the chapel and took Arthur from Phillida with practised ease. I went for a towel and a change. Phillida had given me three new pairs of plus fours and golfing socks. Heaven knows where she got them. I rejoined everybody in time to get another ballocking from Meg for something or other.

Worn out. I wanted to go home.

28

They were waiting for us in the market square at Newginfawr. My
heart sank. Two police cars. Calvin Jones in his splendid red motor,
and Olwen with tons of photographic gear. There was a superb old-
ish motor, rakishly blue, nearby. I'd made love once in one, to
Jessina Mosston. She'd had one on loan from her husband's show-
room. She'd called the car an 'Anglo-American marriage'.

'Good afternoon!' I heard Meg call. Luke's horse took against the
blue police motor lights. Preacher gave a burst of 'To Be A Pilgrim'.
An unfortunate omen. John Bunyan was forever in clink.

Thuds of solid boots sounded. I studied the shops, people standing watching, the cars crawling past. We were the centre of
attention.

'You Lovejoy? Down.'

Like you say to a dog. Tudor had been beside me, but he'd
vanished. I got down. The two Plods were on a winner. One had a
notebook.

'That's him!' Calvin Jones shouted. I swear windows bent in-
wards. 'He stole our films, two cameras, and – '

Two cameras?

The lead Plod said, 'Let's have them.'

'Me? You've got it wrong . . .' et piteous cetera. They wouldn't
listen, I wouldn't concede. They searched anyway.

They undid cupboards, bunks. They dug through Arthur's nappy
bags, the nags' satchels. They prodded vegetables, started Phillida
weeping. They made Rita unzip her twelve makeup purses. They set
Duchess caterwauling. Red-faced, they started taking down Preacher's sermon until they realized. They unhitched hammocks. I
watched, calmly cooling Arthur's bottle in the Nantgarw bowl.
Then, with a cry, they found the box slung underneath my caravan,
and unscrewed it.

'Wait, boys!' Calvin Jones posed by it. 'Ready Olwen? I'll show shock, horror. Get it right for once.'

'Yes, Calvin.' If I'd been her I'd have sloshed him.

'Go!' He registered shock, dismay, anger.

The Old Bill lifted the lid. I didn't need to look. It would be the Page's water clock. I'd get chucked in clink. I'd almost started to walk to the police car, save us all time –

Empty? I looked twice. Nothing. Silently I praised Sir Winston's wisdom. A cased stolen clock is a theft. An empty box is innocent to the casual observer, while constituting a promise to him in the know. It also meant that I'd have to return via Sunderhill, which meant they wanted to do a deal with me. Which meant money. God, I liked that sports club.

One of the peelers saw me mop my brow. I glared back. Out of the blue motor unfolded Sir Winston Delapole. He strolled over, the crowd parting. Authority's great stuff to them that hath.

'Good day,' he said, calm. The peelers saluted. 'Can I help?'

'Hello, Sir Winston,' I greeted. The cunning sod had waited until the search was clean, I noted. 'You've still got your Series Two Sunbeam Tiger! Do you approve of the Mustang 4.7-litre engine? Pity they couldn't use British.' That exhausted my entire knowledge of motor cars. Jessina had bored me to distraction telling me it.

His eyes glinted humour. 'Bags of thrust, Yank engines. A man's drive.' He stood, inspecting troops' progress on some remote campaign. 'Having the time of your life, what?'

'Some misunderstanding. The police seem misled.'

He stood aside while we straightened our things. The rain was merciful and stopped. The sun came out to steam the paving. I saw a sign to a library, cheered up immediately. There was a phone box by a baker's. I liked Newginfawr. Boris was wearing my sou'wester, and sported glasses he didn't need.

The peelers came over. 'In the absence of evidence, you may leave. We'll be watching you. Understand?'

'Why will you be watching us?' I asked.

'Lovejoy.' Luke's word was a warning, a plea, a threat. Boris had disappeared the instant Sir Winston arrived.

'Because, boyo,' the sergeant said, 'we want no trouble.'

We all parted company. The peelers went smarting, Sir Winston affable, Calvin fuming, and Olwen screeching out, 'No, no! I'll manage!' when Phillida went to give her a hand.

Meg relented in relief and let us order some bread and cakes from the bakery. I gobbled mine and hurried away.

The library was small, neat, from another era. The lady was pleased to find somebody keen to learn about local history. I asked about the old ruined chapel. She told me addresses, of troubles between Unitarians and Methodists. I loved her, told her so. She got even more zealous to impart knowledge. I could tell she was disappointed when six o'clock came. I left celibate, but promising to return, and had a real meal in a chip shop to tide me over until supper time.

Then I bumped into Humphrey, just when I didn't want to, because in the market square was a great lovely vehicle I recognized. Relief almost bowled me over. A chance of a woman.

'Lovejoy. Have you a second?'

'Er.' The traffic was sparse. Seeing Mrs Arden had come for me, I didn't want her to waste her journey. A fine old tavern stood opposite. Its rooms would be really comfortable, if she had the money. The place was possibly hers anyway. I could see her looking across at the caravans under the three trees. The horses had been unshipped, or whatever, and stood looking out of place. I drew Humphrey into the doorway of an outfitter's. I didn't want Mrs Arden to see me not rushing to her instantly. Humphrey was beginning to be a pest.

'Lovejoy.' He harrumphed. Something momentous was coming.

'Yes?' I couldn't concentrate. Mrs Arden, coming to seduce me. Ecstasy's ecstasy, and rare.

He paused, letting some shoppers by. 'It was five months ago. I was in practice.'

'Well, never mind,' I said heartily. 'Things blow over.' My mouth watered. Mrs Arden . . . 'Eh? What baby?'

'It was in the drawer.' He was telling me something horrible. 'Shut in. Cigarette burns on its skin. Both arms broken, its hip joint displaced. Fingernail marks on its abdomen.'

'A what?' I thought stupidly, what's he saying?

'There'd been rumours. I dropped by, on the pretence of checking up on its vaccinations. They were a young couple. We chatted.

I heard a noise, went to the drawer. It had pneumonia, was battered.'

'What?' I couldn't stop saying what. The lights were on now, a bank, security check, uniforms testing locks.

'I couldn't speak.' Humphrey sounded so tired. 'I asked why the baby was in the drawer. Covered in vomit, it stank. They'd just finished their meal, a Chinese take-away. Watching television. The place was a tip.'

'What . . . ?' I meant, What did they say?

He smiled a smile I hope I never see again. 'The man said, "What's it got to do with you?" So I hit him.' He stopped, worried. 'No. I don't mean *therefore* I hit him. I mean I *started* hitting him. You see? The woman came at me with a knife. I beat them both to the floor. They couldn't stand up.' My silence gave him time. 'If the baby hadn't cried out, I'd have carried on pounding them both until they were dead. Murder, you see? Me, a murderer. I took the baby to hospital.'

'?' I asked, zero syllables.

'One of my colleagues is a consultant there. I could trust him to keep the baby in. I went to the police station. By then the couple had reported me. I was arrested.' I listened, stricken. 'It never recovered. Poor little mite died, day three.'

'But that was . . .' I dried up. 'Justice?' The word is a laugh. A bitter legal laugh, but still a hoot.

'Is there such a thing? I resigned, wrote to all my patients. Sent word to the General Medical Council.' That terrible smile. 'A doctor can't take an oath to save folk, then smash them about.' He almost snorted. 'My patients organized a support petition.'

'Anybody would have done the same, Doc.'

'Humphrey, please, Lovejoy. Not Doctor.' He heaved a breath. 'Just thought to tell you that reporter was right. My wife left. Shame, you see.'

'You get my medal, Humphrey,' I said. 'Is this why . . . ?' You can't really say suicide. How do doctors ask?

'I was down. I'd lost my chlordiazepoxide.'

I remembered the plastic bottle. 'Ah, Phillida's found them. Only, doctor's handwriting, eh?' I chuckled unconvincingly. Doctors don't write their own names on prescription bottles. The pharmacist writes the patient's. So why 'Dr Lancaster'? Therefore

Humphrey shared that name. Only one way for that. 'Just tell her I'll smack her wrist if she finds them again, okay?'

'Oh, good.' He gestured. 'Coming? Suppertime.'

'Not yet. I want to find a, er, bookshop.'

He left. I gave him a couple of beats, then started into the square with a loving smile. It died before I'd gone a yard. I ducked back swiftly. They hadn't seen me. Luke, in Mrs Arden's motor. They seemed very good friends. I checked that no windowpanes reflected me for the eagle-eyed Luke, and sloped away.

Which gave me time to ring Doc Lancaster. There was some jiggery-pokery about getting through. Some bird made me listen to Delius's *Sea Drift*.

'Wotcher, Doc. It's me, in Walia Pura, a.k.a. Welsh Wales.'

'Lovejoy?' He tried to sound bored. 'All well?'

'The constabulary are anti us nutcases.'

'So Wales has sussed you, Lovejoy! Nothing amiss?'

'Is he your brother, Doc?' I came straight out with it, sick of mucking about. It was Mrs Arden knowing Luke narked me.

He hesitated for a beat, 'Mmmh. Nice chap, get to know him.'

I said. 'Doc. Did *you* organize the whole farce?'

'What's wrong, Lovejoy?' he asked quickly.

'Is there a word?' Like teaching a kiddie to say please.

'Organize the trip? No, of course not. Why would I?'

'Then why's your brother on it, and not on some cruise with willing ladies with stars in their eyes?'

'Because you were going, Lovejoy.' I listened in disbelief. *Me?* Doc thinks I'm a prat, always has. 'I couldn't risk him on holiday without a friend to turn to. Superb doctor, but solitary.'

'Me?' I got out.

'I trust you, Lovejoy. Knew you'd give it a go.'

God, but it was cold. The Carmarthen wind stings your eyes sometimes when you don't expect. I wiped my nose. 'Why didn't you tell me about him?'

'Humphrey wanted to go incognito. In fact it was only when Vana said that I – '

Headache time. 'Vana who?' I asked, cunning Lovejoy.

'Mrs Farahar. Wife of a senior American Air Force officer. It's her charity, Cardiganshire's her home county. Her family's on my list. She was raising funds . . .'

Too simple. I must be blind as a bloody bat. Vana Farahar's voice had elided its Welshness, but now I detected it in a mental re-run. I suddenly knew all, nearly.

'Doc? Any chance of you getting to these parts?'

'Not really, Lovejoy. I'm on call. Keep in touch?'

'Right.' Well, it wasn't my fault I hadn't rung the blighter before now. 'Cheers, Doc.'

'Cheers, Lovejoy.' I plonked the receiver down and started briskly towards the square. But it's a kind of law with me: when a doctor wishes you good health, look out for plagues.

Luke had the nerve to demand what I fed my dog on. I looked at Tudor, who'd magically reappeared.

'Don't they fend for themselves?' I said.

'In the Bronze Age, maybe. Now, you feed them.'

Great, I thought bitterly. Another sponger, just when I wanted a clean pair of heels. 'Luke,' I called. 'What on, mate?'

He made no answer, uncooperative swine. See what I mean about being kind?

29

Newginfawr was relieved to see us go. No crowds to jeer us out, nothing like that. But the whole town heaved a breath. I didn't care, case-hardened.

We were a rum lot, pulling out. I'd been up in the night, hearing Arthur blow soon after four. I'd looked across to see the pink caravan's light. I'd pulled my mac on and gone across. Phillida was weeping on the caravan steps, Arthur in her arms. I went in, heated his bottle, took over. It felt funny, because I sleep naked mostly and had to sit on the steps with my knees together. Makes you wonder how women manage. Hell of a draught.

'It'll be okay,' I told her quietly. Arthur's mouth leeched on the bottle with a yell of approval. 'Mynydd Mal'll be marvellous.' I couldn't even pronounce the blinking place.

'It won't, Lovejoy,' she said. She'd pulled on her overcoat. The traffic lights by the church changed. Gripping. 'He won't be there.'

'Course he will!' I said, thinking, Who?

'Gwyn said he would, but he won't.' She sniffed, rummaged, brought out a string of pearls, silver matchbox, a computer mouse, fountain pen and, fanfare, a hankie. 'He made me come. I didn't want to, Lovejoy.' Tears flowed. I always want to clear off.

'Why'd he make you?'

'He said it'd give him an in, chance of a lifetime.' She dropped a man's wallet finding a new tissue. I picked it up, slammed my knees together. God, it's a wonder women get anything done at all, knee problems all day long.

'Did he?' Gwyn who?

'Typical,' she wept on, answering obliquely like they do. 'He's always on about the big score.' She made it a mocking citation. 'As if he was buying the Derby winner. He can't boil an egg.'

I shifted uneasily. Women usually moan about me in identical terms. 'Oh, give him the benefit of the doubt, love.'

'Gwyn? You don't know, Lovejoy. He's been in business two years, and nothing. All my dad's money. Even took the maternity money, bought a Russell Flint painting. It was a forgery. Typical. Everything he touches.'

'What a shame.' Arthur farted blissfully into the air of New-ginfawr, grunted, sucked, gave me the bent eye at the artist's name. I glared. It's easy for infants. You should be out here, mate, I beamed back at him. I withdrew the bottle. He belched, G sharp.

'It's not, Lovejoy. It's for life. He bought into the Arcade, near his friend's car business.'

'Gwyn in the car business?' I asked, my heart griping.

'With his friend, Mossie. Gwyn did his books, took calls, ship-ments, spares.' She sat, elbows on knees. 'Gwyn borrowed from a moneylender at Tey. I know he'll mess it up.'

Arthur cackled, kicked at the thought of impending disaster. I didn't join in. Big John Sheehan is the only financier in Tey. He is very sombre news. Gwyn Hughes, Florence's husband, was Jessina Mosston's hubby's pal. Christ.

'Are you married?' I asked. 'Maybe – '

'He's getting a divorce. She's a bitch. She claimed he stole her pottery collection, but he didn't.'

Oh but he did, love, I answered inside. Florence told me. I'm basically a coward. I should have come right out. What can you do, though, when you're feeding a bird's babe and she's brokenhearted? Her nerk was in Simon Doussy's syndicate. Gwyn bought in with Florence's valuable W. H. Taylor collection.

Arthur got off to sleep, me singing 'Marching To Pretoria', my unfailing soporific for infants. It woke half the town centre. Cheap at the price.

Like I said, they were relieved to see us go from Newginfawr.

The journey was suddenly harder. Preacher took the lead arguing transubstantiation with fence posts. Then Meg, edgy and cross. Then Luke, blue caravan, me last. Corinda had trotted in a state of wild nudity to the public loos screaming joyously when netted by Meg. Humphrey I'd inveigled into sitting with Phillida in my wag-gon. Rita was still doing her makeup after two hours. Duchess was screeching into the bright morning. Mr Lloyd was watchful. Situation normal, you might say.

Until the lumbering old bus chugged past.

It'd been coming for some time, gears grinding, engine coughing, pistons sandpaper. I heard it hooting. The horses skittered. I just sat there holding the reins hoping that Pulse understood roadhogs.

When finally it passed – Luke led us off – I gaped. The most derelict bus you ever did see. I've ridden in some, but never seen anything like this Leyland. It was a carnival. The windows were mostly cardboarded. Its paint was rust, mudguards gone. The tyres shone bald. The engine was exposed, the bonnet had disappeared. A goat – a *goat* – peered out beside the driver, a bearded bloke of immense girth. Folk waved. I waved back, smiling.

The creation pulled in. People poured out like a football crowd. I jumped down. Anything was an improvement. The driver came through his mob, parting them like a biblical inundation. I went forward, hand out.

'Good to see you. Lovejoy. You on the road?'

He bellowed a laugh that made our nags wilt. I'd underestimated him. He was sumo-sized, with straggly black hair, a beard you could hide in. His shirt fungated pubic hair, his chest wire wool behind an enormous gold pendant. His jeans were a symphony of holes. The seven children were unwashed, tattered, the three women threadbare in caftans with earrings you could swing on, given the circumstances. The goat brayed or whatever. Kaliyuga, the fourth age of global degeneracy, was upon us. I began to think critical things, then remembered that I'd called my caravan friends a menagerie.

'Lovejoy! Love of . . . ' he twinkled, ' . . . joy! Get it?' He boomed. I wished Calvin Jones had been here. He'd have met his match. His tribe laughed, applauded. He grabbed my hand in some complicated palm-rolling ritual I couldn't follow but which set the children doing it amongst themselves. 'Baptation C. Morris, bro,' he thundered. 'Ah stands foh friendship, right, each en every all?'

'Right, right!' his mob agreed. I found myself agreeing along, wondering what he was on about.

'You going – ?' I started. I liked him.

'Sure, Bro Love!' His eyes closed. 'To the one true fezzie!'

'Are you short of anything, er, bro?'

'Spoken like a true travvie!' He leant over me for a confidence. 'Sister Cruza will unify you through prayer. She's with Bro Bon foh a few holy moments.' The women looked shy. 'You know what Cruza means, each an every all?'

'Hey,' I said, 'are you American, er, bro?'

'Bro Bap to friends!' His correction set Ash whinnying away from this savage. 'American in mah heart!'

Thank God for that, I thought with relief. I'd enough problems, without having to weed American spies out. I saw Meg jump down and start towards us, fuming. I switched into my oblivious mode.

'Bro Bap. Meet mah friends.' It sounded weird, but was all I could manage. 'There's Luke. Here's Meg. Preacher in the lead, still, er, praying – '

'Praise the Lord!' Baptation thundered, raising his hand.

'Er, quite.' I raised mine, feeling daft. 'Humphrey.' Humphrey was carrying Arthur. Rita was peering from the window. Corinda started to strip. I quickly ran through the names, including Mr Lloyd's. 'Some of us are not, er, usual, Bro Bap.'

'Is anybody usual, Bro Lovejoy?' Tears flowed in an instantaneous torrent. I stepped back astonished. The children and women gathered about him, patting him like some great wounded animal while he wept. Meg had frozen. She peered into the goat's face. It decided to come down the steps. The horses didn't like that. Baptation beckoned one of his women, ripped off part of her blouse and dabbed his eyes. She murmured gratitude. I thought, whatever turns you on. His tears dwindled.

'You're right. Ain't he, each an every all?' Tumultuous concurrence set us all grinning and patting. The goat sniffed me. I've heard they're the cleanest of animals. 'Look, bro,' I chanced. 'Please don't take offence. But we've food, paraffin, milk.' With a stroke of genius I added, 'And a ton of oats.' The once Meg'd made porridge it had proved inedible. Luke had stocked up in Newginfawr. I kept the goat between me and Meg. 'Sugar, and . . .' We'd bacon, but I guessed Baptation's lot to be hedge-huggers. 'And bread.'

'You . . .' His tears gushed forth. Meg turned puce. Luke interposed, talked softly to her. I started to cull our stores, mostly held in Preacher's waggon. The children were marvellous, only taking what they were told. The women started prattling, and went ahead into their bus. I gave Meg a sack to carry as punishment for her rotten porridge.

She stopped, aghast. I blundered into her, almost dropped six cartons of milk. 'Lovejoy!' she said.

'Well,' I excused politely, 'it's their place.' They'd got washing strung between two window frames. Heaps of blankets, altars with alchemical symbols, sleeping bags, a sink piled with crockery. It seemed pretty normal, but Meg dropped her oats and shoved rudely out. I handed my milk to the women, smiled. Luke called a halt. He thought we'd given enough. Meg was tapping her elbows in fury.

'That was pretty rude, Meg,' I told her.

'Not the mess, Lovejoy!' She was apoplectic. 'Those two . . . *doing* it!'

'Who?' I asked, blank.

'On the floor! It's *animal*!' Cries of an orgasm came.

There actually had been a couple. Sister Cruza, I supposed, kneeling astride Bro Bon, her lovely body riding each thrust up into her, but I hadn't taken any notice. It isn't right to.

I said, 'But it's their own home.'

She spat her words. She was tiresome. 'You're even more of an animal than they are, Lovejoy! Don't think I've forgotten. I'll see you punished for taking advantage of Rita at Sunderhill.' I honestly can't see the point of Megs. 'For *depravity*!' She rushed to her caravan. I was mystified. Bap had said copulation was going on. Women never listen.

'Listen up, y'all,' said this non-American American. I looked round. Tudor was eyeing the goat. The loading was finished. 'Come fezzie sunrise,' he held a pose, arm aloft, chest dangling bells, 'we travvies will *joi-yern*, y'all, with these holy Bro Luvvah uv Joy travvies!' We had an invitation.

He cut the scattered applause. The bus rocked with diminishing amplitude. I listened, reverent in holiness.

'Amen,' I said, feeling Bap wanted a response.

'I feel wholly unworthy.' A trio of motorbikes roared, dopplering him into inaudibility. They pounded past, engines beating our eardrums, stones spitting. I gaped, never having seen motorbikes so vast, chrome so brilliant, handlebars so high. Replicas of Baptation sat at a reclining angle. Their horns squealed, blew, hooted, howled, whined in salute. Bap waved, shouted after them. We watched them recede. He went on, 'See how we're travellin'? By stinking oil-smearing engine! It's given to Bro Lovejoy to show us the way, using the living creatures for trans-port-a-tion! Pray!'

Preacher seized the chance of his first ever willing congregation. I gave up and went to see that Boris was all right. He was in our cara-van, tapping his knees, staring.

'You all right, Boris?'

'Thank you, yes.' From another person such abruptness would have been insolent. He almost snapped, 'Carry on!'

'Look. My nag's ankle isn't right. Do horses get corns?' I waited hopefully. 'Only, Luke's narked I gave those folk our grub.'

He said, 'I might take a gander. When everybody's gone.'

'Ta, mate. It'd be a load off my mind.'

'Not at all,' he said. 'Carry on.'

Closer and closer! I was so pleased that I didn't see Luke until I bumped into the sly sod. 'Sorry.'

He nodded, checked Boris with a glance, came back with me to where Preacher was belting out St Paul gibberish.

'Don't, Lovejoy.' Luke stood affably by.

'Don't what, Luke?' I asked, amazed. 'Somebody's got to speak with the poor bloke.'

He said quietly, 'Leave well alone.'

'What have I done?' I asked. We both kept our voices low.

'Don't be friendly with travvies.' He was really narked now, but I'd been too docile too long. It was time I acted.

'No?' I said evenly. 'Then who'll help?'

'Heed me, Lovejoy. Last warning.'

'Amen! Amen!' I cried at a crack in the sermon, hoping to hurry it all to a conclusion. I never could stand St Paul. I think he's a fraud. Ancient scrolls call him The Liar.

If the syndicate had each other, I now had more helpers than any-body, with this load of travelling people. About time.

30

Time was on my side for once. Whatever would happen, couldn't yet. We had to reach Mynydd Mal first. There my rewards waited: Vana Farahar and the Romano-Celtic lanx. I'd accept them in any order. I settled to the Romany life.

And watched passing hamlets, cottages, for antiques. Oddly, the most prolific source in the next few days was taverns. The first was a William Adams pottery serving jug, about 1790. I almost fell into my ale seeing that unbelievably beautiful blue on pearl, displayed up there in a four-ale bar. I didn't say a word, just pencilled a note in my – Liffy's – notebook. The same incredible day, I bought for two quid a Swiss fob seal some bloke was wearing as a lapel badge – he'd never tried twisting it (gently!) and realized it was a cunning minuscule musical toy worth a mint.

Two days later, I pencilled in a 'ring pillar' in a teashop. An inverted hollow glass cone, on show among fancy modern dross. Trailing design, looking unbelievably clumsy up there on a shelf. But turn it the right way up – point down – and it becomes a beautiful sixth-century drinking vessel. Experts tell us these glasses are pathetic, that the early glassmakers had forgotten Rome's trick of putting a flat foot on. Codswallop. Their misunderstood shape was deliberate – you can fill it with wine and stick it upright in a sand or clay tray. Ever hopeful, I made a note to offer up to a thousand quid, on IOU, of course. (If you collect these, incidentally, only buy when they have a genuine certificate of dating by infrared spectroscopy – they modify it by Faurier transform interferometry now. God knows how.)

Pretty soon I'd a list of eleven antiques. Good old Wales. I didn't tell Meg.

We were now often passed by odd vehicles. They looked a ghastly retreat. Lorries converted to mobile homes, rusting buses, three-wheelers like magnified invalid carriages, and once – I swear – a houseboat swaying dangerously behind a thing like a forklifter. As they careered past in showers of gravel, you could see that children abounded, the females were lithe and straggly, and the blokes . . . well. They were either skeletal, smoking, or were replicas of Baptation. Tin cans clattered from windows, pots were emptied as they ground past. Inside seemed a riot. Cheerful, though. Dogs flourished. Motor horns were constant. You could hear one of the vehicles coming three miles off. The way we were heading! I cheered up.

We reached a nice village only to find Calvin Jones there with his camera-toting serf, Olwen. He was sickeningly ebullient, but now wary.

'Photos, lined here,' he announced. The villagers eyed us. 'The mad doctor, too.' He saw me. 'We missed somebody last time. Lovejoy's friend, a loony in a sou'wester.'

I said amiably, 'He's called Boris. You'll like him.'

'And, Olwen. This grass lunatic can be eating the horses' food, right? Will he do that to cue, somebody?'

I came grinning. 'You want the mad baby, too?'

Luke arranged the caravans with the local bobby pointing. The village green was minute. Stalls already occupied most of it. Meg was at the reins of her caravan, Preacher likewise. It was a good opportunity.

'Hey!' Calvin laughed. 'He's not so crazy!'

Olwen went frantic with lenses and camera boxes. I beckoned Calvin, grinning my idiot's grin, and pointed to Pulse. 'How about here, mister? I pulled the reins. 'It's funny. Can I be in the picture?'

What happened wasn't my fault. Tudor was with me. On the road I'd taught him a sponge ball game. Flick it, and Tudor'd leap. He always yelped as the ball emerged. A dog without sheep's bored. It was just bad luck that the sponge ball accidentally fell out of my pocket as Golden Boy Calvin came smiling by the near front wheel. It was even worse luck that it bounced against Pulse's back left leg. Tudor barked, leapt excitedly forward on to Pulse.

You couldn't blame the nag. It must have been thinking it had done its job, dragged that lousy caravan over hill and dale. A few minutes' rest, and a mad dog scrabbles at its haunch. Pulse veered, neighing, bounced up and lashed its back hoof, dragged the caravan so the wheel grazed my knee. It really stung. A split second, that was all.

Calvin screeched, eardrums perforating everywhere. Pulse's hoof cracked his leg in mid-thigh. I gaped, because a docile nag like Pulse, well, you don't think, do you? But it did. Calvin hurtled past, his foot almost catching my ear, thoughtless sod. He might have brained me. What with Tudor wagging, the ball in his mouth, and the caravan jerking forward, Pulse plunging, my knee stinging, Calvin screeching like a party balloon, it was mayhem.

Luke was there in a trice, shoving me aside and catching Pulse's reins. I sat moaning, Tudor wriggling. My knee was almost nearly in real pain. Calvin was still sounding off, selfish burke. If I'd not moved smartish, I'd have caught it instead of him.

'No,' Luke was saying. 'It's fine. All in hand.'

He was talking to Boris, reporting in, you might say. Boris had appeared, but now ducked back. I heard Luke address Meg, who was shouting as usual. Preacher sang 'Lead Kindly Light'.

Things settled. I was a picture of agony. Rita emerged, Corinda jubilantly applauded with laughter, Arthur started bawling for minions to fawn, and old Mr Lloyd started taking every second item from a haberdasher's. Duchess keened.

'Ambulance!' somebody called.

'It's okay,' I told Rita. 'I don't need an ambulance.'

'Let me look, Lovejoy.' She slit my trouser leg with scissors, real skill. Humphrey knelt by Calvin Jones who was retching, making a real meal of it while I was practically dying.

'A graze, Lovejoy,' Rita said. 'The skin's not broken.'

'Oh, sorry,' I shot back, narked. 'Should I have had my leg off then?' People are really hard-hearted. Luke was standing there. 'I know. All my fault. Go on, start.'

'That dog,' Luke said. Tudor hadn't got rid of the ball, stupid mongrel. A dog's supposed to be man's friend. I decided to blame Tudor, because people like dogs.

'Tudor was playing. I didn't see what happened.' I peered about. 'Did anybody see what happened?'

'That crazy bastard made the horse kick me,' Calvin cut in. Everybody was paying him attention. 'Deliberate.'

Well, that did it. I erupted. 'I saved your life, you stupid sod! He poked Pulse. You can't blame the horse. It was him, the stupid – '

Humphrey was binding a walking stick to Calvin's leg.

'Lovejoy. A word.' Luke stepped away.

'Help me up, somebody.' I gave a realistic groan but nobody offered. It just shows. Weep loudest for sympathy. Save a bloke's life, you get disdain. Even Rita had gone to help Humphrey, unsympathetic cow.

'Broken,' Humphrey announced. 'Hospital.'

'Here, Doc,' I offered helpfully. 'Doesn't that stick go higher up? A first-aid lady once told me – '

'Lovejoy,' Luke said. I hobbled over. Meg came up, her features contorted with rage. I felt really down. There's no pleasing some people.

'Lovejoy!' she began.

'Excuse me, Meg.' I was determined not to be scapegoat for the nth time. 'Calvin deliberately – '

Meg's idea of tact was to shriek louder. 'I resign here and now! I will not tolerate . . .'

Take the rest as said. Righteous endeavour (a.k.a. Meg) against crass stupidity (a.k.a. me). She flounced off to the phone to call an air strike.

'Quite honestly, Luke,' I admitted, 'I'm not sorry to see her go. She'll never change if she lives a million years – '

'Lovejoy.' I swear the bloke hadn't taken a blind bit of notice. I hate people who can't be persuaded. 'No more doing things off your own bat.'

'Me?' I was frankly amazed. 'All I did was – '

'Secondly, leave Boris alone, Humphrey, Rita, Phillida.'

'Oh, that's great!' I said quiet, because I get narked too. 'Your naval officer is incognito because of some stable love with Her Royal – '

Suddenly I was on the grass, and him saying in a calm voice, 'It's his epilepsy, Constable. Stand well back, please, no fuss . . .' And the world was black with dots because he had hold of my neck, the frigging maniac. I patted the grass twice, wrestler's submission. Slowly air wheezed into me. I coughed, came dizzily to. Tudor barked happily. He thought it some new game and crouched, tongue out.

'He'll have a headache presently,' Luke was assuring some elderly dame keen to put an umbrella handle under my tongue. 'Lovejoy's seizures are short,' Luke assured her, 'but thank you.'

He waited until the ambulance hiked Calvin Jones off. Olwen would get ballocked for not getting it on celluloid, sure as eggs. She went weeping and scattering equipment. I saw one little lad walking off examining an enormous camera. I felt my neck. People's intolerance.

Luke crouched by me. 'Boris was aide to a certain royal family.' I listened. Luke was starting to scare me. A 'certain', though? How many had we got? 'Boris acquired notoriety from certain allegations. You don't repeat tabloid guesses. Follow?'

'One maintains a certain silence.' He did not smile, which was okay. He didn't relax, which wasn't.

'No more fun.' I shook my head. The bloke was off his frigging trolley. 'You saved Humphrey at the chapel. You twice saved Boris from reaching the front pages, by thieving cameras and breaking Jones' leg. And you got Rita from under. But no more interference will be tolerated.' He sounded like a headmaster, dry, omnipotent.

'Right, Luke.'

'Henceforward, you ask. Every time, every yard. You return within a stipulated time. You report every word, every person encountered.'

'Yes, Luke.'

'Lovejoy?' I looked up slowly so my neck didn't fall off. 'You have been warned.'

Disconsolately I rubbed my leg. Everybody would come out of this okay except me. At first I'd assumed Luke was along to keep Boris out of the press's excoriating eyes while the royal scandal cooled and Her Highness got her Brownie pack badges back. If he was in with the Arden-Farahar-Mrs Divine pack I was sunk. Who'd notice one Lovejoy less?

Answer: Tinker, Dolly, the landlord of the Tudor Arms, a crooked golf club committee who happened to be working a shuff – as we call clandestine swap-and-drop theft. And, for perhaps one millisec, Bap's travelling tribe.

And me. Mustn't forget me.

*

When the fuss died down, I wandered about lost. Phillida'd taken Arthur to Humphrey. The little turncoat glimpsed me and cackled. A few people came to stare. I had my menagerie feeling, would have scratched under my arms but Luke'd have got mad. Meg swept off in a taxi. A travellers' bus creaked its way through.

Children were grouped about a small booth. I went to see. A puppeteer, real genuine limewood marionettes, too, none of your hideous plastic replicas. They looked aged.

Dunno about you, but Punch and Judy shows give me the willies. I mean, the baby, crocodile, hanging Jack Ketch, the policeman truncheoning hell out of everyone. It's not a laugh a minute, though the children fall about. And the voices are enough to turn your stomach, that evil-sounding thing these puppeteers use.

Before I go on, I wasn't sulking. I don't. I'm a realist, out for myself. It was my job, for God's sake. Nobody owed me a living. As I stood there watching Punch and Judy, it came to me that maybe I should cut and run. Meg had, because her publicity scheme had suffered a setback. Luke had let her go. That was quite odd. Superfluous old me was chained, yet essential Meg sweeps out unhindered? Even more stranger.

Looking back, I waved to the caravans. Luke appeared in a flash. I wrote a great question mark in the air. He nodded. I could attend a children's booth, then, nothing too subversive. I stayed in sight, only forty yards off, and watched the show, wincing as the noose jerked Jack Ketch's body. The children howled with laughter. I closed my eyes as the crocodile's jaws opened . . . I walked, shutting the screams of laughter out. Jesus, but comedy has a lot to answer for.

The collection was taken by a girl. I put in, last of the dissolving crowd.

'Liked your show,' I said. 'Your bloke got time for a word?'

'Thanks.' She waited until the children had gone. 'Da?'

The old bloke came out. I shook his hand. 'Lovejoy, antiques. Masterpiece. Real limewood, eh? Brilliant!' I talked of acts about East Anglia.

He was pleased, shoved back his thin grey hair. 'Kind, *bach*. Getting long in the tooth.' He smiled ruefully. 'I'm on the lookout for somebody to take it on. Too much telly, computer games.' He nodded at the lass. 'Ceinwen's not the voice – women haven't, see. And children aren't children more than a few minutes.'

'You're right there.' I explained how I was accompanying inmates from a psychiatric unit. 'We need people like you.'

'Bless you, *bach*,' he said, laughing. 'Hear that, Ceinwen? We're the only indigenous people for miles!'

'You live here?'

'Always have. I do the villages, field days.'

'Now, Da.' Ceinwen's money was paltry. 'We do all right.'

'Lovely place,' I said admiringly, thinking the opposite.

'Wales is a man's dream,' he said. Dylan Williams, going on eighty, and Ceinwen, his granddaughter, who pulled a face as the old gent waxed lyrical. They lived on a smallholding. 'Dolwar Fach's been my home for all but a few war years, Lovejoy.'

'Near Mynydd Mal?' I'd never heard of Dolwar Fach, couldn't pronounce it if I had. 'The travelling folk are gathering.' Feelers, always feelers, when desperate.

His face clouded, Ceinwen snorted in anger. 'Lovejoy, *bach*, who'd want to roam, to prove yourself aimless?'

Ceinwen shot at her granddad, 'Ruining Wales, ruining the kingdom! Despoiling fields! All take, no give! Drawing unemployment money! They descend like Philistines . . .' Her diatribe was a Sunday fire-and-brimstone. I switched off, but kept nodding, while old Dylan tried to mollify her. Their ancient controversy.

'Ceinwen has to cope. Things go missing.'

'Things don't *go missing*, Da,' Ceinwen corrected, stung. '*Stolen* is the word!' She gave him a mouthful of Welsh.

'Your farm must be lovely,' I said wistfully. 'My granddad farmed, Lancashire fells.'

'You'll be near us, Lovejoy,' Old Dylan said, bless his heart. A real trouper. 'A fellow Tudor! You would be welcome – not that we have any antiques. Mynydd Mal is the next valley.'

'Thanks, Dylan.' I stifled my joy. 'I shall.'

Ceinwen was less delighted. She started to talk him out of it, the woman's gambit, remembering the million things they had to do.

Hastily I interrupted. 'Your show has opportunities. I've a couple of ideas. Talent's always underpaid.'

That shut her up. She'd sussed me out as a chiseller and fly-by-night. Now, she hesitated long enough for Dylan to give me directions.

I helped my new friends load the booth into their old Austin, and waved them off. Then reported to Luke. I bored him witless with the structure of marionettes, puppets, the preparation of limewood, the prices in recent sales. He broke after ten minutes, told me to get gone. I asked could I phone a lady. He said he'd listen. The swine actually did.

With effort, I got Ted to take a message for Dolly. I actually went red dictating it. 'Write it exact, Ted,' I grumbled, 'in case Tinker's sloshed.' It was simple: 'Sorry, but please come if you can with love.' It set Ted laughing. I said I'd kill him if he told the lads. I asked Luke could I let her know where to come. He said no.

Ted asked me, 'What if her husband answers, Lovejoy?' A compassionate soul. 'No Welsh girls, then?'

You can't telephone a sneer. I hung up, stumped off hoping I'd got the acting right for once.

Luke seemed satisfied. We hit the road, after pausing fifteen minutes while a column of crumbling vehicles reeled through. And two tinkers' donkey carts, I was pleasead to see.

'Tomorrow's the last lap,' Phillida told me. Rita nursed Arthur, the lucky little swine warbling on her lap. 'Will it be as nice as they say?'

'Hope so,' I said. Humphrey had gone to drive Meg's waggon. 'Look, love. Why don't you get Gwyn to come?'

'Oh, Lovejoy,' she said, hopeless, 'don't you think I haven't tried? I've *begged*.'

I timed the suggestion. 'Maybe you haven't offered the right . . .' I coughed delicately. They don't like the word bait except in fun, and this was no laughing matter, God's truth.

'How, Lovejoy?' She turned her helpless stare on me.

'Well,' I said, my voice down. Rita was indoors, Arthur screaming with laughter. 'Gwyn's an antique dealer.'

'Yes!' She was all eager. 'He's really quite expert.'

I winced. If Gwyn was 'expert', I knew budgerigars that would qualify. 'Say there's an antique here that's priceless. Tell him you've got it.'

'I'll phone, Lovejoy!' she cried, filling with hope. 'Once he's away from that cow of a wife, I'll keep him.'

'No, love.' I looked grim. Such weighty matters. 'Phone a message through some intermediary. Then he'll come, see?'

We hit on the right phraseology. I explained that Luke had placed me under restriction. She was thrilled, but I was a bit downcast. Phillida was just my type, and here I was bringing her other bloke in. Doing everybody else good turns. I'm what saints are made of.

If God was fair, he'd bring Dolly stuttering to my rescue. I needed her now more than ever, and it wasn't only lust. An hour later Phillida phoned a message on Gwyn's machine, carefully reading out what I'd written. It was pretty good. Luke gave his imprimatur.

That night we camped by a watermill, drawing up the caravans in the mill yard. It rained heavily. The old waterwheel tried to make a go of it, but failed as it obviously had for a century. Everybody slept soundly except me. I listened to the water tumbling over the paddles, the rotting wood striving to get free. The scene was so pretty – a millwheel like they sing about on music halls. But me and the old mill knew what it felt like.

31

Next morning Corinda surprised me. Any other dawn she'd have abandoned her clothes, if any, and done a fandango in the mill-stream. Boris was his reticent self. Humphrey seemed jaded. Little Arthur bawled with gusto, of course, but Phillida snapped at Rita who wept alone and shunned breakfast. Preacher prayed on his knees, a figure of the past. Mr Lloyd was fetched out, sat staring, his face a-dribble. Duchess had fouled herself, and took some cleaning up. Phillida snappishly gave help. I warmed enough water to see Duchess was washed and dressed. Luke made eggs, bread, cereals, milk, said little. Exactly as camping in God's clean air usually is.

A tinker was camped down the road. He was a phoney, not real Kalderari, tin-smithing gypsies of the Continent. Nor did he seem a Romany, one of our own. Our stupor got me down so I got Luke's permission and strolled to see them. Four children, a shrewd wife, and a patriarch with a bent for bent.

'Wotcher,' I said. The tinker looked sloshed. Their donkey cart had enough utensils to stock Birmingham.

'Morning.' The woman started clearing away, meaning nothing doing so push off.

The children were grinding powders with a pestle and mortar. The mangy donkeys looked on disconsolately. One's knees were a mass of sores.

'Your donkeys need feeding, do they?'

The woman brightened. She was cagey. 'We can't afford to buy them food, poor animals.'

'I'll ask our boss if you like.'

'You're not travvies,' she said. 'You're to the fezzie?'

'Want a smoke?' the bloke asked. He beckoned. 'I've got plenty.' Newcastle accent.

'What is it?' I crouched. 'I don't use just any.'

'Not just any.' The bloke sat heavily on the cart steps. The vehicle's hooped top shook. It was signed *Mercury* in faded letters. A dog emerged, yawned, crawled back. 'Genuine.'

'Fool!' the woman snapped. 'Can't you tell he's trouble?'

'Everybody's got friends.' The bloke winked, managed to stay upright. I leant away from the aroma. His eyes seemed wrong. One of the children fell over. The pong was horrible.

'Any good?' I asked.

'Any good!' He crowed, hummed, held on to prevent a glide onto the grass. 'Perfection. They're on about Mexican toads, right? The bufo toad shit! Milk and scrape them, dry it on tissue, chop it, sell and see heaven! Toadstools and minced bark, *nu-nu*, five quid for one cigarette paper.' He snorted disgust, shedding tears of anger. 'Everybody wants Mexican, Peru, South American. But I got our own plants, toadstools.'

'Real country lore, eh?' I chuckled admiringly.

'You got it, friend!' He recovered. He had four saucers, each with a powder. He was wrapping salt-spoon quantities in fag papers, but was making a hash (sorry) of it. He lit and began to smoke one. Hardly a factory. His pipe fumed forgotten. 'Any fezzie, I make a killing. My stuff's currency! In Wiltshire I had money stuffed in the donkeys' feed bags! 'Cking glorious! I started selling bran and chalk. Jesus, paradise.'

His missus said, 'Can't you see what he's up to?'

'Me? Look. I just got fed up with our own camp,' I said indignantly. 'They're mental, see.' A Meg-type word. I brought it out proudly. 'We're to the fezzie. Recreation.'

'Mad?' The woman didn't move, but she'd fled a mile.

'The lot,' I said, sighing. 'One went off her head two nights since. You should have seen her. I've no drugs. It's a liberty, leaving me without help.'

'My mixes'd see her happy.' The bloke wobbled, poked one of the saucers spilling some stuff.

I set it right. 'Would they? Which one?'

'This.' It looked hideous, flakes of bark in grey powder. 'Long as Bufo Brown, and happy happy happy.'

'How much?'

'Tenner,' the woman said. I paid twenty for a big dose. I might need this currency.

193

For quite a while I sat. Mercury talked on and on. I learnt more than I'd done all my life. I was surprised when Humphrey called me. The caravans were drawn up ready to go. I said so long to Mercury and his family.

Oddly, they never caught us up. Maybe something I'd said put them off. He looked sensitive, deep down.

Luke had me at the front this time, just pointed to lead position. I clicked my tongue, but Luke had to pull Pulse forward by its mouth to set us going. Humphrey smiled as I drove. Luke said straight on, eight miles, implying that even I couldn't mistake it.

We were nearing our destination. I was suffering withdrawal. Apart from the Tudor Arms, and the old Punch and Judy, and a ton of other things, I felt I'd not seen any antiques lately. It was a terrible ache for antiques. There were diversions, erratic trucks, limping buses, lorries, charabancs. We clopped past small fields where bonfires smouldered. We saw three encampments, packs of dogs, sprinting sheep, goats, horses. We also passed rubbish, bin bags strewing debris.

And we got stoned, chased by dogs that farmers set on us.

The first time, I was smiling a greeting, as a bloke with three serfs advanced as we trundled to pass his gate.

'Good morning,' I chirruped like a fool. '*Bore da!*'

'*Bore da*, is it, you thieving wastrels? Two of my sheep killed and six more savaged? Heathens! Despoilers!'

'Clear off!' a minion bawled. I quaked. He had a shotgun. 'And tell your pals what they'll get!'

'We're not travellers, lads,' I called out, trying to pull the reins tight. The horse edged across, worried. 'We're from the psychiatric – '

'Bastards!'

'We're going, we're going!' I cried, shaking. I tried to gee Pulse up. We passed at a slow plod. Luke was last. Boris drove second in a deerstalker hat, smoking a pipe, then Preacher. For my money, we had one caravan too many. I was to remember that later.

Preacher, bloody fool, chose exactly that moment to sing the old Gospel, ' "Why do ye linger, why do ye stay, In the broad road, that most dangerous way – " '

'Sorry, sir,' I called to the angry lot, flapping Pulse's reins. 'The Holy bloke's not right in the head – '

We escaped, thank God, but no thanks to the Almighty's repertoire. I fumed. The silly goon would carol us all to perdition, with his Sankey. Luke tied his rein on to Preacher's caravan, and jogged up.

'Lovejoy? We'll arrive in three hours. Don't stop.'

Even I could see the sense in that. Across a valley four more fires, several groups of ramshackle vehicles like mobile farms. I could have sworn I heard a gunshot.

'Look, mate.' I was uneasy. 'Shouldn't we take a detour? Why force our way in?'

'We carry on, Lovejoy.' In another reincarnation, he'd have smiled. 'Left at the eight-mile junction. An uphill pull.'

'No galloping, Pulse, okay?' I said. It took no notice. I whistled Tudor but he was excited, forever ferreting the hedgerows. In the end, I picked him up bodily, made him sit there.

Rita managed us a cup of coffee from an enterprising roadside stall – a farmhouse with a pleasant lady. She returned my *Shwmae*, hello, smiled the loveliest smile, pointing to little Arthur in his wicker basket.

'Not mine, missus,' I disclaimed. 'I'm still in the market.'

'Get on with you,' she scolded. I cheered up. Maybe it wouldn't all be threats and squalor.

There civilization ended. We reached Mynydd Mal.

We'd been climbing for a thousand leagues – well, miles, maybe two. Boris'd called to rest the horses. It wasn't wise. We were driven off by two gamekeeperish blokes with shotguns and four huge dogs. We left, reviled. It happened six or seven more times, our briefest halt interrupted by people chucking stones.

It wasn't fair. Starting out, we'd been hated because we were mental – this, note, when law, that joke, forbids discrimination against the ill. Now we were abused for looking like some other people. I was getting narked, but Luke sussed and said keep quiet, going, silent, obedient.

The countryside was now mountainous. Distantly, we saw purplish rims of mountains, shifting greens. Sheep grazed, and you could occasionally see a figure with dogs. We were now watched every yard, one farmer on some promontory to see us pass so his neighbour could take over. Usually, though, as we passed hacked trees and scattered filth, or after we'd been overtaken by another clutch of makeshift vehicles, we got stoning and curses.

At one confrontation I discovered a most astonishing thing. Boris spoke Welsh, fluent, too. We'd slowed on a steep slope the nags made heavy weather of. A farmer stomped into the road with a shotgun. I tried my affable -- by now aghast – grin, but was met by a torrent of defilement in Welsh.

Boris answered in Welsh. The man hesitated, stepped to see who'd spoken. Boris spoke on. Pulse clopped by. The man looked, watched the second caravan pass. Not a word. He stayed silent. He was there, stock still, even after Luke's trailing waggon lumbered past. And all the time Boris had been speaking his fluent Welsh, not raising his voice. We rounded a tangle of thickets, out of sight. Boris stopped speaking.

'Why didn't you do that earlier, cleverclogs?' I bawled back.

'Luke said not to, Lovejoy.'

Another hour and we came to it. On a hill crest, before us lay a vast encampment of the festival. I reined in, appalled. Mynydd Mal in all its glory.

Ten thousand people, maybe plenty more, sprawled in one vast camp beneath a towering mountain. Fires, cooking smells and latrines, smoke, plastic blowing, a turmoil. A score of cack-handed vehicles limped in, a jubilant mob dancing to greet them. Horses, goats, sheep, dogs, dogs, dogs. Children with bare bums played around campfires, hencoops, geese honking. The pandemonium was unimaginable.

'God Almighty!' I said.

'Quite a crowd.' Boris and Phillida were with me. We had a vantage point. Behind us loured a mountain. Across, the taller monster, Mynydd Mal. Slung between but still high was this vale and its broiling layer of humanity. Guitarists sat and strummed. No fighting, I noticed. Two young blokes were digging latrines, canvas shelters. Pigs rummaged, lads hacked firewood.

Luke came up with Rita. Humphrey exclaimed, deploring the sanitary arrangements, thinking cholera.

'This it, Luke? The Promised Land?' from me.

'Not our bit, Lovejoy.'

'*Deo gratias*.' I didn't give a hoot now I was here. I'd be off soon. Dolly would be blundering around looking for me, ballocking thousands for improper behaviour. I could see a couple copulating with abandon. A dog nuzzled the undulating flesh. Whatever turns you on, I suppose, but in a crowd . . .

Preacher cleared his throat. ' "Yet there is room!" ' he bellowed, the old Ira Sankey. ' "The Lamb's bright hall of song, with its fair glo-o-ry, beckons thee al-o-o-ong." '

'Knock it off, Preacher,' I said, tired. 'The shoulder road, Luke?'

'That's it, Lovejoy.' And I swear Luke looked sad. Old Ironsides himself with a suggestion of sorrow? 'Take your time,' he said, the blighter. 'No hurry now.'

That's what you think, pal, I thought. We clambered into our waggons. Somebody said it was two miles, left branch.

We clopped into civilization forty minutes later. No Dolly, silly cow. I didn't care. A new one-storey building, guarded by two smart guards with pick-handles. They knew we were coming. Several motors were already there. The place looked spic and span. Bath, clean clothes, a proper meal! I was free.

Preacher sang a celebration Sankey, ' "Look not be-hind thee; O sinner be-ware!" ' I wanted no more community living. I'd be sorry to part, even from Duchess and Mr Lloyd, but I was on the starting block.

'Hey, Preacher,' I interrupted. 'You know a hymn my Gran used to sing, "Hasten, Sinner"?'

Preacher bellowed, slightly off key, as we disembarked and looked about. 'Stay not for the morrow's sun' was the bit I liked. I hummed along.

32

That welcome was curious. Rejoicing, I still had strange feelings. A constant background hum made me imagine being somewhere sleepy. The huge brawling encampment of the Visigoths on Mynydd Mal?

We took our belongings in. Then Luke, the pest, said to drive the caravans to a layby overlooking a lake, uncommonly high up. We did, backed the waggons to the edge, scotched the wheels with stones. I said ta to Ash and Pulse and walked back. Luke took the nags to some pasture.

There we were. We each had a room – bed, bathroom tacked on, smelling of new paint, window opening on a garden. In the reception lounge a pale Meg welcomed us among dignitaries. Her enthusiasm was meagre.

In this strained atmosphere Valerie Arden came smiling. There was a halting little ceremony amid flowers. Mrs Arden spoke with conviction about the benefit patients were going to receive at the Myndydd Mal Rehabilitation Centre. Carl Arden was there. Mrs Farahar sent word she would arrive with the Colonel. There were interviews for radio, irritable interviewers cursing until they read from the idiot boards with lifelike smiles.

A local dignitary presented something, and we were sent to unpack. We obeyed. Phillida and little Arthur were next door, Meg next to her and Rita across the corridor.

After an hour we were summoned to a banquet, the Farahars among us. Simon Doussy arrived, and Raddie and Chuck were said to be around somewhere. Carl Arden told me, when I wondered aloud, that Mrs Divine'd be along shortly.

Dull as ditchwater, but great, for it was the end. The meal was a bore like all meals, though Arthur's singing stole the show. I changed him before the pudding.

Luke gave a short speech saying thanks. I got a message from reception saying that one Dolly had visited earlier. She'd come for me about eleven tomorrow morning. I was so relieved. Colonel Farahar spoke emotionally of Wales and glory. We of the four caravans seemed to be the only patients so far. He promised great things for the universe. People clapped, though applause for a political speech means somebody's being conned. After, we were dismissed, I caught Luke, who was with Mrs Arden. She looked good enough to eat.

'Luke?' I didn't ignore her. God knows I tried.

'Yes, you can wander. Sign at reception.'

Better still. Stuck in Mynydd Mal I was freer plodding the roads. Dolly would come tomorrow, and I'd take off. The question, why was I here, I ignored, like a fool.

The evening was down to twilight when I walked from the rehab centre. I did a hesitation to show watchers I lacked plans. Then I ambled left.

It was a contour path. The fells were heather-strewn. The stunted trees had a rough time. Boulders were sharpened by primaeval forces. Lichens, moss, rugged mountains. I moved quicker. A glow rebounded from the slopes.

I came on to a promontory and stood. It was almost unbelievable. I'd seen one travvie trek years ago. That had been staggering enough. Here, it looked like a population drift, a city.

The smoke, the lantern pinpoints, campfires, the windows of a myriad vehicles, the sound made up of shouts, music, chants, singing, laughter, the din stopped thought. Children everywhere, couples in sexual throes with nobody taking a blind bit of notice. I'd be hard put to find Baptation. I didn't think of Sister Cruza, honestly. I had my powder, Mercury's universal coinage.

The ground was muddy. Plastic bags drifted across the scene like tumbleweed. Dogs squabbled. Children trotted industriously. Two lasses knelt astride blokes, their breasts swinging, chatting to each other, one leaning her elbows on her bloke's chest like a navvie at a bar. I found somebody not so busily employed, and asked for Baptation.

'A bus,' I explained. 'He came two days since.'

The youth I asked was far gone. I stopped him from tumbling into his fire, propped him against some sacks. He was eating porridge from a cauldron. 'Bro Bap's headwind, bro.'

'Headwind? Where's headwind?'

He snored. Worried, I dragged him to flop in safety. Better muddy than charred. I asked a band, bongos and stringed instruments, no antiques. The drummer helped by pointing. I picked my way through the camp trying to avoid muck and animals. Was headwind some pop group? There was a notice. Torches burnt, tar on plaited sticks stinking the place out.

'Headwind?' I started saying. A toddler, tugged me to Baptation's vehicle.

'Can you find your way home?' I asked the little one, but it was off. I knocked, hung about. The old bus stood at an alarming angle, done for. Three goats nestled under a mudguard. Lanterns only now, I noticed, no battery power. A fire nearby had ashed to grey.

The camp had thinned. A road started a hundred yards off, lit by smoky torches, but downhill the main sprawl thrummed on max. Bap's bus was guardian of the gate.

'Headwind means riding point,' a voice said.

Sister Cruza, in some garment that was half – as in vertically sectioned – stood in the vehicle's doorway. She was as beautiful as when I'd fallen for her.

'Er, I'm Lovejoy. I met . . .'

She smiled, tranquil, the firelight gold on her lovely hair. 'I saw you in the driving mirror. You were very taken. I was at prayer.'

My throat managed to swallow. 'Is Bap around, love?'

'No. Come in.' She moved ahead, sleepy. 'Point is standing sentry duty.'

I entered the shambles. A regular thumping sounded on the upper deck, prayer going on. The sink was piled with crockery. Bus seats were heaped in a corner. The controls were a mass of wires. 'What happened, er, Cruza?'

She sank to her knees, beckoned me close. I stood there like a lemon. An oil lantern burnt. The windows let in drizzle and noise. With patient indolence she undid my belt.

'Bap's at a meet about the threat.' She looked surprised as I backed away. 'I owe you one prayer, Lovejoy.'

'I don't feel like praying, love. I've said my . . .'

She reached in, fingers stroking away my willpower. 'You must, Lovejoy. Prayer is godly.'

'Look, love.' I felt hot. 'The children. You're gorgeous, but I mustn't offend Bap.'

'The littles are abed.' She pointed to the stack of seats, and sure enough several children kipped on them. 'Bro Bon is praying with Sister Mela. We must share their funda.'

'Funda?' I saw her half-dress come away as she lay back. 'Sex isn't sharing anything, love.'

She drew me down. 'In the name of Holy Earth . . .' I honestly tried hard to stay in control, but there's never a hope.

'Amen,' I said in a thick voice. Well, it was a Welsh poet who once said, 'Isn't life terrible, thank God.'

'Threat?' It had been bothering me as I slowly came to. She'd been superb. I still floated. Better still, she'd dreamt along until I surfaced. A woman worth praying with.

'The others across the valley.'

'Who?' I wasn't scared, but a threat's a threat.

She smoked a small hubble-bubble. The water clacked rhythmically in the glass, the children watching sleepily. Oh well, us making love was her fault, not mine.

'Some mental health unit.' She pointed the mouthpiece, naked, her legs folded. 'It's just built. They have an injunction, to arrest us.'

'Where'll you go?'

'Nowhere, Lovejoy.' She smiled, fondling me. I was as naked, a bag of spanners with a dangling spring. 'Police always do an Avon on us – turn us back for unroadworthy vehicles.'

'The mental unit's clearing you from the valley?'

'Yes.' She searched until her eyes found me. 'I love you, Lovejoy. Have you an owner?'

Owner? 'Eh? Oh, aye.' The children slept.

'Will she sell you? I can barter much.'

My headaches hadn't been too bad lately, but now three hit, clamouring to throb quickest. 'I'll come to you if I can escape.'

'Please, Lovejoy.' She drifted, hung on. 'You're so selfish. You make the holiness carnal.'

'Here, knock it off.' I was narked. I'm kind.

She purred, twisting sinuously. 'I displease you?'

She hauled at me so suddenly I gasped and clouted her one. She gave a throaty laugh, head back in rapture. 'Like one of Baptation's explosions, Lovejoy!' She examined her handiwork, cupping me and murmuring.

'Explosions?'

'Trint.' She giggled, head lowering. I gasped, she laughed. 'Semmy, seef. Better than old ammy!'

Then I was gone, sucked into her vortex and out of control on the palliasse. I woke later, Cruza sleeping like a babe. I was frightened to death and scrabbling for my clothes, wondering how to get back and stop everybody, including me, from being blown to blazes.

Trint's the anarchist's nickname for trinitroluene, made from toluene and sulphuric and nitric acids. It's the old one-pound TNT sticks you see in gangster flicks. Semmy is Semtex, the putty-like stuff that's safe until you detonate it. Seef is the famed American C-Four, also like putty, explodes with a shattering 9,000 yards per second. Her 'ammy' was ammonium nitrate, fertilizer mixed with diesel exploded with a battery timer. Only one-eighth seef's power, but corner shop ingredients.

I shook Cruza, gouged her eyes open. I'd learnt my lesson about eavesdroppers since Meg, and whispered, 'I'm in love with you, er, darling. Honest, most sincerely. Where's Baptation? I need Bap to, er, get free. For you!'

She coiled. I struggled not to get drawn, as it were, in. Her eyes were suddenly clear. 'You mean it?'

'Promise! Oh, er, Mother Earth, everything.'

'He meets the American by the lake. Shall I come?'

'Er, no. Stay with the ducks. I'll be along.' I flung her down, and hopped one-legged into my trousers.

33

As a lad, I was taken to see *Henry V*. The carnage, the mêlée, stunned me. No consolation that the actors lined up unscathed to take a bow. It comes anew on bad nights. Hurrying through the endless encampment in the darkness the same appalled feeling was there. I was lost, blundering from one light to the next, asking, calling, only finding chaos.

My directional sense is useless at the best of times. I was numb with shock, every minute expecting to hear Baptation's semmy, trint or ammy go off whoomph and me still stumbling.

The whole spread was made of mini-camps, each one around a fire or music. Small herds rummaged, children idling, some couples copulating in duplicate. I literally fell over a cluster of five on the go, with one bloke wearing a bushman's hat. And among the broiling smoky nocturnal tumult stood the vehicles, lit any old how. I fell over wires and batteries, peered through choked windows. Piles of tyres, rubbish, people asleep, others wandering as lost as me. I felt I glimpsed something unbelievably familiar in the maelstrom but couldn't recognize it . . . It felt like the end of the world. I honestly don't know why film makers don't cotton on. I've seen pictures where nine extras pretend they're thousands of Zulus/Indians/Russians. Directors could minicam this whole populace. Cost nowt, wrap in half an hour.

It finished me. Forty, fifty minutes I raced, then finally was spent, my mind spinning, and collapsed against a tent, fagged out. A dog came, sat by. I was drenched with sweat. The dog nuzzled. I shoved it away. It didn't shift. With my first usable puff I got out, 'Sod off. I'm busy.'

The dog snickered in the flickering gold light. Tudor.

'Busy?' a voice said. I looked about.

Nobody, if you ignore some ten thousand folk, a couple of thousand shambled vehicles looking like a nightmarish pile-up. The place seemed a vast convoy torpedoed on some horrendous static sea. Nearby a wood fire smoked untended, more goats, a baby's cot, two children skipping, and a trio under blankets, kipping Mexican fashion.

'You got what, busy man?'

Inside the tent. 'Beg pardon?' I'd given up, all hopeless. A woman rolled out, straggly, under a leather poncho.

'Got what for what?' She waited. Scandinavian? 'Ganja, squab, bufo, crad, ekkie? What busy *with*?'

Nothing that this bird'd want . . . Then I thought, hey, those names, and pulled out Mercury's packet. 'Lovejoy,' I said.

'Noo, huh?' She eyed the packet. 'Lovejoy, y'say?'

'Yes, it's new.' Well, a couple of days.

'What'll you take for it? I got me, petrol, batteries . . . ' She reeled off a list. I listened in bafflement. Barter, Mercury's coin?

'Er, none of the above.' I inhaled, plunged. 'I want guiding out, to the lake, please.'

She struggled to kneel up, toppled, made it. We eyed each other, worn out. 'Hey, bro,' she said, admiring. 'You'm gone, yeah?'

'True, love.'

'Gimme that Lovejoy,' she said, wobbling erect. 'You got Dimity. What's you?'

'Er . . .' I thought we'd done all this. 'Lovejoy.'

'I like it!' she crooned. 'The product is the man!' We started off, stumbling over guy ropes and folk in various states of uncommunication. I felt uneasy, not wanting her tribe hunting me down for nicking their bird.

Tudor came. Makes you wonder sometimes what dogs actually think of us. I mean, Tudor could be forgiven for seeing us as one weird despoiling multitude. We seemed to blunder for ever. I swear we passed through the same identical rock concert three times, but Dimity seemed sure.

'Lovejoy?' I stumbled into her. 'There.'

'Where?' I couldn't see a damned thing, just a wall.

'The rehab. The lake's up, two hundred yards. That's the road. The Lovejoy, bro. And the way in.'

'Eh? Oh.' I gave her the packet. 'Way in?' Then I remembered this is how addicts ask how a drug needs to be taken. I didn't want the damned stuff harming her. 'Er, you smoke the, er, toke,' I said with embarrassed vocab. Lucky it was night, or she'd have seen me go red.

She put her lips full on mine. 'Go godly, Lovejoy.'

'Ta, love.' I unwound her. 'You go godly too, Dimity.' She'd gone. I found the road, annoyed to see the low building suddenly emerge. A light showed as I rounded the curve. Tudor was eager to be in. Had the silly hound known the way all the time? I approached.

It was the weirdest sensation, expecting carnage and finding everything exactly at peace. Had I been imagining things? Maybe I had jumped to ridiculous conclusions among the lost tribes, breathing in heaven-knows what intoxicants and engulfed by Cruza.

The entrance was ajar. Nobody was on the gate. I pushed the revolving door, entered with relief, sure I'd done the right thing. I stood at the reception desk, dinged the bell.

Nobody. I looked at Tudor. 'Everybody's out, mate?' He said nothing.

Another ding.

Nobody.

Well, I'd been ordered to clock in, so I found the book and wrote my name. Eleven o'clock. Maybe the night staff went for a meal about now?

Daft just to stand here, I thought. It felt odd. You know how some houses have a feel? As if the very place itself was alive, perhaps hating? Like that. It wasn't anything tangible. Over in the immense sprawl of travvies I'd been whacked, exhausted, but it hadn't felt so horrid. An old auntie of mine once decided never to go down a certain street: 'It mislikes me,' she said calmly. And I was relieved when they pulled Foundry Street down for good.

'Tudor?' His ears had pricked up. He stood tongue out, front paw lifted. 'What've you heard, lad?'

No answer, but the same intensity. I wondered if I should take my chances with Sister Cruza and Dimity. But people go to bed at night, right? And what point was there in night staff? Tell me that. Dolly would bowl up come dawn, and we'd be off collecting the antiques as I went.

From the reception desk I couldn't see the lounge. I edged slowly across the foyer. 'Come lad,' I told the dog. He hesitated. 'Go first, you frigging coward.'

Open glass double doors. I could hear the fire lurch as a log settled. I steadied, moved cautiously to peer. Nobody that side. But the corridor was to the right. I took a pace. I looked back to the main door, saw only darkness. I craned, sweat trickling down my temple.

'Boo.'

My belly relaxed. I straightened, and tried to stroll.

'Wotcher, Mrs. Farahar.'

'Vana, please.' She was reading one of those glossies. I felt a duckegg, casually sat on the couch. She looked stunning in a long gold sheath-dress. Emeralds and citrons, gold bracelets.

'Where is everybody?'

'Oh, around.' She smiled a dazzle that made me squint. 'Why?' Her amusement was unconcealed. 'Won't I do?'

'I was out for a walk,' I said feebly. She made me feel helpless. It reminded me of being up for auction. 'Looking at . . .' No, that wouldn't do. I hadn't gone to gape at a circus. I'd gone to Cruza, who'd shown me mercy. 'Calling on friends.'

Vana eyed my state. 'They gave you a boisterous welcome, Lovejoy. You aren't too tired to perform?'

'Can't it wait?'

Her glance flicked towards the lounge clock. 'Not really, Lovejoy.' She scrutinized me. 'I owe you explanations, and a reward. If,' she added languidly, 'you recall?'

My throat needed a couple of coughs. She sat, indolent, in control the way women always are. Shopsoiled, I worried in case I'd got the wrong end of the stick.

'Is it far?'

'Down the corridor.' She rose, sort of swooping upright without effort. She walked towards my corridor, me trailing her like a mutt on a lead. It's a woman's world, always was.

At the glass door she waited. I fumbled it open. She swept through. Her fragrance made me giddier, I swear, than all the fumes of Araby. She paused in the corridor, facing a solid door. I opened it, dizzy from her proximity. She stepped inside.

And suddenly it wasn't the woman, her perfume, the hint of love. It was the array on the snooker table. I'd never seen so much gold. No wonder there were auto cameras at every pelmet. And no wonder I felt odd.

You can talk about the physics of light on metallic surfaces, art down the ages, production figures for gold mines. But when it comes to it, there's no actual *meaning* in those numbers. Like, *all* the gold ever mined would fit in the space under the Eiffel Tower. And like, there's ten billion tons of gold dissolved in the world's oceans. But so? Statistics mean zilch.

There was a croaking sound. It was me. Vana walked round to face me. The gold pieces were on the green felt in a stunning display. There must have been sixty, from twisted neck torcs imitating the ancient Celtic tribal kings' ornaments, to rings, bangles, clasps, chalices, a monstrance, pattens, lunas, all showing simulated excavation trauma.

'Well, Lovejoy?'

'Can I touch?'

I picked up Fair Rosamund's Ring, my hand tingling.

Some things are holy. To some tribes, a couple of feathers and a shell equals pure sanctity. To others, it's a fragment of wood said to be from the True Cross, Veronica's Veil, a long-dead saint's fingernail, a shroud from Turin, a glossopetra – fossilised shark tooth you hang round your neck . . . Everybody's holiness differs. A Buddhist might think you barmy for praying before a piece of consecrated bread. Christians wonder at chaps who wear yarmulkes, whatever. But there's one place we all meet.

It's called gold. The most ductile, resistant stuff, lovely in colour. It's still only metal, when all's said and done. Poor deluded goons adore it for its worth. Which is barmy, in my book, for the same reason it's lunacy to value women by the ounce. You can't.

But when one piece *is* different *then* you're into life itself. That's why every woman has her own beauty.

Like in antiques. Now, gold is old as the world because, along with carbon, hydrogen, all that, it's stuff of which the world is made. But dig and shape it, suddenly the game changes. Each gold atom's the same whether dug up in Johannesburg or the Welsh hills, sure. It's only the human factor alters things. Here on the green baize lay an ancient ring known to scholars the world over, a miracle. It's where logic fails.

They call it the 'Godstow Ring'. Experts date it about AD 1420. It was found in the Godstow Nunnery, Oxford. Chased, and supposedly once enamelled, it's wide, peculiarly graceless. The Mother and Children are depicted on it, some saintly bloke, and the Trinity. It was a love ring, from a passionate incription on the inside. It's in the British Museum. (For emphasis: It *is in* the British Museum.) Us common folk call it Fair Rosamund's Ring, always will unless they educate us.

Which made me think, as chimes echoed in my skull. Because it was in the British Museum. *And* here?

'You like that, Lovejoy?' asked Vana. 'What about the rest?'

'They're duff, replicas made yesterday.'

She came round the table. I couldn't let go of Fair Rosamund's Ring until she practically overpowered me. 'Thank you for that demonstration, Lovejoy. Shall we chat?'

'Er . . .?'

'The gold will be quite safe.' She glided ahead.

Sod the gold, I was thinking. What about Fair Rosamund's Ring. The rest included some excellent fakes. But it's humanity that imparts soul, and only the Gostow Ring had one. The other golds were worth their weight in, well, gold, but who cared?

She swept ahead to my room, rattled the handle.

'Shhhh,' I went, like a fool. 'You'll wake Arthur.'

'Oh, of course.' She was smiling the woman's smile, a sin within. But at what?

My door was unlocked. Some mental unit rule, I shouldn't wonder, as if we were all imbeciles. I meant they, not me.

She surveyed the room. 'Quite pleasant, Lovejoy.'

I was shaking from wondering how on earth they'd managed to borrow the Godstow Ring from the British Museum. Also, I wasn't sure why she was in my room near midnight. Still, her presence quietened my fears.

'It's one piece, Lovejoy,' she said, standing there.

'One piece?' Like a genteel vicar discussing croquet.

'My *dress*, Lovejoy. Come here.' She meant I was stupid.

That smile was driving me out of my skull. She lifted her hair from her nape. My fingers were clumsy. I'm sure I tore the clasp, dexterity to the winds. She sighed as the dress came into my hands.

'For God's sake, Lovejoy,' she said, yanking at my clothes. 'We have two hours before you collect your Romano-Celtic lanx, to end the bargain.'

She knelt hauling my shirt, slapping my leg crossly, impatient. From my standing position she was breathtaking. With so little time left, I was glad to help. We didn't have time to put the light out. I suppressed the chimes reaching across the corridor, of that ancient love ring, famed the world over, glowing on the green baize.

34

Thoughts don't stop just because you sleep. It was pitch black. Awake, I remembered Fruit. A parson who's a firework expert. No kidding. Makes a fortune arranging displays for pageants. The only time I saw him go berserk was my fault. I'd strolled in, said hello. He ran me out into his garden, bellowing, 'Of all the . . .' The rest is unreportable.

His licence depended on keeping sulphur separate from chlorate. I'd walked some yellow sulphur into his chlorate space on my shoes. 'Think of coupling, Lovejoy. You'll blow us to . . .' et abusive cetera, his rotten old Factories Act (Explosives) my fault.

Moral: Sulphur is innocent. Chlorate, innocent. Couple them, varoom. It kept coming into my mind.

In semi-coma I roused, tottered to the bathroom in the dark, stumbled back to bed. She was there, asleep. She must have switched our light off. So? Fruit's furious words went dozily round and round.

Being warm helps you to sleep. And there was the warmth of love beside me, Vana sleeping. Plus, for me, the resonant heat radiating from Fair Rosamund's exquisite golden band lying among the dross. I slept like a babe, like Arthur himself, who seemed to be having a slumbersome night.

Then I woke, cold as a frog.

The warmth had gone.

You're never really sure how long you've slept, are you? Not even what your sleep's been about, if you follow. Sleep varies. Some bits of sleep are simply empty. Other chunks are frantic, mind a-whirl. Other patches are a happy drift, dreams firing through like rockets. I opened my eyes. Darkness. Closed them, felt beside me.

No Vana. So? She was in the bathroom. No noise, though. So

she'd flitted. Well, a married lady . . . Woman cannot live by smiles alone – she has to deliver, or lose all.

Roll over. What sort of sleep this time? Sleep varies, moment by moment. *Una momenta* by . . .

The *warmth* had *gone*. Suddenly I was wide awake, scared. The warmth I missed wasn't Vana's pure unadulterated love, no. It was that musical radiant warmth from across the corridor.

But you don't set out a display of precious ornaments then remove them in the middle of the night, not even if you've let somebody – me – in to glimpse the one that mattered. Do you?

I got underpants, trousers. Maybe Vana was supervising security arrangements?

Or not?

I opened the door, except it wouldn't. It was locked. Me inside. The window? I must have still been moribund because my addled brain said reasonably that the door couldn't be locked because there were no locks, mental patients needing help now and then.

Some central locking device? More awake, I rushed at the bed, felt Vana's side. Coldish. What did that tell me? That she'd been gone an hour, twenty minutes? How long did it take for a bed to cool when you stole away in silence while your thick-witted idiot bloke snored on? How had she wakened? She always wore a watch. Horror stole over me. Orchestra conductors have watches that tap you, don't they? Prompter watches, giving a little needle stab, make sure you wake silently. House doctors have them on baby units.

Were we all trapped? Boris, little Arthur, Rita, the rest? Or just me? I thought of the cameras in the snooker room. Window. I tried it. Sealed fast. Okay, you smash sealed windows to get out. I fumbled about for a chair, but there was no chair.

So what? There was a small bedside locker. I felt my way to it, and lifted it. . .

Except it wouldn't lift. Its feet were metal, screwed to the floor. I tried hauling the foot of the bed upright. No go, its metal legs screwed . . . I rushed into the bathroom, almost knocking myself senseless on something, but nothing in there was movable. I started whimpering. I tried looking out. The blinds were those roller things. I could raise it easily enough, but the sodding things never stay up. I wrenched it away in worsening fright, tried stabbing it at the window but those rotten swine in St. Helens glassworks make glass rock

211

hard. The rod bent like cotton. I thought explosions, on dark hillsides.

I could hear myself whining in terror. I beat on the wall, bawling, hoping to wake Arthur. The place was soundproofed. I should have worked that out, if only from the way Vana yelped before her love fire . . . *Fire*?

On the ceiling. I remembered a fawn-coloured disc. Smoke alarm, yes. And hadn't there been a red glass-covered thing above the door? I tried to reach up, feeling in the dark. I wasn't tall enough.

Distantly, I heard a smart crack. I froze. A rumble followed, only faint but the floor definitely quivering. Crazed, I leapt up, touched something cold. The red fire alarm? Gibbering, I leapt and smashed my fist at the cold something, missed and hit the bloody wall. Maddened by failure I jumped, jumped, kept jumping, smashing at the thing.

Even when the bell sounded and the door I opened kept on jumping, smashing my fist into the sodding thing. It was only when I actually fell forward that I realized I was in the corridor. The door had slid back, central unlocking. I could faintly see the night sky's glow, the end of the corridor.

Another crack sounded, louder this time, then a louder gathering rumble. I was off like a bat, racing towards the fresh cold air. I skittered to a halt, yelled for little Arthur, tore back into the baby's room, fell over the cot, felt about like a maniac, felt the bed, nobody, and hurtled out, crashing into the glass doors at the lounge entrance, past reception where the single red fire panel flicked on and off.

Outside the ground shook. The approaching rumble was louder, steady but exacerbated by deafening cracks and sharp explosive retorts. Where did skiers go in an avalanche? Up? Down? Across? I blubbered, yelling out which way, which way. Then I ran like a hare on to the road and towards the patch of night that was more orangey, hoping to Christ they weren't crazy enough to blast a great mountainside on to their own people like they were trying to do to me.

Shrinks tell us that people who are rescued suffer less trauma than the shrinks who advise. It's codswallop. I know. The nerk who gets out from under as the world caves in is the one. Never mind the others. Get marooned on some desert island, stuck on some iceberg, be lost in some arid desert, you know. Psychiatrists maybe miss the cheese and biscuits at their ten-course nosh, wring their hands – it's a load of dross. The bloke who makes it to land, the oasis, Camp Safety, is the one. He knows.

I only stopped running when a tree swayed out of the gloaming and sideswiped me. I lay retching, croaking like an old man. I couldn't get up. Stars were soaring into the night sky, if that's what the velvet black-blue stuff was up there. I closed my eyes, spread-eagled on rocky terrain.

The roaring had stopped. I kept my eyes closed because it was less frightening. I hoped I was in hiding, so long as it wasn't a hole in some mountain, because they'd suddenly become dangerously unstable.

It's difficult to take a look at yourself. I had a swollen eye, judging by my lopsided vision. My right hand was hurting like hell. It was a horrible mess.

Firelight, sparks crackling up in swirls, red glims against the darkness. Several fires, in fact, one ten yards off. Oddly, people moved about, dogs snuffled. Music, a rhythmic chanting, heavy metal pounding, shouts, the New Age dawning in the candle hours. Most vehicles showed no lights. Batteries given out, maybe? Or the travvies' metabolisms, spotting a diurnal clue or two, finally recognizing nightfall?

When I could, I stood slowly, not wanting another mountain chucked my way. Behind and slightly across, a couple of vehicles stood: the fire services, with more red status lamps than the police's lone blue.

They were well back from the mound where the rehabilitation unit had been. Their headlights shone on to the landslide. No caravans, no people in there . . . But then there wouldn't be, would there? I'd not noticed cars, or anybody, when returning for Vana to show me that lovely gold under the recording eyes of those cameras.

All those'd be gone too. I wondered what they'd told the patients. Move to a safe hotel, on account of threats from the travvies, I guessed. They didn't need any body, literally, to be buried under that mountain. Only mine.

Singularly few rescue workers about. Not much you can do when the world starts sliding about, except pick at the edges and shout. For a while I stayed put, just seeing what the police and the fire people were doing. Nothing, it seemed, except talk. I shook, realizing how close it had come. The centre of the slide was three hundred yards off. It had gone sideways, not down on to the travvies. Clever old mountain. I was freezing, went nearer a fire, sat with a couple smoking some cheroot. They inspected my blooded frame, bleeding feet, hands, swollen face, and brought me a blanket without a word. I dozed sitting upright, until some silly sod cracked the sky and let the light in.

My new friends had gone during the night. Their dog woke me by wanting to play. Where was Tudor? Cleared off at the first sign of trouble. I lay down, smoke drifting over me. Children came out. A little girl asked me to hold her skipping rope while she skipped 'Salt, mustard, vinegar, pepper'.

'All right, love,' I said. 'Don't expect me to skip, too.'

'Why're your feet like Bertie's?' she asked. 'A fight?'

'I fell.' Poor old Bertie. I sat in my blanket, scratching because of arthropods sharing my shelter, and chanted with her, 'One, two, three, Mother caught a flea.' Funny how well you remember them, skipping ropes on pavement . . .

Coming to, I perused the expanse of tilted vehicles. The scene was like a mediaeval battlefield, occasional creatures stirring about embers. One or two called. Dogs barked, not really caring. Music sounded, defining the ravers' area over where the hillside started an ominously steep rise.

The little girl let me go when her pal came, accusing me of singing the song wrong. We had a brisk argument. I lost when the little brat challenged me to do 'Over the mountains, under the sea . . .' I squirmed out of that. They taunted me out of sight. I would have washed in somebody's water butt, but goats wouldn't let me near.

A tall illuminated cross towered half a mile away. I'd been too giddy last night to recognize it. Sty's Relevant Harmony place. Well, well. It stood tall among the higgledy-piggledy forest of TV masts and washing poles. A neon Canterbury cross, rounded ends and scalloped arms. The Temple of Relevant Harmony flourished everywhere. I remembered Sty's litter of mobile homes. I went warily towards it through the wakening morning litter of folk and engines. Moment. Momenta.

Maybe that was it, really. I'd let myself be duped. There'd seemed to be no connection between Mynydd Mal and East Anglia. Okay, a genealogy-hankering American wasn't much. Not enough to draw in the county set. His daft *hiraeth* for Stonehenge's great monoliths only made it barmier still.

But throw in a traveller with his own religion, his own antiques auction meadow in East Anglia. Add to that scams in mid-Wales whereby richly endowed sports clubs milked antiques into his trailers on the way to the travvies' fezzie, and it all became one. At the centre Sty, busily pretending to be a New Age traveller, religionist, guru. Add Gee Omen – diamond merchant in a collapsed world diamond market. Add Simon Doussy, posh resourceful Continental dealer. Add Twentyman, a crashed Lloyd's underwriter. Add the rich Carl Arden, and the influential Valerie. Add Farahar's wide acres – source of umpteen priceless finds, which said acres would be the sites of numerous future planted 'finds' of Welsh golds. Add syndicated lesser fry. And you had a glorious money engine, for ever and ever.

The marquee seemed dowdy now. Bunting flapped, each piece bearing occult symbols. A couple of panels gaped. A cat shot out as a small dog tore in pursuit. Vomit stained some canvas swathes. A stench arose from a trampled area by the entrance. The fastenings were latched. The cross rotated, glowing feebly.

A mess. Near a crescent of trailers an astonishingly grand saloon motor glistening in dew and wealth. Presumably Momenta was about, girding up her Staff of Relevant Life. It all looked derelict. I entered through one of the rips. The aroma was soporific.

Folk were scattered about in groups, twos, threes, one exotic plurality I couldn't disentangle. A raised altar stood in the centre. One couple moved, as if recalling a dream dance of some previous incarnation. Momenta was lying naked near them, a naked bloke snoring under one of her luscious legs, lucky swine.

'Momenta?' I shook her. Blearily she tried to focus.

'Lovejoy? Is it time?' Her boyfriend struggled up.

'No. Three hours to go.' I grabbed a caftan.

He was fuddled. 'I'm the master's servant in the morning . . .'

'It's barely four o'clock yet.' I spoke softly to Momenta. 'Where's Sty?' I didn't want this kipping horde to wake.

'Are you already dead, Lovejoy?' She did well to see through those pupils. Her voice was dreamily syllabic.

'No, love. There's been a mistake.' What would seem logical to Momenta in space. 'I must see Sty, tell him. It's a matter of life or death.' I didn't say whose.

God, she tried. I almost saw her mind like a submerged creature trying to surface. It failed, tried once more. 'The master prays with the lake lords . . .'

'Ta, love.' I let her head fall. I'd been helping her to remember by yanking her hair.

Only one road touched the lake. Near the dam. It was marked by a star, scenery vantage point, on the map.

35

The caftan thing I nicked engulfed me. It was covered in alchemical symbols stitched by Temple Vestals in lax hours. I passed through the camp, now stirring. Several bands played. Fires were on the go. A few pans made a fitful clank. Some folk called out exotic greetings. I returned them, making signs, giving blessings.

Very little of the camp was recognizable. It went on beyond eyesight. I got offered a hard-boiled egg by a lass at a cauldron. I took it with gratitude, did a chant of appreciation, trudged on.

Glimpses of the landslip showed in the distance. I skirted round, heading for the lake. I didn't want to be discovered alive until there was some advantage. They'd wanted me dead underneath all that minced granite. While they harboured the delusion, I'd be safe. I'd had enough. No amount of Vana could make up for being eliminated. Better an incognito acolyte until things cleared.

Somebody called my name. I looked, but smoke intervened. I broke into a shuffle. My feet hurt like hell. I kept my eye out for shoes, but saw none.

The slope up from the camp was steep. The vehicles petered out to rubbish and latrines, nettles everywhere. Then there was only heather and a loose scree, stuff that gave under you. One part was almost vertical, like a small cliff. I found myself near the dam's incline, didn't like the thought of being underneath that. I tackled the slipping scree, holding on, scrabbling footholds. Wise not to use the road. Even the Old Bill might notice a blood-besmirched bloke in a magician's cloak.

There were voices. I scrambled along the upper limit of the scree. The police could be in two places. Down by the engulfed rehab centre, or where they thought the explosion had started the landfall. Here, there was only the road curving to the dam. If Farahar had wanted the travvies flooded out, he could have blown the dam. But he hadn't. He'd exploded the charge above the mental unit. If anywhere, they were where the dam and road met.

The scree was interesting. It's in these places, virtually untrodden, that people find ancient artefacts. It was from such an ancient place in Palestine that the Bedouin carried some sacks into Mr Kando's antique shop in Bethlehem in the 1940s, and offered the Dead Sea Scrolls for sale.

Those voices. Familiar, with one megaphonic. God Almighty, I thought, weary. Not Calvin Jones's dulcet tones? I was close to the rim, lurking. I remembered – wasn't this the place near the lake where we'd put the caravans? I'm good at cowardice. I was silence and invisibility, as I crept to peer through the thin hawthorns. And gave a muffled yelp as somebody clutched my ankle.

'Lovejoy'

I stifled the silly cow before she could shriek. They were all listening to Calvin Jones on the sloping layby, thank God. Dimity looked rapturous in spite of my hand over her mouth.

'Shhhh.' I touched her hand to her temple in the age-old gesture signifying police. I nodded, slowly let her go.

She beckoned, whispered, 'Is this the drop?'

The drugs place. I nodded. She lay beside me below the rim of the road. I peered out. Calvin Jones, interviewing Vana Farahar – startling in a red suit with a smart hat, lovely legs – and Sty, even more astonishing in a sharp double-breasted suit. They were standing before the end caravan. Its wheel was inches from my face. Olwen was moving, directional mike, camera churning. Calvin was perched on his motor, signalling Olwen to avoid his plastered leg. It hung obscenely down, a pleasing sight. The caravans were still ranged in the layby, shafts to the road. Nobody else, just the interview. No Colonel Farahar, either.

'Mrs. Vana Farahar.' Calvin, doing the lead-in. 'You will surrender to the anarchy that cruelly despoiled your dream of mental health for all?'

Vana said fervently, 'No, Calvin. Certainly not. I shall fight on, with Mr Stivanovitch, and my gallant generous husband. We believe in a Wales free from these wreckers. Those.' She flung out an arm dramatically. I ducked.

'Cut.' Calvin shouted at Olwen. 'Pan the valley, okay? Filth, druggies, injections, spaced out, rolling in the fire, okay?'

'Yes, Calvin.'

He donned his telly voice. 'How do you feel about the explosion?'

'It is clear,' Vana said, a catch in her voice, 'that the forces of evil had sabotaged our dreams. Reprobates who make explosives are here among his filthy mob. They must be removed once and for all.'

'And does Mr Stivano . . . Mr Stivan feel the same?'

'Indeed he does.' Vana sniffed, emotional. 'Through his translator he has expressed his determination to rebuild the centre down in that valley, providing jobs and health care for Wales.'

There was more twaddle. Translator? Sty's from Wolverhampton, for God's sake. He's only ever been on a day trip to Dieppe. He's called Sty because he tells pig jokes.

'When's the greed?' Dimity whispered. Greed's talk for drugs.

'Any minute now, love,' I whispered back.

'We want teens, okay?' Teens mean an unlimited amount. Mercury's sachet must have been dynamite.

'Done,' I promised, furious with her.

'Final shot,' Calvin shouted. 'Both inside waving. Where the fuck are the horses?'

'They've been taken to graze. The farrier – '

Calvin swore at Olwen. 'One at each window, like the caravan's rolling. Go, go, go!'

I shushed Dimity and slid up to peer. I saw Vana's lovely legs ascend. Sty followed. Through the wheel spokes I saw Olwen's feet splay for stability on the opposite side. The waggon was almost end on. Calvin was bawling instructions. I heard the clump, clump of feet inside the caravan. I looked down.

The drop was sheer. A couple of yards to my right, the scree ended. The cliff fell almost vertical down to the lake. I saw Olwen's feet appear further away, the caravan between us.

Vana and Sty were inside, obeying Calvin's instruction to wave, dammit. I crawled, thinking possibly to stand up, maybe confront them with the attempt to murder me, right into the camera.

It was there, me slowly standing up, not wanting to interrupt Olwen's filming, that I felt something catch. My caftan maybe, but definitely something. I gave an impatient tug. I crouched, maybe changing my mind, get the police, I don't know.

The caravan moved, only a fraction, but moved. I heard Calvin say, angry, 'Olwen, fix that effing waggon, okay?' And Olwen scurrying, saying 'Right, Calvin!' and then exclaiming, things beyond her redemption.

The caravan rolled. I heard Vana say, 'Is this . . . ?'

Trouble. I sensed it, slid over into the scree on to Dimity, suddenly clutching at her because the lake surface was a gillion miles below. I clung to Dimity, then scrabbled sideways. The caravan above rumbled, its iron tyres chewing the tarmac like I'd heard so often.

Somebody screamed – Olwen, I think. The caravan rolled a few yards, left the layby's camber.

I honestly didn't do a thing, not *me*. I mean, the best of intentions. I was simply going to turn them in, maybe make a statement to the peelers. And I wasn't thinking vengeance. I don't believe in it, never have. Civilized man can't. It was accidental. My caftan really did catch on the brake – else why did the caravan go? A horse-drawn vehicle's brake is only a single stick, for God's sake. All in a split millisec. I saw it. I still do, on bad nights. I lay there stunned. The caravan passed – it didn't race, leap, shoot, merely passed in a gentle glide – into the air a few yards away. I saw, maybe *thought* I saw, Vana's aghast face at her window. The caravan rotated with slow grace, in space, down and down. To smash into the lake with a horrendous lack of noise. Like in a silent film where the ratchets make do for sound.

Olwen was screaming. I stared appalled at Dimity.

'Didn't deliver, huh?' she said knowingly.

'Shut it, silly bitch.' I could feel my face drain as the implication entered by thick skull. She knew, had seen, maybe could turn me in, when I'd done nothing wrong. Everybody who knows me'd say that.

'You got it, man,' she said. 'That police?'

Calvin was babbling into some car phone. The police car at the engulfed rehab unit was wahwahing. Olwen was screaming still. Calvin shouted her his one question.

'You got it? You got every fucking frame?'

'No,' she babbled.

He hit her, shouting abuse. Really cruel. I mean, she'd been taken completely by surprise. I hate cruelty to women. It's totally wrong. He'd have kicked her if he'd been able.

Me and Dimity slid down the scree. I shoved her first because skittering on fragments of granite would have cut my feet even more. This way, she was useful.

It took a horrible long minute to make the first vehicles. We were sharing somebody's grotty porridge when the Old Bill came stumbling after with their daft questions. Me and Dimity answered in a yeah-man-wowee lingo, me copying everybody else.

They gave up, and left grumbling at the climb back to the scene of the crime – no, accident, pure and simple. I told Dimity I needed to find Sister Cruza, and was conducted through the impi of wondering travvies all asking what the Old Bill were doing at the lake end of the camp when the road block was at the other. I told everybody there'd be a camp meeting at eight o'clock.

By then I'd be off, *Deo volente*. Let them hold a durbar. Count me out.

36

If you go to Leptis Magna, in beautiful Libya, there is a forum place that looks so-o-o distinguished. Stone benching all round the open city centre space. Sit, and chat across to your neighbours. The give-away clue lies underneath. A runnel, gulley. The marble benching has significantly shaped holes. Because it's simply a loo, a *public* public lavatory where Romans sat and read newspapers – on wax – while slaves poured jars of water beneath. Cool, those Romans. Nearby are immense baths – cold, tepid, warmish, hot – where travellers were soaped by delectable birds. I used to marvel how it must have felt. Momenta showed me.

They were just mobile when I reached the Temple. Dimity didn't want me to go in, but I had an alibi to see to. Momenta's acolyte was on his dawn smoke.

'Momenta?' I shook her, a lovely experience. 'The plan's changed. Sty won't need you. I'm to take his place. Bath, clothes, breakfast. Okay?'

'Yes, Lovejoy.'

She took over, moving among the throng, rousing serfs. It took some time before I was in a bath – carried in, cleaned of chicken dung and two rabbits. Perfumes, soaps from fantastical bottles, and I was stripped and lowered into the scented water. The Temple Vestals, seven strong, gently washed me free of blood and muck and earth. One even did my nails. They washed my hair, had a hair drier. They cooed with pity over my feet.

They towelled me dry, dressed me in a cotton singlet, silk shirt, jodhpurs. I felt and smelt like a fencing master. I commanded a breakfast alone with Momenta, and told the rest of the kulaks where to produce a motor car, sparing no expense. The grub was a serious disappointment, cereals, water, unleavened bread, tea made from dubious grass. If this was religion, give me paganism. Momenta sat on the floor, me on a canvas throne thing. She wore her Greek set, her exposed breast distracting me.

'Momenta,' I said when we were alone, 'I have serious news. The master, my, er, partner, Sty, has ascended.' I felt a prat saying it, but the acolytes were already chanting and clinking handbells. They must have heard.

'I suspected it, Lovejoy,' she said, without a qualm. 'Consort with evil, evil takes you. Are you in his place?'

'Er, yes.' I brightened at the lie. 'I require all the places where Sty had dealings. You understand?' I added hastily, a bloody lentil stuck in my teeth, 'To undo the wrong done.'

'Harmony.' She nodded, a lovely moment. 'All seventy-nine addresses are in my memory.'

Seventy-*nine*? A gold mine! Remembering the caravan falling, I wished I'd not thought that. I meant a lucky break.

'Write what antiques Sty would have collected. Mark which are paid for, which are not. Then leave. Take two acolytes. I shall be with you in, er, spirit, and see you in East Anglia, at the Temple meadow. Collect the antiques as you journey on.'

'Who will rule there?'

'Me,' I said, spirits soaring. I'd be good at it, with Preacher, part time, for hymns only. 'Have you funds?'

'Yes. Plenteous instruments of sordid commerce.'

Did she mean money? 'Take half, give me half. Leave about noon. The others must wait here for, er, orders.'

'Very well, Lovejoy. And the antiques we gather up?'

She sounded like the Old Testament. 'You will keep them for me. One thing. I want a written message taken to the American officer named Farahar. You know him by sight. Urgent, within minutes. Possibly up near the landslide.'

She got me a jacket. I said to her, ' You have duties. Go.' I think from a Charlton Heston feature. 'Someone will come alone, wanting to speak with me. I might need four stalwart acolytes nearby in case I call.' I almost said to gird up their loins.

Momenta went with my scrawled message. I waited for the foe to drop by. He had to. Somehow I couldn't see Farahar killing Liffy. I could see Sty, or Doussy and Sty. Which left Doussy.

*

He came after about an hour, me by now hungry and wanting at least another lentil. The tent flap went, and there he stood. He looked, came slowly in. I'd had a good go at making myself look in charge.

'Lovejoy?' As if he still couldn't believe it.

'Doussy?' As if I could.

'God.' He sighed in reluctant admiration. 'You're a sod to get . . .' *Get rid of*, he wanted to say.

'You're not on tape. Chat's safe today.'

'What now? A deal?'

'Aye. You pay Dashboard twenty years' salary, for killing Liffy. One-off or drip feed, I don't care.'

He thought a bit, standing there. A less decisive bloke would have made out he wasn't to blame. He said, 'Very well. I'll pay him one sum.'

'Do it, or you're for it.' I saw a glimmer in his eye, and smiled. 'Anything happens to me or Dashboard, you'll have one hour before the sky falls in.'

He hesitated, wondering if it already had. 'These people are Sty's. He was my ally, not yours.'

'Your scam slew Liffy, Vana, Sty.'

'Not everything was me. Vana and Sty were accidents.'

'Oh, aye.' I didn't want my one listener to reach the right conclusion. 'Whose scam was it? Who'll get the profit?'

'My syndicate, my idea to include Farahar.'

That was what I wanted. I relaxed. 'The Roman gold mines lie under this very ground, eh?' I drew a circle. 'Two miles northwest of Glan-y-nant, the old lead mines. Silver at Llywernog. But nothing quite like Dolaucothy.' I cursed myself for trying to threaten with Welsh pronunciation. 'Except for places like Mynydd Mal, eh, Doussy?'

The blighter actually smiled cheerfully. 'Well, the temptation, Lovejoy! The scam screamed to be played. Can you imagine? Re-open the old Romano-Celtic gold mines here, clandestinely. Small amounts. We craft the artefacts, plant them in Farahar's Suffolk lands. We "accidentally" plough them up. And sell to the highest bidder. We mine ten gold ounces in Mynydd Mal, they become six million dollars overnight.'

I heard him out, the murdering sod. 'Is it worth deaths?'

'Don't be foolish. Liffy stole my motor. I couldn't take the risk of you having the Kungsholm. You'd have traced the legit owner, realized it was a plant.' So Liffy had tried to nick the Swedish glass, and not told me. Well, I'd have done the same. Doussy spread his hands. 'You'd have done the same.'

See? They go off their heads. No wonder Jessina Mosston had mouthed a sorry, she with the husband who owned East Anglia's posh motor concession. 'Churchill said once that even if a strategy's beautiful, you must occasionally examine the results.'

'My results justify it all, Lovejoy. Easy to hire travvies with explosives, Lovejoy. Obliterate the heath unit, to get – '

' – the travvies blamed and moved out, leaving the valley free.'

'Concealing the gold workings that Farahar rediscovered in the fly-over photographs. Welsh gold mined today is pricey, yes. But Welsh gold made into ancient artefacts authenticated by a divvy . . . well.' He was in heaven. I swear he almost floated.

'Valerie Arden's first husband was a chemistry don. Was it a genuine mistake, those Brummy lads – Des, Sass – picking on Wolfie in The Ship?'

He laughed, rueful. 'Mistaken identity, Lovejoy. Meg.'

'And me?' I answered myself. 'On camera, picking out the one genuine gold. Vana Farahar inveigled me in to be filmed doing it. An advertising video for you, Sty, Vana, your syndicate. You planned to eliminate me under the landslide. So you could say I was still alive somewhere overseas, providing certificates of authenticity for each antique.'

'True, Lovejoy.' He was in agony at how things had gone. 'The video tape went over with Vana.'

'You want me to film it again?'

'Yes. I couldn't believe you were still alive!'

'Then you'd kill me a second time?'

'Now, Lovejoy.' He was placating me. 'God murders us all and gets away with it.'

'What do I get?'

'Five per cent.' The answer was ready. 'Every single "find" on Farahar's land, you get cash on the nail.'

The argument took a while over the percentage, Doussy beating me down. We settled on eight, as if I cared. It was only to convince him I was sincere. I told him to leave first and I watched him go, disdaining the people all around. He actually leant away when somebody spoke.

'Bye, Simon,' I said to myself. 'Remember me to Liffy.' And slowly counted to a thousand. 'Colonel?'

He stepped from behind the hangings, thank God.

'I heard.' He was pale, overweight, sweating. He'd thought himself in control. 'Lovejoy. I must know. Was Vana – ?'

'All women are faithful,' I said. Like hoping there's a God.

'It was a fraud, then? Vana included?'

'Only to prove your theories,' I lied gravely. 'Pity Doussy was so evil.'

'That arrangement with him, Lovejoy?' he asked heavily.

'I had to pretend along. He killed Liffy, a pal, by burning him. I'll try to get even. After he's paid up.' I sighed. 'A self-confessed murderer, of Liffy, your wife, Sty.' I made my voice bitter. 'He'll walk away scotage-free. Killers do.'

'Do they?' he said, white, intense.

'Every time.' I was so sorrowful. 'Report him to the police, he'll have alibis. Some innocent bloke will get sentenced instead.' I swallowed. Horrible thought.

He said, 'How long did you say?'

'A week. I'll tell you when Dashboard gets his gelt.'

'Do that, Lovejoy.' I wondered how he'd do it. It wouldn't matter. He'd settle Simon Doussy's hash. He looked outside through the flap. 'These people, on holy ground. It amazes me. All nogoods.'

'Why don't you do something else, beside buy East Anglia?'

'Like what?'

'Cut a new Stonehenge from the Welsh mountains. Transport it to the USA. Set it up, a tourist attraction. Use it to teach America about Wales. Books, tours, university lectures, magazines. It doesn't have to be genuine. Look at the famous story of Llewelyn, who left his dog Celert to guard his baby son. Came home to blood everywhere. He killed the dog, mistakenly fearing the worst – to find his baby safe under a wolf's body. It's all made up, pinched from a Norwegian folk tale . . . ' I halted. He'd got that Meg look. 'Er, such romantic stories!' I ended lamely.

He stood for a long time. 'The Vana Farahar Memorial!' His eyes ran tears. I wondered if I'd get a percentage. The USA successfully sells do-it-yourself coffins. Yanks are brilliant salesmen. 'Thank you, Lovejoy,' he said.

37

Momenta came with a small canvas case. It contained money, more than I'd every seen at one go. And this was half? I bussed her, whispered an infinity of promises, and sent her off. I waited a good span, then walked through the camp and up to the road. It took about twenty minutes. Police were blocking off the entrance to the valley. A queue of yet more lopsided vehicles filled with several species of refugees from civilization waited.

It took me some time to reach where the three caravans stood among swivelling police lights. I talked to an Old Bill. He gave me enough gist to alibi my knowledge of events. No Dolly. Her so-say message must have been false.

Luke inspected me gravely. 'Safe then, Lovejoy.'

Aye, I thought, no thanks to anybody. 'Anybody hurt?'

'No.' We were apart from the rest. Boris wasn't about, just Humphrey with the rescue people looking down at the lake. Tudor, the turncoat, sat by Humphrey. It looked away. Can you believe it? 'You heard about Mrs. Farahar and Mr. Stivanovitch?'

'Terrible,' I said evenly.

He said nothing. 'Remember we scotched the caravans?' I said mmmh. 'The rocks came away. It's a physical impossibility. The wheels' weight holds them.'

'Dunno,' I said. 'What's the plan now?'

Finally he said, 'They'll build again, when the travvies go.'

'Won't happen,' I said. 'Many a slip twixt cup and lip.'

He stared in that way I hated. People are too suspicious. 'You make a habit of guessing right, Lovejoy.'

'Hardly.' I tried to lighten it. 'Humphrey's got Phillida and Arthur. And Tudor, I see. And Mrs. Arden?'

He did not smile. 'I was security chief for her first husband's government laboratories. Then with the Commander.'

Lucky man to have her. 'I should have guessed. Tell Commander Boris I hope he gets his princess. I can do him a genuine Welsh gold wedding ring, smashing price.'

He walked away. He could please himself.

Which left Humphrey. I stood by him. 'Congrats, Doc?'

'Well, me and Phillida thought we'd . . .'

'Take care of little Arthur,' I said. 'Don't give him chocolate buttons with wrong additives, okay? One thing. How'll you manage?'

'God knows.' He stared across the lake. 'Train all your life to become a doctor, then hand in your licence.'

'Want a job?' I drew him aside. 'I've spotted some antiques. If they come to nothing, don't worry. But if they do . . .'

'Antiques?' He was startled. 'I wouldn't know a Sheraton – '

'Same as all antique dealers, Humphrey, present company excepted. Tell Luke you'll drive a caravan back free of charge. See you in East Anglia. I'll give you a list, where, who to see, how much. Follow it exactly.'

'You're serious, Lovejoy?'

'Shortest unemployment ever, eh? Love to Arthur.' I gave him the notebook, with its details of antiques I'd seen on the way, with prices. 'Keep it. Stop Phillida from nicking it.'

I'd lost patience. I gave him the bag of gelt, a wrench.

'Use this. If there's any over, there's a pale lad called Jerry, hospital paediatric ward. See him right. The little sod cheats at bowls.'

For a few moments I paused, wondering who to go with. Momenta? She could run me to a railway station. Dimity, enthusing over my pharmaceuticals? But I'd no frog droppings, or whatever it was she smoked. Cruza would have me, but they'd soon arrest Baptation. I went down the road. Calvin was closing the interview with Meg.

She was waxing to Olwen's camera, 'We shall prevail. Health care is vital, see. We will conquer for social equality . . .'

A sociologist praising herself means . . . 'And the sponsors?'

'Are firm,' she proclaimed. She'd had her hair done. 'The Ardens from East Anglia, Mrs. Divine, Mrs. Hughes, Mr. Gee Omen. And Mr. Doussy, whose scheme . . .'

I nodded hello to Olwen, stepped over and kicked Calvin's dangling leg. He screeched. I kicked it with my other foot. Luckily it also dented his red motor.

'So long, Calvin. D'you film that, Olwen?' I walked away. I had the address of the puppeteer Dylan Williams and his lovely grand-daughter Ceinwen, pr. Kine-wen.

When I got home I'd have to settle with Mrs. Arden. Carl was innocent, and Deirdre Divine, Florence also. Raddie and Chuck hadn't the brains, so I'd exempt them.

A car caught me up after I'd gone a hundred yards.

Meg. 'Lovejoy? Get in. I'm glad you kicked him.'

'Ta.' We sat in silence.

'What a *mess*, Lovejoy. Sergeant Corran back there wants you.'

'Eh? Oh, my cousin. He'll wait. Nice chap.'

Quiet.

'Give me a lift? I know a Punch and Judy man. Dolwar Fach.'

Her eyes burned. 'Raping our heritage, Lovejoy?'

I sighed. 'It's honest. One thing, Meg.'

'Yes?'

'Your unit's short of money, right? That artist who invented those phoney druidical breastplate things. Herbert Hekover, wasn't it? What if I knocked up a few forgeries? And you sell them at the next Eisteddfod?'

'That's an insult, Lovejoy!' She wanted to clobber me.

'Then how about some of those phoney "traditional" costumes that Lady Llanover made up – wife of Ben Hall, the original Big Ben? We'd make a fortune.'

'You swine, Lovejoy! I heard about Rita, Humphrey and Boris. But all the time you were up to something!'

'I give you my word, love. Honest.' I was thinking, if I could inveigle old Dylan and the luscious Ceinwen into letting me use their croft to hide a few things – gold artefacts manufactured secretly by somebody decent like me – and maybe to ship a few antiques through mid-Wales, why, Dylan Williams would be in clover! Lovely Ceinwen would be grateful! And I'd not exactly starve. I'd need some old Welsh gold, like that mined at Llanpumsaint, second most prolific goldmine in the Roman Empire.

I said casually, 'We far from Llanpumsaint, Meg?'

'Oh no! Travvies!' I looked back – at a little yellow motor that could only be Dolly's. And a decrepit lorry. The driver looked uncommonly like Cruza. And behind that reeled a bus, smoke

230

clouding the air. Dimity? We were miles from anywhere. I started to sweat.

'Look, Meg,' I said, desperate. 'I've just remembered a clue I didn't tell the police. I know how Vana and Sty died.'

'Don't lie, Lovejoy. Here's Dolwar Fach.' She pulled in before an old stone farmhouse. Ceinwen was looking down at us, pretty as a picture. 'Who's Little Miss Prim?' Meg demanded, her voice hard. 'You said an old man?'

'That's his daily help.'

I leapt out and ran towards the lovely Ceinwen.

'Lovejoy?' Meg called, angry.

Ceinwen came forward with a smile of welcome. She didn't yet know me, and might believe my promises. If I could work some out quick.